LONG
TIME
DEAD

LONG TIME DEAD

A DETECTIVE SHERIDAN HOLLER THRILLER

T. M. PAYNE

THOMAS & MERCER

Text copyright © 2024 by T. M. Payne
All rights reserved.

Published by Thomas & Mercer, Seattle

www.apub.com

Amazon, the Amazon logo, and Thomas & Mercer are trademarks of Amazon.com, Inc., or its affiliates.

ISBN-13: 9781662511301
eISBN: 9781662511295

Cover design by Dan Mogford
Cover image: © Rekha Garton / Arcangel; © Alexander Spatari / Getty Images

Printed in the United States of America

For Susie
Always by my side

Why bury me here in another man's grave
And leave no candle to show me the way
You can't hide from the devil, he knows what
you've done
And now he's coming to play

Does no one care to look for my bones
Am I gone from this life without trace
You put me here, forever to fear
I'll be a long time dead in this place

PROLOGUE

Saturday 13 December 1997

Sally Doneghy pulled into the supermarket car park just as her petrol warning light came on. 'Shit,' she said, a little too loudly.

Her daughter Abby chastised her with a wave of her finger. 'That's a bad word, Mummy' – Abby shook her head – 'and I'm telling Daddy.'

Sally grinned as she pulled into a parking space. 'Or . . . how about you don't tell Daddy, and I let you open one present on Christmas Eve?'

Surely this offer's tempting enough for a seven-year-old, Sally thought, waiting as Abby undid her seatbelt and picked up her woolly giraffe. A handmade gift from her grandmother when she was born, 'Gerald' was never more than an inch away from her.

'So, that will leave me six presents to open on Christmas Day then.' Abby wiped Gerald's grubby face.

Sally turned in her seat to face her daughter. 'How do you know how many presents you've got?'

'They're under your bed. Gerald found them and told me.'

Sally shook her head. 'Santa knows if you're lying,' she said, looking past Abby at the flurry of shoppers scurrying in and out of the supermarket, pushing trolleys piled high with food and drink. The usual pre-Christmas pandemonium.

'That's God, not Santa,' Abby announced, bouncing Gerald up and down on her knee.

How did my daughter get to be such a smartarse? Sally got out of the car and walked around to the passenger side, putting her hand out for Abby to take hold of and smiling as she heard Christmas music being played outside the store.

'Is Santa here, Mummy?' Abby asked excitedly, swinging Gerald around by his scrawny neck.

'I'm not sure, darling.' Not after last year's 'Jolly Santa' was sacked, having been caught handing out gifts while stinking of alcohol. Sally, failing to hide her smile, recalled the 'Santa's Blotto' headline in the local paper.

Abby pointed to a little girl walking past them wearing an elf hat. 'Can I get one of those?'

'We'll see.' Sally glanced down at the icy ground as they neared the store entrance. 'Now, what have you got to remind Mummy to do when we get home?'

'Give Gerald a bath.'

'That's right. Good girl,' Sally replied. Gerald's 'bath' was actually half an hour of his worn and tattered body clonking around in the washing machine, accompanied by the dread that he wouldn't survive the spin cycle. Usually, Abby would protest for hours that Gerald didn't need a bath, but the thought of Christmas looming appeared to distract her.

'And what else?' Sally asked.

'Shave your legs.' Abby tilted her head to look up at her mother. 'I heard you tell Daddy this morning.'

Sally threw her head back and burst out laughing, hoping the two women walking in front of them hadn't heard. The blonde one appeared to look round for a second, but the taller, dark-haired

2

one seemed totally oblivious. Just then, Sally saw the taller woman raise her hand and scream, 'No, Lively!' and suddenly there was a loud crack, then another and another as Sally felt warm, thick fluid spatter across her face. She could taste it in her mouth, coppery and bitter, and it took her a moment to realise she was covered in blood, just as the two women fell to the floor.

Now, right in front of her, Sally could see a man on a motorbike, pointing a gun at where the two women had been standing. He went to ride off but was fumbling with the gun, which fell from his grip and clattered to the ground. He hesitated for a moment before speeding off. Sally remained frozen to the spot.

Eerily, the only sound was a Christmas carol playing, the music drifting across the car park from the speakers next to her. Abruptly, the music stopped. Everyone stopped. And then all hell broke loose.

Shoppers fled in every direction. Some were running into the store for cover while others ducked down behind their trolleys. Parents were scooping up their children and fleeing to their cars. Some people just stayed where they were. Staring. Confused and disbelieving.

Sally quickly wiped the blood from her mouth and face with her coat sleeve before dropping to her knees to shield Abby from the horror of the scene before them. A thick, dark river of blood slowly flowed out on to the icy ground from the blonde woman's head. The dark-haired woman was lying awkwardly, her legs tucked under her body and her arms outstretched, blood oozing from a bullet hole in her neck.

Sally closed her eyes. *Oh my God, they're dead. They're both dead.*

CHAPTER 1

SEVEN YEARS LATER

Tuesday 14 December 2004
Liverpool Crown Court

Defence barrister Simon Calvin-Jones rolled his pen between his fingers and frowned. 'So, tell me, Detective Inspector Holler, did you at any time ask the defendant any questions in relation to the alleged assault, outside of the interview room?' He eyed the judge over his glasses before turning his attention to the witness.

Detective Inspector Sheridan Holler shook her head once. 'No.' She raised an eyebrow. *Yes, I bloody did*, she thought. Trying not to smile.

Calvin-Jones flicked a look at the jury and then back at Sheridan. 'You didn't speak to him in the corridor of the cells and ask him any questions at all about the case?' He smirked, and Sheridan felt the urge to grab his stupid wig and stick it up his pretentious arse.

'No, I did not.' Sheridan gave a slight shake of her head.

He continued. 'You interviewed the defendant several times. Can you be sure that at no time did you have a conversation with him about the assault – alleged assault – that was not in the confines of the taped interview room, with myself present?'

'Yes, I can be sure.' Sheridan tilted her head. She could feel the jury staring at her. The woman in the front row shifted in her seat and leaned forward slightly.

Sheridan knew that her colleague, Detective Sergeant Anna Markinson, who was sat in the row of seats behind her, would not be flinching, but rather trying not to show her reaction. Anna knew that Sheridan had, on two occasions, asked the defendant if he liked assaulting women and attacking defenceless animals and if he didn't tell her where he had hidden the weapon, she would make sure he had a very difficult time in prison. Well, something to that effect.

The defendant's partner, Donna Hunter, had previously called the police twenty-six times to report domestic violence. Each time, either making no formal complaint once officers arrived or withdrawing her statement before the case ever got to court.

Their two children remained under the watchful eye of social services and even with the constant threat that they might be taken away, the victim had always supported her partner. *'He's lovely when he's sober,'* she would say. *'He'd never hurt the kids, he adores them,'* she would say. *'He was abused as a child and his dad used to hit his mum, it's not his fault,'* she would say. Every time, the same thing, the same words, the same excuses.

Except this time, he'd stabbed her in the cheek with a screwdriver before killing the family dog. And this time, she'd made a statement and stuck to it.

Sheridan had spent hours with her, carefully and quietly letting her divulge and describe all the previous assaults she had endured. All the times he had forced himself on her, punched her and kicked her until she was on her knees. All the times he had spat at her, told her she was fat, told her she was ugly, how she dressed like a fucking

6

tramp, how she should be grateful that he even wanted to be with her because no other man would look at her twice.

Eleven years of domestic abuse tumbled out of her and on to the pages of a statement that the jury had now heard. Sheridan had called the victim every week, praying as she dialled the number that she hadn't changed her mind, that she would still support the prosecution and give evidence in court. In the months leading up to the trial, Sheridan watched as the broken woman before her, slowly but surely, became whole again.

Sheridan had dealt with thousands of victims over the years. She'd put her heart and soul into every investigation, supporting the victims from the moment they'd found the courage to call the police. She was passionate about her job. About every case she dealt with. Cases where families were so deeply affected by the crime that even years on, they would still reel from the devastating effects. She wanted to fix everyone, put the broken pieces back together.

Like she wanted to with her own family, after her brother's murder.

And so yes, when Donna Hunter had finally decided to testify against her partner, Sheridan was determined to secure the prosecution, whatever it took. The only thing that was missing from the mountain of evidence was the weapon he'd used. And so, Sheridan had indeed threatened him. She'd put her face up to his and whispered that his life would be very difficult in prison. Especially if it accidentally slipped out what he was in for. He wouldn't be the big man inside prison walls if it was made common knowledge that he was a woman-beater. His reaction was to smile at her and tell her that he wasn't going to prison, because his partner would never go to court and give evidence against him. That was the moment Sheridan knew Stuart Conner had to be convicted because if he wasn't, his partner would never trust the criminal justice system again.

Now, as she stood in the witness box, she just had to keep her cool for a little bit longer.

Calvin-Jones shook his head and raised his eyes to the ceiling. 'I put it to you, Detective Inspector' – he spat the words as if mentioning her rank left a bad taste in his mouth – 'that you did in fact have such a conversation.'

Sheridan hated this little weasel. She'd been the investigating officer on a number of cases where he was the cross-examiner, and he annoyed the shit out of her every time. He took forever to get to the point, clearly disliked successful, strong women and always tried to humiliate police officers at every given opportunity.

Sheridan sighed. 'I did not.' She glanced at the judge who also appeared to have lost interest in this line of questioning. The devil on her shoulder gave her a nudge, and she hesitated for a moment before she said, 'I assume your client has told you that we discussed the case while I was walking him to the interview room? Well, there was one conversation that could be related, I suppose, but it's really not relevant.'

Calvin-Jones held his hands out, palms up. 'Oh, I think that would be for the court to decide, don't you?'

'I assure you, it really isn't relevant.' Sheridan turned to the judge. 'Perhaps in chambers, your honour?'

Anna Markinson watched the jury's reaction. The judge agreed and as the courtroom was cleared, the judge removed his wig and wove his hands together. 'Detective Sergeant Markinson may stay,' he said, nodding at Anna, who was on her feet and ready to leave.

Once the courtroom had emptied, the judge turned to Sheridan. 'So, Detective Inspector Holler, what was this conversation with the defendant?' he asked.

Sheridan bit her lip. 'I was walking him back to the cell one day and he asked me if we had any evidence that could tie him to the assault.' She paused. 'I told him that I couldn't discuss it with him until we were in interview.'

'Is that it?' the judge asked, clearly a little indignant that the trial had been halted for this non-revelation.

'My client,' Calvin-Jones jumped in, 'advises me that you threatened him if he didn't tell you where the alleged weapon was.'

'Absolutely not.' Sheridan shook her head. *I absolutely did.*

'So, that's it, that's all that was said between you?' The judge unravelled his hands and tapped his index finger against his knuckle.

'Well, there was one other thing.' Sheridan focused on the defence barrister.

'Go on.' He grinned, thinking quite incorrectly that he was about to hear some big admission of a breach of the Police and Criminal Evidence Act.

'He said that he . . .' She hesitated. 'Do I really have to say?' Her eyes turned to the judge, as she savoured the moment. This was going to be fun.

'Yes, you do,' the judge replied.

Sheridan looked Calvin-Jones straight in the eye. 'He said that he thought you were a complete prick and that your incompetence would probably result in him getting banged up.'

Anna Markinson swallowed as hard as she could to suppress the laugh that was bursting to come out.

'That's why I didn't want to say anything in front of the jury.' Sheridan put her hands behind her back and stuck her middle finger up. For Anna's eyes only.

An hour later, they were making their way back to Hale Street Police Station. 'Well, you've pulled some corkers in your time, Sheridan, but that was pure gold.' Anna threw her head back, laughing.

Sheridan pulled up to the traffic lights. 'I couldn't resist. He's such an arse-wipe.' She tapped the steering wheel.

Anna turned to her. 'Did you see the judge's face? I think he wanted to give you a commendation.'

Sheridan's phone rang just as the lights turned green, so she reached into her pocket and passed the handset to Anna. 'Can you answer that for me?'

Anna squinted at the screen. 'It's your mum.'

'Oh, don't answer it, I'll call her back.'

Anna held the ringing mobile in her palm. 'Do you fancy grabbing a quick coffee before we go back to the nick? Celebrate getting one over on dickhead Calvin-Jones?'

'I can't. I've got a quick enquiry to do. I'll drop you off, but I promise to buy cakes later for everyone.'

'Now you're talking. What enquiry? Anything I can help with?'

'No, you're alright mate.'

After dropping Anna off in the back yard of Hale Street nick, Sheridan made her way to the house, her stomach churning as she drove.

CHAPTER 2

Sheridan couldn't park in her normal spot, so had to find a space further down the road, which still just about gave her a clear view of his house. She turned off her engine and settled in to watch. She could knock on the door today. She had to do it sometime. Her parents weren't getting any younger and they deserved to know. They deserved to know the truth about their son. The truth about her brother, Matthew.

She knew she might only have one shot at this. One chance to knock on his door and tell him who she was. She had sat outside Andrew Longford's house so many times over the years, building up the courage to walk up that path.

He was the last person to have seen Matthew alive, apart from his killer. Andrew Longford had been Matthew's best friend, the friend he'd played football with on the day he was murdered. Andrew was fourteen at the time, Matthew twelve. Andrew had given a statement to the police, but the enquiry had gone nowhere. No witnesses had come forward and all these years later, the Matthew Holler murder remained unsolved.

But Sheridan was never going to give up in her quest for the truth. All she had to do was knock on Andrew Longford's door, introduce herself and pray that he would let her in. Maybe he'd remember something about that day that hadn't occurred to him at the time. Her parents had spoken to Andrew and his family right after the murder, but not since then. It always felt too raw.

But every time Sheridan had sat outside his house, the doubts crept in.

What if he slams the door in my face? What if he tells me to leave him alone and never make contact again? I only have one chance.

This time, as she sat in her car, Matthew's face came into her head, as clear as day. Usually when she thought of him, she could only see his blurred outline, his features obscured in her memory. She felt the familiar tightness in her chest that always surfaced when she remembered him. And then, without warning, heavy salty tears fell down her face as she gasped. It was a sensation that overwhelmed her, consumed her. She hadn't held him for nearly twenty-eight years, hadn't ruffled his hair or told him to tidy his room before their mother saw the state of it.

Suddenly, she made the decision to get out of the car and walk over to the house, but as quickly as she opened the car door, she slammed it shut. Frustrated at herself, she whacked the steering wheel. Flames of doubt engulfed her. *How many times will I sit in this road and stare at his front door? How many more times before I finally walk up his path and ring the bell?*

She closed her eyes. And, suddenly, her mobile rang.

'Hi, Mum. Sorry I missed your call earlier. You okay?'

'We're fine, love. Just wanted to see how you're doing?'

They chatted for a few minutes before her mum asked the question. 'Any news on Matthew? I know you're busy, but I just wanted to check. Any new information?'

Sheridan swallowed as she stared at Andrew Longford's door. 'I'm still working on it, Mum. I'm always looking for new leads,

12

you know I'll never give up. I promise I'll let you know if I find anything out.'

'Okay sweetheart, well, I won't keep you. We love you.'

'I love you too.'

She ended the call, started the engine and glanced at his house before making her way back to Hale Street.

CHAPTER 3

DC Rob Wills raised his head as Sheridan walked into the CID office. 'So how was Mr Calvin-Jones today?' he asked. 'Still a complete prick?'

'Absolutely.' Sheridan nodded and made her way to the front of the room, quickly scanning her team to make sure no one was on the phone.

'Right, everyone,' she said loudly, 'I need your total and undivided attention.' She perched on the edge of a desk before continuing. 'So, we all know that Christmas is almost upon us and some of you have managed over the last few weeks to use unscrupulous methods to get me to sign your annual leave requests.' She pointed her finger at several DCs. 'You know who you are.' She tried to hide a grin.

'Anyway, I just want to say that for those of you who are lucky enough to be spending the festive season with family and friends, please don't choke on your stuffing balls.'

Everyone smiled including Sheridan herself, who couldn't keep that straight face forever.

'Now, yesterday I went through everyone's workload and I'm happy to report that you're all pretty much up to date with your cases.' She put her hands together in mock prayer. 'So, let us pray that the Christmas gods are kind and don't throw any shit at us for the next couple of weeks.'

The phone rang on Rob Wills' desk, and as he answered it, he put his finger in his ear to drown out the chatter and banter going around the office. Straining to hear, he put his head down, listening intently, a slight frown spreading across his face. As he ended the call, he puffed out his cheeks and looked at Sheridan. 'Sorry, boss.'

'What?' Sheridan tilted her head as her shoulders slumped.

'Got a job just come in. Murder.'

'You're bloody joking.' She stood up.

'Nope. Apparently, someone's been murdered. And they want us to solve it before Christmas.' Rob bit his bottom lip.

'You dickhead.' Sheridan threw her pen at him. 'Why do I ever believe anything you say?' She put her hand out as she walked towards him. 'Give me my bloody pen back.'

Rob Wills grinned, bending down to retrieve the pen from under his desk, banging his head as he came back up.

'That bloody hurt.' He rubbed his head with one hand and handed Sheridan her pen with the other.

'God did that,' Sheridan replied. 'Right, as I was saying, you're all pretty much up to date with your cases and as you've all done such a great job this year, I'm off out to buy cakes for everyone.' She made her way to the door. 'Except Rob.' She threw him an exaggerated frown, which quickly dissolved.

CHAPTER 4

Gary Lee took a flask out of his holdall and poured himself a cup of tea. He stretched his back and gazed around the cemetery. Four years of digging graves here and he still loved his job. A qualified teacher, he had thrown his career away after discovering that he didn't like children. They were evil. Put on the earth to make his life a misery. He had endured three years of hell at the hands of his pupils, finally resigning after one had thrown a chair at him, hitting him full in the chest. Enough was enough.

Now, he was away from all that. Working outside in all weathers, freezing in the winter, sweating in the summer sun. And he loved it. Dead people didn't laugh at you. He knew the cemetery like the back of his hand. He loved to work alone, with no one to bother him.

He looked down at the grave he was preparing. The deceased was an eighty-one-year-old man – Brian Walters – now joining his beloved wife Heather, who had died seven years before at the age of seventy-seven.

Gary Lee put his flask away and picked up his shovel. He didn't mind that he had to dig by hand. He took his time. He always took his time, especially when a grave was being reopened, respecting the person already buried there. He worked slowly, methodically, humming as he went.

Then three feet down, he suddenly stopped when his spade hit something. Something hard, something odd.

He knelt down and moved the dirt away with his hand. 'What the hell?'

He felt the hard bone with his fingers as he brushed the earth away and stared down in disbelief. He knew he hadn't dug deep enough to have hit the body buried there. And there was no coffin. He shifted his position and took a deep breath, feeling his heart quicken as he realised what he was touching.

The earth was cold and hard. He used the tip of his spade to break it away carefully, slowly revealing a skull with empty eye sockets looking blankly at him. He worked his way along, ribs, arms, legs. Then, slowly, he eased himself up, staring at the partially clothed remains. 'Oh, God,' he gasped. 'Oh, God.'

CHAPTER 5

Sheridan carefully carried two large boxes of cakes up the stairs, one hand firmly placed on the top box, walking quickly and trying to avoid attracting attention as she headed for the safety of the CID office. Cakes brought into a police station stood literally no chance of lasting more than a few minutes; it was like running the gauntlet to reach the top of the stairs as a stream of uniformed officers filed past her.

'For us?' one of them asked, cheekily, as he passed. 'You're too kind, ma'am.'

'You can all feck off,' she called out, shaking her head defiantly, leaving an echo of teasing jeers behind her. She couldn't help but smile as she strutted into CID, victoriously raising the cakes above her head. 'Tuck in, fine warriors. I bring . . .' She stopped, suddenly noticing the deflated expressions on everyone's faces. 'What?' she asked, placing the cakes on the desk in front of her.

Rob Wills inhaled before he spoke. 'A job's just come in. A body's been found in Bordersfield Cemetery.'

She let a grin slowly sneak across her face. She wasn't the kind of person to be fooled twice. 'Oh no. Really? A body found in a cemetery? How suspicious.' She opened the box of cakes. 'Nice try, Rob. Dig in, folks.'

No one moved. Sheridan wasn't buying it and selected a cream horn, amused that her team were resisting her wares. She licked the cream from the top and gave an exaggerated, 'Hmmmmmm, delicious,' before nibbling the flaky pastry around the edge. 'I'm just going to eat all these cakes myself. Don't think for a second that I won't.' She lifted the cream horn for all to see and then shoved it in her mouth. Thick white cream spurted out, covering her nose and chin.

'Sheridan?' The voice took her by surprise. She turned to see DCI Max Hall standing in the doorway.

'Yes boss?' Sheridan stood facing him, wiping flaky pastry off her cheek.

'You heard about the body in Bordersfield Cemetery?'

'Er, yes, boss. Rob's just filling me in now.' She nodded her head, and Max frowned slightly as a lump of fresh cream dropped off her chin and on to the carpet.

CHAPTER 6

Wednesday 15 December

There was a knock on Sheridan's door. 'Come in,' she said, looking up from her computer.

Anna Markinson put her head around the door. 'The DCI wants everyone in the CID office.'

'Okay.' Sheridan got up and followed Anna down the corridor. As they walked into the room, Sheridan spotted DCI Max Hall, who was standing with his sleeves rolled up and his tie loosened. A little less smart than he had appeared earlier on TV, giving the press as little as possible. He hated journalists.

'Morning everyone.' DCI Max Hall scanned the room. 'I just wanted to pull everyone together so that I can go through what we have so far and who's going to be tasked with what.' He coughed and took a sip of tea.

Turning to the whiteboard behind him, he began. 'As you're all aware, yesterday the partially clothed remains of what is believed to be a male victim was found in Bordersfield Cemetery. The body was buried approximately three feet under the earth, so, basically three feet above the coffin of a female called Heather Walters who died on the first of December 1997. The grave was being reopened because her husband Brian Walters had recently passed away, and they were due to be buried beside each other. The male body has been removed for identification, cause of death, unknown DNA and so forth. There's a seal on the grave at the moment but I'm hoping that CSI will be done fairly quickly. Once we know who the male is, and how he died, we can crack on.' He looked up. 'Sheridan, can we find out when Heather Walters was actually buried? How she died, family and all that, just in case there's a link between her and the deceased male, once we know who he is. We also need to start checking out missing persons reports from around that time.'

Sheridan responded, 'No problem.' She had already made herself a note, *Check out missing persons around 1997.*

She eyeballed her team, mentally picking out who she was going to task with what. The room was humming as DCI Max Hall departed, off to keep the press at bay.

Anna Markinson plonked herself down on to the chair opposite Sheridan. 'You look tired. Are you okay?' she asked.

'I'm fine, mate.'

'Any gorgeous woman on the horizon?' Anna asked, pouting.

'Nope.'

'We could set you up online . . .'

'Don't even think about it.' Sheridan pointed a finger towards Anna.

Anna shrugged. 'I'm just saying, you need a woman. I mean, how long has it been since you—'

'Let's sit here and discuss my shite love life, shall we?' Sheridan furtively scanned the room to check that no one had overheard. 'Anyway, how's Steve?'

'He's fine. I think he sometimes gets a bit pissed off that I'm at work most of the time, but such is the life of a copper, eh?'

'Yeah, you got that right. It takes a certain kind of person to understand that we don't get to do the nine-to-five. Trust me, if after seven years Steve is only just starting to get pissed off, then you're not doing too badly.' Sheridan stood up. 'Anyway, let's crack on. Can you task someone to check out missing persons around 1997?'

'Yeah, of course,' Anna replied, before hastily getting up and making her way back to her office.

Sheridan's phone rang: DCI Max Hall summoning her to his office. He waved her in as she peered around the door.

'That's fantastic,' he said, speaking to someone else on his phone. 'Thanks for everything. DI Holler is here with me, so I'll let her know.' He hung up, smiling broadly.

'The jury found Stuart Conner guilty on all eleven counts. The judge gave him sixteen years.'

Sheridan nodded, biting her bottom lip. Feeling tears pricking her eyes, she put her head down. 'He should have got longer, but it's still a good result. I'll ring Donna and let her know.'

Max walked around his desk and lifted her face with his enormous hands. 'Well, would you believe it, Sheridan Holler isn't made of wood. Are these tears I see before me?'

Sheridan slapped his hands away and grinned. 'Bugger off.'

Max laughed and squeezed himself back behind his desk.

Sheridan noticed droplets of sweat on his forehead. Max Hall was fifty-one, six foot tall and heavily built. A large belly hung over his trousers and his cheeks glowed red most of the time. He was the best DCI that Sheridan had ever worked with. He was old school, and considered his team as his family and would go to any lengths to support them. And Sheridan adored him. Not that she'd ever tell him that.

'You look flustered, boss. You okay?' she asked, casually, sitting down and sticking a foot up on his desk.

He eyed her over the top of his glasses and crossed his arms. 'I'm fine, just got a lot on at the moment.'

Sheridan knew what he meant. His daughter was due to be married. His wife Sheila – whom Sheridan had met a number of times and knew to be loving and utterly devoted to her husband – was beginning to get broody in a grandmotherly fashion. Always hinting that she wanted her daughter to get pregnant sooner rather than later. The daughter, of course, wasn't in such a hurry, and Max often found himself caught in the middle.

'I want my girl to be proud of me when I walk her down the aisle,' Max said, before sneezing, blowing his nose and throwing the tissue into the bin under his desk.

'She *will* be proud of you, what are you worried about?'

'I'm worried that I won't fit into my suit,' he said, patting his stomach. 'Sheila and I went shopping for it months ago, but I've put on weight and it doesn't fit me any more. The belt's too tight and at this rate my feet will be too fat for my bloody shoes. I haven't told the wife.' He shook his head. 'I try to hint that I need to go on a diet, but she just says that she loves me no matter how big I am and then shoves a roast dinner under my nose. Don't get me wrong, she's a wonderful woman but I really need to lose some bloody weight.'

Sheridan had heard Max talk about his wife's amazing cooking over the years, hearty meals for her hard-working husband. Hearty meals that increased his waistline, as well as his chances of a heart attack.

Sheridan pulled her foot off his desk and sat upright. 'Bring the belt in tomorrow.'

'What for?'

Sheridan stood up and headed for the door. 'Just bring the belt in.'

CHAPTER 7

The Gables Nursing Home, Crosby, Merseyside

'Good morning!' Joni Summers breezed through the nursing home doors and smiled at Mrs Overson, who had yet again escaped the confines of her room on the first floor and ridden the lift up and down several times before finding herself in reception.

'Now, Mrs Overson, what are you doing down here?' Joni gently took her arm.

'My son has called me a taxi and I'm going home.' Mrs Overson gave a gummy smile, having left her dentures in her room.

'Well, I think we should wait upstairs in your room for him. Come on, I'll take you back up for now.' Joni ushered Mrs Overson back to the lift. Mrs Overson didn't have a son, and her home had been sold to pay for her care. What she did have was dementia. On a good day she remembered where she was and why she was there. On a bad day her mind played the cruellest of tricks, such as believing she was twenty-five years old again, walking along the beach hand in hand with her fiancé.

Joni settled her back into her room and promised to bring her a 'nice cuppa'. Mrs Overson stared blankly at the bare branches of the tree outside her window.

◆ ◆ ◆

Joni made her way to the staffroom and flicked the kettle on, enjoying a moment of peace before the rest of the dayshift staff began to arrive.

Just then, Mo Chase crashed through the door. 'It's bloody freezing out there!' She plonked her sizeable backside against the radiator before blowing into her cupped hands. 'Oh good, you've got the kettle on, nice one!' She rubbed her hands together.

Mo Chase was thirty-four, loud and annoying with an uncanny knack for pissing everyone off just with her mere presence.

Joni pulled two mugs out of the cupboard and earmarked the one with the massive chip in it for Mo. Joni was the same age as Mo, and she had only been working at The Gables for a year – whereas Mo acted like she'd been here forever. Joni loved her job. She was compassionate and kind.

'So, Mo, how's lover boy?' Joni raised her eyebrows and smirked. She loved winding Mo up.

'He's fine. Actually, he's not fine. I'm thinking of dumping him.' Mo sighed.

'I thought you were going to dump him last week when he blew you off?'

'He didn't blow me off. Something came up at work,' Mo retorted. She was growing a little impatient with the other girls' constant piss-taking about her relationship with Harry Minton.

All the staff had at some point heard Mo talking about Harry Minton. Either when she was bragging, or needlessly complaining about, her relationship. Mo had met Harry a year earlier when he had come to The Gables, looking for a suitable home to place his elderly mother in. Mo would tell anyone who would listen how Harry was a jet-setting sales executive and was often out of the country. Mo had never been to his house, had never met his friends or family. The rumour among the rest of the staff was that Harry Minton was married, probably with a couple of kids. And, of course, Harry's mother never actually ended up at The Gables.

'I haven't got time to sit chatting. See you later.' Mo took her coffee and made her way upstairs, all ready to start the day in a bad mood.

Joni pulled a jumper over her head. Winter had taken hold and a bitter wind whistled around the building as she embarked on her rounds, starting with Ellie Sands, who was fast asleep. As Joni walked around Ellie's bed to open the curtains, Ellie suddenly opened her eyes and let out a loud shriek. Although Joni was used to her outbursts, it still made her jump.

'Good morning, Ellie! How are you today?' Joni asked. 'Would you like some breakfast?'

As quickly as Ellie had awoken, she snapped her eyes shut and fell straight back to sleep.

Joni filled a bowl of water and, taking a flannel from the cupboard, she dipped it into the warm water and ran it gently over Ellie's face. Ellie's eyes opened again, and Joni smiled at her. 'Is that nice?' Joni asked. 'We'll get you showered later and pop you in your chair.'

'How's it going?' A voice from behind her made Joni turn to see the nursing home owner, Yvonne Lopes, standing there, leaning up against the door.

'Pretty good.'

'How's Ellie today?' Yvonne walked in.

'She's okay, even if she doesn't always know I'm here.'

'Oh, she knows you're there, trust me.' Yvonne Lopes was tall, with short-cut greying hair that she refused to dye. She had gentle lines around her face and her warm hazel eyes didn't miss a single thing. She was firm but fair and was passionate about The Gables.

Having retired from nursing some ten years before, she had taken over the home following a highly critical report for lack of patient care. She had rebuilt its reputation and now dedicated her life to the place and its residents.

Joni carried on wiping Ellie's face. 'So, have you got a big family Christmas planned?' she asked without looking up.

'Yes, my son and his family are coming for dinner.' Yvonne smoothed the covers on Ellie's bed. 'You?'

'It's just me and my mate, Sam. She's coming to stay for a bit. It's going to be wild.' Joni grinned.

Ellie let out a cry that made Joni jump. 'It's okay, Ellie.'

'Pissy, pissy knickers!' Ellie cried out. It was one of her usual phrases; often yelled whether she'd had an accident or not. It seemed to be one of her greatest fears.

'I'd better check her.' Joni gently pulled back the covers and checked Ellie. 'You're alright Ellie, you're nice and dry.'

Yvonne watched as Joni wiped Ellie's face with such care, quietly talking to her, calming and reassuring.

'Can I ask you a question?' Joni whispered.

'Of course.' Yvonne crossed her arms.

'I just wondered if Ellie ever had friends or family visit before I came to work here?'

'She did. Initially.' Yvonne kept her voice low. 'She didn't have any children, but the odd family member or friend would pop in every now and then.'

Joni noticed that Ellie had closed her eyes. 'Why'd they stop coming?'

'I guess it was just too hard for them. What we see isn't the Ellie they knew, I suppose.'

Joni nodded. 'I can understand that. It must be too much for some people.' She sighed. 'At least her nephew comes occasionally.'

'Yes, I suppose so. Anyway, I'll leave you to it.' Yvonne glanced sadly back at Ellie before she left the room.

Joni recognised the look on Yvonne's face as she left. Ellie's nephew had that same look whenever he came to visit. He would at least sit and talk kindly to her, but he always left looking so sad and disheartened by her lack of response.

CHAPTER 8

Joni Summers had been home for an hour when the phone rang. 'Hello, Mum,' she said, taking a deep breath.

'Hello love, how are you? How's work? When's Sam arriving?' Her mother always asked questions in multiples of three. Sometimes more.

'I'm fine. Work's fine. And Sam should be here any minute. You okay?'

'Apart from my hair doing its own thing, I'm fine. Anyway, I won't keep you. Don't work too hard. Love to Sam.'

'Okay, bye, Mum.' Joni smiled and pushed herself up from the sofa. She finished her coffee and lit a cigarette, immediately stubbing it out. She didn't want to fall into the usual New Year's resolution tradition of quitting her bad habits. She would give up before then, stand out from the crowd, be different. She busied herself tidying up.

Life was good. She had her own place, with an amazing view over Crosby Beach and the River Mersey beyond. A flat she would never have been able to afford had her adoring grandmother not left it to her. She had a job that she loved, and her best friend, Sam, was coming to stay with her. Sam was a schoolteacher and had been based at a school in Manchester but had recently accepted a new post in Liverpool. She'd found a flat in Bootle and had been due to move in when the landlord suddenly decided he wanted to sell, leaving Sam high and dry.

Sam and Joni had met in school when they were seven. Joni was getting the shit kicked out of her by a couple of eight-year-olds and Sam punched her way into the fight, taking out the tall, lanky girl first and then her little friend. And so, the friendship had begun. That was twenty-six years ago and the bond between them was still rock solid. Joni nodded to herself. Yeah, life was good. She picked the cigarette out of the ashtray and relit it. She'd definitely give up tomorrow.

Ten minutes later, she opened her front door and threw herself at her best friend. 'Oh, it's so good to see you, come in!'

Sam Sloan puffed out her cheeks, dragging a bulging suitcase through the front door. 'Thanks.' She hugged Joni with her spare arm. 'Good to see you, too.'

'Is that all your stuff?' Joni asked, frowning.

'No. There's a few more bits in the car.' Sam kissed Joni on the cheek and pushed the suitcase into the hallway. 'Thanks for letting us stay, you're a lifesaver.'

'Hang on. Us? Who's us?' Joni asked.

'Me and Maud.'

'Oh God, I'd forgotten about her. You know your cat hates me.'

'No, she doesn't. Actually . . . I'd better get her out of the car before she starts puking on the seats. She doesn't travel well.' Sam caught the look on Joni's face. 'She is litter trained, however.'

'Fantastic,' Joni said sarcastically, shaking her head.

Later that evening, Joni and Sam talked while Maud the cat wandered the flat, taking in her new surroundings. She jumped on to the window ledge, watching wide-eyed as rain landed on the misted-up pane, tapping her paw against the cold glass.

'So, how's the job?' Sam took a sip of her Jack Daniel's and settled herself in the armchair.

'It's good. Bit knackering but I enjoy it.' Joni eased her head back against the sofa cushion. 'It's such a shame though, you spend all your life working or whatever and then you end up in a nursing home with strangers washing and feeding you.' Joni sighed. Ellie Sands' face came into her head. And just for a moment, feeling the joy of having her best friend there made her feel guilty.

She suddenly changed the subject. 'Anyway, let's toast to happy times,' she said, raising her glass and pointing it towards Sam.

After finishing the bottle of bourbon, they crashed into their beds, leaving Maud to continue investigating her temporary home, finally settling on the back of the sofa. After weeing on the kitchen floor. Twice.

CHAPTER 9

Thursday 16 December

Sheridan met Anna in the corridor. 'You okay?' she asked.

Anna nodded as she was about to crunch into an enormous apple. 'Yeah, good, I've got an update on mispers from the late nineties for you.'

'Ah, good,' Sheridan replied as they headed towards her office.

Anna studied the sheet of paper in her hand.

'Okay, there are two strong possibles. One was a male who disappeared in 1996. Martin Samms, aged twenty-three, regularly went missing, had mental health issues. His family believe he might have moved abroad, possibly somewhere in Africa. They've had no contact with him since he disappeared.' She paused. 'The second isn't technically a misper, but he's been wanted for seven years. And those of us who've been here for a while remember him all too well. John Lively. Main suspect in the shooting of Kate Armitage – off-duty police officer who was based at this nick. She was shot and killed in a supermarket car park on the thirteenth of December 1997. He also shot a female who was walking near to PC Armitage at the time, but she survived. John Lively disappeared after the incident but is still wanted in connection with the shooting.'

Sheridan absorbed the information. 'I remember that case. I was in Hampshire Police at the time. It was all over the news. Did you know Kate Armitage?'

'Yeah. Sort of.' Anna took a bite of her apple.

'Can you get me the original file on her shooting?' Sheridan sat back in her chair.

'You think the body's John Lively?'

'Could be,' Sheridan replied.

'I'll get the file sent over,' Anna said as she left the office.

A moment later and Anna peered around her door. 'Sorry, the DCI wants us all in the briefing.'

Sheridan nodded. 'Okay.' She pushed her chair back, stood up and followed Anna down the corridor.

DCI Max Hall wheezed his way to the front of the room to stand by the whiteboard.

'Okay. Now that everyone's here, we have an update on the body.' He blew his nose. 'Sorry, I've got a stinking bloody cold.'

He coughed and blew his nose again. 'Right . . . body's been identified as John Lively, born eleventh of November 1972. Cause of death was a single gunshot wound to the chest. The bullet has been recovered. We're still waiting for the results of any unknown DNA evidence on his remains and clothes, although he was only wearing boxer shorts when he was buried. Now, I'm sure you're all aware of who John Lively is, or was. He's the suspect in the fatal shooting of Kate Armitage, a police officer who was based here for most of her police service. She was shot by Lively on the thirteenth of December 1997, in Mason's supermarket car park. He rode up to her on his motorbike, fired off five bullets in quick succession. Two bullets hit Kate Armitage. Two missed their intended target, and the fifth hit a nearby female, who fortunately survived. John Lively has been missing since the shooting. He was a local druggie and Kate Armitage had had many dealings with him before he disappeared. He'd also made threats towards her before he shot her. Now, clearly, we're opening a murder enquiry into John Lively's death.'

Max Hall pointed at DC Rob Wills. 'Rob, what have you got on the lady whose grave Lively was found in, Heather Walters?'

Rob Wills referred to his notes. 'She was seventy-seven when she died of breast cancer on the first of December 1997, and was buried on the twelfth of December. She was a retired accounts clerk. The family are all of good character, no links to any known criminal activity. Her husband Brian died at the age of eighty-one of heart failure.'

Max Hall nodded. 'Okay. Keep digging and see if we can find any link at all between Heather Walters, her family and John Lively.'

'Will do.' Rob tapped his pen on the desk.

Max Hall took a sip of water. 'The condition of John Lively's remains indicate that he's been dead for approximately seven years, which ties in with when Heather Walters was buried, and when Kate Armitage was killed by John Lively. It also appears that his body has been in the ground for that entire time, so whoever shot him was likely to have buried him soon after. So, Lively could have shot her, but was then killed himself shortly afterwards. Possibly a drug deal that went wrong.'

One of the detectives quickly shot his hand up. 'I take it we can't rule out that this was a revenge shooting in retaliation for Kate Armitage's death?'

There was an awkward silence around the room.

Sheridan jumped in. 'We can't rule anything out. We need to go back to the original file on Kate Armitage's shooting, see if anything was missed the last time around.'

Max nodded in agreement.

Anna gave Sheridan a quick wink. Once again, Sheridan was one step ahead.

Max wiped his forehead with the back of his hand as he addressed the room. 'The press are sniffing around like hell on this one, so just be aware of that. You all know the protocol.' He coughed, a heavy, chesty cough. 'I'm off to die in my office.' He looked at Sheridan. 'I'll leave you to it.'

Sheridan returned to her own office, closely followed by Anna who lingered in the doorway with her arms crossed. 'So, what are your thoughts?' She grinned.

'What do you mean?'

'Well, you've normally got a case sussed before we even start an investigation, so I figured you've got this one all worked out and we can all go home.'

Sheridan leaned back with her hands behind her head. 'What was Kate Armitage like?'

'Bit of a firecracker.'

'What do you mean?'

'From what I can remember she was quite outspoken, didn't take any shit and had a reputation for, well, sleeping around. She was having an affair with her crew partner, Jeff Nichols, at the time of the shooting.'

'That's interesting.' Sheridan wrote Jeff Nichols' name down. 'Was Kate Armitage married? Kids?'

'No, she was single. But Jeff Nichols was married. With a couple of kids, too.'

'Did you work on the original case?'

'No, I wasn't in CID then.'

Sheridan tapped her fingers on top of her head. 'Okay, well, I'll look forward to reading the original file.'

'I'll get it to you as soon as.' And with that, Anna left.

Sheridan got up and walked down the corridor, meeting Max Hall coming out of the men's toilet.

'Did you bring it in?' she whispered.

'I did.' He walked back to his office as Sheridan followed, closing the door behind her.

Max took the belt out of his desk drawer and wrapped it around his waist. Sheridan adjusted it and stood back, leaving him holding it in place.

'You're breathing in.' She slapped his arm. 'Don't breathe in.'

Max raised his eyes to the ceiling, and reluctantly relaxed his stomach. Sheridan squinted at the belt and then at Max.

'You're going to have to lose at least two inches for that to fit.'

'I could have bloody told *you* that.' He flung the belt on his desk. 'The trousers are the same, they're so tight I can feel my innards trying to escape.'

Sheridan tried not to laugh and put her hand to her mouth as if imagining the dilemma.

'Okay, here's the plan . . .'

Sheridan wrote him out a diet sheet and gave him simple exercises he could do to help reduce his waistline. They agreed it would be difficult for him when he was at home, but during his working day, he could replace the junk food he'd normally consume with fruit and drink plenty of water.

'How do you know all this stuff about diets?' Max asked.

'I'm a woman, Max, we just know these things.'

'And if I do all that, you reckon I'll get into my suit in time for the wedding?'

'Absolutely.' She smiled, folding up the sheet of paper and handing it to him.

'And you won't tell anyone?'

'I won't tell a soul.'

'Promise?'

'Pinky promise.'

CHAPTER 10

Jeff Nichols stood at his front door and opened his mouth to speak, but his ex-wife Carly put her hand up. 'I don't want an argument, Jeff. I just want to have a civilised conversation.'

Jeff raised his voice. 'Then don't ring me and tell me you're taking my kids away.'

'Can I come in?' Carly stepped towards him. 'Or do you want to discuss this out here?' She raised her eyebrows and followed Jeff into the house, shaking her head at the state of the place.

Jeff pushed the living room door open and walked in, turning to face Carly with his arms crossed.

'Well?'

'I'm moving to Norfolk to be with my parents.' Carly sighed. 'They're getting older. Mum struggles with Dad sometimes; he's getting less mobile with his arthritis. I told you ages ago I was thinking of moving. I'm not stopping you from seeing the kids.'

'No, of course you're not . . . you're just taking them so far away that it makes it difficult for me to see them.' He sat on the edge of the coffee table and sank his head into his hands.

'It's not the other side of the bloody world, it's a five-hour drive and it doesn't wash with me Jeff, this bloody "poor old me" pretentious bollocks. You never gave a shit about the kids when we were together, and you never see them now because you've spent the last seven years drowning in your own self-pity.' Carly took a breath. 'Look, I know what happened was bloody awful and I know you feel guilty because of it, but you have to remember that you were unfaithful to me, you were screwing her and all the time I was at home bringing up our children.'

He raised his head to look at her. 'I've lost everything and now you're taking my kids away.'

'You've lost everything because you couldn't keep it in your bloody pants!' She sighed heavily, tired of this conversation. The same conversation they had had over and over again for the last seven years.

'Let it go, Carly. I've said I'm sorry a thousand times. If I could change it all I would, but I can't. Please just don't take my kids away from me.'

'I'm not taking them away from you, Jeff, you lost your kids a long time ago. Christ, you forgot Amy's birthday last year, do you have any idea how devastated she was? So, don't play this bloody game with me, everything that has happened between you, me and your kids was your own doing.'

Jeff stood up and put his face an inch from Carly's. 'You've poisoned their minds.' His voice was low, trembling with anger.

'You're a bloody loser, Jeff. I have no sympathy for you. I'm going now.'

'That's it? That's all you have to say? Jesus Christ.' He looked straight into her eyes. 'Please don't hate me, Carly.'

'Don't.' Carly remained face to face with him. 'Don't do this, Jeff.' She put her hand on his shoulder but took a step away from him. She remembered the pain his affair had caused. The nights she had lain awake crying into her pillow, praying her instincts were wrong. Convincing herself that her husband, the police officer, wouldn't risk everything for a quick fuck with a colleague. But her instincts were bang on and she couldn't erase the gut-wrenching feelings that had struck her when the truth finally came out.

'So we'll be leaving in a couple of days.' An uncomfortable moment passed as they just stood there. 'I'm going now.' Carly removed her hand from his shoulder and turned around.

Jeff slumped back down as he heard the front door close behind her.

CHAPTER 11

'What do you think?' Sam raised her arms and spun round to show off pale blue jeans that sat comfortably on her slim figure. The collar of her crisp white shirt was turned up and her brown boots squeaked slightly as she walked, new boots that needed some walking in.

Joni looked up. 'You look lovely, dear.'

'Not too butch?' Sam checked herself in the mirror, running her fingers through her long brown hair. She was naturally beautiful with olive skin and hazel eyes.

'No, not too butch. Who's this mystery girl again?' Joni asked, opening the oven door and waving away the black smoke that poured out. 'Shit!'

'What *is* that?' Sam bent down to take a closer look.

'It *was* chicken-in-something-marinade.' Joni turned the oven off and lifted out the cremated chicken.

Maud stood behind her and put her paws up against the cupboard.

'Maud said she'll eat it,' said Sam.

'I wouldn't do that to her. Mind you, she did eat the corner of my magazine the other day.' Joni opened the cupboard and began hunting for something she could cook without destroying it. 'Anyway, you didn't answer me . . . who's this mysterious girl?'

'Harriet, she's a fireman, firewoman.' Sam looked back at the mirror. 'And she is bloody fit.'

'Didn't you have a date with her ages ago, and she called it off?' Joni took a packet of Jaffa Cakes out of the cupboard and put one on the floor for Maud.

Sam glanced down as Maud walked out of the kitchen with the Jaffa Cake in her mouth. 'Yeah, that's the one, but I'm willing to give her a second chance. Did I mention how fit she is? Are cats supposed to eat chocolate?'

'I don't think so. But she only eats the spongey bit.'

'Right, I'll leave you to it.' Sam headed for the door. 'Don't wait up!'

An hour later, and Sam was back.

'What are you doing home so early?' Joni called out.

'She rang me just as I got to the pub saying she'd forgotten about our date and couldn't make it now because she was out with a mate and staying in Manchester.' Sam sat on the arm of the sofa and pulled her boots off. 'That's twice now, so she can fuck off. And these stupid boots are bloody killing me.'

'I feel bad for you, I bet you thought you were going to get laid.' Joni yawned.

'What kind of woman do you take me for? Anyway, talking of getting laid, how long's it been since you got some?'

'We're not talking about me.' Joni counted her fingers. 'Eight months.'

'Jesus, it'll dry up, you know.' Sam waved a finger at Joni.

'I'm only thirty-four. Anyway, I'm saving myself for the right guy.'

Sam sat in the armchair, rubbing her feet. 'We'll both find the perfect partner, my friend, you'll marry some handsome blond lumberjack and I'll hook up with some gorgeous dark-haired beauty.' She tapped her legs and Maud obliged, jumping on to her lap and settling down.

'Okay, so describe your perfect woman.' Joni laid herself out, resting her mug on her stomach.

'Well . . . she would be tall, slim or medium build, nice eyes, nice smile, dark hair, not too short, maybe shoulder length, educated, professional and a good sense of humour.' She nodded. 'And likes animals and has a mysterious side to her.'

'That it?' Joni sipped her coffee.

'And isn't all bloody possessive and weird and jealous. Trust me, there's plenty out there like that.'

'That it?'

'And is comfortable with her sexuality and can cook. Actually, scrub that, I don't care if she can't cook.'

'That it?'

'Yep, not too much to ask for, is it?'

CHAPTER 12

Friday 17 December

Sheridan sat at her desk and breathed in the coffee she'd bought on the way to work.

Anna had passed her the original case files into the shooting, which contained copies of PC Kate Armitage's pocket notebook. Taking a sip of steaming coffee, she started reading.

Friday July 11th 1997
09.15 Kingston Road. Stop-search John LIVELY 11/11/72. Search carried out by PC 214 Nichols.

White powder wrapped in cling film found in LIVELY'S bag. Arrested at 09.20 hours. Transported to Hale Street Police Station.

Friday September 19th 1997
14.30 Yale Cross Road. Stop-search John LIVELY 11/11/72

Searched by PC 214 Nichols – nothing found. Escorted to Hale Street PS for drugs search – negative.

Sheridan noted down that PC Kate Armitage and PC Jeff Nichols stop-searched John Lively twice more before the shooting. Nothing was found.

Friday 12th December 1997

PC Kate Armitage reports to Sergeant Alan Harman that John Lively had threatened her when she was off duty. Sergeant Harman's pocket notebook entry read that John Lively had seen her in a coffee shop and told her to 'watch her back'. PC Armitage told Sergeant Harman that she just wanted the incident recorded, as she did not take the threat seriously.

Later the same day – evening – Friday 12th December 1997

Kate Armitage's car, which she had parked around the back garages to her house, is burnt out. She believes John Lively is responsible. No evidence linking him to the fire. When asked why she had parked her car around the back garages instead of outside the front of her property as normal, Armitage explained that she was concerned that Lively may see her getting into her car at work, and if it was then parked outside her home address he would know where she lived.

Saturday 13th December 1997
The shooting.

Summary and eyewitness reports

Kate Armitage is off duty. That morning she hires a car from a local hire company in Liverpool. She is believed to have spent the day at home and is believed to have left her house at around 5.30 p.m. The drive to the supermarket takes approximately fifteen minutes.

She parks her car some distance from the entrance to the supermarket, which is busy due to the time of year. She walks towards the main entrance. A person, believed to be a male riding a motorcycle, rides towards her, stops and pulls out a handgun and fires five times in quick succession. Two bullets hit Kate and the last three missed, one hitting the woman walking beside her. Several witnesses reported that they heard Kate shout 'No, Lively!' just before she was shot. The suspect dropped the gun and rode off. Only John Lively's fingerprints were found on the gun.

All of the witnesses who were close enough believed the motorcyclist was a white male. One stated it could have been a woman. There were differing descriptions of his height, varying between five foot six to six foot. They all said he was slim to medium build. Most of them placed the suspect between twenty and forty years old. Almost all of the witnesses stated he was wearing dark clothes and an open-faced motorcycle helmet with no visor. Only one picked out John Lively from photo identification. There were varying accounts of the timescale from when the male stopped the motorcycle, fired the shots and rode off. Several said it was between five and ten seconds, two said seven to fourteen seconds and one said it was about four seconds.

Sheridan moved on to read the reports following the shooting.

Two witnesses who were near to Kate Armitage stated that they saw the motorcyclist ride out of the car park towards Hollyhock Road. They did not see where he went from there.

One witness, thirty-three-year-old shop assistant Sally Doneghy, stated that she heard three shots, but didn't realise at first what they were. She stated that there could have been more shots fired but she couldn't be sure. She noticed after the shooting that the suspect appeared to fumble with the gun before dropping it. He appeared to hesitate about picking it up and 'clearly wanted to just get away'. She also mentioned that the male's right hand seemed odd, but couldn't be more specific. She remembered staring at the gun in total shock, horrified about what was happening and terrified for her little girl, Abby, who was with her.

The supermarket car park was fairly well lit, bearing in mind it was 6 p.m. on a December evening. There was no CCTV outside the store.

Only one of the witnesses stated that they had seen the motorbike's number plate, but could only recall the first three letters, which were later found to match John Lively's motorbike.

CCTV was checked around the streets leading to and from John Lively's flat and the supermarket. CCTV quality is poor but shows a motorbike on the main road leading to the supermarket and again what is believed to be the same motorbike is seen to ride out of the supermarket, along Hollyhock Road. It then turns left down Montrose Avenue and CCTV coverage ends there.

> *John Lively's motorbike was found outside his flat later that night.*

Sheridan made a note that John Lively could have taken various routes home, but most would have made it more likely he'd be picked up on CCTV.

> *CCTV was checked in relation to Kate Armitage. She was picked up in the hire car at various points from her house to the supermarket. Lively's motorbike was not seen to be following her but picked up as he entered the supermarket car park, moments before Kate's car.*
>
> *Three witnesses remained with Kate Armitage until the ambulance arrived. She did not speak during this time, and all three witnesses stated that they believed she was already deceased by the time the paramedics began working on her. She was treated at the scene but confirmed dead on arrival at hospital.*
>
> *Four witnesses stayed with the woman who had been walking beside Kate Armitage. They stated that she was unconscious throughout and did not regain consciousness while they remained with her.*
>
> *Paramedics treated her at the scene. She was taken to St Anne's Hospital in Liverpool, where she was treated for a single gunshot wound to the head. She survived but suffered a significant brain injury and spent almost a year in hospital.*

Sheridan turned the page. The female with the brain injury was a fifty-one-year-old local newspaper editor by the name of Ellie Sands.

CHAPTER 13

Joni got to work to find most of her colleagues huddled together in the staffroom. The traditional secret Santa was well underway and homemade cakes and mince pies were being devoured. Joni joined in the laughter as the usual useless and inappropriate gifts were exchanged.

As the present swapping came to an end, Joni made her way through to her allocated residents in their rooms, firstly stopping in to check on Ellie Sands. 'Hey Ellie, how are you today?' No response. Dark eyes stared through her. 'It's nearly Christmas, Ellie, I hope you had some nice Christmases before . . . well, you know, before you came here.'

'Shit me.' Ellie's voice was distorted and her mouth drooped awkwardly, making any speech slurred.

'Let's check you, Ellie.' Joni gently reached across Ellie's tiny body and carefully lifted her nightie. 'No, you're fine, Ellie. Nice and clean.'

Ellie's mouth opened and she let out a screeching noise. Clenching her fists, she brought her hands up to her face. 'Peeeesss!' she shouted.

'Come on, Ellie, don't upset yourself.' Joni sat on the bed and held her hand until Ellie relaxed and closed her eyes.

'Hi.' A voice behind her made Joni look up. Ellie's nephew had just arrived, and was hovering in the doorway.

'Hi, Miles,' Joni said. 'How are you?'

'Fine thanks, how's my aunt today?'

'She's good.' Joni turned back to Ellie. 'You've got a visitor, Miles is here.'

Ellie turned her head to face the window.

Miles walked over and kissed Ellie on the forehead. He was gangly and awkward and always looked like he was uncomfortable being there.

'I'm just going to get her out of bed and pop her in her chair.' Joni pulled the big armchair towards the window and Miles helped her lift Ellie's frail body into it. She took a blanket from the bed and laid it over Ellie's legs. 'Can I get you anything?' She smiled at Miles.

'No, I'm fine thanks, I can't stay long actually, my wife and I are visiting friends later,' he replied.

'Oh, well I'll leave you to it. If I don't see you before, have a good Christmas.' Joni quickly looked at Ellie and noticed her eyes were shut.

'You, too,' Miles replied.

CHAPTER 14

Sheridan was feeling peckish, so quickly robbed a packet of crisps from Max's not-so-secret stash in his office. It was the least she could do to help him on his diet. Back at her desk, she returned to the file on PC Kate Armitage.

At the time of the shooting, Armitage had been forty-two years old. Divorced. No children. She had joined the police force when she was twenty-two and was known as a 'go-getter'. Although she had twice sat and failed her sergeant's exam, she had an exemplary record and was described as a credit to the force.

Sheridan then read the file on PC Jeff Nichols. At the time of the shooting, he had been thirty-nine, married, with two children. He had joined the force when he was twenty-nine. His record was exemplary, with his superiors frequently referring to him as a good police officer. A year before the shooting he had been partnered up with PC Kate Armitage. Several of his colleagues had described them as very close, others as always flirting with each other, and most knew they were having an affair.

Sheridan rubbed her eyes and sat back. She looked at the clock and realised she really needed to go home. Yawning, she picked up another pile of papers and carried on reading.

The reports contained officers' accounts of what had happened as they realised that Kate had called out 'No, Lively.' They all agreed she must have recognised John Lively as the shooter. Armed officers attended his address later that evening.

John Lively lived in a ground-floor flat in Kingsway Road, Toxteth. When officers arrived at his address, they found his motorbike parked outside. They gained entry to the property, finding his wallet, crash helmet and keys were missing, as was Lively. His motorbike was examined, but the only prints found were Lively's and those of a male named Stewart Hunt, a friend of Lively's who confirmed that he had previously worked on Lively's motorbike. Neighbours stated that Lively came and went at all times of the day and night and they rarely noticed any visitors. On the evening of the shooting, one of them thought he heard Lively's motorbike although didn't see him or hear him in his flat and never saw him again.

Sheridan turned to the file on John Lively.

He was an only child, born on 11 November 1972 in Toxteth. His mother Angela Lively died of leukaemia aged thirty-nine, when he was thirteen years old, in 1985. His father was unknown. After his mother's death, Lively was put into temporary care until he was placed with a foster family in Childwall, Liverpool. His foster parents, Alan and Judy Martin, were spoken to after Lively disappeared. Lively was fourteen when he went to live with them; they described him as troubled and often went missing. He smoked and drank, and they believed he was taking drugs for the majority of the time he lived with them. He was arrested twice for shoplifting and once for burglary before he was seventeen, when he had left home. They did not see or speak to him after that time.

Sheridan flicked through the file and found two reports on Ellie Sands, both from Kathryn Pullman, an intermediary specialising in speech and communication.

The first report stated that Ellie was seen at St Anne's Hospital in Liverpool. The report was dated 18 March 1998:

I was asked to see Ellie Sands by DCI Broad to assess her current communication skills and difficulties, to establish if there was any hope of obtaining infor-mation about a shooting incident which occurred three months ago, during which Ellie Sands suffered a gunshot wound to the head. Since the incident, Ellie Sands has only regained consciousness on a few occasions and therefore I have only just been able to take this opportunity to assess her.

Summary:

Understanding of questions; requests; comments; instructions.

I could not establish any consistent way in which Ellie Sands was able to indicate choices, either by pointing to individual words or pictures or by gesture (eg consistent head nod or shake or blink or other gesture such as a hand squeeze to indicate yes or no or by speech). This makes it difficult to assess whether someone is understanding – they can't clearly choose an answer whether gesture/spoken/written/signal.

Expressive language.

Ellie Sands has a few words, but these are so distorted and slurred that it is hard for anyone to know (rather than guess) what they mean; although they sound like the same words each time she speaks. They do not seem to be attached to any particular activity or request, though usually they are delivered with some excitement and upset. Hospital staff report that it is often when someone mentions the shooting that these words come out.

(Repetitive utterances like this are very common after severe head injury of any sort – including swearing from someone who never swore before. They may be words which have meaning for the speaker – or random words which have nothing to do with what is happening or what the person needs.)

Ellie Sands does not at this time have sufficient hand movement for accurate gestures such as pointing or miming an action such as eating/drinking/ combing hair etc.

Recommendations:

I therefore could not recommend any strategies to validate evidence given during an interview at this stage, as it would be difficult to know if anything she tried to indicate was accurate.

I also recommend that she is further assessed prior to her release from hospital. I note that it is likely she will require full-time care based on the significance of her injury. An assessment will be required to ascertain the appropriate care facility for her.

Sheridan then read the second report from Kathryn Pullman dated 11 January 1999:

This assessment is to establish the progress of Ellie Sands who has been in hospital for thirteen months after suffering a significant head injury by gunshot wound. I have spent several hours with Ellie Sands over the last few days and her condition remains the same. She has gained no increase in her ability to communicate in any way. She shows the same gestures and speech as is documented in my original report. My recommendation is that she is placed in an appropriate care facility which will need to be assessed to ensure that she receives the most appropriate care for her condition.

> *Kathryn Pullman*
> *Speech and language therapist.*
> *Specialist in head injury.*
> *Registered intermediary for the Criminal Courts.*

Sheridan noted that Kathryn Pullman and the police had visited Ellie Sands at The Gables nursing home on four more occasions between 1999 and 2003. Ellie's speech and communication ability had not changed or improved during that time.

Sheridan closed the file and quickly scanned her own notes.

> *Locate foster parents – check if Lively made contact after shooting.*
> *Visit Ellie Sands – need update on current condition – consider family/friends re possible revenge for shooting.*

CHAPTER 15

Sunday 19 December

Jeff Nichols pulled up outside his parents' house, tyres skidding slightly on the gravel drive. He looked up at the place and as usual, practically every light was on. His mother loved this house but was adamant it was haunted and insisted on having the place lit up as soon as it got dark. His father had given up arguing about the bills. He gripped the steering wheel and was about to drive away when the front door opened and his mother made her way towards him. He gave a false smile and put his hand up, now resigned to going in.

'Hello, come in! Your dad's just on the phone. I'll put the kettle on, do you want tea or coffee? I've just made a pot of tea, but I can make coffee if you want.' His mother paused for breath.

'Hello, Mum.' Jeff got out of his car and kissed her on the cheek before following her into the house, dutifully wiping his feet on the hallway mat.

Half an hour later and Jeff's father finally joined them. 'Sorry about that, business call. You okay, son?' He patted Jeff on the back as he sat down at the huge wooden table that was far too big for the kitchen.

'Yeah, I'm okay, Dad. Business good then?' Jeff asked, not really interested.

'Yeah, not bad, can't complain,' Bill Nichols replied.

'You should think about retiring, Dad.' Jeff looked at his mother who instantly raised her eyebrows at her husband.

'He keeps promising me a holiday, don't you, Bill?' She handed Bill a cup of tea. 'Been promising for years.' Deirdre Nichols shook her head. She was a slight woman; hard-faced and miserable. She had always been strict with Jeff when he was growing up, and had rarely shown him any affection. Unlike his father, who had doted on his only child. Four years earlier, his father had suffered a stroke, so Jeff was forced to look after the family business while he recovered. Jeff had been reluctant to begin with, but his father had begged, making him feel compelled to step in.

Bill Nichols had started up a small haulage business after being made redundant some thirty years earlier. He had used his severance to buy an old transit van, and started doing local deliveries, eventually employing five staff and expanding his fleet of vehicles. Rising costs and fierce competition from larger, cheaper haulage companies had almost put him out of business several times and now he only employed two drivers, but he'd kept his head above water and provided for his family. Jeff had no interest in ever taking over the business. He'd made his feelings quite clear whenever the subject came up.

His father rubbed the palm of his hand against his chin. 'I'd think about retiring if you took over the business, son.'

'Dad . . . I . . .' Jeff put his head down.

'I know that's not what you want. I'd just like someone I can trust to take over, that's all.'

'I know you do.' Jeff ran his hand through his hair. 'I just can't.'

56

'Jeff.' Bill put his tea down and laid his hands on his knees. 'I'm worried about you. We're both worried. You don't seem to be moving on and—'

Jeff cut him short. 'I'm fine, Dad.'

'You're not fine, and we all know it,' Bill continued, while Deirdre stood at the sink washing the dishes. 'You don't go anywhere. You have no interest in anything or anyone. And you seem to have nothing going on in your life. Professionally or personally. You need to let things go, son. Enough grieving now, it won't change anything, you being like this.'

Jeff blew out his cheeks and stood up. 'I'll sort myself out, I'll be fine. I'm happy to do the odd driving job for you, Dad, but I've been thinking of maybe getting away for a while.' He nodded as he spoke.

'You should, son. Get away from it all for a bit. What are you doing for Christmas? We'd love to have you here.' His father got up to help Deirdre, picking up a tea towel.

'I can't. I've arranged to spend it with some mates,' Jeff lied, as he watched his parents doing the dishes together. They had been together for over fifty years and Jeff couldn't remember ever seeing them holding hands or even kissing on the cheek. They must have loved each other once.

CHAPTER 16

Monday 20 December

Anna opened Sheridan's door and, finding her office was empty, she turned to walk away.

'Looking for me?' Sheridan called as she came out of the ladies' toilets.

'Yeah, the DCI's called in sick. He wants you to brief the team.'

'Did he say what's wrong?'

'Stinking cold,' Anna replied. 'I've got the results from Lively's remains, and his boxers. There was no other DNA found on him.'

Sheridan nodded. 'Okay.' She followed Anna into the main briefing room where the CID team were all talking. 'Morning, everyone,' she said as she made her way to the front of the room. The talking ceased, and all heads turned towards her. 'Okay, the DCI's off sick, so he's asked me to brief you all.'

She paused, turning to glance at the whiteboard. Out-of-date information stared back at her. 'As you're aware, the body of the male found in Bordersfield Cemetery has been formally identified as that of John Lively. I've had an update from Anna that his body and clothing have been examined, and no evidence of any other DNA has been found.' She cleared her throat and looked around the room. 'Dipesh, I know you're checking out Lively's associates at the time of the shooting. Anything yet?'

'Still working on it, ma'am,' Dipesh replied. Dipesh Mois was a diligent detective, always impeccably dressed, and with manners to suit. He held Sheridan in the highest esteem and was well liked by his colleagues.

'Okay.' Sheridan pointed at Rob Wills. 'Rob, you were checking out any links with the woman whose grave John Lively was found in, Heather Walters. Anything?'

'Nothing. We've checked her and her family's background. There's no known link to Lively.'

'Okay, cheers Rob. Now, let's also not forget that this could be a revenge killing for either Kate Armitage or Ellie Sands. So, we need to check out their families, friends and colleagues. However, it's quite likely that Lively was killed by someone he knew, maybe a drug deal that went wrong.' She looked up. 'Rob, can you speak to the press officer? No doubt this will be a big story for them, bearing in mind that Ellie Sands was a local newspaper editor when she was shot. Can you also contact Kate's parents, offer them a family liaison officer? Get someone to locate Lively's foster parents. Their details are in the original file, so let them know he's been found. Actually, can you speak to Ellie Sands' family first? Let them know Lively's body's been found. Can we check that she's still at The Gables Nursing Home? I want to speak to her. Get as many details as you can about her family and associates, and in particular anyone who may have had a reason to seek revenge for what happened. I don't want to rule anyone or anything out.'

Sheridan looked at Anna. 'Can you contact Jeff Nichols and ask him to come in and see me?'

'No problem.'

She addressed the room. 'Okay, let's get on with it, keep me updated as soon as you have anything.'

Sheridan made her way back to her office and sat at her desk, thinking about John Lively. A low-level drug dealer who killed a police officer. One of their own. She thought about her team, how they must feel deep down, investigating his murder. Would they look at it the same way as any other case? She quickly dismissed the thought. She knew her team. But she also knew that she wouldn't share with them her own suspicions about who killed John Lively. That one she was keeping to herself for now.

CHAPTER 17

Joni walked into the staffroom to find Mo Chase talking away on her mobile. 'I'll see you when you get back, then.' Mo ran her finger across the worktop as she continued to speak, unaware that Joni was there. 'Alright, have a good trip.'

She ended the call and turned around, flinching when she saw Joni. 'Shit, you made me jump, how long have you been there?' she hissed.

'Just walked in. Trouble in paradise?' Joni reached into the cupboard and retrieved her mug, the words I LOVE MAUD emblazoned across it: an early Christmas present from Sam.

'No, actually everything's fine, thank you. Harry's just off on a business trip.' Mo sat down heavily on the now-creaking arm of the tatty old chair in the corner of the small staffroom.

'What does he do again?' Joni asked.

'He works in sales, something to do with advertising space. He's got to go to Germany for a few days.'

'Blimey, don't you find that a strain on your relationship, being apart so much?' Joni asked as she waited for the kettle to boil.

'No, it suits me. I'm not the possessive type and I like that we don't see each other a lot, I like having time to myself. I mean, we're not bloody married or anything.' She looked at Joni. 'Anyway, how about you? Never hear you mention a man,' Mo said sarcastically, pulling out a lump of foam from the arm of the chair and flicking it on the floor. 'You're not a lezza, are you? I mean it's okay if you are, I don't have a problem with them.'

'No. I'm not a lezza, as you so eloquently put it. And maybe you should look up some more derogatory words to describe gay women, add them to your atrocious vocabulary.' Before Mo could respond, Joni's mobile pinged and she looked down at the screen. It was a text message from Sam: *Car's knackered, can u pick me up after work, about 4?*

Joni texted back: *No probs. Your car is shit*

Sam replied: *Would buy a new one but then couldn't pay the rent*

Joni smiled. *When are you moving out anyway?*

Sam texted back: *When I meet the woman of my dreams*

Joni sent back a single kiss.

'Well, better crack on.' Joni nodded at Mo, who was staring inquisitively at the mug in Joni's hand . . . probably wondering who the fuck Maud was.

CHAPTER 18

Joni pulled up at the front of Avery Primary School's gates, having arrived early to pick Sam up.

They'd both gone to school here, and just the sight of the building was enough to bring memories flooding back, both good and bad. She walked up to the main reception, where she was met by a tiny young woman with pink streaks in her hair.

'Can I help you?' Very polite, very smiley. Very pink. Joni wondered for a moment if the pink woman was actually a member of staff or just a very helpful pupil.

'I'm here to pick up Sam Sloan, her car's broken down.'

'Oh yes, she said you were coming, her class should be finished soon, please take a seat.' The pink girl turned to pick up the phone.

As Joni sat down, she could hear the sound of children reciting the alphabet in a nearby classroom, then a teacher calling out, 'Henry, will you stop that now, please?'

Joni scanned the walls. Paintings of Picasso-esque faces were Blu-Tacked all around. A tree that looked like a nuclear mushroom with a man standing on top of it holding what appeared to be a strange tortoise-like creature. Across the other side of the wall was the alphabet written in different colours, each letter decorated differently.

Joni stared at the alphabet wall for a moment, remembering how they used to sound out the different letters when she was at school. And then it hit her. She had an idea. She might just have a way of helping Ellie Sands to communicate.

CHAPTER 19

Anna poked her head around Sheridan's door. 'Fancy a drink?'

Sheridan looked up from her computer screen. 'Absolutely, just give me ten minutes.'

'I got hold of Jeff Nichols by the way, he'll come and see you on Wednesday at two,' Anna said as she stepped into the office.

'Great, thanks. How did he seem?'

'Quite emotional actually, said he saw it on the news about Lively being found.'

'Emotional, how?' Sheridan asked.

'He sounded kind of shaky, if that makes sense? And at one point I thought he was going to cry. He went really quiet.'

Sheridan absorbed Anna's comment. She'd never met Jeff Nichols, and was looking forward to the opportunity to assess his reactions for herself. She'd make sure there was a familiar face present when he came to see her, someone Jeff had worked alongside and felt comfortable with. And then she'd start asking questions.

Half an hour later, they walked into The Black Cat pub, which sat snuggled down a cobbled street at the back of the police station. One half of the pub's walls were covered with framed pictures of Everton footballers and the other half with Liverpool teams. It was a long-standing joke among the regulars that the landlord, known as 'Blue', would only serve Evertonians. His wife, known as 'Red', a life-long Liverpool supporter, would only serve Liverpool fans. So, either way, you were guaranteed to get a drink.

Anna and Sheridan chose a quiet corner.

'I'll get them in,' Anna said as she dropped her bag next to her seat and made her way to the bar. Sheridan noted that the place was pretty empty; just two lads sitting by the window laughing loudly and an elderly couple near the bar, drinking slowly and not talking.

Sheridan sighed, her head aching a little. She loved getting her teeth into difficult cases, loved the challenge of it all, but she often let it consume her. She always pushed herself, challenged evidence, looked for the one clue that maybe others had missed. Or dismissed. She had joined the police force to make the streets safer, safer than they were when her little brother was murdered. It ate into her every thought that his killer was still out there. Maybe even still killing children. She wanted to rid her world of evil. One case at a time.

Soon enough, Anna returned with the drinks and took a sip of her own before plonking down opposite Sheridan. 'Something's bugging you. Is it work or personal life?' Anna put her drink on the table and picked up the beer mat, folding it in half, a habit she'd picked up when she'd finally managed to give up smoking.

'Well, why don't you be direct about it?'

'I'm a copper, I can't help it.' Anna picked at the corner of the beer mat, then took another sip of her drink.

'Well, it's not my personal life, because I don't have one at the moment. I'm at work all the bloody time.'

'So, it's work.' Anna raised her eyebrows.

'No, not really, just got my head full of this case. You know what I'm like, I want to do everything myself, make sure nothing's missed.' Sheridan quickly scanned the pub, always conscious of who might be lurking in a corner somewhere, listening.

'You've got a good team behind you, Sheridan. They respect you so much, and they're willing to go all out to get a result just to please you. Anyway, come on, I want to hear your theory. I know you already have one.' Anna cradled her drink.

'How do you know I have a theory?' Sheridan frowned.

'Because you live, eat and breathe every case you work on. And I know *you*.' Anna pointed a finger at her.

Sheridan sighed. 'Okay, yes, I have a theory.' She leaned forward, keeping her voice low. 'I think Jeff Nichols could have something to do with John Lively's death.'

She waited for Anna's response.

'Really?' Anna instinctively looked around, and then gave her full attention to Sheridan. 'Seriously?'

'Yep.'

'Why?'

Sheridan took a sip of her drink and ran her hand through her long hair. 'Well, I've been reading the history on this case . . . basically we know that Jeff Nichols was married with two kids. Kate Armitage was divorced and – as you put it – a bit of a firecracker. They were crewed up together, and clearly were having an affair. There's also a lot of history between Kate, Jeff and John Lively. They stop-searched him numerous times, and locked him up more than once for drug offences.' She paused, sipping her drink before continuing. 'So, Lively could have had a grudge against both of them. But for some reason his main issue was with Kate. He made a threat to her the day before she was shot and then her car got burnt out. Okay, there's no evidence that it was Lively who was the arsonist, but it's fairly obvious it was him. Then, the following day Kate goes to the supermarket and Lively shoots her. Jeff's devastated. He's lost Kate, the affair is exposed, his marriage breaks down, and he leaves the job because he can't face it any more. I think he either lured Lively to the cemetery and shot him, or got someone else to do it.

Heather Walters had just been buried, so, let's say Lively was killed very soon after that. Heather Walters' grave was fresh and easy to dig up. Jeff buried Lively, or again got someone else to, and then carries on living his sad little life.' She paused, inhaled deeply and bit her lip. 'There's just something I can't figure out.'

'Go on.' Anna nodded once, listening intently.

'Why did Lively shoot Kate Armitage in a busy supermarket car park? Why not just shoot her outside her house? He knew where she lived because he'd burnt her car out. Why take the chance in such a public place?' She ran her finger around the rim of her glass. 'Unless it wasn't planned. Unless he was out on his motorbike, happened to see her and just snapped. But then she was in a hire car, so unless he saw her driving it, he wouldn't have known to follow her. There's CCTV of some of his movements before the shooting, but he doesn't take a direct route to the supermarket. He doesn't follow her all the way, his bike is picked up in various places and a lot of his journey isn't caught on CCTV. Mind you, the CCTV wasn't very good, and it was dark.'

'Maybe he knew where the CCTV was. You know what these local shit-bags are like; they always know this kind of stuff.' Anna shifted in her seat.

'Yeah, true, but why potentially go to all that trouble to avoid CCTV and then shoot her in full view of the public?'

Anna nodded and for a moment they sat in silence. 'You really think Jeff Nichols could have been involved?'

'Possibly. Whoever killed Lively removed all his clothes except his boxers, so they knew that evidence could have been obtained from whatever he'd been wearing. Mind you, I suppose there's enough programmes on TV for Joe Public to know that.' She sighed. 'Anyway, I want to see what Jeff Nichols is like when he comes in to see me.' She finished her drink. 'Another?'

68

'Yeah, why not?' Anna drained the last drops from her glass and handed it to Sheridan. 'Are you going to share your theory with the team?'

'No, not yet.'

When Sheridan returned with the drinks, Anna continued pulling the beer mat apart. 'I'm thinking of sitting the inspector's exam; what do you reckon?'

'Go for it. You'd be brilliant. Although not as good as me, of course,' Sheridan replied, grinning and lifting her glass to clink against Anna's.

'I just doubt myself all the time. I could have sat it ages ago . . . but I bottled it.'

'We all doubt ourselves, mate. But you have to go for it.'

'I guess so,' Anna replied. 'Anyway, I take it there's no update on your brother?' she asked, trying to put the thought of the inspector's exam out of her head.

'No, nothing. I need to concentrate on this case right now. Anyway, how's Steve?' Sheridan replied, quickly changing the subject to Anna's partner. She didn't want to talk about her brother.

'He's fine. Even if I'm forever having to put the loo seat down and clear his hair shavings out of the sink.' She screwed up her face. 'You're lucky, you don't have that problem.'

'No, you're quite right, none of my ex-girlfriends ever left hair shavings in the sink. Leg hairs in the bath maybe.' She laughed and Ann laughed with her. 'Anyway, the way my love life's going, I'll end up a lonely old spinster.'

'No, you won't, anyway I thought you didn't have time for a relationship.' Anna yawned.

'I would if the right woman came along, they just always seem so bloody demanding.' She looked at her drink. 'I just want to meet someone who isn't weird or possessive and who gets me and understands the job I do. Someone I look forward to being with at the end of the day and who doesn't care if my breath stinks in the morning.'

'That it?' Anna grinned.

'And is funny and caring and intelligent, has gorgeous eyes and a nice bum.'

CHAPTER 20

Tuesday 21 December

Joni looked up as Sam walked in. Maud was lying on some paper spread out across the floor. Helping. Apparently.

'How sweet, the two of you playing together with your crayons.'

'Did you get your car sorted?' Joni moved her leg from under her and rubbed away the pins and needles.

'Yeah, new starter motor and something else I can't pronounce.' Sam put her bag on the chair. 'What are you two actually doing?'

'We're writing the letters of the alphabet out.' She smiled.

'Good luck with that. I've tried teaching Maud the alphabet loads of times, but she never gets past the letter C.' She sat on the arm of the chair, chuckling at her own joke.

Joni looked at her. 'It's for Ellie Sands, you muppet.'

'Is that the one who was shot?'

'Yes, that's her. I got the idea when I picked you up from school. I'm going to get her to point to letters of the alphabet. I want to see if she can spell out what she wants to say.'

'Can't you try her with a keyboard?'

'I don't think that would work, she can't really control her hands and fingers that well, so I thought I'd try this. I know it's all been tried before. When I first took over as Ellie's primary carer from Mo Chase, Yvonne told me that since Ellie's been at The Gables, the police and a head injury expert have tried several times to get her to communicate, but she's never made any progress. It's just that sometimes when I'm with Ellie, she looks at me like she's really trying to say something.'

'Maybe it's because you get to spend more time with her, so she recognises and responds to you. There was a kid in my last school who would hardly respond to the other teachers, but with me, he was like a different child. So there may not be a *specific* reason why Ellie reacts to you, beyond simple familiarity, but if you think you can get her to communicate then that's brilliant. And keeping it simple with the alphabet might work.'

'I hope so. How lovely would it be for Ellie to finally be able to communicate with the world.' The thought lingered with Joni for a moment. She knew how hard the doctors and experts had worked to try and get Ellie to speak. Could she really succeed where so many others had failed?

CHAPTER 21

Wednesday 22 December

Jeff Nichols felt his stomach turn over as he pulled into the back yard of the police station. He sat for a moment, glumly staring at the building that housed so many good memories alongside so many painful ones. He had spent years trying to work out what would bring him back here. And now he knew. The events of seven years earlier were never going to let him go.

He walked around to the front counter, where he was greeted with a smile from some of the staff who remembered him.

'I'll take you upstairs, Jeff.' Sergeant Parry – who'd aged twenty years in seven by the look of him – said, putting a hand on his shoulder. 'It's good to see you; you keeping alright?'

'Yeah, not too bad.' Jeff swallowed a little and nodded. The corridors were somewhat daunting now. The smell was still familiar somehow. Echoes of his years here all around him.

'So, you're here about Lively?' Sergeant Parry asked.

Jeff nodded. 'Yeah. Apparently, they found him buried in Bordersfield Cemetery?'

Sergeant Parry kept his voice low. 'Best place for him. Fucking cop killer.'

Jeff nodded again. 'Do they know how long he's been there?' He put his foot on the first stair and felt his legs weaken. The memories of seven years ago swept over him, and he felt sick.

'Quite a while from what I hear. Anyway, the DI will fill you in.' He put his hand back on Jeff's shoulder.

'Who's the DI?' Jeff asked.

'Sheridan Holler. You probably don't know her, but Mike Jacobs is with her, so there'll be one familiar face, at least.'

Jeff was shown into a room that he remembered as the old cramped CID office, now filled with desks and a conference table.

Inspector Mike Jacobs stood up and shook his hand. 'Jeff, good to see you. Thanks for coming in.'

Jeff took a deep breath. 'No problem.'

'Jeff, this is Detective Inspector Sheridan Holler.'

He accepted her hand and shook it. 'Ma'am.'

'Hello, Jeff. Please take a seat.'

Jeff sat down and crossed his legs. Then uncrossed them.

'Firstly, I want to say that I understand that this might be very difficult for you.' Sheridan had a sympathetic note in her voice. She had a strong face with perfectly shaped features and was rather beautiful. Her long brown hair sat comfortably on her shoulders, and she was dressed impeccably in an expensive grey suit. Her voice was soft and yet commanding.

She had 'copper' written all over her.

'What do you mean?' Jeff shifted in his seat, staring at her.

'Sorry, it's just that I understand that the shooting of PC Kate Armitage had a huge impact on you, being your crew partner and everything.' She didn't wait for him to respond. 'So, you're aware that John Lively's body has been found?' This time, she left a space for him to respond.

Jeff swallowed and felt his heart pump furiously in his chest. 'Yeah.' He blew out his cheeks, fighting the bile in his throat.

Sheridan continued: 'The body was found by a grave digger in Bordersfield Cemetery, buried three feet under the ground in an elderly woman's grave. Her husband has passed away and the grave digger found him when he was reopening the grave.' She looked at Jeff, whose eyes were full of tears.

'Are you alright?' she asked. 'I know this probably opens old wounds for you, Jeff, but at least now you know he's not out there any more.' She reached over and picked up her coffee. 'The post-mortem results show he was shot in the chest. We've opened a murder enquiry.'

Jeff stood up. 'I'm sorry, I feel a bit sick, I just need to go to the toilet.' He quickly left the room.

When he was gone, Sheridan frowned at Mike Jacobs.

'He never got over it, you know.' Mike Jacobs sat back in his chair. 'It was fairly common knowledge that Jeff and Kate were having an affair and when Kate was shot, he was absolutely devastated. As you've read, she'd told her sergeant the day before she was shot that Lively was threatening her, and probably had some grudge against her for getting him banged up for dealing. Jeff didn't want to let her out of his sight. To be honest, no one believed Lively was a real threat to anyone. He was regarded as a bit of a meathead. He wasn't known to be violent, always seemed a bit slow, if I remember. It was like he wanted to be the big man – you know, some big bloody drug lord – but he was a nobody.'

'Until he shot a police officer in a crowded supermarket car park,' Sheridan said bluntly.

'Well, yeah.' Mike Jacobs looked at Sheridan. 'Jeff lost everything after it happened, he eventually left the job, his marriage broke down and he's ended up like a bloody recluse.'

Sheridan knew all of this but politely listened anyway.

A few minutes later, Jeff Nichols walked back into the room. 'I'm sorry about that,' he said as he sat down.

'It's okay, are you alright?' Mike Jacobs asked, his voice full of genuine empathy.

'Yeah, you know, I've spent seven years trying to forget about what happened and now it's here again.'

'I know, I'm sorry. I know you and Kate were close,' Mike replied.

'Everyone knows we were having an affair, Mike,' Jeff snapped, crossing his legs and quickly wiping a rogue tear from his face. 'You don't have to bloody skirt around it. It all came out in the murder enquiry.'

Sheridan put her coffee down and sat forward. 'I'm working with DCI Max Hall on this enquiry, and as hard as this is, I need to go over a couple of things with you, if that's alright?'

Jeff nodded, clasping his hands in front of him. 'Yes of course, it's fine.'

'You and Kate were crewed up for a year before she was shot, and you had a lot of dealings with John Lively. You must have had knowledge of his associates. Is there anyone you can recall who would have wanted him dead?' She looked Jeff in the eye.

Jeff exhaled and blew out his cheeks again. 'Lively mixed with a few druggies, he was a bit slow to be honest. Unassuming even. He wasn't the main man if you know what I mean? Small fish. Not the sort to rile anyone.' He paused. 'You said he was shot.' He looked first at Mike Jacobs and then at Sheridan.

'Yes,' Sheridan replied.

'Do we know how long he's been dead?' Jeff asked.

'About seven years, so possibly not too long after he shot Kate.' Sheridan watched his reaction. She observed his body language, how he tensed up at the mention of Kate's shooting, his eyes filling with tears, which he constantly seemed to fight against. The more she watched him, the more she convinced herself that he had killed John Lively. Simply out of revenge for taking Kate away from him.

After a long silence, Jeff finally responded. 'Do you think it could have been revenge for her? Maybe it wasn't one of his shit-bag associates? I hate to throw this out there, but Kate was well liked and really popular, maybe someone close to *her* got to Lively?'

Sheridan didn't respond at first. She hadn't expected Jeff to throw the idea of a revenge killing at them. He had to know it put him into the mix, too, as someone with a reason to have killed Lively. But maybe bringing up the past had struck a nerve with him. Maybe he was just expressing what he wished he could have done at the time. 'Possibly,' she finally replied. 'We're not ruling anything out.'

Jeff nodded. 'I suppose then that you probably think I'm a suspect.' He paused. 'I don't deny that I loved her, I really did and yes, I was devastated when she was killed. The affair came out and my marriage was destroyed, I lost everything. So, I can understand if you think I could have killed Lively.' He focused on Sheridan. 'I didn't kill him.' He shook his head. 'Am I glad he's dead? Yes, I am. I won't deny that. He took Kate from me, and the knock-on effect that her death had on my life was huge, but no, I didn't kill him. Even if I wanted to, I couldn't have. I don't have that in me.' He rubbed his face. Tears filled his eyes and he swallowed. 'I wish, I just wish so much that none of this had ever happened, I wish I'd never hurt my family. I wish that Lively had never existed. And I wish I hadn't fallen in love with Kate.' He choked a little, trying to hold back tears. 'I'm sorry. It just upsets me so much.'

'It's okay, I can't imagine what you've been through, Jeff.' Sheridan tried to allow empathy into her voice, reminding herself that he wasn't a prisoner; this wasn't an interview with a suspect or person of interest. And she didn't want him to pick up on the fact that she had doubts about him.

'If there's anything I can do to help with this enquiry please just ask.' He looked Sheridan in the eye. 'I mean it. I know that you might have your suspicions about me. But that aside, I really want to help if I can.'

'Thanks Jeff. I appreciate that.' Sheridan forced a reassuring smile, which he returned. 'I'll be in touch.' She stood up and put out her hand. 'Jeff, we're releasing as little as possible to the press at the moment, so I just need to ask that you don't discuss this with anyone.'

'Of course.' Jeff shook her hand.

Sheridan watched from the window as Mike Jacobs walked Jeff to his car and as he drove away, she went back to her office. A moment later Mike Jacobs appeared at her door, arms crossed. 'Poor bloke, I know he was in the wrong with what happened, the affair I mean, but he's a good lad, he was a good copper too.'

'Was he?'

'Yeah, he was quite quiet, but steady, got the job done, you know.' Mike Jacobs put his hands in his pockets. 'You don't think he shot Lively, do you?'

Sheridan shook her head. 'No, I don't.' She still had her suspicions, but didn't want this theory spread around the nick. In her eyes, the fact that Jeff Nichols had suggested that he himself was a suspect was a potential double bluff; the old reverse psychology trick.

'Good, because I honestly don't think he did it, you just get a feeling, don't you, about someone, and I knew Jeff for most of his time in the job. I really don't believe for a second that he has it in him to do something like that.'

Sheridan nodded. 'Yeah, he seems very genuine.'

CHAPTER 22

Joni stood at the foot of Ellie Sands' bed, watching as she slept. She picked up the sheet of paper with the alphabet written on it and ran her fingers over the letters.

Ellie woke up and looked at her, lifting her arm. More of an involuntary movement than anything purposeful. Or at least that was what others seemed to believe about most things Ellie did.

'Hey Ellie, how are you doing?' When Ellie had sat up, Joni gently took hold of her hand and laid it on the paper. 'Point out what you want to say, Ellie. Can you point to a letter?' Joni felt Ellie's hand pull away from hers slightly and then she pointed to the letter P, then B, then N, then I. Joni sighed. 'That's good Ellie, that's really good.' *That doesn't spell out bloody anything*, Joni thought, wondering if this was really such a good idea. Had she thought that she could really get Ellie to communicate after everyone else had tried and failed? Maybe the truth was that Ellie would never be able to communicate.

For a moment, Joni felt deflated. But her determination soon took over and she continued. 'Ellie, just point to one letter and I'll write it down. Then you can tell me if that's right, okay?'

Again, Joni guided Ellie's hand towards the paper and Ellie touched the letter P, before her head dropped to one side and she closed her eyes, frowning. 'Piss.' Ellie's voice echoed around the room.

'What's going on?' Mo walked in, carrying an armful of towels.

Joni didn't look up. 'Just trying something.'

Mo dumped the towels on the armchair and walked over to the bed. 'What's that? The alphabet?' she said sarcastically.

'Yeah, I'm just seeing if Ellie can point out what she's trying to say.' Joni felt her face flush a little, partly with embarrassment and partly annoyance at Mo's mocking tone.

'What's she said so far? . . . "pissy knickers"?' Mo chuckled to herself. 'It's all been tried before. You're wasting your time. I've known her since she came here and trust me, she's not going to suddenly point to all the letters and spell out that she likes her toast done on both sides.'

'At least I'm trying to communicate with her, instead of taking the piss,' Joni snapped.

'Alright, calm down, I'm just having a laugh,' Mo retorted. 'But I'm telling you, you're not going to get anywhere with her. Her mind's gone.' Mo crossed her arms.

Anger crept into Joni's voice. 'Thank you, Dr Genius, for your expert opinion.'

'It doesn't take an expert to see that's not going to work. You're wasting your time.'

'Everything okay?' They both snapped around to see Yvonne Lopes standing in the doorway.

'Yeah, fine. Joni's trying to communicate with old Ellie here.' Mo chuckled again as she ambled towards the door.

'How's it going?' Yvonne looked past Mo to Joni.

'Slowly.' Joni sighed. 'But I've only just started, to be fair.'

Yvonne nodded and followed Mo down the corridor. 'Mo, can I have a quick word?'

'Sure.' Mo crossed her arms.

'I just want to be sure that the residents are treated with care and respect and are not referred to as "Old Ellie" or "Pissy Knickers".' Yvonne's voice was low, controlled.

'I was just messing about . . .'

'This is a nursing home for vulnerable people. We don't mock the residents and we encourage communication. It doesn't matter that everyone thinks that Ellie can't communicate, at least Joni's trying. Even if you think the whole thing is futile, I like my staff to show initiative. Maybe you could learn something. Now, wind your neck in and get on with your job.'

'Fine.' Mo walked away looking pissed off. Really pissed off.

CHAPTER 23

Jeff dialled Carly's number.

'Hello?' She sounded out of breath.

'Hi, it's only me, I just wanted to see how you were settling in.' Jeff looked at himself in the hallway mirror as he spoke.

'We're fine, thanks. The kids love it here.' She took a breath. 'Sorry, I'm a bit puffed. Just been for a run.'

'Oh, right.'

There was an awkward silence. Jeff could hear Carly breathing deeply and he closed his eyes, imagining she was beside him. 'I'm sorry Carly, for everything. I never meant to hurt you.' He felt tears sting his eyes.

'Where's that come from?' Carly asked, trying not to sound exasperated.

'I just wanted you to know, that's all.'

'What's going on, Jeff?'

'They've found John Lively's body.'

'So, he's dead,' Carly said bluntly, sighing down the phone. 'That's why you've called, I knew there'd be a reason.' She inhaled deeply before continuing. 'Look, Jeff, I'm sorry. I know how bad things were for you back then and how Lively ruined everything . . . But you have to understand that you were sleeping with that woman, and it cost us our marriage.' She paused. 'Maybe now that he's dead you can move on. Let it go. Get your bloody life back.'

'They've had me in. It's all going to get dragged up and I don't know if I can go through it all again.' He ran a hand over his head and gripped a clump of hair in his fist.

'What do you want me to say, Jeff?'

'Nothing. I just wanted to talk to someone who was there, you know, who knows how it was back then. I just wanted to hear your voice.'

'Are you okay?' Carly could hear his voice breaking.

'Yeah, I'll be fine. I'd better let you go. Tell the kids I love them.'

'Jeff, you're not going to do anything stupid, are you? I mean like hurt yourself?'

'Oh God, no, of course not. I might be a bit low at the moment, but I wouldn't do anything like that.'

'Okay. Look, I don't hate you, Jeff. I just can't forgive what you did to us. To your family.'

'If I could turn the clock back and change it all, I would, you know. I'd go back to when we were happy, and everything was normal.' He held the receiver close to his ear. 'I'm so sorry Carly, I really am.'

'I know you are. I know.'

'Did the kids get my Christmas cards? I put some money in there for them.'

'Yes, they got them. Thanks.'

'I didn't know what to buy them, so I thought they could buy themselves something.'

'Yeah, fine,' Carly answered. *You didn't buy them anything because you don't know your own children*, she thought.

'Anyway, I'd better go.'

'Okay, bye.'

'Bye.'

Jeff dropped the receiver and it clattered to the floor. He sat on his sofa for an hour, not moving, just thinking. Kate's face came into his head, then John Lively's. He wanted to run away from everyone. From everything.

The conversation with DI Holler had made him realise how real it all was. Kate was dead, and now John Lively's body had been found. Did the police suspect him? Or had he now made himself a suspect?

CHAPTER 24

Joni walked through the front door. She had been on a split shift and decided to go home for her two-hour break.

As she walked into the living room, Sam put her hand up. 'I have a confession to make. Actually, Maud has a confession . . . but I will speak on her behalf.' Sam crossed her legs and turned the music down. Stacks of textbooks were piled around her.

'Go on.' Joni sat on the arm of the chair and folded her arms. 'Confess away.'

Sam took a deep breath. 'Maud ate three of your photographs.' She pulled a face and looked at Maud who sat there, looking like she didn't really give a shit.

'What photographs?' Joni frowned.

'The ones you were sorting through for your mum for Christmas, the old family ones.'

'How did she eat them?'

'Well, I found them in the hallway on the floor. I think she licked the faces off and then kind of chewed the rest of them a little bit. She seems okay, so I don't think she's poisoned or anything.' Sam scowled at Maud. 'She is *very* sorry.'

Joni looked at Maud and she did not look one bit fucking sorry.

'It's fine, I can make copies.' Joni smiled. 'Do you fancy a coffee?' She got up and slipped off her coat, tossing it on to her bed as she walked past.

'Absolutely.' Sam remained where she was on the floor. 'How's your day going?' she called.

'It's okay. I tried out the alphabet thing on Ellie.' Joni bent down to get two mugs out of the cupboard.

'How did it go?'

'Not good. She kept pointing to the letter P but then went off on to random letters that didn't make any sense.' Joni flicked the kettle on and opened a packet of biscuits.

'The letter P?'

'Yeah, every time, but then pointed to an I or a C or N or O. And bloody Mo just stood there taking the piss. She really hacks me off sometimes.' Joni leaned back against the worktop.

'Is this the one shagging the sales guy who you all think is married?' Sam asked, burping involuntarily.

'Yeah, that's the one. She's so miserable, and gets really uptight if you ask her about him. Harry Munchkin or whatever his bloody name is.' Joni shook her head just as Maud swanned into the kitchen.

It was then that she noticed something on the kitchen floor and knelt down, tentatively poking at the strange object, which resembled a tiny furry animal that had been through a washing machine.

'What the hell is that?' She pulled off a sheet of kitchen roll and carefully picked the object up, studying it closely. After giving it a few curious sniffs, she headed into the living room and shoved it under Sam's nose. 'What do you think that is?'

Sam squinted at it. 'It's a furball.'

'A what?'

'A furball. You know, those things that cats puke up.'

'How nice.' Joni looked at it again. 'And some people say that having pets isn't fun.' She carried the furball back into the kitchen and tossed it in the bin, watched by Maud. 'You're gross.' She pointed at Maud who yawned at her.

'I had a thought about your alphabet thing,' Sam called from the other room.

'Hang on.' Joni turned and went back into the living room. 'What?'

'Your alphabet thing, I was thinking, it might be easier for Ellie if you had one piece of paper for each letter instead of the whole alphabet on one sheet. It might make it easier for her to indicate which letter she wants.' She handed Joni the sheets of paper with a letter written on each one. 'I've done them for you to try.'

Joni patted Sam's head. 'Actually, my queer friend, that's quite a good idea.'

'Why thank you, now where's my bloody coffee?'

'Oh, I am sorry! I got caught up in the excitement of the whole furball shenanigans.'

◆ ◆ ◆

Joni went back to work shortly after the furball drama. At the end of her shift, she made herself a coffee and headed upstairs to Ellie's room, finding her sitting and staring blankly out of the window. Joni pulled up a chair and sat opposite her. 'Hi, Ellie.'

Ellie didn't respond.

Joni took out the alphabet. 'Ellie, I'm going to show you a letter and I want you to tell me if it's the right one for what you want to say, okay?' Ellie looked at her and opened her mouth. 'Paaaan.'

Joni held up the letter A first and Ellie turned her head away. Then B, C, D. Nothing. Joni then skipped the other letters and went straight to the letter P. Ellie looked at it and let out a cry, tears

87

filled her eyes, and she banged her hand on the arm of her chair. 'Okay Ellie, it's okay.' Joni held her hand, waiting for her to calm down. Joni knew that in the past, everyone had assumed that Ellie's movements meant nothing. But in the time they had spent together over the last year, Joni had learned these outbursts were Ellie's way of showing her frustration.

When Ellie was quiet again, Joni continued: 'So, the letter P is the first letter of what you want to say?' She watched Ellie's face and smiled as Ellie nodded. A clear, definite nod. 'Well, it's a start.' Joni put her thumb up. 'It's a really good start. How would you like to sit in the garden for a while?' she asked and saw a glimmer of a smile on Ellie's face.

After getting Yvonne to help settle Ellie into a wheelchair, Joni was about to get her into the lift when she spotted Ellie's nephew, Miles, coming along the corridor. 'Hi.'

'Hi, Miles.' Joni pressed the lift button. 'I'm just taking Ellie down to the garden.'

'I won't disturb you, just wanted to see how she is today.' Miles stepped towards them and kissed Ellie on the cheek. 'Yvonne told me you were trying to get my aunt to communicate, how's it going?'

'Slowly, but she likes the letter P.'

Miles frowned. 'The letter P?' He looked at Ellie who had closed her eyes. 'Do you think she's really able to communicate? I mean, for the last seven years no one seems to have had much success talking to her.'

'I don't know, to be honest. But I thought it was worth trying. You never know, eh?' Joni waited for the lift doors to open and carefully pushed the wheelchair inside, turning to Miles. 'Can I ask you something?'

'Of course.' Miles joined them and pressed the button for the ground floor.

'What was Ellie like before it happened?'

'She was a character. A real character.'

As they sat on a bench in the care home garden, Joni carefully listened as Miles recounted how his aunt had been so career-driven her whole life. She knew when she was at school that she wanted to be a journalist. She'd studied hard, always chasing her dream of working for one of the big newspapers, travelling the world. She never married and never wanted children of her own. In her mind, that would have been a distraction.

When Miles was little, she had once asked him what he wanted to be when he grew up and he said, as he always did at that age, a lorry driver. Ellie would smile and say, 'Then you make sure you're the best lorry driver in the world.'

Miles looked at Ellie. 'She always said that you should never give up on your dreams, no matter how big or small they were, as long as you were happy, you worked hard and tried to be a good person.' He turned to face Joni, his voice breaking slightly. 'She would have made a brilliant mother.'

He went on to tell Joni of the childhood memories he had, staying over at Ellie's house. His parents were strict and always insisted that Ellie should never let him eat junk food, make sure he was in bed by seven and didn't watch anything on television that was inappropriate.

Ellie would promise all of those things and the moment her brother and his wife had left, the promises fluttered out of the window.

'She had a huge sweet jar that she'd bring out, plonk it on the floor and we'd sit there on cushions, huddled together, watching all sorts of rubbish on TV until one of us fell asleep. Usually Ellie.' He smiled at the memory. 'We had a deal that I didn't tell Mum and Dad.' He looked at Joni with a cheeky grin on his face. 'I still haven't told them to this day.'

For a moment, Miles didn't speak as his eyes rested on Ellie, who was breathing gently. Her eyes were closed. She looked totally at peace.

'The truth is, when she was in her forties, she accepted that she was never going to be the high-flying journalist she always dreamt of and she could have actually had a family of her own, but in her eyes, she'd left it too late.' Miles bit his top lip. 'She used to tell me that I was the son she never had.' He blew out his cheeks. 'I miss her.'

Joni noticed tears running down his face and instinctively reached into her pocket and pulled out a packet of tissues, which she handed to him.

'Sorry about that,' he said, clearing his throat. 'Anyway, I'd better be off. I can't come on Christmas Day, but I'll pop in when I can. Thanks Joni, for trying to get her to communicate, I mean.' He got up and gently touched Ellie's face before turning to leave.

'I have one last quick question,' Joni said.

'Go on.'

'Did you become a lorry driver?' She grinned.

'No. I'm an IT consultant.' He smiled. 'But I *am* the best IT consultant in the world.'

CHAPTER 25

Thursday 23 December

Sheridan got out of her car.

'Morning, ma'am,' a young PC said, smiling at her as he drove out of the back yard.

'Good morning,' Sheridan replied, realising that the lad looked about sixteen. Christ, she felt old.

She popped her head around Anna's door, finding her office empty, before making her way to the main CID office, also empty. She shrugged; hopefully everyone was out gathering evidence. She read her emails before opening her desk drawer to take out her diary, just as her phone rang. 'DI Holler.'

'It's Anna. I've spoken to Ellie Sands' nephew. She's still at The Gables Nursing Home in Crosby. I've just called and spoken to the owner, Yvonne Lopes. She said we can go and see Ellie, now.'

'Where are you? I'll go with you.' Sheridan stood up and pulled her jacket from the back of her chair.

'Pulling into the back yard. See you in a sec.'

Anna stopped by the back door of the police station and Sheridan got in.

'You okay?' Anna asked.

'Yeah good, you?'

'Fine. How did it go with Jeff Nichols?' Anna waited for a police car to go flying out of the back yard, blue lights flashing.

'He was very convincing.' Sheridan put her seatbelt on.

'What do you mean?'

'When we talked about Lively's body being found. He said almost straight away that we probably suspect he had something to do with it. He admitted that he loved Kate and when she was killed his whole life was ruined, but he said that he didn't kill him, and then said that he wanted to help in any way he could.'

'So, you still think he could have something to do with it?'

'Yeah, I do,' Sheridan replied.

'Why?'

'I just can't get it out of my head that he would be the one person that would want John Lively dead. He's clearly devastated about what happened to Kate and I think he could have got to Lively. Once Lively shot Kate, he disappeared, but did he really have the resources to go very far? Jeff Nichols had a lot of dealings with Lively before Kate died and probably knew all his hang-outs and where his associates lived and dealt drugs. I think Nichols went on his own little hunt for Lively, found him and killed him. If anyone knows how to dispose of a body and leave no evidence on it, it's a police officer. When he was talking to me yesterday, I just felt there was something about him that made me really uncomfortable. And I have to trust my gut.'

'Where would he have got the gun from?'

'He was a police officer. I'm sure he knew enough dodgy characters who would sell him a gun.'

'But would they have kept their mouth shut about it?'

'I don't know.' Sheridan turned to Anna. 'Anyway, let's go and see what Ellie Sands can tell us.'

CHAPTER 26

Joni parked her car outside the main doors of The Gables and buzzed herself in.

'Joni, can you pop into my office?' Yvonne was coming down the stairs as Joni came in.

'Sounds ominous,' Joni replied, turning into Yvonne's office and putting her bag on one of the chairs.

'The police are on their way to speak to me about Ellie Sands,' Yvonne said, closing her door.

'Really? Why's that?' Joni felt a sudden rush of adrenaline course through her body. She knew what had happened to Ellie but had almost disconnected it from her normal daily routine of caring for her. Learning that the police were coming to see Ellie instantly reminded her that she had been the victim of a horrific crime.

'They didn't say too much other than they have an update on the man that shot her and they want to talk to her. Now, I've explained that she still doesn't really speak but that you're her main carer and you've been trying to communicate with her, so they just want a quick chat with you.'

'No problem. Although I can't really tell them much.'

'Pop your things in the staffroom and I'll give you a shout when they get here.' Yvonne opened her office door as Joni picked up her bag again.

Walking towards the staffroom, she suddenly spotted Sam standing at the main doors, pressing the buzzer. Joni opened the door. 'What are you doing here?'

'You left your mobile at home . . . and being such a good friend, I thought I'd drop it in to you.' Sam curtsied and handed Joni her phone.

'Ah . . . thank you! You *are* a true friend.' Joni looked past her to see a car pull up and watched as two women got out and made their way towards her.

Sam turned round and noticed the taller one, who also noticed *her*. They looked at each other for a moment. Sam smiled and she smiled back. 'After you,' the woman said.

'Oh, I'm not going in, just dropping something off.' Sam felt her stomach flip. She turned back to Joni. 'Well, I'd better leave you to it, see you later.' Sam nodded at Sheridan and made her way back to her car, glancing up in time to see Sheridan showing Joni a card before being let in. Before the door closed, she turned back to Sam, who grinned and got into her car.

'Can I get either of you a drink?' Yvonne said, closing the door to her office.

'I'm fine, thanks.' Sheridan looked at Anna, who also declined the offer.

'This is Joni,' Yvonne said, indicating the other woman who had now joined them. 'Ellie's main carer.'

The two officers acknowledged Joni who wasn't sure if she was supposed to shake their hands or not, so she tucked them behind her back.

'You said there was an update on the man that shot Ellie?' Yvonne sat behind her desk.

'Yes, but we're trying to keep it very low key at the moment, so we'd ask that whatever we discuss stays here for now. I'm sure the press will be very interested, seeing as Ellie was one of theirs, and this case attracted a lot of interest when it happened.' Sheridan cleared her throat. 'You've probably seen on the local news that a body was found hidden in a grave at Bordersfield Cemetery recently?' She looked at Yvonne and then Joni.

'Yes, I saw it,' Yvonne replied, standing up to retrieve Ellie Sands' file from the locked cabinet behind her desk.

Joni shook her head. 'I didn't see it,' she said, consciously noting that she really needed to watch more television.

'Well, we've identified the body as being John Lively, who we believe shot and killed PC Kate Armitage, and shot Ellie Sands seven years ago.'

'Does Ellie's family know?' Yvonne asked. 'She has a nephew, Miles.'

'Yes, we've spoken to him and he's aware we're coming to see Ellie. I understand from previous reports that each time she's been seen by police and Kathryn Pullman that she doesn't talk much, if at all, and her communication hasn't improved over the years. But we'd like to see her anyway. Does she understand what's being said to her?' Sheridan turned to Joni for the answer.

'I think she does sometimes, but it's really hit and miss. I've been trying to get her to point to letters of the alphabet to see what she's trying to say, but I haven't really got very far, although she does like the letter P.'

'P?' Sheridan crossed her legs.

'Yes, whenever I start going through the alphabet with her, she seems to want to always point to the letter P first, but then goes off on to random letters that don't make much sense.'

'Have you noticed any change in her communication skills at all?' Sheridan asked.

Yvonne opened Ellie's file and flicked through the pages. 'No, not really. I take it you've seen Kathryn Pullman's reports?'

'Yes, they're in the original file. Can we see her?' Sheridan asked.

'Of course. Are you going to try and tell her that John Lively's dead?' Yvonne got up and made her way to the door.

'Yes. Do you think she'd understand, or will it upset her? You know, bring it all back to her?' Sheridan looked at Joni.

'I really don't know. Maybe it'll bring her some peace,' Joni replied, holding the door open.

They made their way to Ellie's room and Joni sat on the edge of her bed. Ellie opened her eyes, immediately turning her head away.

'Ellie, these officers are here to talk to you, can you look at them for a second?' Joni took Ellie's hand.

Ellie turned her head from left to right as her hand came up and then flopped back on to the pillow. Sheridan walked slowly towards her. 'Hello Ellie, I'm Detective Inspector Sheridan Holler.' Sheridan's voice was low and gentle. 'Ellie, we've come to tell you something about the man who shot you.'

Ellie let out a cry and she blinked fast, before shouting, 'Ammmmmm!'

Joni kept hold of Ellie's hand.

'Ellie, the police have found the man who shot you.' Joni felt awkward for a moment and conscious of herself. 'Do you under-stand me, Ellie?'

Ellie's head moved back and forth, and she opened her mouth, but no sound emerged.

Joni turned to Sheridan for guidance. 'Can I tell her his name?' Sheridan nodded.

Joni squeezed Ellie's hand gently. 'Ellie, the man who shot you, John Lively, is gone, he's dead, Ellie.' Joni felt her hand tense and saw tears fill Ellie's eyes.

'Naaaaa!' Ellie's mouth drooped slightly as she cried out. 'Piss, piss.'

'Okay Ellie, just rest now.' Joni got up.

'Does Ellie's speech change from day to day?' Sheridan asked, her voice at a whisper. She stared at Ellie and felt so sorry for her. It dawned on Sheridan that her hopes of Ellie being able to tell them something – anything – about what had happened to her were futile.

'Kind of.' Joni looked back at Ellie.

'Okay, I think we'll leave it there,' Sheridan said. Anna nodded in agreement, and the four of them walked out of Ellie's room.

They stood outside her door for a moment. 'Thanks for letting us see her.' Sheridan smiled at Yvonne and Joni. 'I'd like to contact the intermediary, Kathryn Pullman. I just want to see if she or someone else in her field can come and speak to Ellie again. To see if there is any chance at all they could communicate with her.'

'No problem,' Yvonne replied.

'Unfortunately, the press will be all over this soon. Can you speak to your staff about reporters hanging around? They're pretty devious when they want a story. They might even pretend to be a relative of one of your residents. So just make sure that you don't discuss this with anyone outside of here and let me know if the press gives you any problems.' Sheridan handed her card to Yvonne.

'Thanks.' Yvonne took the card, and they made their way to the main doors.

Sheridan walked back to the car with Anna. 'I'll drive.'

Anna handed her the keys and they climbed in.

Once she was in the driver's seat, Sheridan leaned on the steering wheel. 'What a bloody tragedy, that poor woman.'

'Yeah, it's awful, I guess after all this time she'll never get any better than that.'

They sat in silence for a moment before Anna grinned at her. 'I know what you're thinking.'

'What's that?'

'You're wondering who that gorgeous woman was that was at the home when we got here.'

Sheridan smiled. 'She was rather nice, wasn't she?'

'Not exactly my type, but I couldn't help see the looks between you.' Anna sat forward. 'Look at you, grinning like a Cheshire cat. She said she was dropping something off, so, I would guess she has a relative at the home.'

'Well, when we do come back, maybe the trip won't be a complete waste, then.' Sheridan pulled away, still smiling.

CHAPTER 27

Joni switched on the television and flicked through the channels. The local news would be on soon and she wanted to see if there was anything on about John Lively.

The front door opened, and Sam waltzed in. 'Hi, honey! I'm home!' She walked into the kitchen and plonked the shopping bag on the work surface before joining Joni in the living room. 'How was your day?'

'You're very cheerful. My day was weird.'

'Weird how?' Sam perched on the arm of the chair. 'Where's Maud?'

'In the bath.'

'Sorry?'

'She's sitting in the bath staring at the taps.' Joni turned the TV volume down.

'Right, okay.' Sam pursed her lips. 'Anyway, why was your day weird?'

'The police came to see me. Apparently, that body they found in Bordersfield Cemetery is the man who shot Ellie.' She shook her head at Sam, who was looking confused. 'You really need to start watching television.'

'I hate television. It's all bullshit and bad news.' Sam pulled her boots off. 'So, what does that mean? Case closed I guess?'

'Yeah, I guess so. We tried to tell Ellie, but I don't think she understood.'

'So, these police officers, were they the two women who turned up when I was there?' Sam asked, trying very hard but failing to sound nonchalant.

'Yes.' Joni knew where this was going.

'So . . . will they need to speak to you again?' Sam asked.

'I don't know.' Joni pretended to be interested in something on the television, hiding the grin that was creeping across her face.

'Oh, right.' Sam got up, picking up her boots. 'Right then.' She walked to the door.

'Her name's Sheridan Holler. She's a detective inspector.' Joni didn't look round.

'Thank you.' Sam smiled and went to the bathroom to check on Maud, who was still staring at the taps.

'Your phone's ringing!' Joni called, and Sam went back into the living room to retrieve it from her bag.

'Hello?' Sam's eyes widened when she heard the voice on the other end of the line. 'Oh, hello, Harriet.'

Joni looked at her and mouthed, 'The firewoman?'

Sam nodded before staring down at the floor. 'I can't. I'm busy at the moment, but I've got your number. Maybe I'll give you a call sometime and we'll have a drink or something.' She shook her head and looked at Joni.

'You're free next week?' She kept her eyes on Joni. 'I'm sorry, I can't, I've got my eccentric Aunt Maud staying with me.' Sam shook her head and looked at Joni, who was still grinning. 'Why do I say she's eccentric? Oh, just her funny little ways, living on Jaffa Cakes and sitting in the bath staring at the taps.'

Joni burst out laughing and Sam threw a cushion at her. 'Well, it's nice to talk to you again. I'll give you a call. Okay, take care. Bye.' She ended the call. 'Cheeky fucker. I mean she's fit but I'm not making a twat of myself again. She's blown me off twice.'

'Why didn't you make a date with her and then not turn up? See how she feels,' Joni asked.

'Because I'm not a dickhead.'

Sam put her mobile on the table and went to get changed. 'Call me if that thing comes on the news!' she shouted out from her bedroom.

'What, in case the hot detective's on there?' Joni turned up the volume.

'No, I'm interested in the story.'

'Liar.'

CHAPTER 28

Christmas Eve

Sheridan sat next to Joni in Ellie Sands' room, watching and listening as Kathryn Pullman patiently worked with the woman in the bed. She had been there for an hour, asking Ellie basic questions, showing her pictures, and trying to get her to indicate more clearly what she was trying to say.

An hour later, and Kathryn Pullman stood up. 'Okay, I think I'll leave it there for now.'

Sheridan and Joni followed her out of Ellie's room, and they made their way to Yvonne's office.

'How did it go?'

Yvonne rearranged the office chairs to accommodate them.

'Well, in brief, I can say that Ellie's communication hasn't improved since I last assessed her and I doubt very much that it ever will. I've tried several techniques with her, including one that we call eye gaze.' Kathryn Pullman looked at Yvonne. 'It's where a person has no way of physically pointing to a letter or picture, but they can look at it for a period of time and it's usually clear that they are in fact indicating what they want to say.' She paused. 'Ellie isn't able to do this.'

'Do you think she knows what's being said to her?' Sheridan asked.

'Yes, I think she does. But not all of the time.' Kathryn sat down, crossed her legs and put her notes on her lap. 'She does react quite clearly when the shooting's mentioned. She becomes much more animated. Which is natural, of course. She's probably recalling what happened, and this was an extremely traumatic event. Having said that, she also got agitated when I wasn't talking about the shooting. But this could be her general frustration at not being able to communicate. In Ellie's case, her responses appear so random that it's never clear what she is understanding, or what she might be trying to say.'

'Do you think it's worth Joni carrying on with the alphabet thing with her?' Sheridan asked.

'Absolutely.' Kathryn looked at Joni. 'You said that Ellie almost always points to the letter P first? It could be that this is the first letter of the word she's trying to say. When I tried it with her, though, she pointed to lots of other letters first. But you've built up a rapport with her . . . So, yes, definitely carry on with it.'

'She also seems to try to say words that start with the letter P quite a lot of the time,' Joni said, encouraged by the fact that she was being listened to and her idea of using the alphabet wasn't instantly dismissed.

'That's interesting. Well, like I said: keep going with it, Joni. Ellie seems to react to you so it's worth you taking the time to keep trying.'

Sheridan stood up and held out her hand. 'Thank you, Kathryn. I really appreciate your time. Especially on Christmas Eve.'

Kathryn shook Sheridan's hand. 'No problem at all. I'll email you my report in a day or so. And if you need me to come back at any time, just call.'

'I appreciate that.' Sheridan walked her to the main door with Yvonne.

'Do you think Ellie will ever be able to communicate enough that you understand what she's saying?' Yvonne asked, opening the door.

'If I'm honest, I don't think so, but it's not impossible,' Kathryn replied, stepping outside. 'I have seen cases where people make some improvement, even after several years.'

Yvonne nodded and held the door open. Sheridan stepped outside and Kathryn Pullman turned to her. 'I will say this, though . . . Ellie is *definitely* trying to tell you something. I'm absolutely sure of that.'

CHAPTER 29

Jeff picked up the phone and turned off the television. 'Hello?'

'Hello, Jeff, it's your mother.'

'Hi, you alright?' Jeff tried to sound cheerful.

'I spoke to Carly earlier.' She sniffed; a mannerism that reared its head whenever she was about to lay into Jeff. 'She said you sent the children money for Christmas. Now, I'm not nagging, but I think money is so impersonal. Are you going to call them tomorrow and wish them a merry Christmas?'

Jeff felt a tingling across the back of his neck. 'Yes, I'll ring them,' he replied, doing his best to hide the frustration in his voice.

'Good, make sure you do. Carly told me they've found the man that shot your colleague.' His mother couldn't have sounded less compassionate if she'd tried.

Jeff sighed and felt his stomach turn over. 'Yeah, that's right.'

'Well, I suppose knowing he's dead must be a bit of a relief for you, and at least he won't be costing taxpayers money in prison, that's one good thing.'

'Yeah, I suppose so.' Jeff wanted to throw the phone out of the window.

'Anyway, you paid the price for what happened, and Carly has moved on now. But I just don't want you to lose touch with your children, make sure you ring them. Or maybe you should go and see them?'

'I said I'd call them, Mum. And anyway, I need to be around for a while. The police have opened a murder enquiry and they probably need to speak to me again, so it's best I stay local.'

'Why do they need to speak to you?'

'It's just routine. I dealt with John Lively a few times and they're just making enquiries around him, that's all.'

'Oh, okay. Well, just ring the kids.'

'I will.' Jeff gripped the receiver as his mother abruptly ended the call. He put the phone down and went into the kitchen to pour himself a large Scotch. He could feel his body shaking as he put a hand on the work surface to steady himself. How was he ever going to get through this?

CHAPTER 30

Rosie and Brian Holler were sat in the living room when Sheridan pulled on to their drive. She took comfort from seeing the Christmas tree lights twinkling in the window.

In the first few years after her brother's murder, her parents had struggled to even think about Christmas, but continued to decorate the house for Sheridan's benefit.

Matthew and Sheridan, like most children, had loved Christmas and would sneak downstairs in the middle of the night on Christmas Eve, when they thought their parents were asleep, to quietly take a peek at their presents under the tree. And each year, Brian would sneak down and wait outside the living room door to jump out at them as they tried to creep back upstairs. Rosie, meanwhile, would sit on the stairs, watching through the banister, laughing with delight.

They tried to keep life as normal as they could after Matthew died, for Sheridan's sake. But the truth was, they were falling apart at the seams, and it was Sheridan – who was fourteen at the time – who held them together. Their marriage didn't suffer. In fact, it made them even closer as a couple. However, as the grief consumed her parents, it was Sheridan who was the strongest of them all.

When the original police investigation drew a blank, Sheridan watched as her parents went through another wave of grief, as did she. How had no one seen what happened? Who had killed their little boy? Was any child safe?

Her parents pleaded with her not to ever go to Birkenhead Park, where Matthew's body was found, but Sheridan defied them and spent days there, watching and keeping a notebook detailing the description of anyone who walked past her. She'd note the time and date, what they were wearing, if she'd seen them before. Everyone was a suspect, and at fourteen years old, she knew she was going to join the police force. She had wanted to do anything she could to try and stop other families going through what hers was experiencing.

To lose a son or a brother was devastating enough. But to live with the knowledge that his killer was still out there was intolerable.

And now, almost twenty-eight years on, they still didn't have answers. Sheridan often felt that she'd let her parents down, especially after she'd failed to make any more progress even after joining the police. Each time they asked if there was any news, any hint of a clue that might bring them nearer to the truth, her heart ached for them.

She couldn't tell them that she had sat so many times outside Andrew Longford's house but hadn't yet knocked on his door. The fear of giving her parents hope and then snatching it away wasn't an option. If Andrew Longford slammed the door in her face, then she'd deal with it. She'd find another way, but until she knew his reaction to seeing her again after all these years, she couldn't tell her parents.

She let herself in and called out cheerfully, 'Merry Christmas Eve!'

Rosie got up from the sofa and met her in the hallway, while Brian went into the kitchen to put the kettle on.

They sat around the kitchen table demolishing the home-made mince pies that Rosie had cooked earlier. After swapping presents, they hunkered down in the living room until Sheridan got up to leave.

'You off already?' Rosie asked, wiping crumbs off her chin.

'Yeah, sorry, early start tomorrow.' Sheridan gave her a hug. 'I'll pop in again soon.' And with that she got into her car and reversed off the drive.

Ten minutes later, she was parked opposite Andrew Longford's house. His curtains were closed, and the house was in darkness. She waited for an hour before heading home.

CHAPTER 31

Christmas Day

Jeff Nichols answered his front door and blinked at the brightness.
A light snow had fallen and it took a moment for his eyes to adjust
as he emerged from the gloom of his home.

'Hello, mate.' Tom Hudson wiped his feet and stepped past
Jeff into the hallway. 'Jesus, it's like death in here.' Tom peered into
the kitchen, pulling his crash helmet from his head before ruffling
his hair back into place.

'Come in,' Jeff said sarcastically, shutting the front door.

Tom Hudson was the only colleague who had stayed in any real
contact with Jeff after he left the force. They had been close friends
since Tom had joined the police, and he was Jeff's *only* confidant
when he was having the affair with Kate Armitage. Jeff would often
tell his wife Carly that he was having a boys' night out with Tom
when he was actually at Kate's.

After Kate's death, Tom had tried unsuccessfully to comfort
Jeff, failing to convince him to move on. He'd been there for Jeff
when Carly kicked him out, and was still here for him now.

'Some of the lads are going out for a beer tonight. Do you
fancy it?'

'No thanks.' Jeff sighed.

'Come on, Jeff. Do you good to get out of here, see some of the boys again. It's Christmas Day.'

'I really don't want to, Tom. I'm happy just being here.'

'When are you going to let this go?'

'Leave it, Tom, please.' Jeff put his hands on his hips and dropped his head down, closing his eyes. 'Please, Tom. I really want you to leave.'

Tom sighed. 'Okay, but I want you to call me if you need any-thing. Have you spoken to Carly?' He put a hand on Jeff's shoulder.

'Yeah, I rang her this morning.'

'The kids okay?'

'Yeah, fine.'

'How's the John Lively investigation going? I heard they've had you in.'

'Yeah, it's fine. They just wanted to know if I could think of anyone who'd want him dead.'

'What did you tell them?'

'I just said I couldn't think of anyone.'

'Right. Well, keep me posted and I'm here if you need to talk. I mean it.'

'Thanks, Tom.'

'You're a good bloke, Jeff.'

And, with that, Tom Hudson opened the front door to let him-self out. Jeff watched as he pushed his helmet back on, mounted his motorbike and rode away slowly, hearing the soft crunching of tyres as they left tracks along the road.

Jeff closed the front door, walked into the kitchen and poured himself a whisky before staring out of his living room window, wiping the condensation away with his sleeve.

He watched his neighbours in the house opposite welcoming their family who had turned up to spend Christmas with them, unloading presents from the boot of their car and excitedly hurrying indoors.

He turned around and picked up his cigarettes, lighting one and dragging the smoke deep into his lungs. Then he grabbed his jacket from the back of the chair and slammed the front door shut behind him.

He walked down the empty streets of Liverpool, head hung low. A biting wind made his eyes water, and he shoved his hands deep into his pockets. He walked without purpose or direction, uninterested in the historic buildings that loomed in front and all around him.

Down Castle Street, he glanced into windows of closed coffee shops and restaurants. As he reached the town hall, he made his way down a side street, passing the building where scars from the war could still be seen on its frontage. Pock marks from the past gouged out of the walls. Clearly visible, but rarely recognised for what they were by those who passed them every day.

Eventually, he came to Exchange Flags where Nelson's monument stood silent and cold. Usually bustling with office workers filing out of Moorfields train station, the place was eerily empty. Jeff lit a cigarette and sat on one of the benches, gazing up at all the abandoned tinsel in the office windows above him. A small Christmas tree sat on a window ledge, its lights turned off for the Christmas holiday, sadly waiting to be packed away in some office storage room until next year.

He stretched his legs out before standing up and turning to walk towards Western Approaches museum. Known as the War Rooms, they were secret bunkers used during World War II, and were now a popular tourist attraction.

He moved on aimlessly, passing doorways filled with leaves that had been whipped around by the wind and had settled in heaps, mixed up with sweet wrappers and tissue paper. Eventually he found himself at the Liver Building.

A sudden memory filled his head of his father telling him as a child of the legend that if the Liver Birds on top of the building ever turned to face each other, then Liverpool would no longer exist. As a boy, this legend had always bothered Jeff and he always looked up as he passed to make sure one was still facing the city and the other facing out to sea.

Today, he looked up and for a moment, he wished they were facing each other. He felt a painful loneliness closing in around him, in a city that he loved, a city bursting with affection and warmth despite the sad history of a war that still scorched its grand facades.

After London, Liverpool had been the most heavily bombed city in the country during WWII. But like every other city it had risen from its own ashes, and it had risen high and proud. World-famous for giving birth to The Beatles, their faces etched on memorabilia still snapped up by adoring fans who flocked to the city from across the globe. A place where proud Scousers shrugged off their unjustified reputation for robbing everything that wasn't screwed down. The truth was, a Scouser would more likely give you their last penny.

It was a city where Jeff had been born and raised, where he had always felt safe. Where he had always felt its lungs breathing in and out, a thriving, bustling place. Now, as he walked on, his face started to numb from the icy winds whipping in from the river. Maybe he'd find a pub and drink until everything went numb. He let his mind wander, back to when his life was still in one piece, and he swallowed, desperately trying not to be sick. The feeling subsided and he started walking back and, passing an open pub on his way, he quickly glanced in before deciding to go home instead. Back to his empty house.

CHAPTER 32

Anna came down the stairs and hesitated before opening the living room door. The argument with Steve the night before had kept her awake, crashing around in her head. She looked at him, stretched out on the sofa, his head buried in a pillow. As she stood there watching him, he opened his eyes and strained to focus on her, before sitting up, licking his lips and wiping a hand across his eyes and face. He tapped the sofa. 'Come here, babe.'

Anna sat next to him and he wrapped his arms around her, laying his head on her chest. She felt her jaw tighten as she closed her eyes.

'I'm so sorry, babe. I hate it when we argue.' He lifted his face to hers and kissed her cheek. 'I'll make it up to you, I promise.' Steve stood up, stretched his arms above his head and yawned loudly. 'I'll start by making us a proper Christmas Day breakfast, full English.' He smiled and Anna forced one back.

As he reached the kitchen door, she breathed in deeply before she spoke. 'Steve.'

He turned around. 'Yes, babe?'

'If you ever hit me again, I'll have you arrested so fast, your feet won't touch the ground.'

He was about to answer her when the phone rang, and she picked it up.

'Merry Christmas, you old trout.' Hearing Sheridan's voice made Anna want to burst into tears, but she held back, swallowing before she replied.

'Merry Christmas, mate.' She squeezed the receiver and watched Steve hovering in the doorway.

'Have you opened your presents yet?'

'Not yet. Steve's just making breakfast.'

'Making breakfast, eh? You lucky bugger, bloody spoilt you are.'

'Yeah, he spoils me.' She didn't look up, but knew he was still listening.

'He's a keeper. Right, I'd better go. I'm heading into work. Have a brilliant day, mate.'

'You too.' As she ended the call, she felt his arms around her waist. As he rested his head against her back, she could feel his chest expanding as he burst into tears.

'I love you more than anything in the world,' he said. 'I swear on my life that I will never raise a hand to you again.'

Anna turned to face him. They had been together for seven years and – like all couples, she supposed – they argued. The odd raised voice here and there, the odd day when they weren't speaking. But there had never been any hint of violence. Until last night. When she'd felt his fist against her face, she'd been too shocked to react straight away. He'd immediately apologised. He'd held her close to him, saying sorry over and over until the word seemed insignificant. They hadn't talked about it. Anna had just told him to leave her alone.

Now, as she looked into his eyes, she could see pure and genuine anguish. She loved him. She had loved him for seven years. They told each other every day because they loved each other every day.

'Are you going to tell Sheridan what happened?' he asked.

'No.' Anna held his face in her hands. 'But I meant what I said, Steve, if you ever hit me again, I *will* tell her and trust me, she *will* arrest you.'

'And kick my arse.' He looked sheepish.

'And kick your arse.'

As Steve made the breakfast, Anna went upstairs to shower. For a few moments, she just stared absently at herself in the mirror. The red mark where he had struck her cheek was already fading. She put her finger inside her mouth and could feel her tooth move as she touched it.

Every thought went through her head: *You're a police officer. You deal with victims of crime. Victims of domestic abuse. You listen as they tell you how it had all started. The arguments, the control and the subsequent violence.*

The words of a thousand victims echoed in her ears: *The times they hit you and then got down on their knees to beg forgiveness. And you believed them. You didn't tell anyone because that showed a weakness in you. Your friends would tell you to leave your abuser. And if you didn't leave, they'd eventually give up on you because they got frustrated that you weren't listening. In the end, you'd look around yourself and realise you were alone. Alone with your abuser. They'd isolated you from everyone, making you believe that you didn't need your family and friends. And so it goes.*

Anna knew the statistics. She could hear herself telling victims that two women every week are killed by a current or ex-partner. She had forgotten the number of times she'd said to victim after victim: *It will only get worse. If he's hit you once, he'll hit you again. Even if he swears on his mother's life that he won't.*

She ran her tongue over her tooth and blinked away a tear.

CHAPTER 33

New Year's Eve

Max Hall peered around Sheridan's door. 'Did you miss me?' He grinned.

She shook her head. 'Nope.'

Max proudly dangled his belt in the air, prompting Sheridan to jump up excitedly and grab it from him. He walked to his office with Sheridan following closely behind, and closing the door quickly, she stood facing him. 'Now, bear in mind that most people put on weight over Christmas, so don't get all pissy if you haven't lost any.'

He lifted his arms up as she wrapped the belt around his waist.

'Don't breathe in.'

'I'm not.' He put his arms down.

Sheridan bent down and fed the leather strap through the buckle, checking carefully that the belt was in the right position.

'Well, what do you know? It fits.' Sheridan beamed. 'I can't believe you've lost so much so quickly.'

Max smiled. 'I've literally eaten bugger all over Christmas.'

Sheridan rolled the belt up and handed it to him. 'You should be proud of yourself. Now, just stick to the diet and you won't put it all back on.' She put her hand on his shoulder. 'Proud of you.'

'New year, new me, eh? Anyway, what are you doing tonight? Off out partying?'

'Nope. Quiet night in. You?'

'Just a little get-together with some friends. I'm off for a few days now. But call me if anything comes up.' He stretched his arms out and Sheridan gave him a big bear hug.

'Happy new year, mate.'

'You, too.' Sheridan kissed him on the cheek and patted his belly.

She was still smiling as she walked down the corridor and sat at her desk to log back on to her computer.

Then, she got back up and walked slowly, purposefully, back to Max's office and stood in the doorway with her arms folded.

'You fecker.' She pursed her lips. 'You bought a bigger belt, didn't you?'

Max slouched down in his chair as if it would make him invisible.

CHAPTER 34

Joni was brushing her hair while desperately trying to ignore Maud, who was merrily licking her unmentionables.

'Mathew Street.' Sam walked into Joni's bedroom. 'We could start at Mathew Street and work our wicked way through town, get pissed and make New Year's resolutions.'

'Your cat is licking her lady parts on my bed.' Joni pointed her hairbrush towards Maud.

'Yeah, she's really settled in here, bless her. So, what do you think?'

'Mathew Street is fine. I just want to get drunk and have a laugh. I don't care where we go.' Joni looked at Sam and then back at Maud. 'Seriously, can you get her to do that somewhere else?'

Sam stared at Maud and Maud stared back at her. 'Oh, yeah, okay. Maud, could you please go into the bathroom, close the door and lick yourself in private? You're upsetting our gracious host.'

Maud readjusted her position, tucked her paws under herself and closed her eyes. If a cat could say 'Kiss my arse' that would have been Maud's response. In a sophisticated, elderly feline kind of way.

◆ ◆ ◆

The New Year brought fireworks over the Mersey, lighting up the water across to the Wirral. Flashes of hope for new beginnings, strangers kissed, lovers kissed, promises made of this being 'a good year'.

Joni and Sam hugged at midnight before squeezing themselves from a packed Irish pub, tumbling out on to the streets of Liverpool that heaved with even more partygoers. A group of girls with lyrical Scouse accents staggered down the middle of the road singing 'Auld Lang Syne', clipping along in high heels and tiny skirts. Too happy, and way too drunk to care that they were totally underdressed for the freezing weather.

Music boomed out from every pub and club, mixed with proud renditions of 'You'll Never Walk Alone' drowning out a siren wailing in the distance. In one doorway, a young couple kissed as revellers walked past, whistling at them. In another doorway, a young man with a sleeping bag tucked around him gratefully picked up coins with grubby, cold fingers that an older, well-dressed couple had gently dropped at his feet.

Sam and Joni walked arm in arm, soaking up the atmosphere. 'I bloody love this city,' Sam slurred as they headed towards the taxi queue.

'Best city in the world,' Joni replied, slipping on a discarded kebab, making Sam howl with laughter.

Joni woke the next morning and groaned. Her head thumped and she gingerly turned over and opened her eyes, blinking as she tried to focus on the unfamiliar shape next to her.

'How sweet.' Sam appeared at Joni's bedroom door holding two cups of coffee. 'See? She does like you.' Sam plonked herself on to the bed and Maud opened one eye momentarily before going back to sleep.

'What a night, eh?' Sam handed Joni her coffee.

'We got drunk and came home,' Joni said bluntly, rubbing her hand over her face.

'Yeah, but it was still a good night,' Sam said enthusiastically.

'I repeat . . . we got drunk and came home.' Joni sipped her coffee.

Sam sighed. 'What shall we do today?'

Joni sneezed and reached over to the bedside table for a tissue. 'I think I'm allergic to your cat.' She blew her nose and tutted as she spilt coffee on to her duvet.

'No, you're not.'

'I have allergies, you know.'

'No, you don't.'

'I'm allergic to bananas.'

'Okay, then I'll make sure Maud doesn't eat a banana in front of you.' Sam smiled at her own quick response.

Joni gave in to the grin forcing its way across her face. She turned to look at Maud who was clearly very comfortable curled up with her head buried in the duvet. 'She is a bit cute, even if she has got a miserable face.'

'Are we warming to her?' Sam pursed her lips and frowned. 'Since when were you allergic to bananas?'

'Since I had a violent reaction in Paddy's Bar, last summer.'

'That wasn't an allergic reaction, you pillock. You drank four banana daiquiris and puked up outside.'

'Same thing.' Joni winked.

Sam shook her head. 'Anyway, what do you want to do today? I've got a few days before I have to go back to work, and I want to make the most of every single one of them.'

'I'm back at work tomorrow, so I would like to go back to sleep.' Joni peered at her coffee and noticed a cat hair floating on the top.

121

'Fine, but how about when you do get up, we go for a long walk along the beach, blow the cobwebs away?' Sam asked.

'Okay, but no pubs.' Joni handed her coffee to Sam. 'There's a cat hair in that.'

'Or, how about I buy you a pub lunch but no alcohol?' Sam took the coffee mug and fished out the hair before going to hand it back to Joni.

'I'm not drinking that.' Joni looked at Sam in disgust.

'It was only a cat hair. It won't kill you.'

'It's not the cat hair I'm worried about, you just shoved your finger in it.'

'My fingers are clean.' Sam inspected her own hand. 'You're too fussy.'

Joni lay back down and put her pillow over her head. 'Go away, you weirdo. Wake me in an hour.'

Sam nodded, saluted and left the room, leaving Maud snoring next to Joni.

CHAPTER 35

Monday 3 January 2005

Sheridan threw the remains of her sandwich in the bin and finished her coffee. She checked through her emails until she was forced to looked up as Anna came in. 'I've just spoken to Rob. He's acting as family liaison officer for Kate Armitage's parents and keeping them updated. We're still doing checks around them and Ellie Sands' family and friends. She's got one sibling, a brother living in Canada, both parents are deceased, and it looks like the only family she has here is her nephew, Miles. He's no trace on PNC or any crime system and neither is his wife.'

'Okay, keep me posted.' Sheridan wiped her mouth with a tissue.

Anna sat down. 'We've spoken to as many of Lively's associates that we can locate but none of them are talking. They're all just saying that they didn't really know him that well and can hardly remember him. One of them is a lad called Josh White. He's banged up at the moment, so I've asked Jules Mayfield to go and interview him.'

'You have been busy.'

'Jules is at Lively's foster parents' house, now.' Anna tapped the desk. 'I need to shoot off a bit early today, if that's okay?'

'Yeah, no problem, everything alright?'

'I've got a dodgy tooth, made a dentist appointment.' She shook her head.

'You look tired. Everything else okay apart from your dodgy tooth?'

'Yeah, all good.'

'Okay. I emailed you Kathryn Pullman's report, did you see it?'

'Yeah, makes interesting reading, just a shame that Ellie Sands isn't going to be able to tell us anything.'

'Well, we'll see.' Sheridan blew out her cheeks. 'Anything else?'

'Max called in. He's back tomorrow and wants a full update.' Anna saw Sheridan's face change, the corners of her mouth going down. 'You okay?' she asked.

'I just feel that we need a break in this enquiry. Something to really get our teeth into.'

Sheridan's mobile rang. 'DI Holler.' She sat back. 'Yes, Jules, how's it going?' Sheridan looked at Anna as she listened to the person on the other end. 'What's his full name and date of birth?' Sheridan grabbed her pen and wrote the details down. 'Okay, I'll him run through PNC. Are you on your way back now?' She tapped her pen on the desk. 'Alright, I'll see you in a bit.'

She bit her lip and ended the call. 'Jules has been to see Lively's foster parents. We might just have that break after all.'

CHAPTER 36

Sheridan inhaled before she spoke. 'According to Jules, Alan Martin – John Lively's foster dad – was banging on the whole time about what a little shit Lively was when he lived with them, drinking, taking drugs, shoplifting, but he also kept saying that most of the kids they fostered were all liars and couldn't be trusted, said they gave up fostering because of it.'

'I take it they haven't seen Lively since he left them, then?' Anna asked.

'Nope, but Jules thinks there's more to Alan Martin's story.'

'I'll get him PNC'd right now.' Anna got up and went back to the main CID office.

An hour later she was back with a printout in her hand. Sitting down, she said, 'I've done some digging. Alan Martin was arrested on the fifteenth of June 1992 on suspicion of sexual assault on a twelve-year-old male. One of his foster kids. A lad called Richard Halford.'

Sheridan wrote herself a note. 'Did it get to court?'

'No, he was never charged, the kid withdrew his complaint and Alan Martin denied it in interview. That's his only arrest.'

'What about the wife?' Sheridan asked.

'I thought you'd ask that. She's no trace.'

Sheridan wrote another note. 'So, that's why Alan Martin said that the kids were all liars, and hence they couldn't foster any more.' Sheridan weaved her pen between her fingers. 'He's a potential suspect then.' She noticed the frown on Anna's face. 'Let's say he sexually abused John Lively and Lively went back to him and said he was going to report it. Maybe Alan Martin somehow gets hold of a gun and kills Lively, buries him, job done.' Sheridan stared at the notes she had made. 'What do you think?'

'It's possible, he would have had a motive at least.'

'It's bloody thin, but let's find out everything we can about Alan Martin and his wife, Judy, anyway. Also, double check if Lively ever reported a sexual assault. Maybe he made a report, but Alan Martin was never actually convicted or even arrested. I'm sure we would have picked it up by now if he had, but can we double check anyway? I just need to make sure we haven't missed anything.' Sheridan took a deep breath. 'Can you also locate Richard Halford? It would be really good if he can tell us more about why he withdrew his statement, maybe Alan Martin threatened him.' She sat forward. 'At least I'll have something to tell Max tomorrow.'

'Sure.'

'Thanks, Anna.' Sheridan watched as Anna went to the door. 'Sorry, one more thing, can you contact Jeff Nichols and ask him if we can go and see him tomorrow? I want to ask him if Lively ever mentioned anything to him and Kate about being abused. Maybe he said something, and they never took it further. I'm just thinking that might have been a reason for Lively to shoot Kate, maybe he was pissed off with her because she didn't take him seriously.'

'Why don't I just ring Jeff Nichols and ask him the question?'

Sheridan shook her head. 'No, I'd rather see him face to face.'

Anna nodded in agreement. 'Okay. I'll give him a call, and then I'll get off to the dentist if that's alright?'

'Of course it is. I'll see you in the morning.'

'Okay.' Anna tapped the door frame and left.

Sheridan ran an eye over her notes and drew a line under Alan Martin's name.

CHAPTER 37

Joni was on a nightshift, and busy settling some of the residents into their beds. She turned the light off in Mrs Overson's room, and made her way to visit the next resident, Alice Frank. Passing Ellie Sands' room, she glanced in to see Yvonne leaning over Ellie's bed, talking quietly with her hand on Ellie's cheek.

Joni walked past and into Alice's room and found her sitting in her chair by the window. 'Hey, Alice, can we pop you into bed?'

Alice stood up. 'I haven't had my dinner yet.' She took hold of Joni's arm. 'Mashed potato. I'd like some mashed potato.' Alice smiled. 'Mashed potato.'

'You had your dinner at six Alice, fish pie. Apparently, you thoroughly enjoyed it.' Joni put her hand on Alice's shoulder.

'Did I?' Alice tapped her own forehead. 'Marbles, lost me marbles.' Joni helped her take off her dressing gown. 'How old are you?' Alice asked.

'I'm thirty-four.'

'Am I thirty-four?' Alice sat on her bed. 'I don't bloody feel it.' Joni helped her under the covers and turned off her light.

'Goodnight, Alice.'

'Goodnight,' Alice replied. 'Don't put any pepper on my mashed potato, don't like pepper.'

Joni replied, 'I won't,' as she closed the door and walked along the corridor, suddenly hearing a loud scream she recognised.

Joni quickened her pace and as she entered Ellie's room, she found Yvonne standing over Ellie with Mo next to the bed.

'What's wrong?' Joni walked over to Ellie, who was crying and thrashing her fists.

'She's been like this all day. She just seems really distressed.' Yvonne stepped back as Joni took hold of Ellie's hand.

'Hey, Ellie, it's me. Come on, my love, calm yourself down.' Joni sat on the bed and brushed Ellie's hair from her face.

Ellie's head flopped to one side. 'Jooo, Jo sorry.' Her mouth drooped and she closed her eyes.

'What are you sorry about, Ellie?' Joni looked at Yvonne. 'I'll stay with her for a bit, she'll be okay.'

'Are you sure? I can get her a sedative. Might calm her a bit,' Yvonne said.

'No, it's fine, honestly. She'll be alright in a little while,' Joni replied.

'I don't like her being distressed like this. I think a mild sedative will help.'

'Can I try first? And if that doesn't work, we could give her something to calm her?' Joni asked.

'Alright. But I'll check on her before I go home. Is there anyone that Mo needs to put to bed for you?' Yvonne asked, knowing that Mo would probably protest.

'Yes, just Margaret and Pauline, the others are all done.'

'Mo, can you sort them for Joni, please?'

Mo nodded, hacked off that she had to do Joni's work while she babysat 'Pissy Knickers'.

'I'll come back up before I go.' Yvonne left and Joni opened Ellie's bedside cabinet, retrieving the notepad she had put in there.

She took a pen out of her pocket and wrote the date and time and then the words that Ellie had shouted. *JOOO, JO SORRY.*

Ellie put her hand on Joni's and then touched the pad and Joni looked at her. 'What do you want me to write, Ellie?'

'SHIT, ME NO, SHUT.' Ellie's voice was raised as Joni wrote the words down.

'Shut what?'

'Guummmm, me shut.'

Joni continued writing and then it suddenly hit her. 'Gun,' Joni repeated. 'Gun, me shot.'

Ellie banged her head back on the pillow and shouted, 'Yeeee, yes, gun, shut.' She put her hand back on the pad.

'Yes, you were shot. And the man that shot you is dead.' Joni put the pad next to Ellie.

'Noooo, Jooon, no.' Ellie's face was contorted, and Joni could see the pain in her eyes, the total frustration that she knew what she wanted to say but just couldn't form the words.

'It's okay Ellie, I understand you. I think that's enough for now, you need to get some rest.' Joni picked up the pad and put it back in the cabinet. She thought about trying the alphabet with Ellie but she had closed her eyes and Joni covered her up, gently stroking her arm until she fell asleep.

Joni went downstairs and found Yvonne in her office.

'Ellie's settled. She's asleep.' Joni leaned against the door frame. 'I think she said the words "gun" and "shot". I've written it down.'

'Are you sure?'

'I think so, I wanted to try the alphabet with her but she's sleeping now.'

'Okay. Well thanks, Joni. She was really distressed earlier. Thankfully she responds to you.' Yvonne stood up and looked at the clock. 'I need to go home, it's been a long day, will you be alright?'

'Yeah of course, I love nights.' She grinned.

'Well, hopefully you'll have a quiet one, call me if you need to.'

'We'll be fine, go home and get some sleep.'

Joni walked Yvonne to the front door and lit a cigarette as she stepped outside. 'Goodnight,' she said as Yvonne made her way to her car.

She watched as Yvonne drove away before gazing up at the sky, blowing cigarette smoke into the cold air. She thought about Ellie and just wished that she could understand what she was trying to say. She thought about what had happened to her. Wrong place, wrong time. Just went to get her shopping and gets caught by a stray bullet. *You couldn't make it up*, thought Joni. *What are the chances?* She drew deeply on her cigarette. She'd definitely give up smoking tomorrow. Definitely.

CHAPTER 38

Tuesday 4 January

Max Hall walked down the corridor with a coffee in his hand. Stopping at Sheridan's door and finding it empty, he carried on to the main CID office. There were a handful of detectives there, on their phones or studying computer screens.

Sheridan looked up and nodded at Max. 'Morning, boss. You okay?'

'No, I feel like shit. Can't shift this bloody cold. Anyway, how's it going?'

'Not too bad. Got a possible suspect.' Sheridan grabbed her notes from the desk next to her and sat opposite him.

'Okay, good. Update me.' Max sipped his coffee.

'Firstly, we've located and spoken to a number of Lively's associates. None of them are saying anything. One's in prison and he's being seen today.' She checked her notes. 'Jules Mayfield went out to see Lively's foster parents, Alan and Judy Martin. Alan Martin was banging on about the kids they fostered saying that most of them were liars and that Lively was nothing but trouble, drinking, taking drugs, shoplifting etcetera, etcetera. Anyway, we did some checks on him, and Alan Martin was arrested for sexually assaulting one of their foster kids back in 1992. The victim was a twelve-year-old lad called Richard Halford who later withdrew his statement. Martin denied the offence, so he was never charged. They obviously didn't foster any more kids after that. They're still married and living together. Judy Martin herself is clean.'

'So, have you thought about the possibility that Lively was sexually assaulted by Alan Martin, maybe he found him years later and threatened to report him?' Max Hall wiped his mouth.

'Yes, we have. I've got officers trying to locate Richard Halford to find out why he retracted his complaint. I've also got checks being done on whether Lively ever reported sexual assault. Maybe he did and then never went through with it. We're checking the old crime system and Anna spoke to Jeff Nichols yesterday. I'm going out this morning to see him at home, see if he can remember Lively ever mentioning that he was abused in foster care.'

'So, Alan Martin's a potential suspect in the Lively shooting. What about Lively's motive for having a grudge against Kate? Maybe he told her that Alan Martin abused him, but she never did anything about it? Could be something like that.' Max rubbed his temples. To Sheridan, he looked like he really should have stayed at home.

'Yes, that's what we thought, that's why I'm going out to see Jeff Nichols this morning,' Sheridan replied.

'Good. Sounds like you're all over it.' He stood up. 'I'll be in my office, keep me posted.'

'Max?' Sheridan also got up.

Max turned around. 'Yes?'

'Are you alright?'

'Yes, I'm fine, ignore me. Just don't feel a hundred per cent.' He picked up his coffee and went back to his office.

Sheridan looked around the room at the busy officers all working to get a result. She loved her job. She went back to her office and sat down.

Anna walked in, one side of her face slightly swollen; the result of an hour in the dentist's chair.

'Blimey, you look rough,' Sheridan said, pulling a sympathetic face.

'Thanks, had to have a tooth out, it hurts like a bitch. Have you spoken to the DCI?' Anna touched her cheek with her forefinger.

'Yeah, told him where we are so far. Have you got painkillers?' Sheridan opened her desk drawer.

Anna put her hand up. 'No, I'm fine, honestly, got a high pain threshold, it only hurts when I smile.' She winced.

'Will you be okay to come and see Jeff Nichols with me?'

'Yeah, no problem. I just need to have a quick wee.'

CHAPTER 39

Jeff opened his front door. 'Hello, ma'am. Sergeant. Please come in.'

'Old habits die hard, eh?' Sheridan wiped her feet and stepped into the hallway.

'Sorry?' Jeff closed the door behind Anna.

'Calling me "ma'am". You don't have to, you know. You can call me Inspector or Sheridan if you want.'

Jeff opened the living room door. 'I guess I just feel it's disrespectful. Please come through. Sit down. Can I get you a drink? Tea, coffee?'

'Not for me, thanks.' Anna sat in the armchair by the window. She didn't dare risk a hot drink. Her mouth was bloody killing her.

'I'm fine, thanks.' Sheridan took her notes out of her bag and sat on the sofa.

Jeff was in the armchair near the fireplace. 'So, how can I help?'

Sheridan put her notes on the sofa cushion next to her and took out a pen and notepad. 'We've been doing some checks around John Lively's old associates, who as you can imagine aren't very forthcoming. Most of them say they either can't remember him or hadn't seen him for years. We then spoke to Lively's foster parents, Alan and Judy Martin. Did he ever talk about them?'

'No, doesn't ring any bells. I think I can recall that he was fostered or adopted but I don't think he ever talked about it. It was a long time ago,' Jeff said.

'Well, Alan Martin was nicked back in 1992 for sexual assault on one of his foster kids. Young lad. But the case never went anywhere. We're going to be speaking to him, but I wondered if Lively ever mentioned being abused when he was in foster care?'

'No, I don't recall anything like that.' Jeff shook his head.

'We're just trying to establish if maybe he told you or Kate, and perhaps for whatever reason she didn't pursue it. Might have even been his motive for shooting her. I know he had a grudge against her but it's not entirely clear what the grudge was.' Sheridan watched for Jeff's response, for anything that gave him away, checking for his reaction whenever she mentioned Kate's shooting. This time, there was nothing, but he quickly jumped to Kate's defence.

'No way. If he'd told either of us that he'd been sexually assaulted, we would have taken it further. Kate was always really proactive when it came to jobs like that, in fact with any job she dealt with.'

Sheridan immediately jumped in. 'Don't get me wrong, Jeff. I'm not questioning Kate's integrity or yours.' She shifted in her seat. 'I just need to know if Lively ever said anything or intimated anything about his foster parents.'

'I really can't remember him saying anything to us, but then he hated Kate, so she was probably the last copper he'd disclose that to.'

'Why did he hate her so much?' Anna asked, wishing immediately that she'd kept her mouth shut, or at least taken up Sheridan's offer of a painkiller.

'Kate got him locked up a couple of times for dealing. He blamed her for having a shit time in prison, so he just seemed to focus his hatred on her. I don't know why, because plenty of us had dealings with him and I'm sure plenty of us got him locked up over the years. But he just seemed to want to take it out on her.' Jeff felt his chest tighten. His eyes filled with tears and he stood up quickly. 'Excuse me a second.' He went up to the bathroom and leaned on the sink as he felt a wave of emotion wash over him.

Anna moved towards Sheridan, keeping her voice low. 'He looks so different to when I remember him, he's aged a *lot*.'

Sheridan thought for a moment. 'I still don't trust him.'

'Really?' Anna kept her eye on the door.

'Yeah.'

Jeff blew his nose and splashed water on his face, checking himself in the mirror, then he went back downstairs into the living room and sat back down. 'I'm sorry about that.'

'Don't worry about it. I understand how difficult this is for you, Jeff, I honestly do. Did you ever get counselling?' Anna asked.

'A couple of sessions after Kate was killed. But to be honest, I wasn't in a place then where I felt I could talk about it.' He wiped his hand over his face.

'What about now?' Sheridan asked.

'I'm dealing with it.' He looked at her. 'But thanks, anyway.'

'Well, we've taken up enough of your time.' Sheridan stood up. 'Please call me if you do remember anything.' She picked up her notes and followed him into the hallway.

'Take care, Jeff,' Anna said as they headed out the door.

'I will, and like I said before, if there's anything I can do to help, please let me know.'

He watched as they got into their car before going back inside.

'Jesus, he looks rough.' Anna looked up at the house.

Sheridan sighed. 'How does he come across to you?'

'If I'm honest, I think he's a broken man. I think he's genuine and as much as I hate to disagree with you, I don't think he had

137

anything to do with Lively's death,' Anna said, her mouth aching with every word.

Sheridan started the engine. 'You are allowed to disagree with me, you know.' She smiled, and when Anna smiled back, she said, 'Just don't make a bloody habit of it.'

CHAPTER 40

Sam put Maud's bowl down on the kitchen floor and watched her tuck into her dinner of *Real beef in delicious jelly*.

'I doubt there's much beef in that to be fair,' she muttered.

Joni walked into the kitchen, still in her pyjama bottoms and T-shirt.

'Good afternoon, how was your nightshift?' Sam said, as she started filling the kettle.

'Long.' Joni yawned. 'Ellie was really upset when I got there. I had to calm her down.'

'Upset about what?'

'Who knows? It's like she's so frustrated that she can't communicate. She just doesn't make much sense, although I did work out that she said "gun" and "shot".'

'Did you try her with the alphabet again?'

'No, I didn't want to push her too much. I might try again tonight. I just worry that Ellie's reliving what happened to her. I hate to think that I'm upsetting her . . . but she looks at me sometimes like she's really trying to tell me something.'

Sam raised her eyebrows. 'Do you think Ellie will ever be able to speak properly?'

'I don't think so. I'm not an expert, but she's been like this for so long now, and her speech hasn't improved.'

'But she's saying the words "gun" and "shot" clearly?'

'Yeah. But there's no consistency.'

'Look, I'm happy to try and help. I could come into work with you and see if she responds to me. Obviously it's different but I do teach kids to read, write and communicate. I might just figure out a way to get her to tell you what she's trying to say?'

'You'd do that for me?'

'Of course I would. You're my best mate and that's what mates do for each other. I'm not all self, self, self you know. I'm all for helping the police with their enquiries.'

'You really are quite special.'

'So . . . when do you want me to come in?'

'Let me think. Oh yeah, never.'

'What?'

'You're just hoping that the hot detective is going to be there.'

'What hot detective?' Sam put her hands in the air.

'Sheridan Holler.'

'Well, I'm deeply hurt by your assumption. Here I am, totally and unselfishly trying to solve this case, give up my precious time, use my years of experience and all you can do is accuse me of trying to get in with the hot detective. I'm shocked to the core. Shocked, I tell you.'

Joni started clapping slowly, bowing her head. 'Bravo. Bravo performance.'

Sam performed a dramatic curtsey. 'Thank you.'

CHAPTER 41

Friday 7 January

Sheridan looked up as Anna walked into her office. 'Want the bad news?'

Sheridan sighed. 'Go on.'

'The lad that Alan Martin was accused of sexually assaulting – Richard Halford – committed suicide four years ago.' She sat down. 'He was living on a farm in Scotland, hung himself from a tree. Didn't leave a suicide note. Apparently, he had some mental health problems, history of self-harm, bit of a loner.'

'Bollocks.' Sheridan put her hands behind her head. 'It's hanged, by the way.'

'What?'

'It's hanged, not hung.'

Anna frowned. 'Hanged himself. That doesn't sound right.'

'It's definitely hanged, not hung,' Sheridan said, nodding.

Anna grinned and continued. 'I'm sure you're right. Anyway, Jules went to see Josh White, the lad in prison. All he said was he knew Lively from the area, knew he was a druggie and thought he was, and I quote, "A fucking loser but at least he killed a bent pig, so he wasn't all bad."'

'Bent?'

'You know what these shit-bags are like. They think we're all bent.'

'Yeah, I guess. We'll keep going with everything else, see what comes up.'

'Okay.' Anna headed out of the office.

'You're going to check out the hanged-hung thing, aren't you?' Sheridan called after her.

'Yes, I am,' Anna called back as she walked down the corridor smiling.

Ten minutes later, Sheridan's mobile pinged with a message from Anna: *Okay smart arse, you were right, it's hanged not hung*

Sheridan grinned and text back: *Annoying aren't I?*

Anna replied: *Yes.*

CHAPTER 42

Saturday 8 January

Joni checked her watch. It had just turned two in the morning, but she felt wide awake. All the residents were asleep, and she'd completed all her paperwork. Pouring herself a coffee, she heard Mo come into the break room.

'I bloody hate nights.' Joni looked up as Mo plonked herself on the armchair. 'Do you want a biscuit with that?'

'No, ta,' Joni said. 'Do you want a coffee?'

'Yeah, why not?' Mo rummaged in her bag and heaved out her lunchbox.

'How's Harry?' Joni asked as she reboiled the kettle.

'Fine.'

'Are you thinking of moving in together?'

'No thanks, I like my own space.'

'Where does he live?'

'Chester, I think.'

'Does he live on his own?'

'No, he shares with some of his mates.'

'What's his place like?'

'Don't know. I've never been there. He always stays at mine.'

Joni thought about everyone's assumption that Harry Minton was married. From what Mo was saying, Joni was surprised that Mo couldn't see it, too. It was pretty bloody obvious.

'Has he ever been married?' Joni asked.

'Divorced. Anyway, what's with all the questions?' Mo took her coffee from Joni and dunked a biscuit into it.

'Just interested. We've never really talked about him that much. You must get on pretty well.'

'Yeah, we do, actually. He's not like most of my exes, only interested in themselves. He's always asking about me. And he puts up with me moaning about this bloody place.'

Joni sat down. 'Why don't you look for something else if you hate it here so much?'

'I might do. I suppose you just get used to a job and know what you're doing and can't be bothered to start going for interviews and filling out application forms. Sod that,' Mo said, trying to fish out the dunked biscuit that had fallen into her coffee.

Joni didn't answer and they sat for a moment in silence.

'What happened to Harry's mum?' Joni finally asked.

'What do you mean?'

'I thought he came here looking for a home for his mum?'

'Dunno. I think she died,' Mo said bluntly. 'Anyway, what about you? No man on the scene yet?' Mo licked her fingers, which were now soaked in coffee and crumbs.

'No, not yet. I'm happy on my own.' Joni rested her head back.

'Don't you live with a lesbian?'

'Yeah, my mate Sam.'

'Doesn't she fancy you, then?'

'No, it's nothing like that, we've been friends since we were little. She's just a mate.'

Mo raised her eyebrows. 'Whatever you say.'

144

Joni had the temptation to tell Mo to go fuck herself, but instead she resisted. 'I'm going to do a round, check everyone's okay.'

'Suit yourself, I'm having me butties,' Mo replied, laying out crisps between two slices of bread.

Joni got up and left without another word. *Mo's a prat,* she thought.

She made her way from room to room. The sound of the floorboards creaking slightly with each step wasn't enough to wake anyone. Joni checked in on Ellie and as she opened the door, she noticed Ellie was awake, the hallway light shining on her face. Joni went in. 'You okay, Ellie?'

'Naaaaa,' Ellie's voice rattled.

Joni walked over to her. 'What's wrong?'

'Joooo noo shut.' Ellie lifted her head off the pillow and threw it back down.

Joni took the notepad out of the cupboard and wrote down the words. She noticed that Ellie had said something similar over the last couple of nights.

'Shot, is that what you're saying?' Joni leaned in towards Ellie.

'Johhhhhn . . . naaaa shut me.'

Joni pulled back and frowned. 'Are you saying, "John shot me"?' Joni was surprised that Ellie had remembered the name 'John' from when they mentioned him to her before.

'Naaaaoooo.' Ellie banged her head on the pillow again. 'Nooaaa, John Live noooo shut meeeee.'

Joni wrote down the words quickly. She had realised that she had to write them as soon as Ellie said them, otherwise she wouldn't remember them properly.

Joni wrote as Ellie spoke, looking down at the words. 'Ellie.' Joni was inches from Ellie's face. 'Are you saying John Lively did *not* shoot you?' Joni waited.

'Yeeeeeeee. Peeesse.' Ellie turned her head and Joni noticed tears rolling down her face.

'Is that really what you're saying?' Joni asked.

'Faaaan.' Ellie's mouth drooped and she closed her eyes.

Joni sat back and stared at her. She put the notepad on her lap and read the words again.

'Bloody hell.'

CHAPTER 43

When Yvonne came through the doors of the home at seven that morning, she was surprised to see Joni still there.

'Everything okay?' she asked as Joni followed her into her office.

'I was with Ellie last night and I think she was trying to say to me that John Lively didn't shoot her.' Joni looked at her notebook. 'She said something like, "*No, John Live no shoot me*" and when I asked her if she meant John Lively didn't shoot her, she said yes. It wasn't a clear yes but I'm pretty sure that's what she meant.'

Yvonne opened her desk drawer and took out Sheridan Holler's card. 'I guess you'd better give Inspector Holler a call.' She handed Joni the card.

'It's Saturday. She might not be on duty.'

'She's a police officer. I'm sure she's always on duty. You can call her from here if you want.' Yvonne turned her desk phone around to face Joni.

'It's a bit early. I should probably call her a bit later from home.'

'Okay.' Yvonne held the card up as Joni jotted Sheridan's mobile number down on her notepad.

'Now get yourself off, you must be exhausted.'

'Yeah, I'm pretty tired.' Joni turned to head out of the door.

'Joni?' Yvonne said, as she sat at her desk.

'Yes?'

'Please make sure you update me with whatever DI Holler says.'

CHAPTER 44

Sheridan stepped out of the shower and wrapped a towel around her waist, staring at her reflection in the mirror and noticing how tired she looked. She dried herself off and pulled on a pair of jeans and a white grandad shirt. After sticking a note on her fridge that she needed to pick up her dry-cleaning, she poured herself a glass of orange juice, just as her work mobile rang. She answered quickly. 'DI Holler.'

'Oh, hi. It's Joni Summers from The Gables Nursing Home.'

'Hi, Joni. Is everything okay?'

'Yes, fine. I hope you don't mind me calling you. I just thought you should know that Ellie has been trying to talk and I think she's said something you might need to know. I've written it all down.'

'Okay . . . what kind of things?' Sheridan asked.

Joni told her about the conversation she had had with Ellie.

'When's a good time to come and see you?' Sheridan asked, keen to read the notes that Joni had made. Joni assured her that although she had just finished her nightshift, she was happy for Sheridan to go and see her.

Sheridan noted down Joni's address and grabbed her coat.

CHAPTER 45

Joni had spent the last half an hour tidying up the place, puffing up the cushions on the sofa before going into the bathroom, lifting the toilet seat and squirting blue toilet cleaner down the pan. She then put the notepad on the coffee table, where Maud sniffed at it somewhat disdainfully.

Picking up her mobile she wiped it clean on her top and went to text Sam, just as there was a knock on the door.

She opened it to find Sheridan standing there. 'Hi. Come on in.' Joni pulled the door wide open and quickly looked out to see if Sam was back from shopping.

'Thanks.' Sheridan stepped into the hallway and followed Joni into the living room. 'Hi, cat.' She stroked Maud on the head, instantly making a new best friend.

'That's Maud, my flatmate's cat,' Joni said. 'Can I get you a drink?'

'Coffee would be good, but I don't want to keep you up.'

'Oh, it's fine. I'll crash a bit later.' Joni picked up the notebook and handed it to Sheridan, who sat on the sofa. 'These are the notes I've been making. I'll just get your coffee. Do you take sugar?'

'No, thanks. Just milk.' Sheridan started reading the random words that Joni had jotted down during her conversation with Ellie.

Few of them made any sense, although Joni had written in brackets next to them what she thought Ellie had been trying to say. Sheridan slowly turned the pages.

The front door opened and Sam walked in, turning into the kitchen, clearly unaware that Sheridan was sitting in the living room. 'Five fucking quid for a jar of coffee.' She plonked the bag on the worktop. 'They take the piss.'

Joni whispered, pointing to the living room, 'DI Holler is here.'

'What?' Sam peeked through the gap in the living room door. Her eyes widened. 'Has something happened?'

'No, not really, just some things that Ellie said last night, so DI Holler wants to go through them with me.' She waved at Sam to go into the living room. 'Do you want coffee?'

'I'd love one.' Sam grinned at Joni and brushed her hair back before making her entrance.

'Hi, I'm Sam. Joni's flatmate.' Sheridan stood up and they shook hands.

'Hi . . . we've met before?' Sheridan took a moment to realise why Sam looked familiar. 'At the nursing home.'

'Yes, I was dropping Joni's phone off to her.'

Sheridan sat back down and was joined by Maud, who pushed her head against Sheridan's hand.

'Sorry about Maud . . . she doesn't get personal space.' Sam went to move Maud, but Sheridan put her hand up.

'That's okay. I love cats.' Sheridan stroked Maud, who decided she rather liked the look of Sheridan's lap and promptly parked herself on her.

Joni walked in holding two mugs of coffee, handing one to Sheridan and the other to Sam, who sat in the armchair. Joni went back to the kitchen to get her own drink before joining them.

'You say that Ellie has been trying tell us that John Lively didn't shoot her?' Sheridan reached over to the coffee table to get Joni's notepad, trying not to disturb Maud.

'Yeah, if you look at the last entry, I wrote down something like *John Live no shut me*, so I asked her if she meant John Lively didn't shoot her, and she said yes.' She flicked a look at Sam who raised her eyebrows in surprise at this new revelation.

Joni continued. 'Ellie's been really agitated since you came to the home, her speech is more animated and she cries a lot.'

'You know her better than anyone. Do you really believe that's what she was saying?' Sheridan stroked Maud's head as she spoke.

'I do, yes. I mean, I can't be one hundred per cent sure. She can seem to make sense one minute and the next she's shouting something that makes absolutely no sense at all, as you know.'

Sheridan nodded and carried on reading the notes. 'The thing is, Ellie Sands was simply caught by a stray bullet. John Lively's target was Kate Armitage and Ellie just happened to be walking beside her in the supermarket car park.' She paused. 'Has Ellie ever mentioned John Lively's name before we came to see her?'

'No, last night was the first time.' Joni yawned.

'Right . . . so when we mentioned his name to her, it seems that she's remembered it and perhaps said it in a sentence that sounds like *John Lively didn't shoot me?*' She looked at Joni, 'Could that be possible?'

'Yes, it could be. You know how random her sentences are,' Joni replied, suddenly feeling deflated and a little embarrassed that she may have dragged Sheridan over for nothing.

Sheridan took a sip of her coffee. Thinking. Absorbing.

'Can I ask you something?' Joni said sheepishly, while tucking her legs under her.

'Sure.' Sheridan nodded.

'I know you can't go into detail . . . but is there any doubt that John Lively was the one that shot the police officer and Ellie?'

'All the evidence at the time pointed to him, but I suppose with any case there's always the risk that something doesn't add up or something's missed, but to be honest in this case we're pretty sure it was him. Can I take a copy of these notes?' She held up the pad, making Maud look up.

'Yes, of course. Just take the whole pad. I can start a new one.'

'Thanks.' Sheridan smiled at Maud.

Sam waited until she knew Sheridan wasn't looking and glanced at Joni, moving her head slightly towards the door, in a gesture that said, '*Go to bed.*'

Joni gave an animated yawn and got up. 'Well, unless you need anything else from me, I'm going to get some sleep. I'm back on nights tonight.'

'Of course, I should be going anyway, I've taken up enough of your time already.' Sheridan gently scratched the top of Maud's head and Maud closed her eyes, clearly feeling she had died and gone to heaven.

'At least drink your coffee and then good luck telling Maud that she's got to get up. I haven't wasted your time, have I?'

'Absolutely not, anything like this is always really helpful and if Ellie says anything else that you feel is relevant, don't hesitate to call me. Any time. Day or night.'

'Thanks . . . well, goodnight.' Joni winked at Sam and left the room.

'Goodnight,' Sam and Sheridan replied in unison.

Maud stretched and went back to sleep. 'Your cat has a cool name.' Sheridan tilted her head to look at Maud's face.

'She's named after my late Aunt Maud. It's the whiskers.'

Sheridan laughed out loud and then put her hand over her mouth. 'Sorry.' She looked at the door, realising that she needed to keep the noise down, giving Joni a chance to get to sleep.

'Would you like another coffee?' Sam hoped Sheridan would stay a little longer.

'I'd love one.'

As Sam took the mugs off to the kitchen, Sheridan's eyes wandered around the room. Photographs set out in frames across the sideboard. Joni and Sam dressed as Wonder Woman and Catwoman in a club. A picture of Maud sitting on the carpet surrounded by the remains of what appeared to be a Jaffa Cake. Then one of Sam asleep on the sofa with Maud tucked under her arm. Sheridan chuckled at that one.

Sam came back in with the coffees. 'Can I get you a biscuit or something, we've only got Jaffa Cakes. Joni and Maud have got a thing for them.'

'No, I'm fine thanks, trying to watch my weight.' Sheridan tapped her own stomach.

'Really? Why? You've got a—' Sam stopped short. 'You're fine.'

'So, what do you do for a living?' Sheridan changed the subject, although she really didn't want to.

'I'm a teacher at Avery Primary School.'

'Really?'

'You sound surprised.'

'You just don't look like a schoolteacher. My teachers probably looked more like your Aunt Maud.'

Sam grinned. 'Well, I thought all police officers looked like Columbo, walking around sucking lollies.'

'That was Kojak.'

'Oh, which one was Columbo?'

'Big beige coat, glass eye.'

'Was he bald?'

'No, that was Kojak again.' Sheridan noticed the total confusion on Sam's face.

'Oh. Well anyway, you don't look like either of them.'

154

Sheridan laughed. 'I'll take that as a compliment.'

'So, how long have you been a police officer?' Sam quickly switched the conversation.

They talked about Sheridan's twenty-three years in the force, how she had joined Merseyside police when she was eighteen and always wanted to be a detective. She'd transferred to Hampshire police in 1996 but returned to Merseyside five years later.

'Why the move to Hampshire?' Sam asked her.

'I met someone who lived down there.' She paused. 'It didn't work out, so I came back. To be honest the hardest part was being away from my parents, we're really close and I hated being that far away from them.'

'Do they live near you?'

'Yes, they're on the Wirral too, New Brighton, about a five-minute drive from where I am on Bidston Hill.'

'Do you have any siblings?' Sam shifted in her seat, noticing how Sheridan's jaw tightened before she answered.

'No.' Sheridan moved her legs slightly, feeling pins and needles starting in her feet. Maud was still sound asleep and snoring very quietly. 'So, anyway, enough about me, tell me why you became a schoolteacher.'

'I get to play with plasticine.' Sam grinned again. 'So, does your partner mind you being a police officer?'

'I don't have a partner,' Sheridan answered, a little quicker than she had intended to. 'You?'

'Nope,' Sam answered, a little quicker than she had intended to.

At that moment, Maud woke up and stretched across Sheridan's lap before jumping down.

'Well, I guess that's my cue to leave.'

'Yes, I'm sure you've got better things to do than sit around here all day.'

Not really, thought Sheridan. 'Shopping and housework,' she said, standing up and following Sam into the kitchen with her mug. 'Shall I pop this in the sink?'

'Just leave it on the side there,' Sam replied.

Sheridan went back into the front room to pick up the notebook and stroked Maud on the head. 'See ya, Maud.' She looked at Sam. 'Thanks for the coffee.'

'Any time,' Sam replied.

Sheridan walked to the door, pausing before she opened it, feeling Sam's presence behind her. She didn't want to leave. As she turned around, their eyes locked, Sam's eyes pulling her in. No words passed between them. Sheridan was completely captivated by Sam's features, her flawless skin, those eyes, the tempting shape of her mouth.

Just then, Maud appeared at Sam's feet and let out a murderous 'meow' and they both laughed before Sheridan winked at Sam and headed out the door with a 'Take care' farewell.

'You, too,' Sam said under her breath as she watched Sheridan walking back to her car.

CHAPTER 46

Sheridan turned off the vacuum cleaner to pick up the phone. 'Hello.'

'How are you, love?'

'Hey, Mum. I'm good thanks, you and Dad alright?'

'Yes, he's having a lie-down, got one of his heads. How's work?'

'Busy, but good. Is Dad okay?'

'Oh, he's fine, he just gets tired sometimes. We're getting old, you know. Anyway, I hope you're not working too hard.'

'You know me, got my teeth into the John Lively case.'

'It must be so hard for you, Sheridan. That lad killed a fellow police officer, but you still have to find *his* killer. How do you deal with that?'

'It's my job, Mum.'

'I worry about you, love. About how your job might affect you.' Rosie paused for a moment before continuing. 'Your dad and I were talking about Matthew last night, and how often I ask you if there's any leads yet . . . And it dawned on me that I probably put too much pressure on you. I know you have such a busy life, and here I am ringing you every five minutes asking about his case. It's been twenty-eight years, and—'

'You don't put pressure on me, Mum. I think about Matthew all the time and I'll follow up any new information, and believe me, if anything comes up, you and Dad will be the first to know. But don't ever worry about asking, it's fine.'

'We're so proud of you, Sheridan. You've always had such a beautiful soul. I hope you meet somebody one day who sees just how special you are. And whoever she is, I hope she'll realise just how lucky she is.' Rosie paused for a moment. Then her voice lifted as she continued. 'Talking of which, anyone on the horizon?'

Sam's name was on the tip of Sheridan's tongue, but she held back. 'No, not really, but I'll meet the right woman one day. Anyway, what are you up to today?'

Sheridan listened as her mum talked excitedly about how her golf game had improved. Sheridan knew her mum loved to play crazy golf but talked about her handicap as if she was a professional golfer playing proper eighteen-hole courses. Sheridan loved hearing her mum's chattering. It gave her a sense of peace to know that her parents were still getting on with their lives, even if Matthew was still always in the forefront of their minds.

After a few minutes, her mum signed off. 'Well, I won't keep you any longer, take care, sweetheart, and don't work too hard.'

'I'll pop over for a cuppa soon. Give my love to Dad.'

'I will. Bye, love.'

'Bye, Mum.'

Sheridan ended the call and leaned against the living room wall. A feeling of guilt suddenly washed over her. Walking into the kitchen she stared at Matthew's photograph hanging on the wall and pressed the palm of her hand against his face.

'I miss you so much,' she whispered. 'I'm so sorry if I've let you down.'

CHAPTER 47

Wednesday 12 January

He'd stood there for longer than usual as the wet grass soaked through his shoes, making his feet cold and numb. Breathing frozen air into his lungs, he felt his chest tighten. What had happened here was as vivid in his mind now as it had always been.

Closing his eyes, he could see himself running, shouting at him, and chasing him towards the trees. He remembered the sound, the loud crack, just before his body dropped to the ground. The ground where he'd lain cold and alone in a shallow grave. The scene of the crime. The terrible crime that he had committed. Staring at the ground now he could recall the look on his face, on his dead face. He'd killed him. He knew he'd killed him, but he also knew there was nothing to link him to the killing. There were no witnesses. If there had been, they would have come forward by now. There was no forensic evidence, and the clothes he'd been wearing when he was killed were long gone.

As he looked around, there was hardly a soul to be seen and the sound of the odd car that passed beyond the wall was drowned out by the wind blowing through empty branches on the trees around him.

He pulled his coat sleeve back and checked his watch. 'Shit.' He was late. Time had escaped him, and he needed to go. He quickly made his way back to his car.

CHAPTER 48

Sheridan looked up as she heard the knock on her door. 'Come in.'

DC Dipesh Mois walked in. 'Ma'am, just a quick update on the background checks about whether Lively had ever reported a sexual assault. Basically, we've checked both crime systems twice, we've been through the pocket notebooks of officers around that time . . . and we've also checked with the intel unit. But we can't find anything.' He put his hands up as if in surrender.

'Okay, thanks, Dipesh. Have you updated the DCI?'

'He's not in yet.'

'Really?' Sheridan frowned, looking up at the clock on her wall. 'Okay. Oh, before you go, can you get Jules to come and see me? She went to visit Alan and Judy Martin, and I need to check something with her.'

'Jules is out at the moment, ma'am. I'll get her to come and see you as soon as she's back . . . unless you want me to call her?'

'No, it's fine. Just when she's back.' Sheridan winked as she answered. Dipesh was the most polite and respectful police officer she had ever met, always insisting on calling her ma'am. He was also the sharpest-dressed officer in the station.

'So, what do you think of the suit?' He turned around in a full circle, snapping his fingers as he stood in a pose worthy of a fashion magazine.

'Very nice. Very nice indeed.'

'I haven't told the wife how much it cost,' Dipesh replied, grinning broadly.

He jumped slightly as Anna suddenly appeared in the doorway. She waited for him to leave before stepping into the office.

'You're not going to fucking believe this.' Anna remained standing.

'Go on.'

'Seriously, you're not going to believe it. It changes everything.'

CHAPTER 49

Anna inhaled deeply.

'John Lively was shot with the same gun that was used to kill Kate Armitage.'

She waited for Sheridan to absorb the information.

'What?' Sheridan's mind raced. 'Are you sure?'

'Positive, just got the results back. Not just the same calibre or make. The same gun.'

Sheridan sat back in her chair and let her mind think through what she was being told. As always, she spoke her thoughts aloud. 'John Lively shot Kate and Ellie Sands, dropped the gun at the scene and rode off. The gun was still on the scene when police arrived, so . . . fucking hell! John Lively was already dead. He couldn't have shot Kate. He couldn't have been the shooter.' She sat forward as they just stared at each other for a moment, both realising the enormity of what this meant.

She shook her head. 'So, now we need to look at who would want to kill John Lively *and* Kate.' She tapped a pen on her desk. 'So I got Jeff Nichols all wrong? It can't have been a revenge shooting if Lively was already dead and buried.' She looked to the ceiling. 'I wonder if Alan Martin is more of a suspect than we thought. Dipesh has just confirmed that Lively made no complaint against

Alan Martin, and there's no record of any such allegation. So, maybe Lively threatened to report him . . . said that he'd told Kate Armitage, and maybe Alan Martin killed them both.' She looked at Anna. 'There's a lot of bloody maybes in there.' She sighed.

Sheridan opened her desk drawer and pulled out Joni's note-pad. 'Joni Summers has been working with Ellie Sands and she keeps a notebook of what she's been saying. Apparently, Ellie has said that John Lively didn't shoot her. I know she's random but if that's actually what she's saying then does she know who *did* shoot her?' Sheridan bit her top lip. Anna remained silent, allowing Sheridan to process her thoughts.

Sheridan continued. 'Ellie Sands was an innocent victim in all of this, wrong place, wrong time, caught by a stray bullet. There was nothing to suggest that she was the target. So, why do I now think that she might have been? Why is she saying John Lively didn't shoot her? How would she possibly have a clue that it wasn't him?'

Anna responded, 'Don't forget that as far as we know, Ellie Sands has never mentioned John Lively before we informed her of his death. All she's ever come out with is random words. Then we go and tell her that the guy who shot her is dead, and we tell her his name. It's only then that she starts saying it. She's got a serious brain injury, Sheridan, who knows what's going on in her head?'

'I'm sure John Lively's name will have been mentioned to Ellie before we went to see her, so maybe she was just remembering the *name* rather than actually knowing the person.' She closed her eyes. 'I need to go through this in my head.'

Anna waited; she knew how Sheridan's mind worked, how she thought of every scenario, every possibility. Sheridan was an exceptional police officer and Anna often wished she had her ability to think outside of the proverbial box.

'Okay, there is a link between Lively and Kate Armitage, in that she knew him, arrested him several times, and he clearly had a grudge against her. She made a report that he'd threatened her and then her car is burnt out and she's shot the next day. She sees whoever shot her come towards her on Lively's motorbike, she thinks it's him and calls out, "No, Lively." Whoever the shooter is, he fires off five rounds and kills Kate, while a stray bullet hits Ellie Sands. The gun is dropped at the scene, and Lively's prints are the only ones on it. However, Lively can't have been the shooter because he's already been shot dead with the same gun and buried in Heather Walters' grave. So, he must have had possession of the gun at some point.' Sheridan nodded slowly as if to convince herself of the strength of her deduction.

'Okay, we need to update the team, and then I think we need to try and speak to Ellie Sands again. I'll get hold of Kathryn Pullman and see if she can try and get something more out of Ellie. We need to speak to Ellie's family, Kate Armitage's family and to Jeff Nichols to see if there is any connection between John Lively and Ellie Sands.' She paused. 'Can you also task someone with contacting the original witnesses to the shooting? I want to know if any of them can remember something now that they may have forgotten at the time.'

'Sure.'

Sheridan suddenly put her hand on top of her head. 'Shit.'

'What's wrong?'

'I totally forgot. There was one witness. Sally Doneghy. She gave a statement in which she said that there was something odd about the shooter's hand. Can we speak to her and see if she can be more specific?'

'Of course.' Anna wrote notes as Sheridan spoke.

'I'm going to call Yvonne Lopes at the nursing home.'

'You really think there could be a connection between Lively and Ellie Sands?' Anna asked.

'I don't know, I really don't know but I don't want to assume there isn't.' Sheridan picked up her mobile and called Yvonne Lopes.

Yvonne told her that Joni was on rest days and checked that Sheridan had her mobile number.

'Right, let's go and see if Max is in yet.' Sheridan and Anna stepped out of her office. They were about to head to Max Hall's office when they heard a desperate shout from down the corridor.

'Can I get some help in here, please!?'

CHAPTER 50

Sheridan and Anna turned sharply to see a young probationer coming out of the gents' toilets. 'Ma'am, we need an ambulance, someone's collapsed in there.' The young PC spoke quickly, sheer panic on his face.

'Where's your radio?' Sheridan asked, walking quickly towards the toilets.

'It's in the locker. I'm off duty.'

Sheridan pushed the toilet door open. 'Okay, I'll call an ambulance, you go and get help and then wait out in the back yard and bring the paramedics up here when they arrive.' Sheridan dialled 999 on her mobile.

'Yes, ma'am.' The officer turned and ran down the corridor towards CID.

While Sheridan was on the phone to the ambulance service, she knelt down to peer under the cubicle door where she could see that whoever was inside had fallen awkwardly. His legs were bent under his large frame and his face was pressed against the cubicle wall. She recognised him instantly.

'Shit.' Sheridan turned towards Anna who was just behind her. 'It's Max.'

'Christ.' Anna looked down the corridor to see two DCs running towards her. She stood back as Rob Wills dashed past her and went into the cubicle next to the one Max was in. Standing on the toilet seat he grabbed the partitioning wall and climbed up, lowered himself in and unlocked the door. Sheridan touched Max's face. 'He's breathing but it's very faint.' Sheridan looked at Anna, her face full of disbelief. They waited until the ambulance arrived and by now, a crowd of concerned colleagues had amassed in the corridor.

Anna put her hand on Sheridan's shoulder. 'Are you alright?'

'Yes, I'm fine . . . I just hope he's okay.' Sheridan felt herself shaking. 'I need to call his wife.'

CHAPTER 51

Sheridan sat in the hospital corridor and turned to see Anna walking back from the drinks machine.

'His wife's here,' Anna said, handing Sheridan a cup of coffee in a polystyrene cup.

Sheila Hall came around the corner and walked over to Sheridan.

'He's okay. He's going to be alright. He's had a heart attack but he's stable. Heart disease is in his family, it killed his father and his uncle.' Sheila Hall burst into tears and Sheridan grabbed her, holding her tightly.

'It's okay, it's okay.' Sheridan felt herself welling up.

'I told him to slow down. I told him, Sheridan, but he never listens to me.' She pulled away and wiped her eyes with a tissue. 'Bloody job.' She tried to smile.

'So, is that what they've said? He'll be okay?'

'Well, it's early days. He'll be in here a while, but they seem quite confident that he'll make a good recovery.'

'Is there anyone we can call?' Sheridan asked.

'No, our daughter's on her way from Wales with her fiancé and they'll be here any minute, so you don't need to stay, honestly.' She rubbed Sheridan's arm.

'Are you sure?'

'Yes, really, I'll be fine. I'm going to go back in and sit with him.'

'Okay, we'll let the guys back at the nick know. Call me if you need anything and I mean anything at all, here's my mobile number.'

'Thanks, Sheridan, thank you for everything, and you, Anna.' Sheila Hall made her way back down the corridor.

◆ ◆ ◆

They left and drove to Hale Street nick, with hardly a word said between them until they neared the back yard.

'You never know, do you?' Anna stared out of the car window. 'What's around the corner I mean, where your life is going to go or what's going to happen to you. One minute you're plodding along and the next . . . bang.' She breathed out heavily.

'He'll be alright.' Sheridan looked at the clock on the dashboard: 6 p.m. 'We'll go and tell the guys the news, and then you get yourself home. We'll pick this up again tomorrow.'

'Are you going to the nursing home?'

'No. Not tonight. I might go and see Joni Summers, though.'

As they walked into the CID office, Sheridan wasn't surprised to see everyone still sitting there, even though half of them could have gone home. She told them about Max Hall and tried to sound as positive as his wife had. Relieved faces looked back at her. Max Hall was highly respected in CID, no nonsense, no bullshit, just wanted to get the job done. Sheridan updated the team about the gun being the same one used in the killing of both John Lively and Kate Armitage. The room buzzed at this revelation.

'Now, we have to reopen the Kate Armitage murder. So tomorrow I'll speak to the super in Max's absence, and see if we can pull some more officers in. For now, keep this under wraps and we'll pick it up tomorrow. Get yourselves off home. It's been a long day.'

As Sheridan went to leave, Jules Mayfield got up. 'Sheridan, before you go you wanted to speak to me about Alan and Judy Martin?'

Jules Mayfield had an uncanny way of sounding completely disinterested in everything she said, or what was being said to her, and Sheridan had little time for her.

'Oh yes, you went to see them, what's Alan Martin built like?'

'Brick shit-house.'

'More specific?' Sheridan asked impatiently.

'He's huge, about six-four, and I'd guess maybe twenty stone. Ugly, big head.'

'Big head?'

'Yeah, his head is really big.'

'Did you notice anything about his hands?'

'No, not really, why?'

'It was just something one of the original witnesses said about there being something odd about the shooter's hand, and I just wondered if Alan Martin had anything odd about his hands.'

'I don't think so, nothing that stood out.'

'He doesn't match the description of the shooter on the motorbike,' Sheridan replied. 'What about his wife? What's she built like?'

'Tiny, complete opposite of him, she's like a little mouse, about five foot nothing and skinny as a rake.'

'Okay, thanks,' Sheridan replied curtly before turning to leave. She made her way to her car, where she sat, looking at her mobile. As she scrolled down to Joni Summers' number, a wave of emotion suddenly struck her, and she felt tears fill her eyes. She put her face in her hands and started to sob uncontrollably. She'd held it together all day, as she always did, but now, it completely overwhelmed her. A feeling of utter helplessness washed over her. Her chest felt tight. She breathed in through her nose and slowly out through her mouth as she thought about Max Hall and how he had looked, collapsed on the floor. She thought about the case and how it had now suddenly turned on its head.

As she closed her eyes, Ellie Sands' face came into her mind. Then her mother's face. And, as she knew it would, her brother's face. Everybody needed something from her, and she suddenly felt pulled in a thousand different directions. Then abruptly, she shook her head, wiped her eyes again and started the engine, driving slowly, purposely towards Joni's flat.

CHAPTER 52

Sheridan pulled up opposite Joni's flat and checked to see if a light was on, a bitter breeze across from the Mersey blowing around her as she got out of the car and crossed the road towards Joni's door. She paused momentarily before knocking.

Sam opened the door and was clearly surprised to see her. 'Hello.' She smiled.

'Is Joni in?' Sheridan replied, desperately trying not to burst into tears.

'No, she's gone to see her mum. Is everything alright?' Sam asked, concerned at just how exhausted Sheridan appeared.

'Yeah, I just needed to speak to her about a development in the case. It's fine, I'll call her tomorrow.' Sheridan faked a smile as she felt tears sting her eyes.

She turned to walk away and felt Sam's hand on her arm. 'Hey, are you sure you're alright?' Sam drew her closer, lifting Sheridan's head up to face her.

'I've had a really shit day,' Sheridan replied, her voice breaking as she spoke. Her face crumpled, and suddenly she didn't have the strength to hide her tears.

Sam instinctively put Sheridan's head on to her shoulder and held her. They stood there for a moment, and then Sheridan lifted her head and felt their lips touching. The kiss was soft and slow at first and then as Sam pulled her into the flat, the kiss became more urgent. Sheridan let out a breath and felt her body ache. She pushed Sam against the hallway wall, and they kissed, hard and fast, stopping only when Sam took her by the hand to lead her to the bedroom.

CHAPTER 53

Sam felt Sheridan breathing as she lay her head on her chest and closed her eyes, smiling. 'You okay?' she whispered.

Sheridan turned to face her, kissing the top of her head, and whispering back, 'I'm absolutely fine.'

As Sam pulled herself up on to her elbow, she gently kissed Sheridan's mouth and ran her hand through her hair.

'Are you going to tell me what was wrong earlier?' She looked into Sheridan's eyes.

'Yeah, I had a shit day. And then my DCI had a heart attack.' She swallowed.

'DCI?'

'Detective chief inspector.' Sheridan told Sam what had happened, and then squinted at the bedside clock. 'What time is Joni due home? It's half eight.'

Sam sat up. 'Any time now.'

'We'd better get up, I don't think it's very professional if she walks in and I'm in your bed.' Sheridan grinned. 'Even though I quite like being in your bed.'

◆ ◆ ◆

They were sat in the living room drinking coffee when they heard Joni's key in the door.

'Hi!' Joni called, throwing her bag on to her bed and walking into the living room. 'Oh, hi.' She looked at Sheridan and then at Sam. 'Has something happened?'

Sam glanced for a second at Sheridan and quickly put her head down, feeling her face burning red. *Fucking right something's happened.*

'There's been a development in the case, and I just wanted to have a quick chat with you. I hope you don't mind me coming over?' Sheridan tried not to look at Sam.

'No, of course not.' Joni sat on the sofa.

Sheridan cleared her throat. 'I can't say too much at this stage but I'm going to ask Kathryn Pullman to come and see Ellie again and I need you to keep working on Ellie. I mean, spend as much time with her as you can and try to get her to say as much as she can about the shooting.'

'Okay, can I ask why?' Joni crossed her legs.

'I really can't say a lot. This is an ongoing case and I need to try and keep the press at bay so whatever I say, you need to keep to yourself.' Sheridan looked at Sam. 'I know you two are close, and I know you'll discuss this. But just make sure it's behind closed doors.' She cleared her throat again and hesitated before continuing. 'But basically, if Ellie actually did say that John Lively didn't shoot her then it changes our whole enquiry. I need to establish if she knows something about who did shoot her.'

'But I thought you said before that the evidence proved that John Lively shot her?' Joni said.

'I know, but something's come up and we're not so sure now.'

'Well, you've seen Ellie, her speech is really bad but sometimes she comes out with a word that's quite clear, and I'll be honest, I do think that she said John Lively didn't shoot her.'

'Okay, then hopefully between you and Kathryn Pullman, we can get her to say who did.'

Sheridan agreed that she would speak to Yvonne and check if she would let Joni be relieved of some of her other duties, so that she could concentrate on working with Ellie.

'I'll speak to her in the morning and tell her what I've asked you to do.' Sheridan stood up. 'I'll call you tomorrow and we'll take it from there, but I'd like to be there when Kathryn and you speak to Ellie.'

'Of course.' Joni stood up.

'Well, I'd better get off.' She smiled at Sam.

'I'll see you out,' said Joni, making her way out of the living room.

Sheridan nodded at Sam as she left. 'Bye Sam, thanks for the . . . coffee.'

'It was my pleasure.'

Joni closed the front door behind Sheridan and walked into the kitchen. 'So Ellie *was* talking sense. Do you want a drink?'

Sam leaned against the worktop. 'I'll have a beer, please.'

'So, what time did Sheridan get here?' Joni asked as she handed Sam a beer from the fridge.

'About six thirty.' Sam sheepishly took the beer and coughed.

'She's been here all that time? Why didn't she just call me?'

'I slept with her.'

Joni spun around. 'What?'

'Tonight . . . I ended up in bed with her.'

'You're joking.' Joni stared at Sam. 'Honestly?'

'Honestly.'

Joni shook her head. 'You lesbians don't waste your time, do you?'

CHAPTER 54

Thursday 13 January

Sheridan sat down at her desk just as her mobile rang. 'DI Holler.'

'Oh, hi, Sheridan. It's Sheila Hall. I just wanted to let you know that Max had a good night. He's awake now, and in good spirits.' She sounded upbeat as she spoke.

'That's great news, Sheila.' Sheridan beamed, looking up as Anna walked in. 'Please give him our love and tell him everything's fine here, nothing for him to worry about. I'll come and see him soon. How long do they think he'll be in for?'

Anna put her thumb up, Sheridan likewise, nodding at the same time.

'They're not sure yet, at least a week or so.'

'Okay, I'll come and see him in a few days. Do you need anything?'

'No, we're fine. Our daughter's staying with me for a bit. Please thank everyone for what they did yesterday.'

'I will. You take care and call me if you need anything at all.'

'Thanks, Sheridan.'

She ended the call. 'He's doing okay. He's awake and in good spirits.'

'That's great news,' Anna said. 'Did you go and see Joni Summers yesterday?'

'Yeah, I saw her last night.' Sheridan bit her bottom lip. 'And her flatmate.'

'Flatmate?' Anna pulled a chair back from Sheridan's desk and sat down.

'Yeah, her flatmate. Sam. The one we saw at the home that time, tall, long hair.' Sheridan cleared her throat and saw the confused expression on Anna's face.

'She's Joni's flatmate?'

'She is.'

'You kept that quiet. So . . . what happened?'

'Let's just say that Joni wasn't there when I first arrived.' Sheridan grinned.

Anna flopped back in her chair. 'You didn't.'

'I did.'

'You lesbians don't waste your time, do you?' Anna laughed.

Sheridan stood up. 'Keep it to yourself though, Joni's a potential witness now and I need to keep it professional.'

'By shagging her flatmate?' They both giggled like schoolgirls as they headed down the corridor to go and brief the team.

Sheridan walked into the CID office as everyone looked round. 'Morning everyone. First things first . . . the DCI had a good night. He's awake and doing okay. I'll sort out a card and stuff later to take up to him but Sheila thanks everyone for yesterday.' She walked to the front of the room.

'Now.' She perched on the edge of a desk. 'Like I told you yesterday, we now know that John Lively could not have been the shooter, so we need to reopen the original case. We need to find out who killed him and who *did* shoot Kate Armitage and Ellie Sands. We can possibly assume that it was the same person. It makes sense that Lively was shot and killed, probably buried soon after and then the killer possibly followed Kate and shot her and Ellie Sands. I'm working with Ellie's primary carer, Joni Summers. She's been spending time with Ellie trying to establish what she's been saying. A few days ago, Ellie Sands appeared to say to this carer that John Lively did not shoot her.'

Murmurs echoed around the room.

'Ellie's speech is pretty poor, and we can't be a hundred per cent sure what she's saying. But with what we now know, she is right about the shooter, even though there is the possibility that she's just repeating John Lively's name because she's heard it before, and again more recently. She has also never actually said the name Lively. Only words similar to *John Live no shoot me.* I'm conscious not to rule out that there's a link between Ellie Sands and John Lively, which could also mean there could be a link between all three of them. I'm going to be speaking to Kathryn Pullman again, so I'm hoping between her and Joni, we can get somewhere with Ellie. I know it's a bit vague where Ellie Sands is concerned but Anna will task some of you to speak to her family, ex-colleagues and friends to see if she ever mentioned John Lively. I'm sure that if Ellie did know Lively that these people would have come forward when she was first shot, but I want to cover all bases. However, the main line in this investigation is that we need to establish who would want Kate Armitage and John Lively dead.' She paused, looking at the whiteboard.

'Let's also not rule out the possibility that more than one person could be involved. One person may have shot and buried Lively, and another killed Kate. Unlikely, but possible. Whoever this person or these people are, they managed to obtain a firearm, likely taken from Lively, commit his murder and bury him. So again, there could be more than one person involved, because to get his body to the cemetery and bury him would take some strength, unless of course he was killed in the cemetery and was already near to Heather Walters' grave. Again, unlikely but a possibility.'

Sheridan gave herself a moment before continuing.

'This person or persons have then at some point taken Lively's motorbike, so they must know how to ride one or possibly own one themselves. They've taken his crash helmet, ridden to the super-market and shot Kate, before dropping the gun and leaving the scene. They have then ridden the bike back to Lively's flat and left it there, taking the crash helmet and keys with them.' She paused for a moment, letting the information sink in.

'So, we can assume that the gun was dropped on purpose, because the shooter knew that Lively's prints were on it, framing him for the murder of Kate Armitage. The shooter would then know that the police would be looking for Lively and never find him, because he's already dead and buried.' She looked around the room. Everyone was following what she was telling them.

'The potential suspect for Lively's murder, Alan Martin, doesn't fit the description of the shooter, and neither does his wife. We know from background checks that Lively didn't report any sexual assault to anyone so maybe Alan Martin got to him first, or at least got someone to kill Lively.' She hesitated, thinking out loud. 'It's a big maybe, but maybe Lively told Kate Armitage that Martin sexually assaulted him, and Lively told Martin that he had reported it to Kate. In that case, Martin needed them both dead. I went to see Jeff Nichols recently, and he confirmed that Lively never men-tioned being sexually assaulted to either him or Kate. But maybe he did and Kate just ignored it, and never told Jeff. I don't mean to put Kate's reputation under the cosh, but we can't rule anything out at this stage.'

She waved a hand towards Anna. 'Okay, moving on. Anna will task someone to revisit a witness called Sally Doneghy. She gave a statement at the time of the shooting to say that there was something odd about the shooter's hand. I want to know if she can be more specific. We're also going to speak to Jeff Nichols again to see if he can think of any further connections or information that may be more relevant than suspected at the time.'

She took a breath. 'Any questions? Thoughts?'

Dipesh Mois raised his hand. 'Just a quick update, ma'am. We've been working with uniform doing house to house and talking to locals around Bordersfield Cemetery, to see if anyone can remember anything from around the time Lively was killed. To be fair most of the houses don't back on to the cemetery and the residents we've spoken to so far have come up blank, but we'll keep at it.'

'Okay, thanks, Dipesh.' Sheridan stretched her back. 'Right, now get your hands in your pockets. We need to do a collection for the DCI, so can someone pick up a get well card and we'll get him something. Dig deep, people. Dig deep.'

Briefing delivered, she dashed back to her office, followed by Anna.

'I'm going to speak to Yvonne Lopes at The Gables and give Kathryn Pullman a call, set up a meeting and I want to be there when they talk to Ellie.'

Anna sat down. 'Do you need me to come with you?'

'No, it's fine, I've given you a lot to task out already, so I'll let you crack on. Oh, and I've got three more DCs coming over, so can you brief them and bring them up to speed for me?'

'Sure, no problem.'

CHAPTER 55

Jeff opened his front door. 'Come on in.'

Anna stepped into the hallway. 'Thanks for seeing me, Jeff. How are you?'

'I'm okay . . . please come through.'

Anna followed him into the front room and sat down.

'Jeff, there's been a development in the case. DI Holler wanted me to check some things with you.'

Jeff sat opposite her. 'Okay.'

'John Lively was shot with the same gun that was used to kill Kate.' She paused, waiting for his reaction.

'How's that possible?' He frowned as he spoke.

'Well, it is. It's been confirmed. So, we now need to establish the link between John Lively's killing and Kate's. Clearly, Lively didn't kill her because he was already dead. We also need to check if there's any link between Lively and Ellie Sands.'

Jeff appeared to absorb the information. 'So, John Lively was killed, and then whoever killed him went on to kill Kate. I get that, but why do you think there's a link with Ellie Sands? She was just an innocent victim. I don't understand.'

'Ellie Sands, as you know, has a significant head injury and her speech is poor. Really poor. And to be honest, she has a history of coming out with random stuff. But we think she said the other day that John Lively didn't shoot her. Now if that's right, then maybe she does know who shot her but just can't tell us.'

'I see.' He paused, smiling coyly. 'Well, I guess I'm off the hook at least.'

Anna smiled back. 'We had to consider every possibility, Jeff, you understand that, don't you?'

'Of course I do. To be fair, it would have made sense that I wanted Lively dead in revenge for Kate. I loved her very much and yes, what happened pretty much ruined my life, but I'm not the sort to try and get hold of a gun and go and shoot someone.' He looked Anna in the eye. 'Is there anything I can do to help? I want to find out who did kill Kate as much as anyone.'

'Well, is there anything you can think of that would link all three of them? Or anyone you can think of who would at least want Lively and Kate dead?'

Jeff shook his head, perplexed. 'No, there isn't.' He reached for his pack of cigarettes. 'Do you smoke?'

'No. Used to. Gave up four years ago.'

'Do you mind if I have one?'

'Of course not. Go ahead.'

Jeff lit his cigarette and drew deeply on it. 'What about the guy who fostered Lively, Martin something, wasn't he someone you were looking at?'

'Alan Martin. Yes, we're still checking him and his wife out. But unless they got someone to carry out the killings, we don't think they did it.'

'How come?'

'Well, they don't match the description of the shooter. Completely different builds, he's massive and she's tiny.'

'Oh, right.' Jeff stood up, retrieving the ashtray from the coffee table next to Anna. 'Sounds like a bloody nightmare case.'

'Yeah, it's starting to feel like that to be honest, but we'll get there.'

'Sorry, I haven't even offered you a drink.'

'I'm fine. I'm going to get off now anyway.' Anna stood up. 'If you do think of anything please let us know.'

'Of course I will.' Jeff walked her to the door. 'I'm going to visit my kids for a few days, but I'll call you if I think of anything and please let me know if there is anything I can do. I mean it.'

'I know you do. Thanks, Jeff. So where are your kids?'

'Norfolk, my ex-wife moved there recently, so I don't get to see them much.'

'Well, have a safe trip.'

'I will. I'll be on my mobile.'

Jeff watched her leave, wondering if he really was still a suspect in the police's eyes.

CHAPTER 56

Sheridan pulled up outside The Gables, her mobile ringing as she got out of the car. 'DI Holler.'

'Hi, it's Anna. Just wanted to give you a quick update. I've been to see Jeff Nichols, but he can't think of anyone or any reason why someone would want to kill Kate and Lively. He also can't see a link between them and Ellie, but said he'll let us know if he thinks of anything. He's going to see his kids in Norfolk for a couple of days but he's on his mobile if we need him. He genuinely wants to help if he can.'

'Did he say anything about us not suspecting him now?'

'Yeah, he did.'

'How did he react?'

'He was chilled about it. He understands that we couldn't rule anything out. He just wants to know who killed Kate. Like we all do.'

'Fair enough.'

'I also managed to get hold of Sally Doneghy. She's working until six tonight, so I'm going to see her at her house at seven.'

'Great, thanks.'

'Have you been to The Gables?'

'Just arrived.'

'Okay. Good luck, let's hope you get something out of Ellie this time.'

CHAPTER 57

Sheridan and Joni sat quietly in Ellie's room, watching Kathryn Pullman working with her. 'Ellie, say yes if you know who shot you.' Kathryn's voice was soft and calm as she asked the question.

Ellie put her hand up. 'Sooooo, sorry Jo.'

'Why are you sorry?' Kathryn was asking single, direct questions.

'Sooo, nooo tick Jooo.'

'Can you ask her if "Jo" is John?' Sheridan whispered.

'Ellie, is Jo John?'

'Joooo, nooo.'

'Is Jo John?' Kathryn asked again.

'Jooon, no shut me parrr.' Ellie lifted her head and looked over at Sheridan. 'Piss, me shut meee.' Her head fell back against the pillow.

'Ellie, do you know John Lively?' Kathryn read from the list of questions that Sheridan had prepared for her.

'Yeeesss, you Joo shut me.'

'You do know John Lively?'

'Jooon yees shut me, you tell sooooory.'

Ellie raised her hand towards Kathryn's face. 'Piss.'

'Ellie, who shot you?'

'Piss shut me.'

'Okay Ellie.' Kathryn slowly stood up and gestured to Joni to stand next to her. 'Ellie, who is this?'

'Jooo, Joo shut me.'

'Is this Joni?'

'Yessss, Jooon.'

'Did Joni shoot you?'

'Joon yes shut.'

Kathryn sat down, waiting for a moment before asking the next question. 'Ellie, do you know Kate Armitage?'

'Piss nooo.'

'Ellie, look at me if you know Kate Armitage.'

Ellie lifted her head off the pillow and her eyes closed for a moment. 'Kat.'

Sheridan and Joni watched and listened as Kathryn worked with Ellie, gently asking her to point to or look at the letters of the alphabet. Eventually, Kathryn stood up and nodded to Sheridan and Joni, who both followed her out of the room.

Joni pulled the door closed. 'I'm so sorry, I've wasted your time.' She shook her head.

Sheridan was the first to respond. 'No, you haven't, absolutely not. Look Joni, you've done so well with her, and I appreciate everything you're doing. I really do.'

Kathryn Pullman turned to Sheridan. 'I'm absolutely certain that Ellie is trying to tell you something, she just can't communicate it.' She turned to Joni. 'But I still think you should carry on trying to communicate with her. Just a little every day if you can.'

They walked down the stairs towards Yvonne's office. 'Can you carry on writing down what she says?' Sheridan asked.

'Yeah, no problem.'

They reached the main doors and Sheridan thanked Kathryn for coming.

'I'm happy to try and help. Please don't hesitate to call me if you need anything else.'

'Thank you so much.' Sheridan smiled and watched as Kathryn walked over to her car, before closing the door and turning to Joni.

'We'd better update Yvonne.'

'Yeah, of course.' Joni suddenly grinned. 'So, are you coming over tonight?' she asked, at which point Sheridan looked around quickly, suddenly guilty.

'I wasn't going to . . . I gather Sam told you—'

'Yes, but don't worry, I know when to be discreet.'

'I'm going to give her a call later. It's not awkward for you, is it?'

'Of course not, but I understand that you've got to be professional, so please don't worry.'

Yvonne's office door opened.

Sheridan whispered, 'Thank you' as Joni whispered back, 'You're welcome.'

'How did you get on?' Yvonne asked.

Sheridan gave Yvonne an update on Kathryn Pullman's visit.

'So, does Kathryn think that Ellie will be able to tell you who was responsible for shooting her?' Yvonne asked as they reached the main doors.

'I don't know. Probably not, to be honest.'

'Ever?'

'I suppose we can never say never. But . . . at the moment, no.'

'Right,' Yvonne replied. She watched Sheridan walking to her car and put her hand up as she drove out of the car park. Before she went back inside, Yvonne looked skywards and inhaled deeply.

CHAPTER 58

Mo Chase sat in the corner of the pub, checking the door every time it opened.

Harry Minton – her Harry Minton – walked in, spotting her immediately. He signalled to ask if she wanted a drink. She smiled back and nodded.

He brought the drinks over to the table and kissed her on the cheek. 'Good to see you. How have you been?'

'I'm alright, what's the rush to see me?'

'Tell me about your day first.'

Mo took a sip of her drink and sighed. 'My day was shit, like every other day at that place. And now I have to cover Joni bloody Summers' work, while she babysits Pissy Knickers.'

'Oh dear, what's happened now, then?' He took a mouthful of his pint and wiped his lips with the back of his hand.

'Oh, I don't know, Joni's been asked to spend more time with her to try to get her to talk properly and Yvonne has asked me to cover Joni's work while she plays bloody silly buggers. They're wasting their time. I've seen all these people try to get Ellie to talk over the years and, trust me, she hasn't made one bit of progress. Her head's fucked. And now Yvonne's shafted me.'

'I thought Yvonne was okay. Why would she shaft *you* with it?'

'She doesn't really like me. She thinks I've got an attitude.'

Harry leaned towards her. 'I can't believe she thinks that.'

Mo slapped his leg. 'I just don't kiss her arse like the others do.'

'That's my girl.'

'Ten years I've been working there. Ten years of my life cleaning up shit and sick and wiping arses. I'm bloody sick of it.'

'Well, maybe it's either time you changed your job, or realised that there are worse places to work. Is it worth throwing ten years of your experience away to work somewhere that could be worse?'

Mo turned to look at him. 'I suppose so. Anyway, why are you being all diplomatic all of a sudden?'

'I'm just playing devil's advocate.'

'What did you want to chat about anyway?'

He took another sip of his pint. 'I've got some news. I've got a job in Canada.'

Mo studied her drink. 'So . . . I won't see you any more?' She tried to hide the disappointment in her voice.

'No, I'm afraid not, but we had a good time, didn't we?'

They talked for an hour before Mo left. As she walked home, she thought about their time together; the relationship had suited her, no commitment and no promises, just nice and casual. She thought about the girls at work and what she would say to them, not that it was any of their fucking business. She felt a smile creep across her face. She knew everyone had assumed Harry was married and they probably talked about it every time his name was mentioned. Did they think she was that stupid? Of course he was bloody married. She had never been to his flat, they had never been away together, and he would flit in and out of her life whenever it suited him. It wasn't exactly rocket science. Mo didn't give a shit. She'd had a good time. Plenty more out there. Plenty more married men.

◆ ◆ ◆

After Mo left, Harry Minton stayed in the pub for another half-hour. Once in his car, he took his mobile out of his pocket and called his client.

CHAPTER 59

'It's Jack Lawson. I've just seen Mo Chase and ended our . . . *relationship*. I told her I had a job in Canada. She still maintains that the care home is a good one. There's no question that the residents are treated well, basically the same thing she's said all along. She does have an issue with the owner Yvonne Lopes, who thinks Mo has an attitude . . . which she does. But that's neither here nor there. Mo's just pissed off that she's having to take on extra work while another carer spends time with the one with a speech problem. I think they're trying to get her to talk or something, but Mo, like the others, wouldn't harm a resident. I mean she's a bit fiery, but I honestly don't think she'd hurt one of them.' He sat back. 'I'm going to head back to London now, so we're done. I got the money so you're all paid up. Pleasure doing business with you. I hope you can feel assured that with everything I've reported to you, The Gables is a good nursing home and there's no evidence of abuse to any of the residents, Mr Smith.'

'Thank you, Jack. For everything,' said the voice on the other end of the line.

'No problem. That's what you've been paying me for.'

'Okay, bye.'

Jack Lawson drove away thinking about his job. He loved it, always had. He got to travel – okay, nowhere exotic, but he wasn't stuck in one place. He got to be someone else, got to make up names for himself depending on the job, to pretend to be whoever he wanted, from wherever he wanted. He got paid to do some weird shit for some weird people too, but if they were willing to pay him, then he was usually willing to do it.

Like *this* job. All he had to do was find out if The Gables Nursing Home was a decent enough establishment for his client to feel comfortable putting his elderly mother into it. Jack Lawson told the client it would be tricky and could take some time, but he'd figure out a way. Which was easy when the first day he went there, using the pretence that he wanted to check the place out for his own mother, he met Mo Chase who had smiled when he winked at her. He'd waited outside for her and chatted her up when her shift had finished. She was flattered that he paid her attention. He'd fed her a bullshit story that he was a high-flying salesman, well travelled and wasn't looking for anything serious, just a bit of fun when he wasn't abroad. It suited Mo. It suited him.

She was easy to get information from. She didn't stop moaning about the place, talking endlessly about the staff, the residents, Ellie Sands, the famous Ellie Sands, shot by some guy who killed a police officer seven years ago. 'Pissy Knickers', as Mo called her.

His client wanted to know everything about the home, but most of all he wanted to be one hundred per cent sure that the staff would care for his mother if he put her in there. Jack Lawson didn't ask questions, didn't want to know.

He told his client after a couple of months that he was satisfied that the home was a decent one, but his client was adamant that he stay on the job longer, just to be certain. Jack Lawson didn't care; he had the best of both worlds, he could travel to Liverpool when he didn't have any other work on, get a half-decent blow-job from Mo Chase, get the info he needed, get paid. Life was good, no wife or kids to worry about; the thought of marriage scared the shit out of him. To be tied to one person for the rest of your life. No thanks. He lit a cigarette and considered. Yeah, he loved his life.

CHAPTER 60

Jeff threw his bags on the bed and dialled Carly's number.

'Hello,' Carly answered after just a few rings.

'Hi, it's Jeff. Just thought I'd let you know I arrived okay.'

'You just got here? Was it a bad journey?'

'No, it was fine. Just had some things to sort before I left this morning. I've booked into a B & B in Downham Market. I'm really looking forward to seeing the kids. Are they still alright about seeing me?'

'Yes, they're fine. Look, Jeff, can you come over tomorrow? I just want to talk to you while they're at school so we can set some ground rules.'

'Of course, I understand completely. What time?'

'Say about eleven?'

'That's fine. I'll see you then.'

'Okay, bye.'

Jeff sat on the bed and surveyed the room. Nothing matched. There was a white dressing table opposite the bed and a large pine wardrobe in the corner. The carpet was grey with red stripes. It was hideous. Clean, but hideous. He unpacked his bags and hung the few clothes he had brought with him in the wardrobe. Then he showered, and headed out to find the nearest pub.

CHAPTER 61

Sheridan called Sam's number.

'Hello, Columbo,' Sam answered.

Sheridan laughed. 'Very funny. You okay?'

'I'm good, just getting tomato ketchup off of Maud's tail.'

'Should I ask?'

'It's a long story.'

'Don't you mean it's a long tail?' Sheridan quipped.

'Very good.' Sam laughed.

'Anyway, do you fancy telling me over a glass of wine?'

'Absolutely, give me about an hour.'

As Sam drove through the Kingsway Tunnel, she realised how long it had been since she'd visited the Wirral. She turned the music down as she approached Bidston Hill and pulled into Sheridan's road. Parking outside, she looked up at the house. It was a large, detached property with a dark wooden front door. The path was lined either side by rows of miniature conifers and a bird table stood on the front lawn.

She rang the bell and stood back. She could see Sheridan's outline through the glass and quickly ran her hand through her hair.

'Hi, come on in.' Sheridan was dressed in pale blue jeans and a bright orange T-shirt.

Sam stepped inside as Sheridan closed the door behind her. 'How's Maud?'

'Ketchup free.' Sam smiled.

They settled in the living room and Sheridan handed Sam a glass of wine before they lay top and tail on the sofa.

They chatted happily, swapping stories about their lives, before Sam asked, 'So, tell me, what made you want to be a police officer?' She noticed Sheridan's jaw tense slightly. A silence fell around them until Sheridan finally answered.

'My brother was murdered when he was twelve.'

CHAPTER 62

Sam felt her heart skip a beat. She didn't respond instantly, however, but waited patiently for Sheridan to continue.

'I joined the police because I thought I could become a detective and find his killer.'

Sam's voice almost dropped to a whisper, before she asked, 'And did you?'

'No, not yet.' She went on to tell Sam the details of her brother's death. How, on Saturday 19 March 1977, Matthew Holler went out to play football with two friends in Birkenhead Park, and never came home.

At 2.30 p.m. one of his friends, Chris Hoe, had left to go home. The second friend, fourteen-year-old Andrew Longford, told police that he had carried on playing football with Matthew for around half an hour and at that time they both spotted a male watching them nearby.

The male was white, medium build, with a beard, wearing a brown coat and blue jeans. Andrew said that he and Matthew decided to go home, and they walked to the pathway that crossed a small bridge, where they went their separate ways. Andrew didn't see Matthew again. He was reported missing by Sheridan's parents later that evening.

His body was found the next day, hidden near the bridge where Andrew Longford had last seen him. He had died from a single blow to the forehead. His clothes had been removed but there was no evidence that he had been sexually assaulted. His clothes had never been found. And neither had his killer. Andrew Longford and Chris Hoe both gave statements to the police. Chris Hoe told police that he hadn't noticed anyone hanging around the park while he was there. Eleven years later, he was involved in an accident at work, where he fell from the scaffolding on a block of flats in Bootle. He died three weeks later.

'I promised my parents that I'd find the man who killed Matthew. A couple of years ago, the cold-case team were relooking at unsolved murders in the area and Matthew's case was one of them. They did some work on it, but they didn't get any closer to solving it.' Sheridan sighed, hesitant. And then she continued. 'I sit outside Andrew Longford's house, sometimes. Just watching. Trying to pluck up the courage to knock on his door and ask him if he remembers anything else, anything more about the guy with the beard, but I haven't managed to do it yet. Andrew's the only one left that might be able to help.'

Sam didn't speak. She wanted to, but the words deserted her. She was just getting to know Sheridan, they were just starting out on their journey and already, Sheridan had entrusted her with this. The tragic truth behind what drove her. Sam wanted to wrap her arms around her and never let go. She gently took her hand.

At that moment, Sheridan's mobile rang. 'Sorry, that'll be work. DI Holler,' she said, answering quickly.

'Hi, it's Anna. Not disturbing anything, am I?'

'Hang on a sec.' Sheridan got up off the sofa and sat on the coffee table. 'No, you're fine, what's up?'

'I went to see Sally Doneghy. She said that when she gave her original statement, all she could remember was that she noticed something odd about the shooter's hand, but she was understandably in shock and didn't really take it all in. Anyway, a few months later her mum became ill, and she spent a lot of time at the hospital. It was then that she realised, after seeing the nurses with her mum, that the shooter had been wearing a latex glove. She recalled that he had a black glove on one hand and a latex glove on the other – the one holding the gun. After he shot Kate and Ellie Sands, he seemed to fumble with the gun, then dropped it, before he rode off.'

'Did she report it?' Sheridan got up and winked at Sam before walking into the other room, closing the door behind her.

'Yeah, well, she tried to. She went to the nick and spoke to someone in the public enquiry office. Told them she might have something to add to her original statement, but no one ever got back to her. Then unfortunately her mum died, and she had all that to deal with. She said that when no one called her back she presumed we weren't interested in getting another statement from her.'

Sheridan kept her voice low. 'For Christ's sake, that would have been really bloody useful to know at the time. If we'd had that information, it might have even cast doubts on John Lively being the shooter back then. We would have questioned why he was wearing a latex glove and why he appeared to have *wanted* to drop the gun. We know now that it wasn't him, but back then . . .' Sheridan shook her head. 'Anyway, thanks for letting me know. Was Sally Doneghy okay, though?'

'Yeah, she was really sweet actually.'

'Well, get yourself off home. Thanks again, I'll see you tomorrow and we'll have a proper catch-up then.'

'Okay, have a good night.'

Sheridan walked back into the room. 'Sorry about that.'

Sam put her hand up. 'Don't apologise. You okay?'

'I'm fine, it's just a complicated case.'

'Do you want to talk about it?' Sam handed Sheridan her glass of wine.

'I can't, really.'

'Sorry, of course you can't. It must be so difficult . . . I mean, it's the murder of a police officer. Did you know her?'

'No, but a lot of my colleagues did.'

'That must be so hard for them. Was she married?'

'No, she was . . .' Sheridan hesitated. 'She was seeing someone, another PC, Jeff Nichols.'

'Bloody hell, he must have been devastated. Is he still a police officer?'

'No, he left the job not long after Kate was killed.' She raised a cynical eyebrow at Sam before adding, 'He was married.'

'Oh. So, they were having an affair? Still, I expect he was still devastated.'

'Yeah.' Sheridan took a sip of her wine, slowly swilling it around her mouth before swallowing. 'Yeah, he was.'

'You're not convinced?' Sam finished off the last of the wine and went to get up. 'I'm asking too many questions, aren't I? I'm sorry, I'll stop.'

They grinned at each other.

'It's okay, I've not told you anything that wasn't already public knowledge. It was all over the papers at the time. I just . . . there's something about him . . .' Abruptly, she stood up and kissed Sam on the lips. 'Anyway, enough about work, let's top up these glasses, shall we?'

'Sounds like a plan to me.' Sam followed her into the kitchen and immediately noticed a photograph on the wall. She stepped closer to it.

'Is that you and your family?'

Sheridan walked over to the picture. 'Yeah. That's me and Matthew. And my parents.'

'How old were you?' Sam turned her face and could see the pain in Sheridan's eyes.

'I was thirteen. It was taken a year before Matthew was killed.'

They stood in silence for a moment. Sam linked her arm in Sheridan's and placed a finger gently on the glass that covered the photograph.

'Can I say something?' Sam asked.

'Of course.'

'Please go and knock on Andrew Longford's door.' She looked straight into Sheridan's eyes. 'Soon. Do it soon.'

CHAPTER 63

Anna locked the front door and after hanging her coat in the hallway, she suddenly jumped as the living room door flew open.

'Where have you been? I was worried sick,' Steve slurred, leaning against the door frame.

Anna put her hand up. 'I don't need an argument, Steve, I was working late and I'm tired.'

Pushing past him she headed for the kitchen, picking up the empty wine bottle on her way and dropping it in the recycling bin.

'I'm going to ask you this once.' He was directly behind her, his breath on her neck. 'Are you seeing someone else?'

Anna put her hands on the sink and as she turned round, she leaned into his face. 'I was working. I'm a police officer, I work long hours and if that's a problem for you, then you should just go.' She pointed to the door.

He kissed her on the lips. 'I'm just joking.' He put his hands on her hips and pulled her close.

'Your breath stinks.' She pushed his face away and tried to wriggle herself free. He poked her in the ribs with his fingers, making her jump.

'Give us a kiss.' He breathed on her, grinning.

She quickly kissed him on the lips. 'You're drunk. You're drinking more lately. Don't think I haven't noticed.' She couldn't help smiling, however, as he crossed his eyes and stuck his tongue out.

'I'm not drunk, I'm high on life.' He pecked her on the cheek and turned to open the oven door.

'Why are you drinking more? Is something wrong?'

'No. Everything's fine. I just have a little drink when I get home and I'm waiting for you to get in from work. So, it's your fault really because if you spent more time with me, I wouldn't be knackering my liver.' He smiled broadly. 'I'm joking by the way. Not about you being at work all the time, but about being responsible if I become an alcoholic.'

'It's not funny, Steve, I know when you're joking and when you're hiding the fact that you're pissed off. I know you struggle with the fact that I work long hours, but my job isn't nine-to-five, and never will be.'

'I know. And it was fine when we didn't live together, I just miss you when I'm waiting for you to come home, and I don't know half the time when that's going to be or what you're doing.'

'What I'm doing is my job and half the time I don't know when I'm going to get home. I text you when I can if it's going to be a really late one . . .'

'Anna, it's fine. Now go and sit down and I'll pour you a drink. Dinner's a bit overdone, but I'll make it work.' He flicked her on the backside with a tea towel as she walked away into the living room, taking off her shoes and flopping down on to the sofa, closing her eyes as she rested her head back.

'I'll have a cup of tea. I don't want a drink. And I think you've had enough already, eh?'

Steve felt his jaw tighten as he wrapped the tea towel around his fist. His face flushed with rage as he snatched his wine glass from the counter and knocked his drink back in one go, gripping the glass so tightly it shattered in his hand, the tea towel absorbing some of the splinters before the rest tinkled to the floor.

'What was that?' Anna called out, opening her eyes.

'Sorry love, just broke a glass, stay there, I'll clean it up.'

'Fuck's sake, Steve.' Anna put her hand to her scalp and massaged it. 'I'm going to get changed.' She got up from the sofa and peered into the kitchen.

'I said I was sorry, Anna. It was an accident. It'll be sorted by the time you come back down.' He reached under the kitchen sink and pulled out a dustpan and brush.

She shook her head and made her way upstairs.

Steve stood in the middle of the kitchen, his fists clenched by his side. Drunken tears of anger escaped and ran down his face. And a thousand pieces of shattered glass lay all around him.

CHAPTER 64

Friday 14 January

Sam arrived home and, opening the front door, she was immediately met by Maud. 'Hey you.' She stroked the cat's head and went into the kitchen as Maud danced around her feet.

'Dirty stop-out!' Joni's voice boomed out from her bedroom. 'I'll have a coffee if you're making one.'

Sam put the kettle on and went into Joni's room. 'Good morning.' She smiled.

'I expect you've been up all night, shagging?'

'Actually no. We sat up talking.' She plonked down on to Joni's bed, joined by Maud.

Joni sat up, pulling her knees to her chest as Sam told her the story of Sheridan's brother, how she had listened to the details and seen the raw emotion on Sheridan's face. Sheridan presented herself as a warrior, a tall, mentally and physically strong woman who was made of steel. Unbreakable. But Sam had seen a vulnerability in her, a side to her that, no doubt, few others were even aware of.

Joni got up and Sam followed her into the kitchen.

'Are you seeing Sheridan tonight?' Joni opened the fridge and sniffed the milk.

'No, she's going to the hospital to see her colleague.'

'We could get a pizza and get pissed, then?'

'Absolutely.'

CHAPTER 65

Jeff sat down at the kitchen table and watched Carly pour water into the teapot.

'Still making it the old-fashioned way, then?'

Carly looked round and said, 'Of course.'

'Your mum and dad okay?'

'They're fine, they've gone to Kings Lynn for the day.'

'I take it they didn't want to see me?'

'No, they didn't. You know how they feel about you, Jeff, you can't blame them.'

'I don't. So, what's it like living in a sleepy little village?'

'It's fine.' Carly didn't want to make small talk. This wasn't a friend who had popped round for a coffee and a friendly chat. This was the cheating ex-husband who had torn her world apart. Truth be known, she didn't want him near her. She didn't want him near their children. In her eyes, she was settled and happy now, living with her parents, people she trusted. This man sitting at her kitchen table was like a dangerous insect, one that looked harmless enough but trust it a little too much and it would sting you. That's what he'd done, he'd stung her, hurt her and her children. And now he was here, in her house, in her kitchen. She felt that his mere presence was a contamination of her sterile and safe place.

She poured out the tea and sat down. 'Jeff, I know you want to see the kids, but I need to be sure that you're not going to mess with their heads.'

'I promise I'm not going to do that. I just want to see them. I know I can't make up for all the years I wasn't there and all the times I let them down, I just want to spend some time with them.'

'How long are you thinking of staying?' Carly asked, not looking up.

'Just a couple of days, I'm trying to help the police with the Lively case.'

Carly didn't want to talk about John Lively. Hearing his name made her think about Kate Armitage and the affair. She was tired of it all. 'Oh, right,' was all she could muster, trying to think of another subject to talk about. Any subject.

Jeff sipped his tea. 'They've asked me what I can remember about him and our dealings with him. Kate's and mine, I mean.' He stared at his tea. 'You can't repeat this, but they've got evidence that Lively didn't shoot Kate. So the whole case has turned upside down.' He quickly glanced at her, checking her reaction to the mention of Kate's name.

Carly was staring vaguely out of the kitchen window. 'Well, I'm sure they'll get to the bottom of it,' she said abruptly.

'Yeah, I'm sure they will.'

'Have you met anyone else?' Carly asked. She knew he hadn't, but somehow, she wanted to hear it. Knowing that he had no one to go home to made her feel a small sense of justice.

'No.' Jeff shook his head.

'You can't spend the rest of your life dwelling on it, you know?' Carly said. 'She's gone, and you have to deal with that.'

Jeff felt his face flush as he swallowed.

'You've never got over her, have you?' Carly said, watching his face change. She could see the pain in his eyes and his shoulders dropped slightly. No, she didn't want to talk about Kate Armitage but she would if it meant seeing him hurt. He hadn't given a shit when he was fucking Kate and lying to her, his wife. And she didn't give a shit if he was hurting now.

He shook his head. 'No.'

'You have to let it go, Jeff. You're going to let it destroy you if you don't.' She watched his face and saw tears form in his eyes. 'Do you regret the affair?'

'I regret hurting you and the kids.'

'But not the affair?'

'What's the point in lying now, Carly? I loved her, and I miss her, and I wish she was still here, so I don't regret knowing her, but I do regret the hurt it caused. I'd give anything to take that back.' He sat back as Carly forged on.

'You changed when you crewed up with her, you know? You were like a different person.' She ran her finger around her teacup. 'You didn't want to be at home. You wanted to be at work all the time. Told me you were working overtime, or had to stay on for some drugs bust or some other bullshit. And all the time you were with her.'

He looked up. 'I'm not denying any of it.'

'You were fucking her while I was at home, caring for our children. I can never forgive you for that, Jeff. You know that, don't you?'

He nodded, breathing in deeply, trying to keep his composure. His chest tightened and he wanted to cry out, wanted to tell her to stop talking about it, he wished he had never brought the subject up, but he listened. She deserved that at least.

'And your little mate – the alibi – Tom Hudson? How many times did he cover for you? Or were the three of you in it together? Did Kate know that Tom was covering for you? Or was he fucking her, too? I bet you were all laughing at me. Laughing at the stupid wife at home.'

'No, it wasn't like that,' Jeff snapped.

Carly slowly shook her head. 'There were times when I wished you were dead, do you know that? I wished you were dead and gone because you made me feel that bad, you made me feel worthless and ridiculous and you made our life a complete sham. I hated you. I hated what you did and I hated her.' She closed her eyes. 'But I've had a long time to get over it and although I don't forgive you, I will let you see the kids, but I swear to God, Jeff, if you screw up, or you say or do anything to upset or hurt them, or let them down, I'll make sure you never lay eyes on them ever again . . . do you understand?'

'Yes.' He looked her in the eye. 'I understand.'

'You can see them tomorrow, get here for ten.'

CHAPTER 66

Sheridan rubbed her temples as she stood in the CID office, preparing for another briefing with the team, exhaustion evident on their faces. Everyone was working flat out, chasing leads, desperately trying to find the link between Ellie Sands and John Lively. She knew the evidence was there, but so far they weren't getting the break they needed. That one piece of the puzzle that made all the others fit together still eluded them.

Rob Wills had spent several hours with Kate Armitage's parents, keeping them updated with the enquiry. Keeping them positive that the whole team was devoted to finding their daughter's killer.

Other officers had carried out extensive checks on Ellie's family, friends and ex-colleagues. To date, not one of them could shed any light on a link between her and John Lively.

Sheridan had gone over the evidence, checked and rechecked. And now, as she faced the room, she knew that her team were feeling dejected.

'Right, everyone. I know it's all getting a bit frustrating but I'm confident we're getting closer to an answer.' She picked up her coffee and took a mouthful. 'Rob? How's it going with Kate's family and friends?'

'I've just got a couple of her cousins to talk to. From what her parents tell me she didn't have a lot of friends outside of the job.'

'Okay.' Sheridan turned to Dipesh. 'What about from Ellie's side?'

'We've spoken to her colleagues that still work at the *Liverpool Post*, nothing. We've tracked down a few that don't work there any more and we're speaking to them today. I've spoken to her nephew, Miles and his wife, and they don't know anything about John Lively. They'd never heard of him before the shooting and Ellie had never mentioned him. Her brother, Edward, lives in Canada and Jules has spoken to him. He didn't have much contact with Ellie before she was shot and had never heard her mention Lively's name.'

'Right.' Sheridan nodded. 'Well, someone must know something. If Ellie knew Lively, then someone must have known about it. Keep tracing as many contacts of hers, Lively's and Kate's. We're getting closer, we just need that break.'

She picked up her mug of coffee. 'I'm seeing Max tonight by the way, so can you all make sure you sign his card.'

'How's he doing?' Rob asked.

'Pretty good, as far as I know. I'll let you all know tomorrow.'

'You're not in tomorrow.'

'Oh yeah. Well, I'll call you if there's any big news. And likewise, please let me know if anything comes up at all. And I mean *anything*.'

CHAPTER 67

Sheridan sat in the hospital car park and texted Sam: *Just got to the hospital. U ok?*

Sam replied: *Hope it goes ok. I'm fine. Gonna have pizza and get pissed with Joni X*

Sheridan smiled and texted back: *Have a good night X*

She got out of the car and made her way to the ward.

The curtains were drawn around Max Hall's bed, so she waited back by the main desk.

Five minutes later two doctors emerged, pulling the curtains open. Sheridan waited for them to go past before walking over to Max's bed. 'Hello, boss.'

'Sheridan, you didn't have to come. It's good to see you though.' Max eased his large frame to a sitting position on the bed.

'You too, Max. How you feeling?'

'Lucky.' He reached for a drink of water. 'How's the case going?'

'Oh no you don't, we're not talking shop. I brought you a card from everyone. I apologise if there are any inappropriate comments.' She put the card on the bed. 'We had a whip-round for you too. Unfortunately I left it to Jules Mayfield to get you a gift. She got a book voucher, do you even read books?'

'No, but it's okay. I'll give it to the wife for her birthday.'

'Cheapskate.' Sheridan grinned.

Max whispered, 'Did you see my arse?'

'Sorry?'

'My arse. When I was in the toilet, you were there, weren't you? Before the paramedics came in? I just wondered if you saw my arse?'

Sheridan stifled a laugh as she put her hand to her mouth. 'Is that all you're worried about?'

'No, I just wondered, that was all.'

'No, I did not see your arse. You were facing the wrong way.' She leaned forward and said quietly, 'I saw your willy, though.'

'And?'

'Bit on the small side. Not that I'm an expert.'

'I knew you'd cheer me up. Everyone else that visits looks at me like I'm about to drop dead.'

'They're just worried, that's all. To be honest, you've looked pretty rough lately, like you're carrying the weight of the bloody world on your shoulders.' She winked at him. 'You look a lot better now.'

'If I'm honest, I haven't felt too good for a while, you know your own body, don't you?' He sighed. 'I didn't say anything to anyone, I suppose I hoped it was something silly and nothing to worry about, but . . .' He coughed. 'Anyway, come on, tell me about the case.'

'No.' Sheridan shook her head. 'Absolutely not.'

'Come on Sheridan, give me something else to think about other than my dodgy heart.'

'It's the job that probably gave you a dodgy heart, so we're not discussing the case, Max.' Sheridan crossed her arms.

'If you loved me, you would.' He pouted.

'I do love you, but I'm still not discussing the case.'

Max frowned at her. 'Stroppy fucker.'

Sheridan pointed at him. 'Dodgy ticker.'

Max pointed back. 'Arsehole.'

Sheridan raised an eyebrow. 'Teeny penis.'

CHAPTER 68

Saturday 15 January

Sheridan took a deep breath before getting out of her car. Locking the doors, she felt butterflies in her stomach as she walked slowly over to his front door and for a moment, she felt the urge to get back in her car and drive away. Sam's words rang in her ears. And before she could change her mind, she rang the bell.

He opened the door. 'Can I help you?'

'Hi, I'm really sorry to bother you . . . it's Andrew, isn't it?'

'Yes.'

'My name's Sheridan Holler.' She hesitated, not quite knowing what to say next. She had spent so long playing this moment over and over in her head but now she was here, words escaped her.

'Matthew's sister.' He stepped back. 'Please, come in.'

Sheridan followed him inside to the living room.

Andrew Longford pointed to the sofa before sitting in an armchair that looked like it had been dragged out of a skip. The room was cluttered with old newspapers and piles of old VHS videos were stacked next to the television.

'Matthew's sister,' he repeated, and Sheridan realised how strange it was to hear his voice.

'Yes,' Sheridan replied, suddenly feeling very awkward. 'I hope you don't mind me coming to see you?'

'Not at all. I often think about Matthew and what happened to him.' His voice trailed off.

'I know you've been asked the same questions time and time again, but I just wondered if you ever remembered anything else about the man that was hanging around that day? The man in the brown coat?'

Andrew removed his glasses and rubbed his face. 'I wish I could. The police came here a couple of years ago asking all sorts of questions, they said they were going back over some cold cases and asked if I could remember anything else about what happened that day, but I couldn't really help them. It was such a long time ago.'

'Had you seen the man before or did you ever see him afterwards?' Sheridan knew that these were stale questions, already asked many times before, but she needed to ask them herself.

'No, they asked me that as well. I only saw him that one time and that was it. Blue jeans, brown coat, beard.'

'And you didn't see anyone else around at the time?'

'No, not that I can remember, I'm so sorry.' Andrew Longford stood up. 'Will you excuse me a minute? I need to take my insulin.'

'Of course.'

She watched him slowly make his way into the kitchen. He was tall and heavily built. His once-blond hair had turned peppery grey and there was a large bald patch at the back of his head. He walked slowly and awkwardly, like a man many years older. She stood up to peer through the net curtains, then her eyes wandered around the room, to the glass ornaments lined up along the fireplace, the picture of a farm scene hanging above. Photos standing in frames, an elderly couple at a wedding, Andrew as a boy, wearing white shorts and a tank top, proudly holding up a fish. She walked across the room as her eye caught the picture of a team of young boys lined up

218

in their red football kits; another picture of Andrew with a purple bobble hat on, sitting at the top of a slide with a man, probably his dad, wearing flared jeans, standing at the bottom, waiting to catch him. On the wall hung a huge collage of photographs pieced together, a mishmash of memories clipped into a frame.

'Sorry about that.' Andrew Longford eased himself back into his chair and took a sip of water from a glass on the table next to him. Sheridan could see boxes of medication piled high and more in a bag on the floor at his feet. 'I had cancer a couple of years ago. I'm in remission, but it's caused a few health issues,' he explained.

'Oh, right. I'm sorry. I hope you don't mind me coming to see you.'

'Not at all. If I'm honest, I always wondered if you would.'

Sheridan turned back to the photographs. 'Are some of these taken in Birkenhead Park? I seem to recognise it.'

Andrew pushed himself up and stood next to her. 'Yes, I spent a lot of time there as a kid and my dad always had a camera in his hand.' He breathed in deeply. 'We stopped going there after what happened to Matthew.'

Sheridan nodded, studying one of the photographs. 'Is that you?' She pointed at a chubby blond-haired boy with a beaming smile, standing with his arms crossed and his foot balanced on top of a football.

'Yes.' He smiled.

Another picture caught Sheridan's eye, one taken at a football match. Four young boys in the foreground, running for the ball, a woman smiling as she looked on, a row of proud fathers on the side line, cheering on their sons. She suddenly realised that one of the boys on the pitch was Matthew. Studying the picture closely, she then noticed an older man standing back behind the goal with his hands in his pockets. He was short, with brown greying hair.

His jumper was too tight around his belly and his jeans flared out around his ankles.

'Who's that?' Sheridan pointed him out and Andrew leaned in closer, reaching into his shirt pocket for his glasses.

'That's . . .' He studied the photograph, taking his time before he answered. 'Actually, I can't say I know him.'

'Do you recognise all the other people?'

Andrew went through everyone in the picture. The only person he couldn't name or recognise was the man watching from behind the goal.

She commented how strange it was to see a photograph of Matthew that she'd never seen before and asked if he had any more. He told her that there were boxes up in the loft that he'd kept after his father died and some probably had old photographs in them.

Sheridan was desperate to see them but stopped short of asking him to go up in the loft to retrieve them. She also avoided offering to climb up there herself, although she was dying to. Andrew suggested that he had a friend who regularly visited and would happily bring them down. So he took Sheridan's number and promised he'd call her to arrange for her to come over and go through them. Answering Sheridan's question, he couldn't actually recall if the police had ever seen the photographs when they'd reopened the case a couple of years earlier. He was going through chemo at the time, and his memory was a little fuzzy.

They sat talking for almost an hour. All the while, Sheridan's mind was drawn to the photograph that Andrew had taken out of the frame and given to her.

'I can't imagine what your family have been through and I'm so sorry that you haven't had closure.' Andrew looked to the floor.

'Do you have a family?' Sheridan asked, perched on the edge of the very uncomfortable sofa.

'I was married when I was twenty-seven, but it didn't work out. We never had any children; she didn't want them. I moved around a bit and then settled back here.'

'So, you say your father passed away?'

'Yes, pancreatic cancer. Eleven years ago.'

'I'm sorry.'

'It's okay.' He paused. 'So, tell me, how are your parents? I remember them and you for that matter, you look the same.'

Sheridan smiled. 'I've aged like we all do. My parents are fine, thank you for asking.'

'Do you work? Married? Kids?'

'Yes, I work, not married, no kids.'

'What do you do for a living?'

'I'm a police officer.'

'Is that so? Well' – he cleared his throat – 'do you enjoy your work?'

'I do, but I'm not here in that capacity today, you do understand that, don't you?'

'Of course, you're a sister trying to find out what happened to her brother. Did you join the police because of what happened to Matthew?'

'Yes. I wanted to solve his case. And I will, one day.'

'I hope so, I really do. What happened to Matthew has haunted me all my life.' He paused. 'I blame myself. I always have.'

'It wasn't your fault, Andrew, the only person to blame is the man who killed him.'

Andrew started coughing; he reached over for his glass of water with one hand and held his chest with the other. His face flushed red as he tried to catch his breath. 'Excuse me.' He apologised, putting his hand up.

Sheridan sat quietly, waiting for him to recover. As he took a tissue from the box beside him and wiped his mouth, she stood up.

'I'm going to leave you in peace. Thank you so much for talking to me, Andrew.'

'You're welcome.' He wrote his phone number down and handed it to her as she was leaving. 'I'll give you a ring once I've got the photographs down. But do please call me if you ever fancy a chat.'

Sheridan got back into her car and raised her hand as she drove past his house. He waved at her before going inside.

CHAPTER 69

Sheridan drove through Liverpool, weaving her way through the usual throng of Saturday traffic. She knew the streets well enough to take the back roads, heading for the Mersey ferry. She parked her car and got out, walking with her hands buried in her pockets.

A moment later, she was staring over the river, watching the ferry as it pulled away, headed for the Wirral. She could see the passengers on board and watched as a small boy stood waving. It reminded her of a time when her and Matthew were small; her parents would often take them on the ferry ride across to Liverpool. It was one of Matthew's favourite things to do. He'd hold Sheridan's hand and point to landmarks his father had taught them both.

After Matthew was murdered, Sheridan used to take the ferry on her own, back and forth. She'd study the other passengers to see if they looked like the man that Andrew Longford had described. Blue jeans, brown coat, beard. Maybe he'd been on the ferry and seen Matthew. Maybe he'd followed them when they got off on the Wirral side. Maybe he'd watched their house and followed Matthew to Birkenhead Park. Back then, everyone was a suspect in Sheridan's eyes. And now as she watched the ferry gliding across the Mersey, she could see Matthew waving at her.

Except, it wasn't Matthew. It was another little boy. Someone else's son, someone else's brother. She turned, walked back to her car, and headed for Hale Street nick.

CHAPTER 70

Sheridan walked across the back yard and made her way upstairs. As was usual for a Saturday, the corridors were empty apart from the odd uniformed officer. Rob and Dipesh looked up as she walked into the CID office.

'What are you doing in this morning? Is Max okay?' Rob asked.

'He's fine. Looks pretty well. Badgering me to talk about the case. So, what's new?'

Dipesh leaned back in his chair. 'I spoke to three of Ellie's ex-colleagues yesterday. Nothing.'

Sheridan turned to Rob. 'How about Kate's cousins? Did you get hold of them?'

'Yeah, but none of them had any more info than what they'd given us in the initial inquiry.'

'Okay.' Sheridan sighed. 'Anything else?'

'I'm still working through the CCTV from the original case, see if that throws anything up. Why don't you get out of here and enjoy your weekend off?' Rob tilted his head. 'You look knackered.'

'Yeah.' Sheridan stared at the whiteboard, her mind distracted with thoughts of her brother. Sam came into her head, and she suddenly felt the urge to go and see her.

'Thanks, guys. I'm on my mobile if you need me.' She walked out and headed to her own office to text Sam: *Good morning. Are you hungover?*

Sam texted back: *Good morning. No, on my third coffee. Wanna join us?*

She texted: *Only if you've got some pizza left X*

Sam's reply made her smile: *Yeah but it's cold and Maud's got her eye on it X*

◆ ◆ ◆

When Sheridan knocked on the door, Sam answered, briefly stepping outside to kiss her quickly on the lips.

'Is Joni okay with me coming over?'

'Of course she is. Stop worrying.' Sam ushered Sheridan inside.

'Good morning.' Joni came out of the bathroom wearing her pyjamas. 'I'm making proper coffee. Would you like one?'

'Proper coffee?' Sheridan peeked around the kitchen door.

'Joni's got a new toy.' Sam raised her eyes to the ceiling.

Joni proudly put her hand on top of her new all-singing, all-dancing coffee machine. 'It makes all sorts. Cappuccino?' she asked, excitedly.

'That sounds great. I'd love one.' Sheridan chuckled and headed into the living room to sit next to Sam on the sofa. Maud jumped up immediately and plopped herself on to Sheridan's lap. 'Hello Maud, I hear you've been eating pizza,' she said, stroking Maud's head as she spoke.

'Only the crusts . . . and sorry if her breath stinks. She's been licking the garlic bread,' Sam replied.

Joni came into the room. 'You two have got the place to yourselves later if you want. I'm going out with one of the girls from work.' She looked at Sam. 'Yes, I have other friends.'

'Two-timer. Don't go out on our account,' Sam said.

'I'm not. I just fancied seeing another face other than yours.'

'Suit yourself.'

Joni disappeared back into the kitchen.

'Have you got to go into work today?' Sam asked Sheridan.

'I've already been in. There's not a lot happening, and they've got my mobile if they need me.'

'Do you fancy doing something?'

'I could take you out to lunch later?'

Just then they heard a loud hissing sound coming from the kitchen. 'Oh, shit!' Joni's voice squealed and they both jumped up to see what the commotion was, closely followed by Maud.

Joni was knelt in a puddle of water and milk that she was trying to soak up with a tea towel. 'I forgot to put the bloody tray in.' She shook her head at Sam and Sheridan who were trying desperately not to laugh. 'It's not funny.'

Maud decided she would help and promptly started hoovering up the milk with her tongue. She totally loved Joni's new coffee machine.

CHAPTER 71

Carly opened the front door. 'Come in.'

Jeff followed her into the kitchen where his twelve-year-old daughter, Amy, was sitting reading a book.

'Hello, sweetheart.' Jeff walked over to put his arms around her. He felt her tense slightly and stepped back. 'It's good to see you! Where's your brother?'

'In the other room watching TV,' Amy replied without looking up from the page.

'Cal, your dad's here!' Carly called.

'Hi, Cal.' Jeff smiled as Cal ambled in. He hugged him and they all sat around the table.

'So, tell me what you've been up to.'

Carly busied herself making a pot of tea and watched as slowly but surely her children talked to their father. She listened as four-teen-year-old Cal told him about being in the school football team and how he wanted to be the next England goalie. She listened as Amy told him that she had taken piano lessons and wanted a clarinet. She watched as the man who betrayed her and ripped his family apart sat talking to the children he had abandoned. For an hour they talked and later they were in the garden, Cal and Jeff kicking a football to each other.

It seems so false, thought Carly, *the way Jeff asks questions*. How he laughed too loudly when Cal did a silly walk across the lawn. It wasn't real bonding. She tried to put her reservations aside and let it be. Let her ex-husband play Dad for the day. Then he could go back to his miserable life and let her get on with hers. She agreed to let Jeff take the children out to lunch and waved them goodbye as he drove away. He'd let them eat junk food, then buy them bullshit gifts; a poor token for so many years lost.

He would then go home and feel that his duty was done. Carly just wanted the day to be over. She hated the way he made her feel. Every moment with him took her back seven years. She'd kept all the newspaper reports on Kate Armitage's murder. Read them over and over again. The police officer's face was entrenched in her memory.

And, now, as she stood in the back garden, she lit the match and watched as the flames turned Kate Armitage's face into ashes.

CHAPTER 72

Sheridan and Sam sat at the window of the Blue Bird café, looking out over the Albert Dock. The place was buzzing with people taking a break from post-Christmas shopping in the city. In the summer, the walkway would be partially covered with tables and chairs for customers to enjoy the outside eating experience and watch the world go by. Today, in a cold January wind, Sam and Sheridan managed to get a table for two in a quiet corner by the window.

As they ordered a drink, Sam checked out the menu.

Sheridan inhaled deeply before she said, 'I went to see Andrew Longford this morning.'

Putting down the menu, Sam stared at her, wide-eyed. 'Really? Did he talk to you?'

Sheridan told her about her visit and showed her the photograph of the man in the picture that Andrew couldn't identify.

Sam studied it. 'I see what you mean, he looks a bit creepy, like he doesn't fit in. He's not wearing a brown coat and he doesn't have a beard though. Mind you, that doesn't mean anything, he could have more than one coat and maybe he shaved his beard off every now and then.'

'We'll make a detective of you yet.'

'B B B,' Sam said, and raised her eyebrows.

'B B B?'

'Blue jeans, brown coat, beard.'

'Oh yeah.' Sheridan frowned.

Sheridan put the photograph back in her pocket and intermittently studied the menu as they talked about Matthew and how he was always smiling, always happy and loved being out in the park with his mates. He had equally loved Liverpool, and Sheridan's parents would make it an adventure for her and Matthew to jump on the ferry over the Mersey to spend the day exploring the city. As she talked, Sheridan felt the familiar tightening in her chest as the memories of what had happened to him engulfed her.

'Are you okay?' Sam reached across the small table and put her hand over Sheridan's.

'I'm fine.' She smiled before suddenly changing the subject. 'How did you and Joni meet?'

Sam put the menu down, spotting Sheridan's need to switch the conversation. 'At school. Some kid was kicking the crap out of her, and I jumped in like Superwoman and saved her life, basically. She's latched on to me ever since . . . and now I can't get rid of her.'

Sheridan laughed. 'You have a great relationship. She's a good person.'

'Yes, she is. I love living with her. And as much as she pretends not to, I know she loves Maud.'

'Well, Maud is pretty cool.'

After lunch they strolled back to Sheridan's car. 'Fancy a walk on Crosby Beach before we go back to mine?' Sam asked her, linking her arm in Sheridan's.

'I'd love to.' Sheridan quickly kissed her on the cheek, while no one was looking.

Half an hour later, a bitter wind enveloped them as they strolled along Crosby Beach, feeling the crunch of empty razor clam shells under their feet. They stopped for a moment and Sheridan pointed out towards her home across the Mersey on the Wirral and New Brighton, a bustling seaside town huddled proudly on one corner of the peninsular. It was a cold but clear day, and they could see the outline of North Wales in the distance.

'It's beautiful, isn't it?' Sheridan inhaled the sea air deep into her lungs.

'It really is.' Sam blew her nose with a tissue. 'It's also fucking freezing. Shall we go?'

'Yes please. I can't feel my face.' Sheridan laughed and they started the short walk back to Joni's flat.

As they came through the door, Joni was getting ready to go out.

'You're going out early,' Sam said.

'I'm working tomorrow, so I didn't want a late one. Maud's had three Jaffa Cakes, and now she's in the bathroom, sitting on the toilet seat and staring into the bath.'

Sheridan sat in the living room and listened to the banter between Sam and Joni. As she closed her eyes, Andrew Longford crept into her thoughts. And for the first time in a very long time, she realised that she didn't want him in her head. Just for this moment, sitting in Joni's flat after spending the afternoon with Sam, her mind was at peace. She wanted to savour it, even just for a few seconds.

'Do you want a coffee?' Sam said, as she put her head back around the door.

Sheridan opened her eyes. 'Love one.'

Joni headed out and Sam sat next to Sheridan on the sofa.

Maud joined them and decided to climb in between them, settled down, purred and then farted, making Sheridan laugh.

'Nice,' Sam said.

Sheridan's mobile rang and she eased herself off the sofa, waving the smell away.

'Sheridan, it's Rob Wills. Sorry to bother you, are you okay to talk?'

'Yes of course Rob, what is it?'

'I've been going over the CCTV from the original case and I think I've found something.'

CHAPTER 73

Sheridan held the phone close to her ear. 'Go on.'

Rob continued. 'The CCTV is a bit grainy but there's an image on there of Kate Armitage's car. When I've looked closer at it, I think I can see John Lively on his motorbike, following her. At least it looks like him and his bike.'

'What date is that?' Sheridan asked.

'Eleventh of December, two days before she was shot. It's early in the morning.'

'And where is she?' Sheridan looked at Sam and tilted her head. She mouthed 'Sorry' as she headed into the kitchen. Sam smiled and shrugged her shoulders. She realised, even this early into their relationship, that Sheridan was never off duty.

'Dove Street, it's the back of beyond. She turns off the main road but then the CCTV stops, there's no coverage from there. Then you can see Lively, well I think it's him, a few moments later going in the same direction. Fifteen minutes later she reappears. Lively comes back into shot about a minute after that.'

'Then where do they go?'

'I can't tell. Like I said, the CCTV coverage is pretty non-existent around there.'

'Can you tell if the guy on the bike is wearing gloves?'

'Yeah, possibly. Dark ones.'

'So, that could be either Lively or whoever took his bike after he was killed. Whoever that was, they would have had to have worn gloves. Mind you, it *was* December.' She thought about this for a moment. 'So if it is Lively, he's still alive on the eleventh. How was this missed in the original enquiry?'

'I don't know. But to be fair, the CCTV is really poor. It might not even be Kate and Lively.'

'But it could be?'

'Yeah, I think so.'

'I'm coming in. I'll be there within the hour.'

CHAPTER 74

Sheridan and Rob sat side by side, closely watching the CCTV recording.

'Do you think it's Kate?' Rob stood up and stretched his back.

'Yeah, I do.'

'What about the guy on the motorbike?'

'I think it *could* be Lively. It's hard to tell, wish he'd taken his bloody crash helmet off. It's kind of the right build and I think that is his motorbike. But if it isn't him, then we could be looking at Kate's killer.'

'And Lively's.'

'Exactly.' Sheridan replayed the recording and leaned in closer, pausing it as the male figure came into shot.

'We need to get the tech team to look at this, see if they can enhance it for us.'

'I've already sent it to them. They're looking at it right now.' Rob smiled.

'How the fuck did you manage that?'

'Pulled in a favour.' He winked.

'I love you very much, Rob.' She took his hand and kissed it. 'How do you fancy taking a drive out to Dove Street, see if we can figure out where Kate went to?'

'Only if you buy me a cake on the way back. For being the bestest detective ever.'

'You're on.'

As they drove down Dove Street, Rob pointed to a side road that was little more than a dirt track. Sheridan pulled into it, driving slowly to avoid the potholes and abandoned shopping trolleys.

'Jesus, it's like the road to hell!' Looking from side to side she could only see tree-lined fields.

'I thought I knew this area pretty well, but I've never been down here.' Rob peered out of the windscreen.

They drove for a hundred yards until they came to a large metal gate with a crudely painted 'Closed' sign hanging from it. They got out of the car and walked closer, noticing a small brick building to the right and a row of small lock-ups to the left.

'What the hell is this?' Sheridan rattled the lock on the gate and called out, 'Hello?'

Silence.

'Hello?' Rob shouted. 'Anyone here?'

'Maybe it's closed at weekends. We'll come back on Monday.' Sheridan stood back, surveying the area.

'I'll get some enquiries done in the meantime to see who owns it.'

'Cheers, Rob. We really need to know what this place is.'

CHAPTER 75

Sunday 16 January

Jeff Nichols turned into the service station and pulled up behind a queue of cars. After dialling his parents' number, he noticed a woman at the pump filling her car. She looked so much like Kate that he couldn't take his eyes off her.

His mother answered the call, and he robotically told her about seeing the children, all the while staring at the woman. Even the way she flicked her hair back reminded him of Kate. He was so engrossed that he didn't see the male attendant walking briskly towards him. He tapped on Jeff's window and Jeff jumped slightly before opening it.

'Make sure you turn your phone off before you fill up,' the attendant said abruptly.

'Mum, I've got to go but I'm about an hour away, so I'll pop in on my way home.' Jeff ended the call and held his mobile up to the attendant's face.

'Happy?' he said sarcastically.

The attendant pointed to the sign. 'Do not use your mobile near the pumps, you've been warned.' He tapped his hand on the roof of Jeff's car before ambling away, satisfied that he had stamped his authority all over *this* guy.

Jeff shook his head. 'Fucking jobsworth.'

◆ ◆ ◆

An hour later he pulled up outside his parents' house.

They sat around the large kitchen table and his mother put a cup of tea in front of him.

'So, how are my grandchildren?' his father asked, sitting down opposite Jeff.

'They're fine. It was really good to see them and even Carly was fine with me,' Jeff said, still thinking about the woman at the petrol station; she had looked so much like Kate and her face had haunted him for the rest of the journey.

'That's really good news, son. I miss those children. Me and your mum both do. I know Carly was never keen on us having too much contact with them, but maybe now we'll get to see them every so often.'

'Yeah, maybe.' Jeff sipped his tea. 'She still hates me, but she shouldn't have taken it out on you two. You are their grandparents, and she should let you see them.'

'Well, like I say, maybe now you've built a bridge with her she'll be a bit more accommodating,' his father replied.

'Yeah, I hope so.' Jeff sighed. 'Anyway, I've decided to take a break and have a holiday.'

'Good, it's about time you did. What made you change your mind?' his father asked, watching Deirdre as she cleaned the cooker to within an inch of its life.

'Seeing the kids, I suppose. I feel that things are moving in the right direction and maybe it's time I tried to move on a bit, small steps but I just feel a bit happier in myself.'

'That's good to hear, son. So, where are you off to?'

'I haven't decided exactly where yet, I might check out some last-minute deals.' He looked at his father. 'Is that okay, or have you got any jobs for me?'

'No, son, you just get away, the work will be here when you get back.'

Jeff finished his tea and said his goodbyes, waving to them in the rear-view mirror as he pulled away.

CHAPTER 76

Joni was carrying linen down the stairs when she heard someone call her name. When she reached the bottom steps, she listened in case they called again.

'Joni, are you there?'

She looked back up the stairs and saw Yvonne waiting for her at the top. 'Sorry, can you come and see Ellie, she's in a terrible state.'

Joni took the stairs two at a time and could hear Ellie screaming as she neared her room. She went in and was shocked to see the state of her. Her hair was dishevelled and she was sweating, her arms flailing around as she screamed 'Piss knickers!' over and over.

Joni went to her and gently held her arms, being as careful as she could not to hurt her. 'Ellie, it's okay, it's okay.' She looked at Yvonne. 'Is she wet?'

'She was. But we've changed her.'

'Okay Ellie, calm yourself down.' Joni kept her voice low and soft.

'Shut me shut me shut me.' Ellie put her head back on her pillow and Joni could see her breathing was slowly returning to normal.

Joni took the notepad from the cabinet and wrote down the words.

'She'll be fine, I'll sit with her for a while.'

'Okay, thanks, Joni,' Yvonne replied. 'Let me know if she says anything that makes sense.' Yvonne left the room and went back downstairs.

Joni sat with Ellie who began to calm down, although slowly shaking her head and repeating the word 'Peee'.

Joni got up and laid the alphabet letters on Ellie's bed. 'Okay Ellie, tell me what you want to say. Point to the letters.'

Ellie let out a cry and pointed to the letter P.

'That's good, Ellie.' Joni wrote down the letter P and then waited for the next letter. Over and over Ellie pointed to random letters and Joni wrote them down.

A short while later, Yvonne came in carrying a cup of coffee. 'How's it going?'

Joni stood up and stretched her back. 'Slowly, but at least she's calm. She's managed to point out some letters but they're not making a lot of sense. She's really trying to say something, you know. I just wish I could figure out what it was.'

'Pissy, ahhh shut show,' Ellie cried out.

'You'll get there.' Yvonne touched Joni on the shoulder. 'By the way, I'm not going to be in tomorrow, but I'll have my mobile on if you need to call me.'

'Doing anything nice?' Joni asked, sipping her coffee.

'Just visiting friends down south.'

'Nice. Whereabouts?'

'London.'

CHAPTER 77

Monday 17 January

Anna grinned as she walked into the CID office.

'Happy birthday!' The whole team clapped.

Sheridan walked over to her, carrying a large cake with one candle on it. 'Happy fortieth, mate.'

'I'm thirty-nine,' Anna said, frowning.

'You're forty. Now shut up and make a wish.' Sheridan put the cake down and lit the candle.

'Okay . . . I wish I was thirty-nine,' she said, blowing the candle out.

After the cake was devoured, the team got back to work, and Sheridan and Anna studied the CCTV which the tech team had managed to slightly enhance.

'It's hard to tell, it's still quite fuzzy, but it does look like Kate and her car, and it also looks a bit like Lively. So if that is him, he was following her and he's still alive on the eleventh of December, two days before the shooting. And if it's not him, then this could be the guy who killed them both.' Anna squinted at the screen. 'I'm not surprised it was missed during the initial enquiry.'

'Let's take a drive out there, see if it's open today.' Sheridan grabbed her coat from the back of the chair.

Sheridan shook her head as they approached the tall metal gates. '"Closed" sign's still up.'

They got out of the car and walked over to it. Sheridan called out but there was no sign of anyone.

'Bollocks.' She rattled the lock on the gate while weighing up if she could climb over it.

'What do you reckon?'

'You'll never get over that.' Anna grinned and Sheridan slapped her arm.

'I could if you gave me a leg up.'

'I'm not doing that.' Anna shook her head.

'That's an order.'

'No, it's not.'

Sheridan laughed and rattled the lock again. 'Rob's checking out who owns the place, hopefully he'll find something.'

They made their way back to the station.

CHAPTER 78

Finding a quiet carriage on the train, she sat in the corner by the window and breathed slowly through her nose, trying to calm herself. Her hand shook as she felt her pocket again. It was still there. Of course it was still there, why wouldn't it be? She'd wrapped it in tissue and secured it inside a plastic bag before zipping it into her pocket. The shape and size of it was unrecognisable. She wanted to take it out, unwrap it and feel it in her hand.

She closed her eyes and swallowed nervously, trying to stop the racing heartbeat from rising in her throat. What if something went wrong? What if she fumbled her words and didn't get her story straight? She'd rehearsed it over and over again. She inhaled deeply and slowly, filling her lungs before slowly exhaling. Maybe she should just get off the train, go home and rethink it. Maybe it was too soon.

Looking out of the window, she stared down at the tracks, focusing on them like they would scream the answer at her. She had to know. Once she knew, she could plan what to do next. At that moment, the train nudged slightly as it pulled out of the station, heading south to London.

CHAPTER 79

Anna put her head round Sheridan's door. 'Is it okay if I get off early? Steve's booked a table at Mamma B's.'

'Mamma B's?' Sheridan laughed. 'The shitty pizza place?'

'Yeah, I love it there.' Anna raised her eyes to the ceiling. 'Steve's idea of a romantic birthday meal.'

'Maybe he's winding you up, and he's actually booked a really plush restaurant.'

'No such luck. Trust me.' She sighed. 'He's fucking useless sometimes.'

'Everything okay between you two?'

'Yeah, everything's fine, he's just shit at the romance thing. Anyway, you nearly done?' she asked, leaning against the door frame.

'Yeah.' Sheridan quickly checked the clock. 'Just got a couple of things to do.'

'I meant to ask you, how's it going with Sam?' Anna stepped into the office and perched on the edge of Sheridan's desk.

'Really good. Almost too good to be true if I'm honest. She's amazing.'

'You're different, you know . . . since you've been seeing her. You're cheerful and happy.'

'Wasn't I cheerful and happy before, then?'

'Not really.'

'Cheeky bitch.'

'It's good to see you like this, it really is.'

Sheridan sat back. 'She's really cool. We get on so well and I know it sounds like an old cliché, but I feel like I've known her for years. She's kind of perfect.'

Anna smiled. 'Wow. That's amazing, mate. I'm genuinely over the moon for you. It's about time you met the right one.' She stood up. 'You think she is the one?'

'It's early days, but there's something about her. I haven't felt this way about someone for . . . well . . . never, to be honest. It's like when we talk on the phone, we natter for hours and I mean hours, and she makes me laugh so much.'

'I'm made up for you. If she makes you happy, then I'm happy.'

'Thanks, mate.'

'Anyway, I'd better get off, so enjoy your evening whatever you're up to.'

'Enjoy your food poisoning,' Sheridan replied with a cheeky grin as Anna walked away.

She picked up her mobile and dialled Jeff Nichols' number. Engaged.

DC Rob Wills appeared at the door to her office. 'What's this about food poisoning?'

'Steve's taking Anna to Mamma B's for her birthday.' Sheridan grimaced.

'Oh God.' Rob stuck his tongue out. 'Say no more. Anyway, I've spoken to intel, and they think that place off Dove Street is privately owned. I went to the council earlier and got a download of their CCTV because they cover that area. I just thought it might be worth having a look at any recent activity, might be there's something dodgy going on there. The cameras only record up to two weeks, so there won't be much to view and from what I've seen so far, there's hardly any cars or people around, so it won't take long to go through.'

'Okay, Rob, that's brilliant. Keep me posted.'

'Will do, boss.'

'I've been trying to get hold of Jeff Nichols, I want to ask him if he knows anything about Kate and the lock-ups.'

'You off home after that?' Rob asked.

'Yeah.'

'Okay.' Rob tapped his fingers on the door frame in a *gotta go* sort of way, before heading back to CID.

Sheridan dialled Jeff Nichols' number again. Still engaged.

She grabbed her jacket and texted Sam: *Hey you, how's your day been?*

Sam texted back: *All good. You ok?*

Sheridan typed: *I'm fine, just popping out on a quick enquiry, call you later? X*

Sam responded: *I'll be here X*

Sheridan got into her car and tried Jeff Nichols again. Still engaged. She started the engine and headed to his house.

CHAPTER 80

Joni had spent the last hour working on the alphabet with Ellie. The usual random letters stared back at her from her notepad and she yawned, standing up to stretch her legs. Ellie had drifted off to sleep. Checking her watch, Joni decided it was time to call it a day. She picked up the notepad and tucked Ellie in. 'See you tomorrow, Ellie.'

She headed down to the staffroom to find Mo walking in.

'Hi, Mo.'

'Alright?'

'Yeah, just off home. You on nights?'

'Yeah, I swapped shifts.'

'How's lover boy?'

'I dumped him.'

'Oh, why?'

'Because he was boring me,' Mo snapped.

'Fair enough,' Joni replied. 'You okay though?'

'Yeah, I'm fine. How's old pissy knickers?'

'I wish you wouldn't call her that, she's a person, you know.'

'She's fucked in the head is what she is.' Mo tapped her own forehead and crossed her eyes.

'I'm going home.' And with that, Joni grabbed her coat and left.

Sam poured a coffee and plonked herself on the sofa. Maud joined her and sniffed her mug. Not keen. She looked up as Joni came in and threw her bag on the armchair. 'Oh dear, someone's had a bad day.'

'Bloody Mo Chase, she pisses me off! She's a complete dickhead . . . and I wish she would just leave because she doesn't want to be there. She's lazy, she doesn't stop moaning . . . and if she calls Ellie Sands "pissy knickers" one more time, I swear I'll punch her in the fanny.'

Sam laughed out loud, spitting out a mouthful of coffee, most of which landed on Maud's head. Maud glared at her in complete and total disgust and proceeded to wash herself.

'Punch her in the fanny?' She laughed again. 'That may be the funniest thing you have *ever* said.'

'Well, that's how angry she makes me.' Joni stomped off to the kitchen.

'Forget about her, don't let her get to you. Tell me about your day.'

'It was shit. I need a drink.'

Sam got up and went into the kitchen, pulling off three sheets of kitchen roll. 'Let me dry Maud off and then I'll pour you a large one, dear.'

'It's okay, I'll sort my drink out, you go and dry your pussy.'

Sam laughed again. 'You should have bad days more often, you're hilarious when you're pissed off.'

CHAPTER 81

Jeff answered the door and looked surprised to see Sheridan standing there. 'Oh. Hello, sorry, I thought you were someone else.'

'Sorry, Jeff, I did try calling but your phone's been engaged. Have you got literally two minutes?'

'Yeah sure, come in.'

Sheridan walked into the front room and Jeff followed her.

'I just wanted to ask if you know anything about a lock-up by Dove Street that Kate might have visited?'

Jeff put his hands on his hips and shook his head. 'No, I don't think so. Why?'

'We've found some CCTV dating back to the eleventh of December, two days before the shooting, that we think shows Kate being followed there by John Lively. It's not very clear but it could be her.' Sheridan sat down before continuing. 'I've been there, and the place seems pretty derelict but there's a brick building and what looks like a row of lock-ups.'

Jeff crossed his arms and frowned. 'Dove Street?' He shook his head again. 'I can't even think where that is.'

'Yeah, it's in the middle of nowhere, at the back of Speke, near the docks. If it is Kate on the CCTV, I just need to find out what she was doing there. And if it's not Lively following her, then it could be the killer.'

'Does the CCTV cover the whole area?' Jeff sat on the arm of the chair.

'No, just the main road, but once you come off Dove Street there's not really anywhere else but the lock-ups to go to. Just fields either side. There's a "Closed" sign on the gate, so it might not even be anything any more. It's privately owned, whatever it is.'

Jeff tapped his fingers on his leg. 'Don't intel know anything? They're normally pretty good at finding that sort of stuff out.'

'Not really, just that it's privately owned. We're doing some enquiries and right now I've got one of my DCs, Rob Wills, checking out recent CCTV activity, so that might throw something up.'

'Right.' Jeff nodded.

'But you can't recall Kate ever talking about it or going there?'

Jeff puffed out his cheeks. 'No, I really can't.'

Sheridan's mobile rang. 'Excuse me.' She stood up to take the call. 'DI Holler.'

'Sheridan, it's Rob. Are you free to speak?'

'Yes, Rob. Go ahead.' She looked up at Jeff as he waved a hand at her and whispered, 'Just popping up to the loo.'

She nodded and as Jeff headed upstairs, she wandered over to the window.

'Did you get hold of Jeff Nichols?' Rob asked.

'Yeah. I'm at his place now. He doesn't know anything about any lock-ups.'

'You definitely free to speak?'

'Yes, mate.'

'I've been going through the CCTV. In the last two weeks there are only four cars that are seen turning off Dove Street near to the lock-ups. I've run them all through PNC and one of them belongs to Jeff Nichols' best mate, Tom Hudson.'

'Really? When was this?'

'Last Thursday at 10 a.m.'

'Are you absolutely sure?'

'Positive. It's a white Ford Focus Estate. I did some digging, and there's something else I've discovered.'

'Go on.'

'You said before that whoever killed John Lively would have to know how to ride a motorbike, or maybe even owns one.'

'Yeah.'

'Tom Hudson owns a motorbike.'

'Fuck.'

'I know, that's what I thought.'

'What's the index number of Tom Hudson's Ford Focus?'

Rob read out the index number and then asked, 'Why?'

'Because that car has just pulled up outside here.' Sheridan quickly stepped back from the window.

'Is it Tom Hudson?'

'Yeah, he's getting out of the car.'

'Sheridan, don't say anything to him about the lock-ups, just get yourself out of there and we can figure out how we approach this later.'

Sheridan could see Tom Hudson walking up the path and a moment later the doorbell rang. She heard Jeff Nichols coming down the stairs.

'Jeff's just letting him in the house,' Sheridan whispered. She heard the front door close, and Tom Hudson appeared around the living room door.

'Inspector Holler,' he said, unzipping his jacket.

'Hello, Tom,' Sheridan replied.

Rob was still listening at the other end of the line. And then the line went dead.

CHAPTER 82

Rob Wills quickly called Sheridan back and held the phone closely to his ear, desperately wanting her to answer. It rang out.

'Fuck.' He redialled and closed his eyes. 'Come on, Sheridan.'

'Hello?' Sheridan answered.

'It's Rob. Everything okay?'

'Yes, sorry we got cut off. I've just left Jeff Nichols' place. I'm heading back to the nick now.'

'You scared the shit out of me.'

'Sorry.'

'Where are Jeff and Tom now?'

'In Jeff's house, they're having a boys' night in.'

'Okay. Me and Dipesh will start doing some enquiries around Tom Hudson.'

'Good idea.'

'See you in a bit.'

'Okay.'

Rob looked up as Dipesh walked into the office, carrying two cups of coffee.

'Sheridan's on her way back in.'

'Why?' Dipesh asked.

Rob updated him on his conversation with Sheridan about Tom Hudson.

'Christ, have we missed something in the enquiry then?' Dipesh sat at his desk. 'We weren't even looking at Tom Hudson.'

'We had no reason to. Anyway, let's at least start doing some digging on him before Sheridan gets back.'

'Yeah, okay.' Dipesh took a sip of coffee and logged on to his computer. 'I wish we still had some of Anna's birthday cake. I could murder a piece right now.'

Rob opened his desk drawer and lifted out a small plate with two lumps of cake on it.

Dipesh shook his head. 'That's theft. Have you no shame?'

'Do you want a piece or not?'

'Of course I do. Cut mine in half though, I'll save a piece for Sheridan.'

'You bloody crawler.' Rob muffled his reply with a mouthful of marzipan.

◆ ◆ ◆

Half an hour later Dipesh turned to Rob. 'What day did you say it was that Tom Hudson's car was seen near the lock-ups?'

'Last Thursday. Why?'

'Look at this.' Dipesh nodded at his screen and Rob leaned over to take a look.

'Well, that's *very* interesting.'

CHAPTER 83

Maud was asleep on Sam's lap when Joni walked in, wrapped in her cosy dressing gown after having just showered.

'I might get an early night,' Joni said. 'You seeing Sheridan tonight?'

'No, I don't think so. She's going to call me, though.' Sam smiled.

Yawning loudly, Joni asked, 'How's it going with her? You all loved up yet?'

'She's bloody lush.'

'You do seem well matched.'

'She's perfect. I love being with her. She makes me happy.'

Joni reached into her bag and pulled out her notebook, dropping it on to the coffee table. 'Good. Well, when she calls can you tell her I've made a load more notes on Ellie, although nothing that makes much sense.'

'Yeah, I'll tell her.' Sam rested her head on the back of the sofa.

'Right, I'm going to bed.' Joni yawned again and left the room, followed stealthily by Maud.

Sam, suddenly bored, picked up the notepad and started flicking through the pages. Studying the random letters that Joni had written, she picked up a pen and began writing out the letters that

Ellie Sands had been pointing to. Sam noted that she almost always seemed to start with the letter P.

As she wrote the letters down her eyes scanned the rows, one after the other, swapping them around, trying to make out any words. P, C, N, C, L, S. The next line was similar. P, C, N, I, L, S. All Sam could make out was the word PENCILS. She kept going, writing line after line, trying to make words. Words that made sense.

Feeling her eyes getting tired, she rested her head back, stretched her arms out and yawned. Her mouth felt dry, so she went into the kitchen, returning a moment later with a glass of water. Standing in the middle of the room, she glanced down at the notes.

And then she saw it. As clear as day.

CHAPTER 84

'Oh my God.' Sam gasped out loud, staring down in disbelief at the letters.

P C N I C O L S S H O T M E.

She wrote them out, separating the words clearly, just to be sure.

Pc nicols shot me.

She flew into Joni's room. 'Joni, you need to see this! I've worked out what Ellie's been saying.'

Joni sat up with a jolt. 'Really?'

'Yeah, she hasn't been saying, "Pissy knickers shit me."' She took a breath. 'She's been saying, "PC Nichols shot me."'

'What? . . . Who's PC Nichols?' Joni blinked as Sam turned on the light.

'Jeff Nichols . . . he's the copper that was having an affair with Kate Armitage when she was shot.'

'How would Ellie know his name? How do *you* know his name?'

'She wouldn't know his name. Or she shouldn't.' Sam ran her hand through her hair. 'But Sheridan told me that there was something about this guy, PC Nichols, that she couldn't put her finger on. She hesitated when she was talking about him. Maybe she wasn't supposed to tell me . . . I need to call her, she said she had to pop out on an enquiry, so I guess she's still at work.'

Joni quickly threw the duvet back and shot up, leaving Maud buried in a heap under it.

Sam rang Sheridan's number. When there was no reply, she sent her a text message.

CHAPTER 85

Rob glanced up at the clock, realising that Sheridan had left Jeff Nichols' place half an hour earlier and should have been back by now. He dialled her number.

'Hello?' she answered.

'Sheridan, it's Rob. You driving?'

'Yes, but I'm on loudspeaker.'

'You stuck in traffic or something?'

'Yeah, it's really busy on the roads.'

'Oh right. Well, me and Dipesh have been doing some digging on Tom Hudson. He wasn't driving his own car last Thursday. He was on duty, crewed up with PC James Greenhall. He booked on at 07.00 and booked off at 19.10. At the time his car is seen on the CCTV at 10 a.m. near the lock-ups, Tom Hudson was dealing with a road traffic collision six miles away. So someone else was driving his car.'

'Okay. We'll discuss it when I get back to the nick.'

'Alright. Is there anything more you need us to be doing?'

There was a moment of silence before Sheridan answered. 'You could do me a favour and ring my husband, Sam, for me. He's booked a table at Mamma B's for my birthday, can you let him know he'll have to cancel? He won't shout at *you*.'

Rob hesitated before answering, 'Will do.'

And with that, the line went dead. For the second time that day.

Rob looked at Dipesh. 'We've got a fucking problem.'

CHAPTER 86

Dipesh rang the control room inspector and markers were immediately placed on Sheridan's car as well as Jeff Nichols' and Tom Hudson's cars, along with Tom Hudson's motorbike.

Their mobiles were pinged, and a firearms unit was dispatched to Jeff Nichols' house.

Outside in the corridor, uniformed officers appeared from every direction, racing down the stairs towards the back yard before climbing into patrol cars and screeching out on to the streets.

Rob called Anna and ten minutes later she came flying into the office, having been dropped off by Steve. She was out of breath after taking the stairs two at a time and she had a look of sheer panic on her face.

'Tell me exactly what's happened.' She threw her coat on a chair and stood directly in front of Rob.

'The last we knew, she was at Jeff Nichols' place, where he denied knowing anything about the lock-ups. Then I called her to say that I'd seen Tom Hudson's car on CCTV heading towards the lock-ups last Thursday. While she was on the phone, Tom Hudson turned up at Nichols' and I told her not to ask him anything and just to come back to the nick and we'd figure out what to do then. I heard her say hello to Tom and then the line went dead. I called her back, but she didn't answer. When I called again, she said she was on her way back to the nick, and that Jeff and Tom were having a boys' night in at Jeff's.' Rob took a breath, half-listening to the radio crackling on the desk. 'Then we did some more checks on Tom Hudson. Turns out that he couldn't have been driving his car last Thursday because he was on duty at an RTC. So someone else was driving his car.'

'Jeff Nichols.' Anna put her hands on her head. 'Fuck, it could be Jeff Nichols.' Anna remembered how convinced Sheridan had been about his involvement in John Lively's murder and now it appeared that she could have been right all along. 'Maybe Tom and Jeff are both involved here.' She looked at Rob. 'What *exactly* did she say to you that makes you think she's in trouble?'

'She said she was on loudspeaker and on her way back to the nick and at the end of the call, she asked me if I could ring her husband, Sam, and tell him to cancel her birthday meal at Mamma B's.'

Anna put her hand to her mouth and felt tears sting her eyes. 'Christ. She was trying to tell you something that you'd know was completely wrong. She knew I was at Mamma B's and it was her message to you to call me. She said Sam's name because she knows I need to make sure Sam doesn't call her or go to her house, in case whoever's got her in the car is taking her home for some reason. Maybe both Jeff and Tom are in the car with Sheridan. Fuck.'

'Sorry, who's Sam?' Rob asked.

Anna quickly sat down and logged on to a computer. 'Sheridan's *girlfriend*. I need to call her.' Anna suddenly realised she didn't have Sam's number. But she did have Joni Summers'.

Anna dialled Joni's number. Breathing out slowly, trying to calm herself.

'Hello?'

'Hi, is that Joni?'

'Speaking.'

'Hi, Joni, it's DS Anna Markinson. Sorry to bother you . . . is Sam there?'

'Hang on.' Joni handed the phone to Sam.

'Hi, Sam, it's Anna Markinson.'

'Oh, hi. Did Sheridan get my message?' Sam reached for the notepad.

'What message?' Anna's eyes widened.

'About Ellie Sands. About what she's been trying to say.'

'I don't know, I'm not with Sheridan. What about Ellie Sands?'

'She's been trying to say, "PC Nichols shot me." I was going through the notes that Joni's been making, and I just saw it. She's not saying "pissy knickers", she's saying "PC Nichols". And she wouldn't even know who he was. That's what I texted Sheridan.'

'Right. What exactly did you text her?'

'I said: *Hi. Sorry but I had to text you. I've worked out what Ellie Sands has been saying. She's saying PC Nichols shot me, not pissy knickers shit me. I've written it down. Speak later when you're finished. XX*

Anna absorbed what Sam was telling her. *If Jeff Nichols is with Sheridan, he's probably seen Sam's message. What if he makes Sheridan drive to Sam's? What if he plans to get to Sam?*

'Are you at home right now?' Anna asked.

'Yeah.'

'You're not planning to go out anywhere?'

'No.'

'Is Sheridan due to come to yours tonight?'

'No. She said she was going to call me but that she had to go out on an enquiry first.'

'Okay Sam, just listen to me and don't worry. I want you to stay indoors and not leave the flat, both you and Joni. A police car is going to come to your place. It's just routine, I promise there's no need to worry.'

'Is everything alright? Is Sheridan okay?'

'Yes, Sam, everything's fine. But whatever you do, don't call Sheridan, she's really busy right now. Just stay indoors and I'll be in touch.' Anna tried but was failing to keep her voice from shaking.

'Okay.'

As Anna ended the call, Sam turned to Joni. 'Something's really wrong. They're sending a bloody police car round here.'

CHAPTER 87

Rob turned the radio up and listened as armed units arrived at Jeff Nichols' house. It was quickly established that Sheridan's car wasn't there. Jeff Nichols' car was parked outside, as was Tom Hudson's.

Officers surrounded the property and one of them approached the window, peering through a tiny gap in the curtains. The hallway light was on, shining into the living room, and he suddenly saw it.

'We've got a person face down on the floor, not moving,' he called out to his colleagues.

The firearms team gained entry, making their way through each room, checking for anyone else inside. The sergeant leading the team turned the living room light on and stepped towards the body on the floor. He radioed the control room. 'Oscar Delta one nine, we need an ambulance. We've got a male victim, gunshot wound to the head.'

PC James Greenhall was standing in the doorway. 'Christ, what a mess.' He shook his head at the sight before him. The male was face down, one arm tucked under his body and the other above his head, his mobile phone a few inches away. Blood and brain matter were spattered on the wall and his hair was matted thick with blood.

Noticing a wallet sticking out of the victim's back pocket, James Greenhall carefully pulled it out and opened it. Inside was a bank card and photograph of a little girl and boy, smiling happily with ice cream on their faces. The officer turned the picture over and written on the back were two names. *Amy and Cal.* The officer read the name on the bank card.

'Sarge.'

The sergeant craned his head to look and immediately got back on to his radio. 'Oscar Delta one nine to control.'

'Go ahead,' came the reply.

'Male victim is Jeff Nichols.'

CHAPTER 88

Anna and Rob heard the update come over the radio. Anna suddenly stood up. 'Jesus, it's Nichols.'

Rob sat back. 'So, Sheridan's with Tom Hudson.'

'But Ellie Sands thinks Jeff Nichols shot her.'

'Well, to be fair, they're not dissimilar.'

'But where would she get the name PC Nichols from?'

Dipesh joined them and turned the radio up just as Inspector Mike Jacobs walked in. 'Armed units are on scene at Tom Hudson's house, Sheridan's place, and they're en route to Sam Sloan's,' said Mike Jacobs. 'We've picked up Sheridan's car on CCTV and have got her heading in the direction of the Dock Road. Looks like she's driving and Tom Hudson's in the passenger seat.'

'They're going to the lock-ups,' Anna quickly stated.

'Yeah. We've got armed units heading there now. Sheridan's phone has pinged off the same mast as Tom Hudson's at exactly the same time, so at least their phones are still active. Looks like Jeff Nichols had his phone in his hand when he was shot. Maybe he was trying to call for help.'

'Is he dead?' Anna asked.

'There's an ambulance on its way, but yeah, he's gone.'

'Jesus.' Rob wiped a hand over his face.

Mike Jacobs' mobile rang and he answered it immediately, quickly leaving the room.

'We got it wrong. We never suspected Tom Hudson.' Anna's face crumpled as she fought back the tears. 'And now he's armed and Sheridan's in her car with him. He's going to kill her, isn't he?'

'She's a smart cookie, Anna. If there's a way out of this, she'll figure it. Look how she managed to let me know that something was wrong. She must have been in the house when Tom shot Jeff and yet she still stayed calm enough to give me that message. She'll be okay. Half the force is out looking for her.'

Rob got up to get a drink of water from the machine in the corner of the room.

'I feel helpless. I just want to get out of here and go get her.' Anna blew out her cheeks and put her hands flat on the desk.

'I know you do. Me too. But we have to let the firearms team do what they do best.'

'If it was the other way round, if it was me in danger, what do you think Sheridan would do?'

Rob returned to his desk and sat down. 'Well, she'd break every rule in the book and go hell for leather to get to you.'

'So, why am I sitting here like a twat, doing nothing?'

Rob leaned across the desk and squeezed Anna's hand. 'You're not doing nothing. You're waiting here while the experts do their job and then when it's over, you'll be here when she gets back to the nick.'

Anna nodded slowly. 'She'll probably kick Tom Hudson's arse before anyone else gets a look in, won't she?'

'Absolutely.' Rob smiled. Unconvincingly.

CHAPTER 89

The ambulance pulled up and parked amidst the flashing blue lights of police vehicles that had taken over the road where Jeff Nichols lived. Two paramedics got out and made their way into the house. PC James Greenhall stood in the living room with his colleagues. 'I can't believe Tom Hudson would do something like this.' He slowly shook his head.

'Do you know him well?' the firearms sergeant asked, watching on as the paramedics checked the body for signs of life. A thick pool of blood had soaked into the carpet, and it squelched sickeningly as they turned him over.

'We've worked together a couple of times recently. I was crewed up with him only last week, we went to a nasty RTC. He seemed such a nice bloke, quiet, you know. I can't get my head around it.' He stared at the blood on the wall as he spoke before focusing back on the paramedics.

'Can you pull his sleeve up a bit?' He bent down to get a closer look at the body.

The paramedic looked up at him. 'He's gone.'

'I need to check something.' James Greenhall was now crouching. 'Pull his sleeve up.'

The paramedic shrugged and then pulled the blood-soaked sleeve back.

James Greenhall stared at the tattoo and then at what was left of the victim's face. 'Bloody hell, Sarge.'

'What?'

'That's Tom Hudson.'

'No. We've established it's Jeff Nichols . . .' The sergeant hesitated, then asked, 'How do you know?'

'Because he showed me that tattoo last week.'

'Nichols could have a tattoo like that.'

'He's got one on his other arm. His late mother's face.'

The paramedic pulled the sleeve back on the other arm.

James Greenhall stepped back. 'That's the tattoo,' he said. 'That's Tom Hudson.'

CHAPTER 90

Sheridan gripped the steering wheel tightly to stop her hands trembling as she drove. She turned briefly to look at him. 'Jeff, please think about this. Whatever you're involved in can be sorted out.'

'I'm just carrying out Kate's perfect plan.'

'What plan?'

'It doesn't matter. Don't speak, just drive. Go straight ahead.' He kept tapping the gun on his leg; more of an involuntary movement than a threatening gesture. He kept checking that no cars were following them. His eyes were wide, and every few seconds he quickly licked his lips. Thinking.

'I thought we were going to the lock-up?'

'We're taking a detour. Don't worry, I'm not going to hurt you, Sheridan.'

Sheridan tried to swallow. Her head was filled with the horrific image of Tom Hudson's face being blown apart. She now knew what Jeff Nichols was capable of. She'd trusted her instincts right up until the last. Right up until she'd walked into his house. In that moment, she'd dropped her guard, and now she was helpless.

As they turned on to the Dock Road, he indicated for her to pull over. They got out of the car and he held her arm, guiding her up a flight of stone steps at the edge of the River Mersey. At the top of the steps, he pulled both of her mobile phones and Tom Hudson's out of his pocket and tossed them all into the river, along with Tom Hudson's wallet that he'd swapped for his own.

In the distance Sheridan could hear sirens and felt momentary comfort from their familiar sound.

Had Rob understood what she was trying to tell him? He knew she didn't have a husband and it wasn't her birthday. Had he called Anna? Sheridan could only imagine what was happening. Had her colleagues gone to Jeff Nichols' house and found Tom Hudson? If they had, they'd know she was with Jeff Nichols, and that he was armed. Prepared to kill.

The sirens seemed to be getting closer now. Or was it just her imagination?

'Let's go.' He pushed her towards the car, the gun never far away from her body.

They drove the short distance to Dove Street and pulled into the road leading to the lock-ups. Sensor lights flicked on and as they neared the gates, he pointed for her to park up on a patch of gravel to the right.

'When we get to the gates, you show your warrant card.' He handed her back the card he'd taken from her earlier. 'Tell whoever's in there that we just want a quick word, don't spook them. I just need them to open the gate and then you stay right next to me, and I'll tell you what to do.'

'What if there isn't anyone there?' Sheridan asked.

'There will be, they always have security on site at night,' Jeff snapped.

They both got out of the car and he made her walk in front, keeping his hand on the gun that was tucked inside his jacket pocket.

As they neared the gate, they saw a young man walking over to them. He walked with a limp and as he approached the gate, he peered at them, squinting. 'Can I help you?' Billy Doyle asked. Sheridan and Jeff could smell beer on his breath.

'I'm Detective Inspector Holler. Can we just come in and have a quick word? It won't take a second.' Sheridan held up her warrant card, and Billy Doyle leaned forward to take a closer look at it.

'What's it about? I'm not supposed to let anyone in.' He spoke slowly, over-pronouncing his words.

'Oh, it's okay, what's your name?' Jeff asked, smiling.

'Billy.'

'Hi, Billy, we literally need two minutes and then we'll leave you in peace.' Jeff put one hand on the gate. 'Open the gate for us and we'll be out of your hair before you know it.'

Billy Doyle looked between Jeff and Sheridan. 'Can't you talk to me here?'

'No, Billy, we need to come in for a sec.'

'Let me call my uncle first, I'm not supposed to let people in.'

Sheridan felt Jeff's body stiffen against her. 'Billy, you don't want us to come back with a warrant, do you? We're not here to check around, we just need to speak to you inside for two minutes, or we can ring your uncle when we get into the office if you like?'

Billy Doyle thought about it. And then he opened the gate.

CHAPTER 91

Anna stood up as Inspector Mike Jacobs walked into the room to give them an update.

'We've got Sheridan and Nichols on CCTV heading down the Dock Road. They've then gone down Hove Close, and then Dove Street. There's no sign they've left that area. Her phones have stopped pinging and so has Tom Hudson's.'

'They're definitely headed for the lock-ups.'

'Yeah, and the firearms units are two minutes away from there.' Mike Jacobs breathed in deeply. 'You guys okay?'

'Yes, sir,' Rob replied for himself, Dipesh and Anna. Mike Jacobs nodded and left the office, leaving the three of them huddled around the radio.

'Nichols must have really thought this through,' Rob piped up.

'What do you mean?' Dipesh asked.

'He swapped his own phone and wallet and planted them on Tom Hudson, so when uniform got there, they thought Tom was Jeff.'

'So it bought him some time. But surely someone would have recognised Tom Hudson.'

'He was shot in the face. God knows what a mess that made of him,' Rob said, suddenly realising that if Jeff Nichols could so *easily* kill his mate, what chance did Sheridan have? Judging by Anna's expression, he knew she was likely thinking the very same thing.

'Sorry, Anna.' While Rob tried to comfort her, he quickly threw Dipesh a discreet 'stop talking' shake of the head.

The corridors outside had fallen silent. Gone were the heavy boots of officers running to their cars. The whole station was holding its breath. Liverpool held its breath. Officers sat in their patrol cars, listening in, waiting for updates. One of their own had already been taken. They all prayed that it stopped there. It was going to be a long night. Every officer who was due to book off, ready to hand over to the nightshift, had stayed behind, from probationers, the fresh-faced new recruits, to those within touching distance of their retirement. Not one had gone home. And not one of them would, until they knew that Sheridan Holler was safe.

Anna closed her eyes. She could see Sheridan's face, and she could hear her voice, the voice that had kept telling her that Jeff Nichols was somehow involved. The radio suddenly crackled. 'Oscar Delta two three, ETA for firearms units at the lock-ups, one minute.'

Anna opened her eyes. This was it.

CHAPTER 92

Billy Doyle walked in front of Jeff and Sheridan, looking back suspiciously as they approached the door. Once they were all in the office Jeff noticed a small CCTV monitor in the corner. From the angle of the cameras, he realised they had to be hidden in the trees leading to the lock-up gates.

'Are they recording?' Jeff pointed at the monitor.

Billy Doyle glanced at the monitor as he went to pick up his mobile from the desk. 'No, they just let us see who's coming.'

Jeff reached forward and grabbed the mobile before Billy Doyle managed to reach it. 'What are you doing?' Billy asked, slurring his words.

'We'll call your uncle, but I need the key to the main lock-up gate. Where is it?' Jeff sounded calm and in control.

Billy pointed to a metal box on the wall. 'In there, but I thought you weren't gonna look around?'

Jeff walked over to the metal box. 'What's the code for this, Billy?'

Billy crossed his arms. 'I'm not telling you anything. Not until we call my uncle.'

Jeff shook his head and pulled the gun out, pointing it at Billy. 'Code first and then we'll call him.' Jeff raised his eyebrows.

'Fuck. What's going on?' Billy unfolded his arms and put his hands out in front of him as if surrendering.

'What's the code?' Jeff went to take a step forward.

'One two three five,' Billy blurted out.

Jeff tapped in the code and the box sprang open. Taking out the key, he turned to Billy. 'Is this the only key I need to get into the main lock-up area?'

'Yeah, but you'll need a separate key once you're in there. All the lock-ups have their own.'

Jeff already had his own key to his lock-up. He stepped towards Billy, pointing the gun at his face.

And then he pulled the trigger.

Billy Doyle flew backwards, his body landing awkwardly on the floor. Sheridan let out a cry and put her hand up to her mouth.

'Oh my God.' She felt her heart pounding inside her chest as Jeff turned, pointing the gun at her.

'I'm sorry, Sheridan, I really am. But I don't need you any more, either.'

CHAPTER 93

Jeff stepped towards Sheridan, his gun aimed straight at her head.

Suddenly he saw the CCTV monitor light up behind her: headlights coming up the dirt track.

'Who the fuck is that?' He grabbed her arm and pulled her over to the monitor. He could see them parked up the lane and could just make out their outlines in the sensor lights that lit up the driveway.

Jeff banged his hand on the desk. 'Fucking police are here!' He pushed the gun under her chin. 'You bitch.' Looking back at the monitor, he shouted, 'Move!' Now holding the gun against her temple he quickly wrapped his arm around her neck. 'We're going to the lock-up right now. And I swear if you try anything, I'll put a very big hole in your head.'

He carefully manoeuvred them out of the door, pausing momentarily as he watched armed officers slowly heading towards them.

'I'll fucking kill her if you come anywhere near me!' he yelled.

'Okay, Jeff, we're backing off. We just want everyone to stay safe.' The armed police officers slowly moved away.

Keeping Sheridan tightly in front of him and using her as a barrier, Jeff backed up towards the lock-up, letting go of her only for a moment to retrieve the key from his pocket. 'Open the gate.' He shoved the key into her hand and Sheridan felt her whole body trembling as she fumbled with the lock. Once it was open, Jeff pushed her towards his lock-up, making her open the lock before pushing her inside. It was dark but a faint light from the building opposite gave enough light for him to see. He pushed Sheridan down on to the floor and she landed heavily on her knees, letting out a cry.

'Jeff, please . . .' She tried to get up, but he pushed her back down.

'Shut up.' He peered quickly out of the door. He couldn't see anyone, but he knew how it worked. He knew he was trapped and now the only way he had any chance of getting out of this was to keep Sheridan alive until he could get away. He leaned back against the brick wall and with Sheridan at his feet, he lit a cigarette, all the while keeping the gun pointed at her.

'Jeff, please think about what you're doing,' Sheridan pleaded with him.

'I'm not going to prison. I know that much.' He dragged on his cigarette.

'Tell me what's going on, I can help you.'

'You can't help me!' he shouted as he towered over her, his spit spraying her face. She instinctively wiped it away. 'You have no idea what's happened, and you can't fix it, and you can't help me! It's a mess and I'm fucked!'

'Jeff, tell me what's going on and I swear I'll do everything I can to help you. Whatever it takes, I'll do it.'

He shook his head. 'You're not listening!' His voice trembled and his eyes filled with angry tears. Sheridan's instinct was to ask questions, get him talking, probe him, challenge him, but her head told her to do everything she could to not rile him. She'd witnessed the horror of what he'd done to Tom Hudson and Billy Doyle.

The only reason she was still alive was because she was now his bargaining chip; his last chance of escape. But she was only going to survive if she didn't make a mistake. The only things separating her from the safety of the armed officers outside were a thin brick wall, a door and a cornered killer with a gun.

'I had this all planned out perfectly and then you fuck it all up for me. You have no idea how close I was to getting away.' He focused on the two large canvas holdalls on the floor. 'That's my future in there.'

Sheridan closed her eyes as Jeff placed the gun to the top of her head.

'I've waited for seven years, and then you go and find this place.' Jeff moved the gun away from her head, tapping it against his leg. 'You shouldn't have come to my house tonight. When you told me that Rob Wills was looking at the CCTV near this place, I knew it wouldn't be long before he'd spot that Tom's car was here last Thursday. I'd already denied knowing anything about the lock-ups when you asked me. Then when Tom arrived at my place, I knew you'd question him about it and he'd tell you that I had borrowed his car last Thursday because mine was in for a service. That's when I knew I was fucked. And then to top it all, your fucking husband Sam sent you a text when we were driving here. He'd worked it out.'

Sheridan looked at the bags and then at Jeff. 'Worked what out?' she asked, her voice low. The pain in her legs was excruciating, but she tried to ignore it.

'He texted you to say that he'd worked out what Ellie Sands is saying.' Jeff stood by the cold lock-up wall.

Sheridan felt her heart quicken while they sat in silence for a moment, in the dark, with only a shard of light from the office window coming through the open lock-up door.

While the unnerving silence clung on, Sheridan could feel a strange calmness collapsing over Jeff, even as he maintained a vigilant watch on the door. She could hear faint movement out there, aware that officers would be getting into position and organising the on-call negotiator. She closed her eyes and Sam's face appeared. *How did Sam work out what Ellie Sands was saying?* She imagined her now, at home, safe, waiting for Sheridan to call her. *Does Sam know that I'm with Jeff Nichols? Does she know I'm in trouble?*

Eventually Jeff spoke. 'Pissy knickers.' He put his head back and sighed heavily. 'It was right there all along and none of you figured it out.' He stared at the door. 'Ellie Sands is trying to tell you that I shot her. She's saying "PC Nichols", not "pissy knickers".'

Sheridan stared at him. She opened her mouth to speak, but couldn't find any words. Nothing made sense.

Jeff lit another cigarette and the smoke hung in the air. 'So, now you understand that this mess can't be sorted, Sheridan.' He turned to look at her. 'It's fucked. Thanks to you and your fucking husband.' He chewed the inside of his cheek before taking another lug of his cigarette. 'If you hadn't come to my house tonight, Tom Hudson would still be alive. I didn't need to kill him before you showed up. We were just going to have a couple of beers.' He shook his head. 'I was almost ready to go.'

Sheridan tried not to react, keep it inside, a million questions racing through her head. She couldn't let her emotions overwhelm her. Not now. She had to stay focused, keep him engaged and let the officers outside figure out how to get her out of this alive. She watched as Jeff slowly slid down, his back scraping against the wall. He just sat there, side on to the door, the gun resting in his lap. He looked empty, frail and broken. He was trapped. He put his head down.

'I did love her, you know. I loved Kate, she was like no one I'd ever met before.' He shifted his position slightly. 'I'd seen her around the nick, and we'd always smiled at each other, then I joined B-relief, and we got crewed up together.'

CHAPTER 94

Saturday 3 November 1996
B-relief shift briefing, Hale Street Police Station

'Right, settle down.' Sergeant Ricky Pope addressed the nightshift, briefing them on the local burglary hot spot areas, who was currently wanted and who was being crewed up with who.

'Everyone, let's welcome Jeff Nichols to the team, he's joined us from D-relief, so now he can see how it's really done.'

Jeff Nichols smiled, raising his eyes to the ceiling.

Sergeant Pope pointed at Kate Armitage. 'Kate, you're with the new boy.'

Kate Armitage leaned back in her chair, assessing Jeff Nichols. He returned her smile.

Halfway into the nightshift they were parked up round the back of the Holmes housing estate, a notorious area for drug dealers. Kate knew all of the local shit-bags.

'You're married, aren't you?' Kate said, grinning.

'Yeah, two years,' Jeff answered as he turned to look at her. 'You're divorced, right?'

'A long time ago. Usual story. Got married too young, everyone said it wouldn't last.' Kate paused. 'Just glad we didn't have kids.'

'Carly and I have got two. They're a handful.'

'Rather you than me.'

They sat in silence for a moment until Kate asked, 'Do you regret it?'

'Getting married and having kids?' Jeff gazed out of the window. 'Sometimes.'

They talked about their time in the job, how Kate had twice failed the sergeant's exam and had resigned herself to the fact that she wouldn't take it again. They laughed at each other's stories of the characters they'd arrested over the years, how Jeff had literally shat himself the first time he had to give evidence in court.

'Actual shit?' Kate howled, holding her hand to her face.

'Yep, I was in the witness room and felt my stomach churning. I was bloody sweating. Boxers were a write-off, so they got binned. So basically, I gave evidence in court with no undies on.' Jeff shook his head and grinned at Kate, who was cracking up. He noticed how stunning she was, how comfortable he felt with her and he realised that he couldn't remember the last time he had laughed so much.

She put her hand on his knee. 'I can't wait to tell the lads that story.'

'Don't you dare.' He raised an eyebrow as he wiggled a finger in her face. 'Our secret.'

By 2 a.m. the streets were deathly quiet. They were about to head back to the nick when Kate spotted a male walking quickly with his hands shoved deep into his pockets.

'Well, look who it is . . . Michael Holding. He's worth a tug.' Kate pulled over and quickly jumped out, followed by Jeff.

Michael Holding stopped and turned, spotting the police car. Then he started running. Kate immediately chased after him, following him around a nearby corner and straight into a dead end. Jeff followed, shouting into his radio, 'Alpha Charlie one one, we've got a runner on Main Street. Michael Holding.'

As he reached Kate, he could see Michael Holding had stopped by a fence and had his arms in the air. 'Okay, I'm done.'

Kate Armitage took out her baton and struck him hard across the arm.

'What the fuck!' Michael Holding cradled his arm as he dropped to his knees in agony. Kate grabbed his head and pushed him over.

'What are you running for, Michael?' She put her foot on his chest. 'Search him, Jeff.'

Jeff Nichols pulled his gloves out of his pocket and searched Holding. 'Nothing.' He shook his head at Kate.

She rolled him over and handcuffed him before reaching into her own inside pocket to pull out a lock knife. 'What's this, then?'

Holding turned his head. 'That's not mine, you can't plant that on me, you fuckers.'

Sirens wailed in the background as Jeff spoke into his radio. 'Alpha Charlie one one. One under arrest. Possession of a lock knife and resisting arrest.' He looked at Kate who was grinning.

'I didn't fucking resist,' Michael Holding protested.

'Yes, you did, that's why I had to hit you. Next time don't run, you little prick.'

They sat in the report room an hour later writing their statements.

Sergeant Ricky Pope walked in. 'Well, if it isn't Cagney and Lacey. Good arrest you two, are you both okay?'

Kate nodded. 'Yeah, fine, Sarge.'

'He's spitting bloody feathers in custody, said it was an unlawful arrest and you beat him up.' Sergeant Ricky Pope pointed at Kate, grinning.

'Is that right? He took a bloody swing at me. Lucky he didn't have the knife in his hand.' Kate winked at Jeff.

'He says the knife wasn't his and you planted it on him.'

'Yeah, that's right. I carry a bag full of lock knives around with me purely to plant on shits like him.' Kate shook her head.

Ricky Pope grinned. 'Are your statements nearly done?'

'Yeah, almost.'

Kate had briefed Jeff on the wording in his statement and read through them both before slipping them into the file ready for the dayshift to interview Holding.

As they walked through the back yard at the end of the shift, Jeff stopped at Kate's car. 'Do you always work like that?'

'I've learned two things about this job, Jeff. One, know your audience . . . and two, you'll never get anywhere if you play by the rules. I'll see you tonight.' She pecked him on the cheek and got into her car.

He thought about Kate on the way home; he liked the way she worked, he liked *her*. He was going to enjoy being crewed up with this firecracker. Grinning, he thought about their nightshift, how she was a risk-taker, and that excited him.

When he walked in the front door his wife Carly was up. 'How was your shift?'

'Yeah, fine.' He dropped his bag on the kitchen floor.

'Can you have a look at the tap in the bathroom later? It's leaking again.' Carly picked his bag up and retrieved the empty lunch box. 'I need you to go up in the loft as well.'

'For what?'

'To get the Christmas tree down. I was talking to Alison up the road yesterday and her sister works in a women's refuge. They're collecting stuff to decorate the place for Christmas and I told her they could have our tree. We'll get a new one this year.'

Jeff put the kettle on and sat on the bar stool, unlacing his boots. 'Can't you go up and get it? It's not heavy.'

'I'm not getting up there, you know I never go up there, too many creepy-crawlies.' Carly dried the dishes before throwing the tea towel into the washing machine.

'Fine.' Jeff stood up. 'I'll sort it out later.'

'Do you want tea or coffee?'

'I don't want anything actually. I'm going to bed.'

CHAPTER 95

Jeff lit another cigarette and threw the empty packet on to the lock-up floor.

Sheridan had awkwardly managed to nudge herself into a more comfortable position, which eased the pain in her legs. She sat there in silence as Jeff continued talking.

'Kate and I were permanently crewed up after that, which is basically when the affair started. She was like no one I'd ever met before, she was exciting and we couldn't get enough of each other. I started lying to Carly about working late or being out with the lads, but I was with Kate. It all happened really quickly. I wanted to be with her all the time, she made me feel like I was alive.' He looked at the gun as he spoke.

'I'd go home to Carly and as soon as I got in the door, she'd be banging on about me not pulling my weight around the house, or the kids' rooms needed decorating. I was awful to her. I felt trapped and I didn't know what to do. Whenever I was with Kate we'd laugh and have a good time. Tom Hudson was the only one I really confided in to any extent. He was never the brightest but he was a good lad. I asked him to cover for me a few times when I was seeing Kate. I used to tell Carly I was going out with him, or going round to his for a beer and she bought it every time. When Kate asked me if I would ever leave Carly, I didn't hesitate to say I would. Kate and I would spend hours talking about our future together. I knew she didn't really trust men – she'd been hurt and let down in the past – but it somehow made her stronger. She trusted me, and she believed me when I told her I'd leave Carly. And I would have done it, too.'

Sheridan didn't dare speak as he turned to look directly at her. 'Have you ever been so in love with someone that you'd literally do anything for them?'

She didn't respond but felt her chest tighten as she watched Jeff, who appeared eerily calm and controlled. His demeanour had changed completely and the change unnerved Sheridan. What struck her was the total absence of emotion from Jeff when he mentioned Tom Hudson's name. Tom was his best mate, and yet earlier he'd casually blown his head off.

She always thought that she could read people. She had a reputation for it, and was rarely wrong. She had known there was something about Jeff when she'd first met him, something that she couldn't pinpoint. He had appeared so genuine about wanting to help with the enquiry, but she'd seen through it right from the start. The mask, the facade. And she had been right about him all along.

She'd seen this type of behaviour a thousand times before with prisoners and it always amazed her. The convincing act and total denial that they had done anything wrong but then when they were caught, the change, the sudden change. The admission – the full and frank admission – that they were guilty before they merrily spilled out the details of their crime like it was something to be proud of. She had seen it a thousand times before.

But never with a gun pointed at her head.

'That's how it was with me and Kate. I was so in love with her.' Jeff wiped his mouth as though his lips had dried up. 'We pulled John Lively over a few times. Then one day, sometime in the

November before the shooting, we found a small bag of heroin in his possession. We asked him who his dealer was and told him that we'd use him as a source if he gave us information. Kate fed him a load of bullshit, saying we'd protect him, keep him out of prison. He was on a suspended sentence at the time and really didn't want to go back inside. It was fairly common knowledge that he didn't cope too well in prison, self-harmed a few times. But Lively told us he had people in high places who would look after him and he didn't need our help.' He paused and ran his hand over his head.

'Kate said that she could get him banged up whenever she wanted. Lively wasn't particularly bright and Kate thought that if she could bullshit him that he could become a source for us. He could lead us to the main dealers. At first, Lively wasn't having any of it. We pulled him a couple more times after that, Kate would keep any drugs we found on him and let him go. We asked him again to be a source, but he kept saying he had someone who would look after him and didn't need to be a grass for us. That's when Kate told him that she'd plant drugs on him and nick him for possession with intent, guaranteeing he'd be back inside. He said he'd think about it. Kate always used unregistered mobile phones which Lively used to call her on. We tried to get him to use one, but he hated mobiles, always used phone boxes.'

CHAPTER 96

Saturday 29 November 1997

Kate Armitage was off duty and had spent the day shopping in town, treating herself to lunch at the Albert Dock. She'd called Jeff that morning to ask if he was free, but he'd had to stay at home and cut back some trees in his garden. She knew by his voice that he was fed up and would rather have been with her. He'd whispered that he loved her as he ended the call and she'd closed her eyes and whispered it back to him. She knew she loved him. She would never have said it otherwise.

Kate had been married at nineteen, but divorced two years later. Her parents spent more time telling her that she should never have married so young than they did supporting her through the separation. Desperate to prove them wrong, she had stuck out the relationship even though the cracks were showing just weeks after the wedding.

She had disappointed her parents, but then she had always disappointed them from as far back as she could remember. Never the academic, they had no expectations that she would excel at anything, and Kate spent her early years believing just that. After the divorce, she drifted in and out of pointless and loveless relationships, waking to find strangers in her bed, nameless, faceless strangers. She was spiralling out of control, and she hated it. She saw the way men looked at her, the way her parents looked at her and she realised that not once had she felt respected by anyone, ever. And so, without telling a soul, on 8 April 1977 at the age of twenty-two, she applied to be a police officer.

It was hard being a woman in the job back then, but Kate fitted in well and quickly grew a reputation for being 'one of the lads'. She was fearless, strong-willed and feisty and her male colleagues respected her. The public respected her. She was back in control of her life, making her own decisions, answering to no one except senior officers.

She had it all planned out: she would get promoted, firstly to sergeant, then inspector and by then she'd be a few years off retirement. She'd take her pension, pay off her mortgage, travel and then settle down with all the comforts she had worked so hard for. She had it all planned out. Until she failed her sergeant's exam.

Suddenly, she felt like she had taken a thousand steps backwards and, for a while, she lost herself. Started sleeping with her colleagues, married men who just wanted a quick fuck. Married men who she knew would never give up their wives for her. She once again became disillusioned with the job, with life, with her plans.

But Kate Armitage was a fighter and she never liked to lose. And so, when she was thirty-seven, she sat her sergeant's exam again.

And again, she failed.

That changed everything. Now, she decided she would take what she was owed. Her own way.

She thought about Jeff, and it all fitted so perfectly. He had come into her life at a time when, at forty-two, she wanted to think of a future with someone by her side. Someone who loved her and respected her. Once Jeff left his wife, her life would be perfect. Just like she'd planned.

◆　◆　◆

As she drove home from the city, she sat in a queue of cars waiting for the lights to change and turned the radio up, tapping out the tune on the steering wheel. Checking her mirror, she caught a glance of a motorbike coming alongside the queue of cars and recognised it as John Lively's. He passed her and took the first left turn into Oak Avenue. 'Where are you off to, you little shit?' she said to herself. 'Not your regular patch.'

She tooted the car in front as the lights changed and quickly turned into Oak Avenue, spotting Lively ahead of her as he pulled up outside a tidy semi-detached house. She drove a little closer to get a better view and watched. Lively knocked on the front door and a woman answered; she was in her late forties, maybe fifty, petite with short blonde hair. Kate watched as the woman crossed her arms before saying something to Lively, all the while looking around. Lively appeared animated before walking away. He got back on his motorbike and rode off in the same direction he had come from. Kate ducked down as he passed her and then watched the house.

'Who are *you* then?' Kate muttered to herself. She checked her watch: 3.10 p.m. She waited, curious. Then at 5.35 p.m. the woman appeared at the door with her coat on, got into her car and drove off. Kate again ducked down as she passed her, started her engine and followed slowly behind. Twenty minutes later the woman pulled into Mason's supermarket car park. She parked her car some distance away from the main entrance and got out, walking purposefully towards the main doors. Kate followed and watched her as best she could from outside.

The woman was in the store for almost an hour. When she came out, Kate watched her load her car up before following her back home.

Friday 5 December 1997

Jeff Nichols walked into the report room and sat next to Kate Armitage. 'The skipper wants us out on patrol. You ready?' He put a hand on her leg and squeezed it.

Kate's eyes moved around the room as she whispered to him, 'I've run a voter's check on the woman Lively visited, the one on Oak Avenue. Comes back to an Ellie Sands.'

'Never heard of her,' Jeff replied.

'I've done a search online. Ellie Sands is the editor of the *Liverpool Post*.' Kate kept her voice low. 'So I want to know why Lively's been going to her house.'

'Shit.' Jeff looked at her. 'Do you think he's gone to the papers to tell them about us?'

'I don't know. Maybe? But who would listen to him? He's a two-bit druggie, so I doubt they'd take any notice of him.'

Jeff nodded. 'I hope you're right.' He stood up. 'Come on, we better go.'

Fifteen minutes later, they were out on patrol when Jeff pointed out the car window. 'Well, look who it is: John Lively himself! Shall we have a word?'

Jeff pulled over just ahead of Lively. Kate got out of the car and stepped in front of him. 'Hello, John, where are you going?'

'Just out for a walk, no law against it is there?'

'Where's your bike?'

294

'Clutch is fucked. Got a mate working on it.' He saw Jeff Nichols walking over.

'Alright, John?' Jeff stood next to Kate.

'Yeah, great thanks.' John Lively's response was awash with sarcasm.

'What have you got on you then?'

'Nothing, you can search me if you like.'

Kate smiled. 'We don't need to search you, John. Get in the car.'

'Oh, for fuck's sake! I haven't got anything on me. Come on! I need to be somewhere.'

'Get in the fucking car.'

John Lively hesitated, studying the line of traffic that had slowed down to rubberneck, before eventually getting into the car.

'You haven't rung me, John. Just wondering if you've decided to take us up on our offer?' Kate turned in her seat to catch his reaction. Loving the power she felt over him.

'What offer? To be your grass?' John Lively stared nervously out of the window.

'No, to be a source, you give us information and we look after you.'

'Yeah, a grass. I think I'll leave it.'

'That's a shame. Right then, John Lively, I'm arresting you for possession with intent to supply heroin and cocaine, you do not have to say anything but—'

'Alright.' Lively shook his head. 'I'll do it.' His head dropped in angry resignation, angry at himself. There was no way out for him now, and it was either give in and become the grass or go back to prison. He was not going back to prison.

'That's better. Now, what can you tell us?'

Lively sniffed and scratched his nose before he answered. 'I've got a pick-up next Wednesday night, eleven o'clock at Bordersfield

Cemetery. They drop off a bag at the back, near the tall trees. There's a tree just off the main path with a big hollow bit in it and that's where they leave the bag. I'm supposed to take the bag and keep it at mine and then in a few days someone picks it up.' He sighed. 'There's a hole in the fencing that's big enough to get through.'

'Who's someone?' Kate asked.

'I don't know any names. I really don't.'

'Alright then, that'll do for now,' Kate said.

'So, you'll be there to nick them? And then I get paid, right?'

'Right.' Kate furtively winked at Jeff, who couldn't help but smile.

'How much?' Lively leaned forward.

'Depends on how much the stuff is worth. Don't worry, John, we promised you we'd look after you, keep you out of prison and we will. You've got us protecting you now.'

'I want at least two hundred.'

'Fine. I'll sort you out a mobile phone as well.'

'No thanks, don't like mobiles, I'd rather use payphones. Can I go now?'

'Suit yourself. Yes, you can go, and we'll sort you out once we've made the arrests.' Jeff got out of the car to open the back door for Lively, who climbed out and walked away with his hands in his pockets.

'What do you think?' Jeff watched as John Lively crossed the road. He started the car and checked behind before pulling away.

'I think he's full of shit,' Kate said. 'Telling us a load of bollocks to keep us off his back.' She sighed, rubbing a hand over her face. 'We'll check it out anyway though, it seems quite specific, bags in hollowed-out trees and all that, maybe there's something in it, we'll see. We can meet up at the cemetery about half-nine in case there really is a drop-off, sit up somewhere and just see what happens. What are you going to tell Carly?'

'I'll say I'm on overtime or an operation or something, or I'm going to Tom's. She'll believe anything I tell her.'

'Are you busy later? I'd love to see you tonight.' She ran her hand along his thigh.

'I can't, Carly's sister's coming over for dinner.' He wrapped his fingers around hers. 'I hate that we can't be together.' He took a deep breath. 'I've been thinking about us, Kate. We love each other and I don't want to be sitting here in another year talking about how we're going to be together, I want us to be together *now*.' He looked at her face. 'I'm going to tell Carly that I want us to split up. I'll pick the right moment and just do it.'

Kate squeezed his hand. 'Are you absolutely sure?'

'I'm positive, I can't bear to be apart from you.'

Kate smiled and nodded. 'I'll make you happy, Jeff.'

'You already do.'

'Well, seeing as you're standing me up tonight, I'm going to see if I can find out more about this Ellie Sands.'

Saturday 6 December 1997

It was three o'clock in the afternoon. Kate Armitage got into her car and started the engine, flicking the radio on as she pulled away.

As she turned into Oak Avenue, she noticed Ellie Sands' car wasn't parked outside her house. Kate parked further up the road and waited. She thought about John Lively and how he might have gone to the papers.

But why go to Ellie Sands' house? Maybe he knows her? Is this woman the person in a high place who is supposedly looking out for him?

297

She sat for almost an hour before driving around the corner and back out on to the main road. She didn't want some nosey bloody neighbour calling the police to report a suspect vehicle in the area. She drove past Ellie Sands' house, this time parking on the opposite side of the road before waiting another hour. After checking her watch at 5.10 p.m., she suddenly had a thought and headed straight for Mason's supermarket.

As she drove into the car park, she couldn't see Ellie Sands' car, so she waited near to where she had parked the week before. Maybe this woman was a creature of habit.

Kate was feeling pissed off, and the feeling grew stronger as she waited. Fucking John Lively, thick little shit, she had better things to do than sit for hours on end, bored shitless waiting for this bloody woman to turn up or not, just so that Kate could try to figure out what she had to do with Lively.

Kate was getting cold. She turned her engine on, blowing into her hands and rubbing them together. It was five minutes to six when she noticed a car that looked like Ellie Sands' drive past. The car turned at the top of the car park and, sure enough, pulled up four spaces away from Kate.

She watched as Ellie Sands got out and walked towards the main doors. Kate followed her and again noted that she spent about an hour shopping before loading up her car and driving home.

Kate waited outside her house. She had no visitors for the two hours Kate sat there, so she drove home, made herself some toast and threw a cup of coffee down her throat before heading back to Ellie's. At quarter past ten that evening, Kate watched as the downstairs lights went off and the upstairs lights went on.

'Off to bed for you, then?' Kate bit her lip, thinking about her next move as she drove home.

Kate Armitage parked her car towards the rear entrance of Bordersfield Cemetery and checked the clock on her dashboard: 9.15 p.m. She couldn't see Jeff's car.

At twenty-five past nine, she saw headlights. She watched as Jeff parked further up the road. He got out of the car and walked down to where she was, looking around before quickly getting into the passenger side. He leaned across and kissed her. 'You okay?'

'Yeah, not bad. Just hope this isn't a sodding wild goose chase. What did you tell Carly?'

Jeff smiled. 'Said I was having a boys' night at Tom Hudson's and told Tom I was seeing you, so I haven't actually lied to *him*.'

'Pretty handy having him as a mate. I take it you trust him?'

'Yeah, he's solid.' Jeff suddenly saw headlights coming towards them.

They ducked down as far as they could and waited as they heard a car door close. Jeff inched his head up to see a tall male dressed in dark clothes head towards the gap in the fence. He climbed through, carrying a holdall.

'That's our man. He's early.' Jeff tapped Kate's shoulder and she sat up slowly, turning her head to see the male walk down through the trees. They both put on gloves and got out of the car, easing themselves through the gap and turning right to keep out of sight. They watched him stop, furtively scanning his surroundings, listening, waiting, before heading over to the hollowed-out tree. He lifted the bag up and dropped it into the hole. For the next few moments, he remained deathly still, unmoving, all-hearing. Kate and Jeff matched his motionless silent stance as they remained crouched down behind a headstone.

The man turned around and made his way back towards the fence and they watched as his car headlights lit up and he drove away. They didn't move for a while, unsure if he would come back. After a few minutes Kate signalled to Jeff and they stood up, walking over to the tree.

Jeff reached in and, feeling the leather bag handle, he pulled at it. 'I've got it,' he whispered.

He put the bag on the floor and took a penlight torch out of his pocket, unzipped the bag and shone the torch inside. Kate was scanning the place, making sure no one was there, hiding up.

'Holy shit!' Jeff's eyes widened.

Kate immediately knelt down beside him. 'Jesus.'

She pulled out a large clear bag of white powder and a larger bag of brown. Then she lifted out a wad of twenty-pound notes. Followed by another. And another.

'How much do you reckon there is?' Jeff whispered.

Kate counted the bundles. 'About ten grand.' Her eyes were wide, and her smile even wider.

'Bloody hell.' Jeff stared open-mouthed at her.

They both stayed hunkered down, nervously checking around.

'What are we going to do?' Jeff asked, staring at the money.

'We're going to keep it.'

He let out a muffled laugh. 'Seriously?' He blew out his cheeks. 'Where are we going to stash this amount of money and what about the drugs?'

'Leave that to me. I've got a lock-up. I'll take it there in the morning. Come on, let's go.'

She handed Jeff the bundles of money to put back into the bag. They walked to the fence, looking around the whole time. She put the bag in the boot of her car. 'Come back to mine.'

Jeff followed her to her house and they sat in her kitchen gloating at the hoard. She made them a coffee and put her hands on his shoulders.

'Well, looks like Lively was telling the truth, then.' She kissed the top of Jeff's head and sat on his lap.

'What are we going to tell him, though?' Jeff wrapped his hands around her waist.

'We tell him that we went there and waited and there was no drop-off.'

'But what happens when his mates go round to collect?' Jeff reached for his coffee.

'Lively won't have the gear and his mates will either kick the shit out of him or he'll do a runner. Either way, he's out of our hair and we're about ten grand better off.' She threw her head back and laughed.

'Yeah, but what if Lively tells them that we might have taken it?'

'He's hardly going to tell his druggie mates that he's spoken to a couple of bizzies and told them all about the drop-offs.'

'That's true. Anyway, this lock-up . . . is it safe?'

'As houses. I've been using it for a few years, the guy that runs it is as dodgy as fuck. But he doesn't ask questions, and neither do I. It's Liverpool's best-kept secret.'

'Does he know you're a copper?'

'No, of course not.' She got up and walked to the corner of the kitchen, opening the cupboard drawer to pull out a key. 'I turn up, give the name Julie Smith, then the code-word Candy and the guy lets me in.' She dangled the key in front of him. 'This is the key to my future. *Our* future.'

'How does he know it's actually you turning up? You could be anybody.' Jeff took the key and after reverently studying it for a few moments, he placed it carefully on the kitchen worktop.

'As long as someone gives the name and code-word, he's happy. He takes no responsibility for the stuff stored. Everything's either nicked or fake, and as long as he gets paid, he doesn't care.' Kate put the key back in its place before sitting down.

'Aren't you worried that he'll recognise you?'

'What do you mean?'

'Well, say he sees you on duty somewhere, and realises you're a copper?'

Kate got up and walked back over to the cupboard drawer to produce a wig and pair of glasses. 'I wear these,' she said, flopping the wig on to her head and putting the glasses on. 'Sexy, eh?' She put her hands on his shoulders and grinned.

They sat up into the early hours talking about their future together. How if they worked as a team, they could build upon what Kate had already amassed in the lock-up. She told him how it had all started, from a sudden death she had attended five years earlier.

Kate Armitage had arrived at the property to find paramedics already on the scene, and the on-call doctor ready to certify the death. After confirming there were no suspicious circumstances, Kate radioed through to the control room, asking for the undertakers to be called, and spoke to the old man's neighbour who had found him in the bedroom.

'Has he got any family?' Kate asked, visually inspecting the room.

'No, he hasn't got anyone,' said the neighbour, standing anxiously in the bedroom doorway as she peered down at the old man. 'I pop in every couple of days, bring him a hot meal and make him a cuppa. His wife died a couple of years ago and he became a bit of a recluse. To be honest, he was quite a cantankerous old bugger, but I felt sorry for him. He hasn't got two pennies to rub together and hasn't got anyone apart from me.' She looked at Kate. 'His wife was lovely.'

Kate nodded. 'Well, at least he had some company. It was very kind of you to do what you did for him.' She smiled. 'Are you alright? It must have been a shock for you to find him like this.'

'It was, if I'm honest. He was kneeling on the floor next to his bed, like he was praying. I didn't realise he was dead until I touched him.'

'Will you be okay?'

'Oh, I'll be fine. Do I need to stay for anything?'

After giving Kate as much information as she could for the sudden death form, the neighbour left, allowing Kate to go back upstairs. She stood over the old man, who was now face up after being moved by the paramedics, and wondered if he actually had been praying before he died.

She walked over to the other side of the room and sat on a little wooden chair, turning briefly to check out the window and see if the undertakers had arrived. As she turned back, she noticed something shiny on the floor just under the bed. She walked over, spotting that it was a small silver key, and crouched down to pick it up. As she did, she noticed a long thin black box under the bed and reached for it, pulling it slowly towards her. It was covered in dust and locked. She tried the key and it opened, revealing four rows of varying styles of gold rings neatly set out in the velvet interior. In the corner of the box was a black cloth bag, secured with a drawstring. She pulled it open and peered inside. Thirty-one diamonds glistened back at her.

'Fucking hell,' she said to herself, quickly getting up and checking out of the window to see if the undertakers had arrived yet. She moved the curtains and looked up and down the road before putting the key in her pocket and shoving the ring box inside her jacket. She made her way downstairs and got back into the police car, her hands shaking, and slid the box under the passenger seat mat before quickly returning to the house.

Kate sipped her coffee as Jeff digested what she had told him so far.

After a few moments, she resumed her story. 'Turns out the old guy and his wife used to own a jewellery shop. I guess he kept some of the stock when they retired. I spent the next couple of years shitting myself that the old man had left a will or someone would come forward to claim it all, but no one did.' Kate casually ran a hand through her hair. 'I had one of the diamonds checked out and it was real. All in all, they're worth about two hundred grand.'

'Bloody hell.' Jeff sat up. 'What did you do with them?'

'I kept them, they're still in the lock-up. I sold a couple of the rings though.' She blew out her cheeks. 'I've managed to steal all sorts of shit.'

She told him how she had stolen from burglary victims. She was always careful, selective, and only took something if she was certain the victim wouldn't notice. Then there were the local drug users, always keen not to get nicked. She would seize the drugs and cash and tell them she was doing them a favour. She would get rid of the drugs at the local tip, bagged up in a bin liner, and keep the cash. She'd taken stolen property from various addresses when she was on a search warrant, an expensive watch or necklace, deftly slipped into her pocket. Easy pickings.

'Let's just say that I don't intend to be a copper until I'm at retirement age. I've got enough stuff – or at least I will have in a couple of years – to pack the job up and go live in the sun somewhere. I've got about three hundred grand's worth of stuff at the lock-up already. And by the time we're done, there'll be plenty more for us to jet off with.' She kissed him on the mouth. 'We're going to have a wonderful life, Jeff.'

He nodded. 'You bloody bet we are.' He held her hand across the kitchen table. 'But, why not just keep the stuff here? Why keep it at the lock-up?'

'I'm always conscious that if I ever slipped up and someone sussed out what I was doing, they might search this place and if they did, they wouldn't find a thing.'

'You're bloody amazing, do you know that?' Jeff nodded as he spoke. 'You're always one step ahead, and that's another reason that I love you so much.'

'Good.' She kissed him again. 'Anyway, I've got to get this stuff to the lock-up tomorrow, he only opens up on Tuesdays, Wednesdays and Thursdays.'

'What kind of business only opens three days a week?'

'The dodgy kind.' She glanced at the clock on the wall. 'What time do you have to go?'

'In about an hour.' He kissed her hard on the lips and pulled her up, then pushed her backwards over the table, unzipping her jeans and his own at the same time.

Thursday 11 December 1997

Kate Armitage closed her front door and looked around. Walking to her car, she placed the leather bag from the hollowed-out tree into the boot before then getting in behind the wheel. For a moment she thought about being stopped and her car being searched. *How do I explain the bag away?*

This was how her mind worked. Overtime. Thinking, rethinking, planning and finding a way around things. She was good at it as well. She always had ideas, liked to be one step ahead. Always. And invariably she was. It was 9.15 a.m. when she pulled over just before reaching the lock-ups. She put on the wig and dark glasses, as she always did, then drove up to the main gates and rang the buzzer.

'Hello?' came the crackled reply.

'Julie Smith, Candy . . . drop-off.'

The guy walked out of the little brick building to the right, opened the main gates and Kate drove in, parking at the far end, not far from where her lock-up was. She waited for the guy to open the second gate and she walked in. He didn't make eye contact with her and didn't speak. He then left and went back to the office, while Kate unlocked her storage unit. After quickly surveying the place, she laid the bag on one of the shelves. Everything was just how she had left it, safe as houses. She pulled open the lid of a small plastic crate and looked inside, taking out the cloth and unwrapping it to reveal the gun.

She remembered putting it in her pocket during a drug raid a few years before. She'd been the only police officer in the room at the time and had seen the gun sticking out from under a pillow. In the same room had been two grand in cash, which she also took. *That was a good day,* she thought. She studied the gun for a moment and then wrapped it back up, got in her car and was let out of the main gates. She knew there was CCTV on the main road, but it didn't cover the lock-up.

She'd thought about the possibility of one day the police raiding the lock-up and checking the CCTV and seeing her car on camera in the area. But she had an answer if it ever came up. The lock-up was some way off the main road and there were fields on either side. If she was ever seen and questioned about it, she would simply say that she used to play there as a child and she liked to visit there sometimes when she was feeling nostalgic.

If the lock-up was ever raided there was a slim chance the stuff she had stored could be linked back to her and the burglaries she had been to. None of the shit-bags she had seized anything from would come forward. Plus, she only had to keep the stuff for a couple more years and then she'd be off. Off to start a new life. It was a chance worth taking.

She was almost home when her mobile rang. 'Hello.'

'It's me. John Lively.'

'Hi, John. How's it going?'

'Alright. Did you sort it last night? Did you get them?'

'John, I can't talk right now.' She thought about telling him that the drop hadn't taken place but changed her mind.

'Okay, but I need to speak to you.'

'Make it quick.'

'I had a visit last night. They want me to do another pick-up tonight – same place. These are different blokes to the ones from yesterday, what shall I do?'

Kate pulled the car over. 'Leave it to me, John. What time's the drop-off?'

'Eleven.'

'Okay, you leave it well alone, I'll sort it out. And by the way, next time I see you, I've got a pay cheque for you.'

'Cheque?' he snapped.

'Just a phrase, don't worry, it'll be cash, I'll catch up with you soon.' She ended the call, dropping her mobile on to her lap, and sat for a moment. Thinking. Then she called Jeff's mobile. She told him about the pick-up and arranged to pick him up outside his house at 10 p.m. He'd tell Carly he had been called into work.

Kate yawned and put her arms back over the headrest. 'Where the hell are they? It's gone midnight.'

'Maybe we missed the drop-off?' Jeff replied, rubbing his eyes.

'Maybe. We'll give it another hour and then we'll go take a look.'

An hour passed and nothing. Kate and Jeff got out of the car and climbed through the fence, checking around the whole time, walking slowly, their senses alert. Jeff kept glancing back towards their car, anxious that someone might turn up and catch them. They stopped near the tree. The whole place was silent and eerie. Kate beckoned him forward and he went over to the tree, reaching inside the hollow.

'There's nothing there,' he whispered.

'Shit. Maybe they're late. Let's go back to the car.' Kate turned to walk away.

'You fucking liars.'

They both turned quickly to see John Lively standing there, holding his crash helmet near to his chest, his face twisted in anger.

'John? What's going on?' Kate looked around, trying to see if there was anyone else with him.

'You took the money yesterday and you're keeping it for yourselves. You lied to me.' Lively stepped towards them.

'John, I don't know what you're talking about, there was no money here when we got here yesterday, we must have—'

'Liar!' He shook his head. 'I was here, I saw you take the bag, and I heard you tell him you were keeping it.' He stabbed a finger towards Jeff.

Kate could see the panic on Jeff's face and quickly turned to concentrate on Lively, putting her hands out in front of her. 'John, look—'

'Don't even say anything. Do you know what they'll do to me if I haven't got that bag? They'll fucking kill me. You said you'd sort it and you haven't, you said you'd look after me and all you've done is screw me over. I'm a fucking dead man if I don't get that bag back.' Kate and Jeff could hear the fury in his voice.

'Okay, John, we'll get it back to you, don't worry. I'll bring it round to yours on Tuesday.' Kate knew she couldn't get into the lock-up until then, so all she had to do was convince Lively that he would get the bag back and everything would be sorted.

'That's not good enough, I need it sooner than that, they'll be knocking on my door on Saturday night and you better make sure it's there.'

'I can't get it to you by Saturday, John. The earliest is Tuesday, you'll just have to tell them—'

Lively cut her short. 'Do you know who these guys are? They won't wait. Now you get back to your little lock-up and get me my stuff back.'

Kate felt her face flush, not that Lively could see it in the darkness, their images only lit by the moon that shone serenely across the cemetery. 'What are you talking about?' she asked him.

'I told you, I was here last night, hiding up, and I watched you get the bag and look inside it and then you said you had a lock-up. So, I followed you back to your house and watched you both go inside with my fucking bag. Then I followed you this morning to the lock-up, saw you putting on your stupid fucking wig and go in and I saw you leave. I waited and then I rang you telling you there was another pick-up tonight. I know you planned to keep the money and drugs for yourselves, so I got me a guarantee.' He gripped his crash helmet tighter.

Kate could see Jeff was staring frantically between her and Lively. She could hear him breathing heavily, his breath hanging in the cold air.

'What do you mean, a guarantee?' she asked, hearing the panic in her own voice. She wanted to grab Lively around the throat, furious that he was making her feel this way.

'I told you, I've got someone looking out for me, so I told her that if I haven't rung her by first thing Sunday morning then she needs to go to the police and tell them all about your little scam.'

'You're fucking lying.' Kate clenched her fists.

'Am I?' Lively smiled and raised his eyebrows.

None of them spoke for a moment. It was a stand-off with Lively holding the ace.

'Who's this woman, then? Don't tell me . . . it's your little friend the newspaper editor on Oak Avenue; Ellie Sands?' Kate spat the words out, enraged that Lively had been one step ahead of her.

Lively's face changed immediately, and he hesitated before answering. 'Yeah. She'll go to the police and report in the papers all about your lock-up and the fact that you're dodgy bloody bizzies.' He smiled again. 'You think I'm a mug, don't you? Well, I'm not, so you make sure my bag is back with me by Saturday or you're fucked.'

Kate took a step towards him, pointing her finger in his face. 'Don't you threaten me, you piece of shit.'

She went to take another step forwards but stopped dead as he pulled a gun from inside his crash helmet. Without thinking, she instinctively grabbed his arm and turned it, throwing her full weight against him.

Then she heard the shot. She stepped back in disbelief as Lively slumped to the floor, his head landing hard on the ground.

'Oh fuck, oh, God, Kate.' Jeff put his hand up to his mouth and tried to stifle a cry.

Kate stood there, watching Lively as he tried to move. He was gasping for air and his hand was trying to grip the floor as he made a squealing, sickening sound, like an animal caught in a trap. Then abruptly, the sound ceased, and silence fell around them.

Kate didn't move. Jeff didn't move. They stood there under the light of the moon, staring at Lively's dead body.

Suddenly, Jeff grabbed his mouth and quickly stepped over towards a nearby tree and vomited. He felt like he was choking as he gasped for breath, putting his hand against the trunk to stop

310

himself from falling. Keeping his head down, he retched again, puking up watery sick.

When he had nothing left inside him, he wiped his mouth with his sleeve and coughed. He stood upright, taking deep breaths, his lungs stinging with the cold air as he breathed in through his nose and out through his mouth. Jeff looked across at Kate.

'What are we going to do, Kate?' He walked back over to her.

'Don't move, just let me think.' Her voice was at a whisper. Her pulse hammering in her neck. She closed her eyes, trying to figure out what she was going to do next.

'We need to get him out of here.' She rubbed a hand through her hair. 'Are you alright?' She stepped towards him, putting her hand on his arm, but he didn't reply. 'Jeff, we need to get him out of here,' she repeated.

Jeff nodded, staring at Lively's crumpled body. 'Okay.'

'Go and bring my car closer to the gap in the fence. We'll have to drag him.' Handing Jeff her keys, she watched him walk away.

Now, she had to think. From this moment on, she had to do everything just right. She needed a plan. A perfect plan.

Crouching down and carefully removing the gun from underneath Lively, she held it in her gloved hands, careful not to remove his prints. She flicked it open; five rounds left. *Shit, he brought a fully loaded gun with him. I underestimated him. Totally underestimated him.*

Her mind was racing. She checked his pockets and found his keys, wallet, a lighter and a piece of paper with a mobile phone number on it.

Her mobile number.

They slowly dragged Lively's body through the cemetery, staying off the main pathway. It was exhausting and they stopped every few feet, listening and looking for any sign of witnesses. When they were sure no one was there, they continued dragging the dead

311

weight of Lively's body until they finally reached the fence. Kate opened the boot of her car and after two attempts they finally managed to lift him in.

Kate leaned against the boot and tried to catch her breath. 'Alright, listen to me. Take his motorbike back to his flat. I'll follow you.'

'What are we going to do with him?' Jeff's whole body was shaking, and he tried to blink away the dizziness.

'I need time to think. Don't worry, I'll sort it, but we need to get his bike back, we can't leave it here. We'll go back to his flat and I'll figure out what to do then.'

Kate spent the journey to Lively's flat thinking, remembering what he had said about Ellie Sands. *Did he really tell her? Had he planned it so well? Was he bluffing? What if he wasn't bluffing? What if he had told her everything? Lively's dead and so Ellie Sands won't get the call from him on Sunday morning. What if she knows about the lock-up? Does she know about the drugs and the money? I can't get into the place until Tuesday.* She banged the palm of her hand on the steering wheel. She couldn't even get in there and get rid of everything.

'Fuck you!' she screamed.

She pulled up opposite Lively's flat and turned off the engine. The place was deserted but she sat for a moment just to be sure. She got out of the car and waited down the side alley for Jeff while he parked Lively's bike out of sight. He handed Kate the keys and they went inside, closing the door behind them.

The curtains were closed. Kate felt along the wall for a light switch. The place was surprisingly neat and tidy. His bed was made, draped in a black duvet cover that barely covered the mattress. A small lamp with no shade sat on a bedside table. The floorboards were bare apart from a frayed rug that lay next to the bed.

'Are you alright?' Kate asked Jeff.

'Yeah, I'll be fine.' Jeff looked around.

They both felt strangely calmer now; being inside Lively's flat with no chance of him suddenly walking in seemed to ease them.

Kate walked through to the tiny kitchen and turned the light on before sitting on the chair in the corner. Jeff followed her and stood in the doorway. 'What are we going to do, Kate?'

'I've been thinking. I just need a bit of time. I need to work out what we do from here.' She managed a smile. 'Hey.' She looked at him. 'I'll figure it out.'

He nodded and crossed his arms.

Kate put her hand on his arm. 'We need to search the place, see if there's anything in here to link him to us. You start in here. I'll start in the bedroom.'

CHAPTER 97

Anna swallowed hard and turned her radio up, listening as the situation was being relayed back and forth between the control room and the armed officers outside the lock-up. A trained negotiator had now been called in and was on his way to the scene.

Anna looked up as Rob Wills put a mug of coffee in front of her. She didn't want coffee, but appreciated the gesture.

He put his hand on her shoulder. 'They'll get her out of there, those guys know what they're doing.'

Anna forced a smile. 'Yeah.'

She thought about Sheridan's parents. She wanted to wait for the outcome before she spoke to them, which the superintendent had agreed to. She looked at the coffee and felt her stomach turn over.

CHAPTER 98

Sheridan listened, trying not to react too strongly to Jeff's story. It felt totally surreal. Over the years she had heard domestic violence victims describe their perpetrator as having a Jekyll and Hyde personality. One moment they were calm, smiling and normal, the next it was like they'd been taken over by some entity. They became, without warning or reason, irrational and violent.

Jeff had, within the last hour, shot and killed his best friend and a young defenceless lad, point-blank in the head, and now he was sitting with his back against the wall, talking calmly and stoically, as if he were describing an everyday event. He stared straight ahead as he spoke, every now and then arching his neck to try and see outside the lock-up door. They could hear faint sounds of officers moving around who were keeping their distance for now. They knew Jeff Nichols was armed and that he had taken Sheridan hostage. They had to play this just right. One wrong decision, one mistake and it was all over.

For Sheridan.

Jeff continued. 'We searched Lively's flat and that's when we found the letter that explained his relationship with Ellie Sands.'

CHAPTER 99

Kate Armitage carefully searched each drawer in Lively's bedroom, while Jeff went through the kitchen. Both had been to enough searches in the job to know where criminals like to hide things.

'Look what I've found.' Kate walked into Lively's kitchen, holding up a handwritten letter.

'What's that?' Jeff was on his knees checking the back of the kitchen cupboards. He got up and followed Kate into the bedroom where they sat on Lively's bed as she read the letter to him. It was dated 16 June 1985.

> *My darling John,*
> *Before I start, I want you to know how much I love you. You are my beautiful boy and I know you will make me proud by being strong when I'm not around. You know that I'm poorly and when you read this letter I'll soon be in heaven. Don't be sad, I'm not scared, and neither should you be. You will be okay and just remember I will always be with you, even if you can't see me.*
>
> *I wanted to make sure that you will be looked after when I've gone and so I've arranged for my*

dear friend, Ellie Sands, to take you in. She has been a wonderful friend to me since we met at school, and although our paths haven't crossed as often as we'd like, we have always stayed in touch. Ellie has promised me that she will look after you. You'll go live with her, and I know in my heart that you will have a wonderful life. Ellie is a clever lady. She was certainly the smarter one out of the two of us. She wants to be a journalist and I know one day she will be, who knows, maybe she'll be on the TV one day reporting from some far-off place, maybe she'll take you with her and you'll get to see the world.

Whatever happens, I know you will be safe with her. You will have a good life, my darling. Keep me always in your heart. Be a good boy. Stay out of trouble, get a good job and make sure you always try to be the best you can. Never let anyone think they are better than you. I know you will grow to be a good man. Meet a lovely girl and get married, have children, love them with all your heart, the way that I have loved you and the way I will always love you. I didn't always make the best choices. I didn't always live my life the way I should have. I kept away from family, turned my back on them, they didn't always agree with the lifestyle I chose. I have done some silly things. I've taken drugs and I've mixed with the wrong type of people. I can't change it now, it was what it was. That's why I want Ellie to look after you, she's a good person, she made better choices than I did.

Love her like she will love you.

I know you won't forget me. I am always going
to be in your heart.
I love you, John.
Always,
Mum xxxxxx

Kate looked at Jeff. 'So, that's how Lively knows Ellie Sands.'

'Yeah, but I thought he went into care when his mum died?'

'Maybe Ellie Sands looked after him for a while, and then had him put into care?'

'Yeah, maybe.' Jeff sighed.

'Whatever happened, we now know that Ellie Sands could be a fucking huge problem for us. Lively has probably told her everything.' Kate stood up. 'I've been thinking about how to sort this fucking mess out.'

'And?'

'I've got a plan.' She remained standing. 'Okay, think about it, we've got to get rid of Lively's body from my boot. Then, I've got to get rid of any evidence that his body was ever in there. We've got his motorbike, keys, crash helmet and his gun with only *his* prints on it. So, I'll go back to the cemetery tomorrow, find a newly dug grave and then tomorrow night we'll bury him in it. I'll call in work tomorrow and tell the skipper that Lively saw me the other day and threatened me. I'll just say that I want it noted just in case anything happens. Then I'll park my car around the back of my place, near the garages, and set it alight. That gets rid of any evidence of his body ever being in there. Everyone will presume it's Lively that's torched my car.' She paused, her mind putting things in order. 'I wish I'd bloody thought of it when we were at the cemetery tonight, we could have buried him there and then.' She shook her head.

'What if someone asks you why you've parked your car round the back and not round the front, like you always do?' Jeff asked.

'Simple, I'll just say that I was concerned that Lively might see my car outside my place and know where I live, and after he threatened me, I was just being cautious. I'll just say he saw me in town somewhere and told me to watch my back. No one's going to question that I park my car round the back.' She raised her eyebrows. 'There's no CCTV anywhere near my place, so no one will be able to prove it was me that torched it and no CCTV to check if Lively was seen anywhere nearby.'

'How's it going to work if we put him in a newly dug grave?' Jeff frowned.

'I'll find a grave that someone's just been buried in, we'll put him in there a few feet down. We won't be able to dig a new one, it'll be too suss. Plus, the earth will be easier to dig up.'

'Jesus, Kate.' Jeff rubbed his face and took a deep breath. 'Sorry, it's just messed up that we're talking about burying Lively's body.' He looked at her. 'Anyway, sorry, go on.'

Kate continued. 'Okay, well this is the part where we have to trust each other completely.' She inhaled. 'We have to kill Ellie Sands and make it look like Lively did it. But there's another thing we have to do, or should I say, you have to do.'

She hesitated before saying, 'You have to shoot me.'

CHAPTER 100

Jeff eased himself up from the floor. Sheridan gingerly moved her legs and knew she needed to stand; her feet were numb, and she could feel the cold from the lock-up floor biting into her body.

'Jeff, please can I stand up? I swear I won't try anything. I just need to move my legs.' She watched his every move as she spoke. He appeared to be somewhere else, like he was just recounting memories to a stranger in the pub. Happy to talk, happy to have a captive audience. And all Sheridan could do was listen.

He nodded.

She put her hands on the hard floor and slowly got to her feet as the blood immediately rushed through her body and she felt dizzy. Taking a step forward she steadied herself against the wall. Jeff watched her and then continued.

'We were careful not to leave any evidence on Lively that could link him to us, just in case his body was ever found. So, before we buried him, we took his clothes off, except for his boxers. After we buried him, we went back to her place to go over the plan for the next day. That's when she gave me the key to the lock-up and her wig and glasses. She knew that after the shooting the police would be all over her, worried that Lively might try and get to her, bearing in mind they had no idea he was dead. Kate was worried that if she'd missed something in her plan, we might need to get the stuff out of the lock-up quickly and move it, so she wanted to make sure I could get there and get in. She had it all planned out.'

Jeff sniffed and wiped his face with his sleeve. 'She told me that Ellie Sands had twice been to the same supermarket at about the same time on two Saturdays. So the plan was that I'd keep the gun hidden in my car. I'd then tell Tom Hudson that I was seeing Kate on the Saturday night for a romantic dinner at her place, and I'd tell Carly that I was going round to see Tom for a few beers. Then I'd drive my car to Lively's place, park up nearby, get his motorbike, ride to the supermarket and when I saw Kate walking towards the main doors, she would make sure that she was right next to, or just in front of Ellie Sands, so I'd know who my target was. I would ride up to them, pull the gun and Kate would shout "No, Lively" so that anyone around would hear. The plan was that later she'd say she recognised him as being the guy on the bike.

'I was supposed to shoot her in the leg, just to injure her, and then she would go down to the floor and I was to keep shooting, making sure I killed Ellie Sands. Then I had to drop the gun to make sure it was left at the scene with Lively's prints on it, ride his bike back to his flat, get into my car and drive to Tom Hudson's place.' He paused.

'When I got to Tom's, I'd tell him that Kate wasn't at home and say that she must have stood me up or forgotten. I'd then be at his place if the police went to my house to tell me Kate had been shot. I knew Carly would be at home so if the police did turn up, she'd say I was having a few beers at Tom's, which technically I was, and that's where they found me to tell me about Kate. The first chance I got I went to the tip and got rid of Lively's clothes, crash helmet, keys, wallet and the mobile that Kate had been using for her contact with him.'

Sheridan didn't speak. She was suddenly consumed by her fear of where this was going, how it would end. Jeff was telling her everything. Had he resigned himself to the fact that he wasn't getting away with what he and Kate had done? Or did he intend to tell her before killing her and making a run for it?

But he was surrounded, trapped. He needed her for now. He needed his hostage. Keeping her alive was the only way he had any chance of getting out of the lock-up. Did he really think he could?

She didn't want to say or do anything to anger him. She just had to listen. The truth was, she had nothing else to do. Nothing she had ever learned during her time in the job could have prepared her for this scenario.

Jeff peered quickly out of the lock-up door and then stepped back. He knew he was in control of the situation. The police couldn't and wouldn't just come running in, all guns blazing; this wasn't a movie scene. This was real.

'Kate planned everything to the last detail, even down to my route to the supermarket and back to Lively's flat, avoiding as much CCTV as possible.' Jeff paused. 'The plan was practically perfect.'

Sheridan waited for him to carry on, but he seemed to be lost deep in his own thoughts, recollecting what had happened and putting it in order.

She took the opportunity to speak. 'Jeff, I know you loved Kate, I know you didn't mean to kill her. I know what you both did was wrong, but you didn't know that it would end up like this.' Sheridan would never dream of speaking like this if she had a way out. If she didn't have a gun pointed at her she would tell Jeff Nichols that he was a fucking monster.

He lifted his head and looked her dead in the eye. 'The only thing that went wrong was that Ellie Sands didn't die.'

'What do you mean? The only thing that went wrong?' she asked.

His eyes narrowed like he was trying to focus. 'The only thing that went wrong was that Ellie Sands didn't die.' He repeated his words as he leaned in towards Sheridan's face.

'I always intended to kill Kate.'

CHAPTER 101

Sheridan tried not to react. She couldn't let Jeff see any emotion on her face. What hit her again was the absolute realisation that she had been right about Jeff Nichols from the start. From the very first day she'd met him, she hadn't trusted him; her instincts had been bang on. But she never saw this coming.

He took a step back, staring at the gun again as he spoke.

'I wanted out of my marriage, I wanted to be with Kate at the beginning and I had every intention of leaving Carly for her. But the moment Lively was shot, something changed in me. It was like all the things we'd talked about, our future together, all the money we would have, the great life ahead of us, just disappeared. I saw something different in Kate at that moment. I saw someone I didn't recognise. Suddenly, I almost wanted my normal, boring life back again. I didn't want to be plotting to get rid of a dead body, I didn't want to spend my life wondering if Kate would ever slip up or change her mind about being with me. She was so smart, so manipulative and cunning, that I realised if things went sour between us or we somehow got linked to shooting Lively, she might just decide to frame me for the whole mess, and I knew she was clever enough to do that. It was like one minute I trusted her completely and the next, I didn't trust her at all.' Jeff rubbed a hand over his face. He looked exhausted.

'When Kate first told me about the lock-up and what was in there, I had no intention of screwing her over. But when Lively died, everything changed. I knew I was going to take it all, and I knew I was going to have to get rid of Kate. I just didn't know how. Then when she came up with the plan to kill Ellie Sands and make it look like Lively did it, I knew it was my chance to kill Kate. She'd planned it all. The morning after she torched her car, she hired another car so that she could get to the supermarket. She knew where Ellie Sands usually parked, so she parked nearby. I picked Lively's bike up from his flat and rode it to the supermarket. I asked Kate beforehand what the plan was if Ellie Sands didn't turn up. She said we'd have to go to her house and shoot her there, still leaving the gun at the scene so the police would still link Lively to the shooting, but that wasn't going to work for me. I needed to kill Kate and the supermarket car park plan worked better for me.

'Anyway, I took the route Kate had planned. I'd only seen a black and white picture of Ellie Sands from the newspaper, but I'd never seen her in real life, so Kate had described her to me in as much detail as possible. Kate told me that if Ellie Sands didn't turn up at the supermarket as we expected, then Kate just wouldn't get out of her car. When I saw them, I knew I had to get it right. I had to make sure I shot Kate and Ellie and had to make sure they were both dead.'

He stopped for a moment, a frown crumpling his face. He inhaled long and hard before carrying on.

'When I pulled the gun out, I saw this little girl with her mum, walking just behind Kate and Ellie. Something made me hesitate. I panicked I suppose, I didn't want to shoot the woman by mistake; her little girl was holding her hand. Then I remember looking at Ellie Sands, her face. She stared at me. Like she recognised me somehow. I was thrown for a second and that's why I didn't manage to aim properly. That's probably why she survived. When I rode away, I knew I'd managed to kill Kate and by the time I got to Tom Hudson's place I was completely calm. It was weird. He didn't suspect a thing and about two hours later the police turned up, telling me that Kate had been shot dead and they were looking for John Lively. In my head the plan had worked, then they said that an innocent bystander had also been shot and was in a critical condition in hospital, unlikely to survive.'

He stopped, reaching into his pocket for his cigarettes before remembering he had smoked the last one. 'Don't suppose you've got a cigarette, have you?' he asked Sheridan. She shook her head.

'They might get you a pack if you ask?' She nodded towards the door, hoping he would consider this. At least then there would be some communication between him and the officers outside. Maybe they would convince him to let her go.

But he just carried on talking as if he hadn't even heard her. 'A few days after I shot Kate, I panicked and came here to the lock-up. I convinced myself that Kate might have slipped up somewhere along the line and the police would find everything. So, I put the cash and the rings and diamonds that Kate had taken from the sudden death into those two bags, took them home and hid them in the loft.' He kicked the bag nearest to him. 'I knew Carly would never go up there, so I knew they'd be safe.

'Then of course, during the enquiry it all came out about my affair with Kate, and Carly kicked me out anyway.' He put his head back and looked up at the ceiling. 'I didn't want to stay with my parents, so I asked Tom Hudson if I could stay at his house until I found myself a place. I couldn't take the bags with me, so I brought them back here.' He sighed heavily.

'Then, I needed to know if Ellie Sands had survived – which, clearly, she had – and whether she was able to tell anyone about me and Kate. I had to know if Lively was telling us the truth about her. I knew that all I had to do was wait it out until it was the right time, until the enquiry into the shooting was wound down and I was sure that Ellie Sands wasn't able to talk, and then I was going to go, jet off somewhere and start a new life for myself. Tom Hudson told me that Ellie Sands couldn't really speak and so I thought I was fairly safe. He told me she'd eventually been transferred to The Gables Nursing Home. I was ready to disappear then, but my father had a fucking stroke and I had to look after the family business.

He coughed heavily, clearing his throat before spitting on the floor. 'So, I had to put the plan on hold. Then about a year ago I was ready to set the plan in motion again and I had to know that Ellie Sands wasn't going to suddenly regain her marbles and start talking. So, I hired a private investigator, a guy called Jack Lawson. I made up a story about wanting to put my mother into care because her health was failing, so I wanted him to secretly check the place out. He said it might be difficult, but he'd figure out a way. As luck would have it, he got friendly with a girl that works there, Mo Chase, and he started having a relationship with her, of sorts. She used to tell him all about the place and she always brought up Ellie Sands, or "Pissy Knickers" as they call her. The first time Jack Lawson said those words I didn't put two and two together; it was a while later when he mentioned pissy knickers again that I realised she was trying to say 'PC Nichols' and I knew that I was running out of time, had to make a move.' His jaw tightened.

'But then John Lively's body was found.' He shook his head. 'You couldn't fucking make this shit up, could you? I knew that you'd figure out that Lively couldn't have shot Kate and you'd be all over it. The first time you called me into the nick I knew you didn't trust me, I could see it in your eyes, and as the investigation went on and you suspected I might have shot Lively, I knew I had to stick around. It would have been too suspicious if I'd suddenly taken off then. But I started making plans, figuring out where I could go to start again, what sort of account I could put some of the cash from the lock-up into, when and how to sell the jewellery and diamonds and get rid of this.' He held the gun up again, examining it like he'd only just realised it was there.

'When I saw this gun at the lock-up, I took it, kept it at home just in case Lively had told one of his druggie mates about me and Kate and they paid me a visit. I wanted to make sure I was prepared for anything.' He put his hand on his forehead and rubbed his temples. 'I knew time was probably running out and I had to make the decision to go. So, I went to see Carly and the kids in Norfolk and then my parents. They didn't know I wasn't going to see them again. I was saying goodbye, but they had no idea. I told my parents that I was planning a holiday, I was going to get away for a while. And tonight, I'd invited Tom out for a few beers. He's been a good mate to me and was always encouraging me to get out of the house and go out for a drink with him. I wanted to say goodbye without him knowing.' Jeff paused, a moment of reflection before he continued. 'The stuff in those bags was my future, but then you found the lock-up.' He closed his eyes. 'And now I'm fucked.'

Sheridan swallowed. Her mouth was dry. She would have killed for a glass of water.

She licked her lips. 'But what would link you to the lock-up?'

Jeff shook his head. 'I wanted to be ready to go at a moment's notice, no matter where I was or what I was doing. I needed to be in a position to drop everything, get here, grab the bags and disappear. So, I put everything I needed, including my passport, in there.' He pointed at the bags. 'Even if the place was closed, I knew I could hide up nearby and wait for it to open.'

He suddenly lifted the gun and hit himself in the head with it. 'But *you* fucked it all up!' he screamed at her.

'Jeff, listen to me . . .'

Sheridan took a tentative step forward, but he grabbed her and put his hand around her throat, placing the gun on her lips, pushing it into her mouth. She gagged and tried to grab his hand, but he forced the gun further in, his finger on the trigger. Then he pulled the gun out.

'Tell my kids I love them,' he said, before putting the gun in his own mouth.

Sheridan was still gripping his wrist, pulling as hard as she could as it flashed through her mind that there was no way she was going to let this happen. No way was he going to kill himself now.

He tried to pull away from her, kicking at her legs and she kicked back, desperately trying to keep control of the gun. She managed to hold his wrist and twist it, so the gun was pointing momentarily towards the floor, but he kicked her again and the pain seared through her leg. She fell to the floor, and he went with her, falling with his full weight on top of her. Sheridan heard the shot and felt the bullet rip through her.

And then she felt nothing.

CHAPTER 102

The armed officers outside the lock-up had their weapons pointed at the door. They had to move, and they had to move now. Jeff tried to get up but was quickly overcome and restrained and as the gun dropped to the floor, he felt himself being slammed against the wall and handcuffed. Caught. It was over.

Anna held the radio against her forehead and slumped down into her chair as she burst into tears. Rob Wills came around behind her, pulling her into him as he held her against his chest, her whole body heaving as she wept.

'Oh God Rob, he's shot her,' she cried. 'He's fucking shot her.'

CHAPTER 103

Two weeks later

Anna was in the guard of honour: thirty-two police officers standing in silence, lining the route from the road into the church. The rain had fallen all night and hadn't let up, even for a moment. Dark clouds hung heavily in the sky, unleashing a downfall that lashed sideways against their faces. She turned her head slightly and watched as the back of the hearse was opened and the pall bearers, four detectives in full uniform, including Dipesh Mois and Rob Wills, gently lifted the coffin out and placed it on to their broad, strong shoulders. As the coffin was carried slowly past her, she bowed her head, as did everyone in the line. Anna bit down hard on her lip, desperately trying to fight back the tears that were tumbling down her face.

She felt Steve slip his hand into hers, and together they followed the coffin into the church. Inside was packed full of family and friends, new and ex-colleagues. And the whole of Hale Street CID. Solemn faces watched as the coffin, dressed in a large bouquet of yellow roses, was placed at the altar. The church was full of flowers, hundreds of them everywhere. A sea of colour and beauty on such a dark day.

The vicar stepped to the side of the coffin, his open Bible held steady in his hands.

'A warm welcome to you all on this sad day. Let us begin with a hymn, "The Lord Is My Shepherd".'

Sam closed her eyes, fighting back tears. She had tried to be strong, tried to pretend that she was alright, but the last two weeks had been unbearable. She felt Sheridan's mother's hand on hers as she opened her eyes and looked around her.

She had fallen to her knees when Anna Markinson had turned up at her flat two weeks before. Anna, standing there ashen-faced, asking to come in. Sam had listened as Anna told her what had happened at the lock-up. How the police had got in there moments after Sheridan had been shot. How they had arrested Jeff Nichols for murder.

Sam subconsciously shook her head as if to rid her mind of the memory of that horrific day. She put her head in her hands and blinked away salty tears. She couldn't cry any more.

◆ ◆ ◆

As the final words to the hymn drifted through the church, the vicar lifted his head and began.

'We are here today to celebrate the life of a highly respected and committed police officer, who dedicated their life to serving the public. A colleague, friend, husband and father, Maxfield Hall, who was known to you all as Max.'

Sheila Hall held her daughter's hand and wiped a tissue across her mouth. She hadn't left her husband's side in the week before he died. He'd been making good progress since his first heart attack and had returned home briefly before he suffered a second one, one that he had not recovered from.

She had been overwhelmed by the support she'd received from Max's colleagues after his death, and was equally overwhelmed by the turnout today. Retired officers, serving officers, old and new faces had joined together to say goodbye. Max Hall was respected by all who had worked with him and today was testament to that. Her mind drifted to her husband's colleague and friend, missing from the assembled mourners: Sheridan Holler.

Sheila had visited Sheridan in hospital two days earlier and watching her surrounded by machines, tubes and wires had been difficult for her, a reminder of seeing her husband lying there before he died. She had prayed for Sheridan and as the funeral came to an end, she spoke with Anna outside.

'How's Sheridan doing?' She took Anna's hand.

'She's still very poorly. I'm going to the hospital later to see her. Anyway, how are you holding up?'

'I'm alright. I can't believe how many people turned up today, Max would have been so proud.' Her voice broke slightly and Anna instinctively put her arms around her.

'I'm so sorry, Sheila.' Anna quickly wiped a tear away, reaching into her pocket for a tissue.

'He loved you all, you know. He would have been devastated about what's happened to Sheridan.' She looked around the crowd. 'Please let her family know that my thoughts are with them. And that poor lad, Tom. What a terrible thing to happen. You know, Anna, being married to a police officer for all those years, I thought nothing could shock me, but what's happened in the last few weeks has. Sheridan will need support when she recovers. She's one of the strongest women I've ever known but she is only human, she just needs to be reminded of that every now and then.' She squeezed Anna's hand and made her way over to the vicar.

◆ ◆ ◆

Sam laid her head on the bed as Sheridan's parents left the room to have a break. Joni stood up to stretch her legs and looked at Sheridan's face, just as she opened her eyes.

'Sam,' Joni whispered.

Sam lifted her head and saw Sheridan blink. Her mouth moved as she tried to speak. Sam sat bolt upright. 'Hey,' she said, her voice low and soft.

Sheridan tried to focus before closing her eyes.

'Can you hear me?' Sam took Sheridan's hand. 'Squeeze my hand if you can hear me.'

She felt Sheridan's fingers tighten around hers and tears blurred her eyes. 'You're going to be okay.' Sheridan squeezed her hand three times in succession and she smiled. 'You're going to be just fine.'

CHAPTER 104

Anna grabbed her jacket from the back of her chair and took a last swig of coffee. 'Right, I'm off, I won't be long.'

Jules Mayfield looked up. 'Where are you off to?'

'I'm going to John Lively's funeral.' Anna didn't wait for a response as she quickly headed out of the office.

The service was short. She watched as John Lively's coffin disappeared behind the curtain, and thought about him and his life. Born and placed into care when his mother died, spiralling into drugs and crime. A typical story and one Anna had heard a million times before. She questioned why she had come. She was the only person who had. Walking out of the church she made her way over to a quiet bench within the grounds, where rows of headstones stared back at her.

The enquiry was still ongoing. Jeff Nichols had been interviewed three times, each time refusing to even confirm his name. He had replied 'No comment' to every question put to him, saying only three words at the end of every interview, 'Ask Sheridan Holler.' He had sat, arms crossed and head down, throughout his first hearing at court. Remanded in custody awaiting trial for the abduction and attempted murder of Sheridan Holler, the murders of Tom Hudson and Billy Doyle, along with possession of a firearm with intent.

Anna thought about Sheridan. Had Jeff Nichols told her anything? Everything? She might hold the key to what had happened to Kate and Ellie. Anna knew that Sheridan was lucky to be alive. She had no doubt fought so desperately with Jeff, and maybe if he had had more than three bullets in the gun, he would have shot them both. Once he'd shot Tom Hudson and Billy Doyle, he had to have known there was only one bullet left. He would have had to make a choice between shooting himself or shooting Sheridan.

If Sheridan did know anything, they were going to have to wait until she was well enough to speak. Anna's thoughts drifted back to John Lively. She had no respect for him but she did know that he hadn't killed Kate Armitage and hadn't therefore shot Ellie Sands. The bottom line was that Lively was a murder victim, his killer not caught. Yet. She sighed. What a sad bloody tale. Lively was a crook alright, petty theft, drugs, but what had his childhood been like? Had he been abused? Was he a victim through and through? A victim of the life that he had been dealt?

CHAPTER 105

December 1989

John Lively felt the hand across his face and winced as his foster father Alan Martin grabbed him around the throat. 'I want you out of here, you little shit.'

He grabbed Alan Martin's wrists and managed to pull himself free. 'I'm going, trust me.' He walked into the kitchen and took a black bin liner from the cupboard before storming upstairs. He threw what clothes he had into it, along with the few possessions he had kept when his mother was alive, two photographs, a necklace and the letter she had written to him before she died. He got to the front door and wrenched it open.

'And don't come back!' Alan Martin shouted after him. John didn't respond. He just slammed the door behind him and walked off into the darkness.

He spent two nights sleeping under a tree in Sefton Park, hanging around with low-level drug users, shoplifting to feed himself and his growing cannabis habit. He stole for others, earning himself money to survive, sofa surfing. He was angry and bitter at the life he felt forced to live, often reading the letter his mother had written to him before she died. How different it could have all been if her friend Ellie Sands had taken him in.

And so, eight years after Martin threw him out, he decided to pay her a visit and looked her up in the phone book. It was a Sunday and he stood up the road from her house for two hours. He felt nervous, going over and over in his head what he would say to her. Would he blame her for his life? Would she apologise and let him stay? Did she have a family? Was she married? Maybe she would take him in, even if it was many years too late.

He rang the doorbell.

The woman who answered the door was so different to how he had imagined her to be. She was short with shoulder-length blonde hair and a subtly pretty face. As soon as she had opened the door, he could smell food cooking and his empty stomach churned with hunger.

She frowned at the figure before her. He must have looked a sight, which was no surprise, considering he hadn't washed his hair in a week and his clothes were too big, swallowing up his under-weight body.

'Can I help you?' the woman asked, putting her foot instinctively against the bottom of the door.

'Are you Ellie Sands?'

'Yes, who are you?'

'I'm John Lively, Angela's son.'

Ellie Sands stared at him for a moment and cleared her throat. 'Oh, hello John, how are you?'

'I'm freezing, can I come in?'

'It's not really a good time, I'm afraid.'

'Please, I just want to talk to you. I won't stay long.'

Ellie hesitated before opening the door a little wider. 'Alright, just for a moment.' She pointed into the kitchen, and he stepped inside where the warmth instantly enveloped him. The house was small but spotless and fresh, a world away from the places he was used to living in.

She stood with her arms crossed. 'So, what brings you here, John?'

He reached into his pocket and pulled out his mother's letter, handing it to her.

'What's this?' She looked at him.

'It's a letter my mum gave me before she died.'

Ellie invited John to sit while she remained standing, reading the words her friend had written to her son. When she finished, she handed him back the letter and he folded it carefully, tucking it back into his pocket.

'John, I'm sorry I couldn't take you in when your mum died. But if I'm honest, I only said it to put her mind at ease. She was worried about you – as any mother would be – but I just wasn't in a position to take on a child back then.'

Ellie made him a cup of tea and sat opposite him at the kitchen table. John listened as she told him how his mother and Ellie had been good, albeit unlikely, friends at school. Both from very different backgrounds, and almost complete opposites in terms of their personalities.

Angela had been a wild card. She smoked and swore, and was a difficult pupil. She didn't care about history and biology, she just wanted to have fun, be the class clown. Whereas Ellie was quiet and studious, wanted to be someone, wanted to learn. But somehow the friendship had blossomed. Angela had looked up to Ellie like an older sister, even though they were almost exactly the same age, born four days apart. When they left school, Angela worked in a newsagents' and Ellie went to college and then studied journalism at university. They kept in touch by letter and met up every year or so. Angela became pregnant with John and although they continued writing to each other, they stopped meeting up. Then in

1984, Angela wrote to Ellie, telling her she had been diagnosed with leukaemia and could Ellie visit her in hospital.

'That was when she asked me if I would take you in when she died.' Ellie put another cup of tea in front of John, and he wrapped his hands around it, blowing on the steam. 'She begged me, she had no one else she could trust, but I said no at first. My life was about my career, and I knew I couldn't give you what you needed. I wouldn't ever have the time to be a parent like your mum asked me to be. Then, a couple of weeks before she died, she asked me again. I remember how painfully thin she was and very, very sick. I couldn't bear to think of her worrying about you, so I said I would take you in.' Ellie lifted up her cup to take a sip but put it back down again. 'I know it was wrong of me to lie to her, but I always thought that she died peacefully because of it.'

She watched John, who was staring out of the window. 'I did make sure that you were taken into care, so I knew you would be looked after.'

'My foster father hit me, nearly every day,' he said, and clenched his jaw. 'I'm homeless and I'm hungry and I think you should have told my mum the truth.' His voice trembled as he spoke. 'I would have been happier living with you, at least I would have had a roof over my head.'

He told her about his time in foster care and how he'd turned to drink and drugs, often stealing to survive. How he'd thought about suicide so many times. How he had slept under a tree and spent two nights in his mate's shed. He wanted to get a job and get his own flat, nothing special, just somewhere he could feel safe, maybe give it a lick of paint and get some furniture from a charity shop. As Ellie listened, she realised how much he reminded her of his mother.

'I knew who you were as soon as I opened my door today,' she told him.

340

'Really?' he replied, finishing the last drops of his tea.

'You look just like your mum.' Ellie stood up to rescue the now very overcooked beef in the oven.

'So, you remember what she looked like? You never forgot her?' John stared longingly at the hot beef sizzling in the oven dish that Ellie had placed on the worktop. His stomach groaned.

'I have a very good memory for faces. Maybe it's the journalist in me. Who knows? But, yes, of course I remember what she looked like. You have so many of her characteristics. Be proud of that, John. She was a good person, and she had a good heart.' Ellie remembered that she had a photograph of Angela taken on their last day of school. She thought about giving it to him but was reluctant to leave him on his own in the kitchen while she rummaged upstairs for it, in case he robbed her blind.

'Can you lend me some money? Just a couple of quid to get some food?'

'No, John, I'm not lending you any money. I don't want you buying drugs with it.' She poured water into a saucepan and put it on the stove.

'I don't do drugs any more, I swear. I just want to get a packet of crisps or something.' He grinned as she turned around. 'Or a hit of heroin.' He slapped his hand on the kitchen table and laughed at her expression. 'I'm joking. I honestly just want to get some food.'

An hour later, he put his knife and fork down and sat back. 'That was really good, thank you, Ellie.' He wiped his mouth with the palm of his hand.

'You're welcome.' Ellie took his plate and put it in the sink before sitting down. 'John, I'll never lend you money, but I will help you get a flat if I can.'

An hour later, she stood at her front door and watched him walking away, his hands buried deep into his coat pockets. Part of her wished he had never shown up at her door and part of her was glad he had. She couldn't dismiss the reservations she had about him; she didn't want trouble at her door. She had worked hard to get where she was and although it wasn't the high-flying career she had hoped for, she loved her job. She loved her life, she liked being in control, liked routine and she had no intention of letting John Lively bring his chaos into her life. She had made it clear before he left that she didn't want him turning up unannounced and that he was to call her if he wanted to see her. She made a conscious decision not to mention him to her family. She had never mentioned her friendship with Angela Lively to them; she came from good stock, a respectable family, unlike Angela Lively, and they would have warned her to stay well clear. Then, as she sat on her bed later that evening looking at the photograph of Angela, she felt a wave of guilt wash over her. Hearing John's story made her ache. It was partly her fault that he'd turned out the way he had. If she had stuck to her promise and adopted him, she could have guided him through life, given him a chance. Maybe he would be someone by now.

She looked at Angela's smiling face. 'I'll do what I can for your boy.' She kissed the picture before putting it away.

CHAPTER 106

Several months passed before John made contact with her again, saying he had found a flat on Kingsway Road in Toxteth. He asked her if she could lend him his first month's rent, lying to her that he had a job working with a friend who was a mechanic, but he wouldn't get paid until the end of the month. Ellie agreed, but only if she could see the flat for herself and she would hand the first payment to the landlord.

Two days later she met John outside the building, and they waited in the rain for the landlord to show. When he did turn up, an hour late, Ellie could smell alcohol on his breath and managed to avoid shaking his grubby hand. He showed them around the flat and Ellie's heart sank. It was cold and damp with not a stick of furniture or a thread of carpet in any of the rooms.

She was about to suggest they leave, when John turned to the landlord. 'It's brilliant, I'll take it.' John smiled.

As dumbfounded as Ellie was at how easily John accepted the landlord's offer, she resisted dragging him out of there. Instead, she turned to the landlord. 'Can we see the tenancy agreement?'

The landlord frowned. 'The tenancy agreement is, he pays his rent every Friday and keeps the bloody noise down.' He turned to John and put his hand out. 'Forty quid.'

John looked to Ellie who shook her head and reluctantly handed over the money. 'I don't suppose there's a rent book either?' she said as the landlord shoved the cash into his back pocket and handed John his key.

'Your mum's a comedian.' The landlord pointed his thumb at Ellie before he left.

'Thanks for this, Ellie. I'm going to do the place up,' John said, running his hand along the wall.

Ellie took a deep breath before responding with a resigned, 'It's better than being on the streets, I suppose.'

John rarely made contact after that day. The odd phone call to let her know how he was doing, that he was still working with his friend and was doing well, with plans to train as a car mechanic and set up his own business. Far from the real truth, that he was actually on a suspended sentence for possession of drugs and was now running for a local dealer. Ellie listened as he spun his tales; she knew he was lying to her because his name was on the court listings page of the *Liverpool Post*.

Then one day, he turned up at her door again.

CHAPTER 107

Saturday 29 November 1997

Ellie opened her front door to see John standing there. 'What do you want, John? I told you never to turn up here unannounced, you should have called me first.' She stood with her arms crossed.

'Can I come in?'

'No, John, I'm sorry. I'm busy.'

'I just want to come in for five minutes.' He put his arms out.

'John, I've tried to help you, but you lied to me. I know you've been in trouble with the police, and I know you're still taking drugs. I can't have you turning up here any more.' She went to close the door.

'Ellie, wait. Please.' He put his hand on the door. 'You've been so good to me, I'm sorry I lied but I've still got my flat and I really am working as a trainee mechanic, I've got a motorbike.' He pointed to the bike parked on the road. 'It's insured and everything. I swear down I don't take drugs, Ellie. There's these two coppers who set me up, planted the drugs on me.' He hung his head. 'I know you don't believe me, but I promise I'm telling the truth.' He looked at her. 'I never want to let you down, Ellie, please can we be friends?'

She paused for a moment. 'Okay, we'll see, but you have to go now, I'm expecting company any minute.' And with that she closed the door.

As John walked back to his bike, he didn't notice Kate Armitage watching from her car down the road.

CHAPTER 108

Friday 5 December 1997

John dialled Ellie's number.

'Hello.'

'Hi, it's John. I'm really sorry to bother you, Ellie, but the clutch has gone on my motorbike, I've got a mate looking at it for me, but I just need a lift to go and pick up a part from a mate in Bootle.'

There was a silence. 'I've got to be at work soon, John.'

'It'll only take an hour. I wouldn't ask but I'm stuck without my bike.'

Ellie sighed down the phone. 'Alright, but just this once, John. Where are you?'

'I'll walk to Park Street and wait outside Hanley's.'

John put the phone down and made his way to meet Ellie, anxiously checking his watch. He had an hour to get to Bootle and make the pick-up, ten wraps of heroin. If Ellie collected him in the next half an hour, he'd be in plenty of time. As he walked, he felt a pang of guilt. She had been so good to him and he hated lying to her but he had to make this pick-up. As he turned into Park Street, he saw the police car. 'Shit,' he said under his breath as he spotted PC Jeff Nichols and PC Kate Armitage pull over.

Jeff parked the police car and Kate got out. 'Hello, John. Where are you going?'

'Just out for a walk, no law against it is there?'

'Where's your bike?'

'Clutch is fucked. Got a mate looking at it.' He spotted Jeff Nichols walking over.

Ellie had seen John walking towards Hanley's and was about to sound her horn when she saw the police car pull up. She pulled into a layby and watched as they approached him. She could see John speaking to them before they got back into the car. John was checking the line of traffic and as he saw Ellie, his expression didn't change. He looked at her for a brief moment before getting into the back of the police car. She watched on as the female officer spoke to John in the back seat while the male officer stared out of the window. 'What's going on, John?' she said under her breath, sighing to herself. She was about to drive away when she saw the male officer get out and open the back door. John climbed out and walked up the road a few paces, giving the police car time to drive off before he crossed the road and got into her car.

'I'm sorry about that . . . misunderstanding.' He pulled on his seatbelt.

'What was that all about, John? If you're in trouble with the police, I need to know. I can't have contact with you, I have to put my job first. I'm sorry.' Ellie put her hands on the steering wheel.

'Those two coppers have got it in for me, Ellie. It's like they follow me and pull me over just to piss me off. PC Nichols is a dick, and his mate PC Armitage is just a bitch. Did you see the way they looked at me? Like I'm a piece of shit.'

Ellie sighed. 'Yes, I saw the way they looked at you. Did they threaten you?'

'They're trying to set me up, they want me to give them information about drug dealers, but I told them I'm not into drugs any more and I just want to live a normal life. That's why they let me go,' he said, hoping he'd convinced her.

'You can always make a complaint against them if you feel they're stopping you all the time for no reason.'

'Oh yeah, that'll work. "Dear mister police inspector, I would like to complain that PC Nichols and PC Armitage are bang out of order because they keep asking me to empty my pockets. Oh, and by the way . . . yes, I've been to prison before for theft and drug offences."' He raised his eyebrows at her. 'They're all bloody corrupt, these coppers. They stick together, trust me. And I'll tell you something else: if anything happens to me, you make sure you remember their names and faces, because if I end up in prison, it'll be a fucking set-up.' He checked the time. 'We better go, I've got to be at my mate's soon.'

Ellie started the car and pulled into the line of traffic. 'John, swear to me you're not dealing drugs. Because if I find out you are, I will go to the police myself.'

'Ellie, I swear down, I don't do that shit any more, I've got a life now, I've got a job and a flat, I wouldn't dream of ever getting you involved in any shit.' He looked out of the window. 'You've been so good to me.' He thought about telling her the truth about Jeff Nichols and Kate Armitage, how they had threatened him if he didn't give them information. Maybe he could sell his story to her newspaper. Maybe, if he convinced Jeff and Kate that he'd told Ellie everything, they'd leave him alone. That would put the shits up them. His eyes rested on her face. No, he wouldn't tell her, he didn't want her involved. He wouldn't tell her anything. Protect her. Keep her out of it.

Ellie waited outside while John went into his mate's flat. Two minutes later he emerged and got back into the car. 'He didn't have the right part. I'll have to see if I can get it somewhere else.'

'John, I need to get to work.'

'It's okay, if you can just drop me back in town, I'll sort it.' He kept his hand tightly clasped around the ten wraps of heroin in his pocket.

Half an hour later she dropped him back on Park Street. Leaving the engine running, she turned to look at him. 'John, please take care of yourself, you're still young and you've got your whole life ahead of you. I'd hate to see you waste the life you've been given. Make your mum proud of you.'

He rubbed his face with the palm of his hand. 'My life is what it is, Ellie.'

Ellie sighed. 'Are you happy?'

John shrugged his shoulders. 'I suppose so. Sometimes.'

'You should be enjoying yourself, not running around trying to avoid the police.'

He turned to face her. 'Are *you* happy, Ellie?'

'Yes, to be honest, I am. I think life is a gift and we should never take it for granted.' She put her hand on his. 'I've seen too many stories of young men like you, going wayward and ending up in all sorts of trouble. Just think about it, John. Think about how different your life could be if you learned to enjoy it for what it is. Live it, because you're a long time dead.'

He nodded to her as he got out of the car and she watched him walking away, turning back momentarily to wave at her and smiling as she waved back.

She got home from work that evening to find a bunch of flowers on her doorstep. She took them inside, laid them on the kitchen table and carefully undid the cellophane wrapping. Tucked inside was a card.

> *My darling husband, I miss you every day. You are always in my heart, Love Grace. Xx*

Ellie shook her head and grinned. 'Oh, John, you really are something else,' she muttered to herself.

CHAPTER 109

Saturday 6 December 1997

Ellie Sands made her usual trip to Mason's supermarket. Studying the Christmas cards, she selected a pack that promised a percentage went to a cancer charity. She looked out for the young man on the checkout who always chatted her up, telling her she couldn't possibly be old enough to be his mother. She enjoyed the banter between them and was disappointed that he wasn't there. Maybe she'd see him next Saturday. An hour later and she was done.

As she walked out of the main doors she noticed a woman standing to her right, but as Ellie glanced up the woman looked away. Ellie immediately recognised her as the police officer who had stopped John the day before, obviously off duty. PC Armitage, she remembered the name.

She thought about John and wondered if he was being paranoid, talking of corrupt police officers. Were PC Nichols and PC Armitage just doing their job?

John had a criminal record, so it was more likely that they had every reason to stop him on the street. She had warmed to John; he wasn't overly bright but he was a likeable character, just like his mother had been. Both wild cards, both living chaotic lives. Her heart told her that John was telling the truth and he wasn't involved in drugs. Her head told her he probably was. She didn't want to get too involved in his life. She couldn't afford to let anything damage her career. She had dreamt of becoming a foreign correspondent, travelling the world and writing stories for a major newspaper. But it was a tough business to crack and one that she hadn't conquered. Instead, she had ended up as a local reporter for the *Liverpool Post*. After several years of hard graft, she had eventually made it to editor. She couldn't let John Lively upset her life, her world.

But if he was right about corrupt police officers, well . . . that would make a great story.

CHAPTER 110

Saturday 13 December 1997

Ellie Sands parked her car in her usual spot at Mason's. She hadn't heard from John for over a week, and was honestly grateful for the break. She felt the crunch of ice beneath her feet as she walked slowly and carefully towards the main entrance, excited shoppers milling around.

She had a quiet Christmas planned. Her nephew Miles and her neighbour would probably pop in, but other than that, she would hunker down and enjoy the repeats on television, maybe treat herself to a nice bottle of gin.

The thought warmed her as she walked on, noticing a little girl holding her mother's hand and hugging a giraffe toy. Ellie smiled, and as she neared the door, she was aware of a woman beside her who suddenly slipped on the ice. Ellie instinctively put her hand out to the woman. 'Are you alright?' she asked.

The woman responded abruptly, dismissively, 'I'm fine.' She quickly looked at Ellie, who recognised her immediately. It was PC Armitage.

What was she doing here? Was she following Ellie? Had she seen her with John, and maybe thought she was involved with him in some way?

Ellie thought about saying something to her, but at that moment a motorbike appeared, heading straight towards them. She looked at the rider, recognising him as he got closer: PC Nichols, Ellie was positive it was him. She never forgot a face. What the hell was going on?

She stared at him and then suddenly PC Armitage put her hand up and shouted, 'No, Lively!'

That's when Ellie saw the gun. She heard the gunshot and was aware that PC Armitage had fallen to the floor. More shots cracked out and she felt a searing pain to her head. Then everything went black.

CHAPTER 111

Sheridan put her head back on the pillow. She was clearly exhausted and although at times she'd struggled to keep her composure during the last couple of hours, she had managed to recount everything that had happened in the lock-up.

Anna had watched her throughout as she gave her statement, listening to every detail. There were moments of disbelief as Sheridan had recalled what Jeff Nichols had told her. She felt relieved that Sheridan was finally well enough to be spoken to, relieved that she remembered everything, but more than anything else, she was just so thankful that her best friend had survived.

Anna herself had felt waves of emotion as Sheridan described how the events had unfolded, from the moment Tom Hudson's car had pulled up outside Jeff's house.

Monday 17 January, 6.20 p.m.

Tom Hudson had just arrived at Jeff Nichols' house and as he stepped into the living room, he spotted Sheridan standing by the window.

'Inspector Holler,' Tom said, unzipping his jacket.

'Hello, Tom,' Sheridan replied, her job mobile still in her hand.

Jeff Nichols walked into the room and, sidestepping Tom, he quickly snatched Sheridan's mobile from her hand and cut the call off before tucking it into his back pocket.

And then he pulled the gun and inched back, pointing it at Tom.

'What the fuck are you doing?' Tom went to step forward.

'Stay there, Tom. Don't fucking move.' Jeff raised the gun slightly, aiming it directly at Tom's head. 'Give me your warrant card.'

'I haven't got it. What's going on?'

Jeff's face turned crimson with anger. 'Just give me your fucking warrant card.'

'Jeff, I haven't got it with me.' Tom's face was etched in fear. 'I can go and get it.'

'Is it in your car?'

'No, it's at the nick.'

Jeff ignored Sheridan's mobile that started ringing in his back pocket. 'I don't believe you. If you don't hand it over now, I'll shoot her, I swear to God.' Jeff snapped his arm sideways and aimed the gun at Sheridan.

'Fucking hell, Jeff, I swear I haven't got it with me.' Tom went to reach into his pocket. 'Look, you can check.'

Jeff Nichols shook his head. 'Then you're no good to me.' He swung his arm back and fired, hitting Tom in the middle of his face. Blood and bone shot out and hit the wall behind him just before his body arched backwards, his legs buckling beneath him.

Sheridan had instinctively put her hands out in front of her, horrified at what she had just witnessed and expecting the next bullet to be for her. 'Jeff . . .'

Her mobile began to ring again. With the gun pointed at her in one hand, Jeff reached into his pocket for the phone, seeing Rob Wills' name flashing on the screen. 'When you answer this, you tell

Rob that you've just left and you're on your way back to the nick. Tell him Tom and me are having a boys' night in. If you give any indication that you're in trouble, I will shoot you in the face.' He answered the call and put it on loudspeaker.

'Hello?' Sheridan answered, her eyes fixed on Jeff's finger, poised on the trigger.

'It's Rob. Everything okay?'

'Yes, sorry we got cut off. I've just left Jeff Nichols' place. I'm heading back to the nick now.'

'You scared the shit out of me.'

'Sorry.'

'Where are Jeff and Tom, now?'

'In Jeff's house. They're having a boys' night in.'

'Okay. Me and Dipesh will start doing some enquiries around Tom Hudson.'

'Good idea.'

'See you in a bit.'

'Okay.'

Jeff hit the 'end call' button and put the mobile back in his pocket. 'You'd better have your warrant card on you or you're going to die right here.'

'Yes. I've got it.' Sheridan didn't move, her eyes falling on Tom Hudson's body. A thick mass of blood was soaking into the carpet and dripping down the wall like lava.

'Give it to me.' Jeff held his hand out and Sheridan slowly reached into her coat pocket, pulled out her warrant card and handed it to him. He flipped the black leather wallet open, looked at it and tucked it into his front jeans pocket. 'This has just saved your life.' Jeff stepped back, keeping the gun trained on Sheridan. 'Sit down.'

As Sheridan slowly eased herself down on to the sofa, Jeff knelt next to Tom Hudson's body and searched his pockets, momentarily taking his eyes off Sheridan, who had carefully put her hand into her coat and put her personal mobile on silent.

Jeff pulled Tom's wallet and mobile out of his pockets and set them on the floor. He then rolled Tom over, leaving his lifeless body face down. Taking his own mobile, he placed it on the floor near to Tom's hand and removing everything except a bank card and picture of his children from his wallet, he tucked it into Tom's back pocket, leaving it protruding slightly.

'Why do you need my warrant card, Jeff?' Sheridan felt her whole body coursing with adrenaline.

'Because I need it to get in somewhere.' He looked down at Tom. 'If he'd had his card on him, I could have used it myself to impersonate a police officer.' He turned his head towards her. 'But then I wouldn't need you, and so you'd be lying there next to him. But I do need you because I can't get away with your photo on your warrant card. So, you're coming with me.'

'Where?'

'The lock-up. You're driving.' He waved his hand upward. 'Get up. Let's go.'

Sheridan stood and took one last look at Tom Hudson before Jeff followed her out of the room, switching off the main light.

Sheridan struggled to get the keys into the ignition, stopping momentarily to take a breath.

'Come on,' Jeff barked at her.

'My hands are shaking.' She tried again and the key went in.

As they pulled out of Jeff's road and turned right, the evening traffic was building up and they sat in a queue of cars, all heading home.

Jeff's leg was shaking up and down as he nervously looked around. 'Fuck's sake.'

As he turned to face forward, a faint glow drew his attention to Sheridan's coat pocket. He reached in and took out her personal mobile, the silent text messages flashing up on the screen.

'I swear, I forgot it was there, Jeff.'

Jeff looked at the name on the screen. 'Who's Sam?'

Sheridan's heart suddenly felt like it was going to stop beating. She wanted to avoid answering, giving herself time to think of what to say.

'I'm not going to ask you again, who is Sam? Is he one of your DCs?'

'Does it really matter?'

Jeff didn't answer her, his head bent down, reading the text message.

He looked at Sheridan. 'If he's one of your lot, you must be shagging him, he put two kisses at the end of his text.'

'What was the text message?'

'Never mind.'

The traffic started inching forward and she could feel Jeff's eyes on her.

Then her work mobile began to ring. Jeff saw Rob Wills' name again. 'When I answer this, you tell Rob that you've been waylaid but you're still on your way back to the nick.'

He pressed 'answer' and held the phone up to Sheridan's face.

'Hello?' she answered.

'Sheridan, it's Rob. You driving?'

'Yes, but I'm on loudspeaker.'

'You stuck in traffic or something?'

'Yeah, it's really busy on the roads.'

Jeff listened as Rob spilled out his findings that Tom Hudson could not have been driving his own car the previous Thursday.

Sheridan felt the gun in her side. 'Okay. We'll discuss it when I get back to the nick.'

'Alright. Is there anything more you need us to be doing?'

There was a moment of silence before Sheridan answered. 'You could do me a favour and ring my husband, Sam, for me. He's booked a table at Mamma B's for my birthday, can you let him know he'll have to cancel? He won't shout at *you*.'

The gun was now pushed so far into her ribcage that it made her wince.

Rob replied, 'Will do.'

Jeff cut the call. 'Why did you say that? About your husband?'

'I had to say that, Jeff. He'll keep calling me otherwise, and if I don't respond, he'll get really worried.'

'I don't fucking care.'

'I know you don't.'

'So, he's in the job?'

'I'd rather not talk about him.'

Jeff turned in his seat. 'I know he's in the job because of what he put in his text message.'

Sheridan's mind raced. *What had Sam texted her?* 'What did he say?' she asked.

'It doesn't matter.' The traffic was moving steadily now. 'Tom thought you were a lesbian. He told me once that he fancied you but said you batted for the other team.'

'I get that a lot.'

They reached the Dock Road and Jeff signalled for her to pull over. A moment later, he was tossing the mobile phones and Tom Hudson's wallet into the Mersey, before they continued their journey to the lock-ups.

Anna got up from the chair and sat on the bed, nodding to DS Jane Edwards who had documented everything that Sheridan had remembered. Jane Edwards had met Sheridan on several occasions before moving to another station on Merseyside.

'I'll leave you to it.' She picked up the file and her jacket from the chair and leaned over Sheridan, gently touching her shoulder. 'Take care.' She smiled.

'Thank you, Jane. Thank you for being so patient.'

'You did really well. I know how hard that was for you, Sheridan. Now rest up, okay?' She nodded and left the room, closing the door behind her.

'So, the diamonds weren't real.' Sheridan gingerly lifted herself up and readjusted her pillow. 'Jeff Nichols went through all of that for a few grand, some gold rings and a bag of cubic zirconia worth virtually nothing.'

'Yep.' Anna nodded. 'Do you think Kate was lying to him that she'd had one tested?'

'I don't know. Maybe she did and maybe she swapped them? It could be that she didn't trust him as much as she made out.' Sheridan rested her head back. 'I can't see why the old man would put a bag of zirconia in a box full of genuine gold jewellery, unless he was running a dodgy business and selling them to unsuspecting customers. Maybe he was taking out the real diamonds from his stock and swapping them for imitation ones.'

'Possibly.'

'Or . . . they were real, and Kate made the swap. Hid the real ones somewhere. If that's the case, then we'll never know where they ended up.'

'Or maybe there were never any real diamonds. To think what Jeff did, how many lives he affected . . . and for what?'

Tears suddenly filled Sheridan's eyes. 'I thought I was going to die, Anna, I really did. I couldn't see a way out of it.' She choked on her words. 'I just kept thinking about my parents, about you and Sam . . . I kept thinking about never seeing you all again. I could see Matthew when I closed my eyes and I just prayed I'd stay alive so that there's still hope I can find his killer.' She wiped her eyes. 'I'm so sorry about Tom Hudson and Billy Doyle. I should have done more to try and protect them.'

'Hey, you did what you could, there's no way you could have stopped Jeff. He had a bloody gun. You're not Superwoman, Sheridan. You're not bullet-proof.'

'I know.' She inhaled deeply. 'You, Rob and Dipesh were amazing, do you know that? When I gave Rob that message, I knew it was my only chance of letting him know that something was wrong.'

There was a knock on the door, and Sam's face appeared. 'Is it okay to come in?'

'Of course.' Sheridan tapped the sheet and Sam sat on the bed.

'You feeling okay?' she asked, holding Sheridan's hand and trying not to knock the cannula out.

'I'm fine. We were just talking about how amazing people are and then you walk in.'

'Why am I amazing?'

'You were the one that figured out what Ellie Sands was saying.' She squeezed Sam's hand.

'Well then, I'm a bloody hero and I want a certificate.' Sam grinned.

'Right, I'm going to leave you two to it. I'll keep you posted.' Anna kissed Sheridan on the forehead and turned to Sam. 'Look after her.' And with that, she left.

Sheridan closed her eyes. 'Will you stay with me a while?'

'I'll have to cancel my facial hair laser treatment, but yeah, I'll stay.'

Sheridan smiled before slowly drifting off to sleep.

CHAPTER 112

Two months later

Anna left the courtroom and dialled Sheridan's number.

Sheridan was lying on the sofa. Sam had left the phone next to her while she went shopping, and had called three times in the last hour to make sure she was alright. 'Hello,' Sheridan answered.

'It's me. You ready for this?' Anna walked over to her car.

'Yeah, go on.' Sheridan laid her head on the cushion and closed her eyes. She knew Jeff Nichols was appearing at Liverpool Crown Court, and had expected Anna's call.

'He pleaded guilty to everything. He's being sentenced next month.'

'That's brilliant, just brilliant. Thanks, mate. You've done a fantastic job. Tell the team I'll come and see them in a couple of days.' She hesitated. 'How did he look?'

'Like shit, to be honest,' Anna replied as she got into her car. 'The best bit was when they mentioned again that the diamonds weren't real – he looked like he was going to explode. Anyway, you okay?'

'Yeah, fine. It's just nice to be getting back to some sort of normality,' she replied. 'And now there's not going to be a trial, we can all move on I guess.' She slowly sat herself up, holding her side. 'I want to go and see Ellie Sands. Will you come with me if I arrange it with Yvonne and Joni?'

'Of course I will. Just give me a call when you've sorted it and I'll pick you up.'

'Will do. You take care, mate. Speak soon. Love ya.'

'Love ya, too.'

Sheridan put the phone down and carefully stood up.

Jeff Nichols' face came into her head. He was always in her head, now. She'd wake in the night, conscious not to disturb Sam, and would lie there going over what happened in his house and the lock-up. She could see Tom Hudson standing there, smiling at her. The smile that had turned to a look of pure horror when Jeff Nichols pointed the gun at him. The desperation in his voice. She felt her muscles stiffen as Tom's dead body appeared when she closed her eyes. She remembered everything that Jeff Nichols had told her, how he believed that he and Kate were going to be set for life. How he was prepared to kill for what he believed were diamonds, worth a small fortune.

Sheridan thought about what could have happened in the lock-up that day; how, in that second Jeff put the gun in her mouth, it could have all been over. How it would have been so different if Tom Hudson had carried his warrant card with him that day. He'd still be dead, but so would Sheridan. How would her parents have ever recovered from that? How would Sam?

Then she thought about Max Hall, her dear friend, her colleague. She wasn't there for his funeral, she didn't pay her last respects to the man she adored. She tried to push the thoughts from her mind, thoughts that haunted her every day. She realised her hands were shaking and she clasped them together as she stepped towards the window, looking out at the trees in her front garden.

She hated feeling like this, she hated being alone, it frightened her. Her exterior had been torn away to expose her vulnerability. She thought about the victims she had dealt with over the years. And now she was one of them. She tried to swallow, but couldn't; she started to panic, she wanted to run out of the house, get some air. Then she saw Sam's car pull up and watched as she got out, lifting shopping bags out of the boot. Sam looked up and saw Sheridan standing there, then reached back into the car and held up an enormous bar of chocolate, waving it at her. Sheridan smiled. Her hands had stopped shaking. *You'll be alright*, she thought. *You've got Sam. And Sam has chocolate. You'll be just fine.*

CHAPTER 113

Joni sat on Ellie's bed and held her hand while Sheridan pulled up a chair. Anna stood quietly at the back of the room.

'Ellie, I've come to talk to you about Jeff Nichols. PC Nichols.' Sheridan kept her voice low and controlled, hoping that somewhere in Ellie's mind, she could understand.

Ellie let out a cry: 'Pess shit.'

Sheridan continued. 'Ellie, we know that PC Nichols shot you.'

She waited for a response, and after a moment, Ellie let out a loud cry. Her eyes filled with tears and Joni squeezed her hand a little tighter.

'PC Nichols shot you and he's now in prison. We know that you've been trying to say that PC Nichols shot you, we know that now, so thank you.' Sheridan swallowed. She watched as tears fell down Ellie's face, while fighting back her own.

'We know how you knew John Lively. And we know he didn't hurt anyone. We've proved that, Ellie.'

No response.

'Ellie, I'm so sorry that this happened to you, I really am. I hope you can take some comfort from this now.'

Ellie closed her eyes.

Sheridan turned to Joni. 'Do you think she understands?'

Before Joni could answer, Ellie opened her eyes and looked straight at Sheridan. 'Fan,' she said.

'What did she say?' Sheridan asked.

Joni smiled. 'She said, "Thank you."'

CHAPTER 114

THREE WEEKS LATER

Sheridan waved Sam off to work before making herself a coffee, and as she stood gazing out of the kitchen window, her mobile rang: Andrew Longford's number. She had contacted him after her release from hospital and he'd told her how sorry he was to hear what had happened to her and the other officer, having seen it on the news. He explained that he had tried to call her but her phone was out of service. She hadn't bothered explaining that her phone was out of service because it was somewhere at the bottom of the River Mersey. He'd also apologised for not having had a chance to go through the photographs, but promised to call her once his friend had retrieved them from the loft.

'Hi, Andrew,' she answered.

'Hello, Sheridan, I've got the photos you wanted.'

'Great, when can I pop over?'

'Now, if you like. I've had a look through them, and I think there's something you need to see.'

Half an hour later, she arrived at Andrew's house and as she followed him into the living room, he quickly shifted a stack of photo albums from the sofa to make space for her to sit down. Handing her a photograph, she started studying it. It was of Matthew's football team, all lined up before the game, their skinny legs protruding out of oversized shorts and one taller lad grinning cheekily as he towered over the rest of them. Standing in the background was the same man as before. Hands in his pockets.

'The same guy.' Sheridan pointed him out. 'Does he look anything like the man you saw on the day Matthew was killed?'

Andrew shook his head. 'I can't be sure, I never really saw his face clearly, just mainly what he was wearing. Blue jeans, brown coat and a beard. I've been through all the pictures and the ones with this guy in, so far, all show him clean-shaven and not wearing a brown coat.'

He handed Sheridan a second photograph, another one taken during a football match. She recognised the same lads, the same parents. Then her eyes fell on Matthew's smiling face, just visible under a pile of bodies, celebrating a goal. As she scanned the picture, she saw the same man standing in the background. Her eyes widened.

This time, he had a beard. And he was wearing a brown coat.

CHAPTER 115

Jeff Nichols sat alone in the canteen picking at his food, ignoring everyone around him. He scooped up a mouthful of mashed potato and felt it roll around in his mouth. He was about to spit it out when another prisoner appeared, standing opposite him holding a dinner tray. He stood six feet five and smiled at Jeff before sitting down.

'I like to eat alone,' Jeff said, looking down at his plate. He had waived his right to Rule 43 segregation. He refused to be banged up on what was known as 'the nonces' wing'. Mainly housing sex offenders, Rule 43 prison conditions were often inadequate, with poor sanitation and limited opportunities for the inmates. He'd never lower himself to be locked up with a bunch of dirty fuckers like that. He was safer where he was. He'd spent a month on suicide watch before being deemed at low risk of self-harm. When he was eventually placed on A wing, two inmates had approached him and offered to look out for him. For a fee.

Jeff knew the police had found all but one of the false accounts he had set up and he used that to pay his 'boys', as he referred to them. It worked well for him. He paid them and they made sure no one gave him any grief. He was untouchable. A handful of the inmates even showed him a morsel of respect for killing a serving police officer.

'You Jeff Nichols, ain't ya? They call me Bones. Pleased to make your acquaintance.'

'Fuck off.' Jeff put his spoon down before calmly taking a sip of water.

'You don't know me. But you owe me.' Bones' voice was so deep it was like he spoke from his stomach. He had beautiful white teeth and a tiny but perfectly trimmed goatee beard.

'Go away.' Jeff put his plastic cup down and stood up, about to clear his tray.

'Sit down,' Bones said under his breath, standing up and placing his enormous hand on Jeff's shoulder. Jeff sat down.

'What do you want?' Jeff held Bones' stare, completely unfazed by him.

'I want what you took from my boy, John Lively.' Bones put his finger into Jeff's food and scooped up a mouthful, licking it from his finger.

Jeff looked around. He couldn't see his boys but he knew they wouldn't be too far away, so he pushed his tray towards Bones, stood up and walked back to his cell.

He sat on his bunk and picked up his book, just as Bones appeared at his door, bending down and stepping into the cell, almost filling it with his massive frame. 'That's not good, you walking away from me.'

Jeff stood up and went chest to chest with him. 'I told you to fuck off, so I suggest you do just that.'

'It's just you and me now, Nichols.' Bones took hold of Jeff's chin and dug his fingernails in. 'Do you know why they call me Bones?'

Jeff didn't respond.

'I like the cracking sound they make when I break them.' He smiled. 'Other people's of course, not my own.'

'You can't touch me, I've got protection.' Jeff saw two figures appear in the doorway; his boys were always there when he needed them. 'And here they are, alright boys?' He stepped back and leaned against his bunk. 'Get this piece of shit out of my cell, will you?'

His two boys stepped into the cell and brushed past Bones, taking their positions on either side of Jeff, who crossed his arms and grinned. 'You see, Bones, I pay these lads well to make sure I stay safe in here.' He turned to the one on his left. 'Alright Joe? Your missus get the money okay?'

'Yeah, all good, ta,' Joe replied, taking hold of Jeff's left arm.

Jeff frowned just as he felt his other boy take a firm hold of his right arm. 'What you doing, lads?'

Bones stepped forward and put his face close to Jeff's. 'You haven't been paying these boys to look after you, Nichols, all you been doing is paying back what you owe me, what you took off my boy, John Lively.' He rubbed his stubble against Jeff Nichols' cheek. 'You see, they work for me, not you.' Bones threw his enormous head back and laughed. 'You're a fucking loser, Nichols. You think you're something you're not. What was it you stole? Oh yeah, a big bag of glass or something. You think you were a diamond smuggler?' Bones laughed again. 'Or have you still got them diamonds? Did you swap them? Cos if you did, I think you're gonna tell me where they are one day.' He inhaled deeply. 'I don't like you, Nichols. I don't like what you did to my boy, John Lively.' He grabbed Jeff's face with his shovel-sized hand and licked his cheek. 'But I'm a reasonable man, so you keep paying up as you been doin' and think about telling me where them diamonds are and I'll leave you in one piece. But if the money runs out, then your bones are all mine.'

Without another word, they stepped out of the cell. Bones blew Jeff a kiss as he left. Jeff slumped down on to his bunk, wiped the saliva from his face with his sleeve and punched his cell wall, immediately feeling his knuckle crack and swell.

His face was contorted with rage, and he started to breathe heavily, his chest rising and filling his lungs with stale prison air. 'Fucking bitch!' He grabbed his hair and pulled it, clenching his fists. He closed his eyes and could see Kate Armitage's face laughing at him. He'd gone over it in his mind so many times. She'd told him the diamonds were real; had it simply been her way of convincing him to get involved with her? Had everything she'd told him been a lie?

'You fucking bitch,' he said under his breath, lying on his bunk and curling himself into a ball, tears of anger and rage pouring down his face.

CHAPTER 116

Sheridan and Sam stood gazing into the shop window.

'If you could pick one, which one would you go for?' Sheridan peered closer at the display.

'I'm not sure, I didn't realise there'd be such a selection.' Sam took a deep breath. 'Do you think we're ready for this?'

'I think so.'

'It's a big commitment, you know. I mean, I've never done this before, and I want to get it right.' Sam squeezed Sheridan's hand.

'We will get it right. We'll choose carefully, but we can't put it off any longer.' Sheridan dragged Sam through the door.

'Can I help you?' the assistant asked as they walked in.

'Yes,' Sheridan answered, 'our kettle blew up this morning and we can't decide which one to buy.'

Sam smiled at the assistant. 'It's our first kettle, I mean, we have had kettles before, but separate ones. This is the first one we've bought together.'

The assistant grinned. 'I see.' She walked around from behind the counter. 'Then let's make sure you ladies get one you both like.'

Half an hour later they left the shop, arm in arm with their new kettle. And a coffee machine.

CHAPTER 117

She was making the most of having the place to herself. Checking her watch, she was assured they'd be at least another hour. Taking a sip of wine and placing the glass down on the garden table, she closed her eyes and let the sun kiss her face, cooled by a gentle breeze from across the back field.

She knew she shouldn't, but she just couldn't help herself. Carefully, she unwrapped the little cloth bag and picked out one of the shimmering diamonds.

Holding it up, she watched the light bounce and play around its edges. She recalled the day she'd got on the train to London and taken it to the dealer and he'd confirmed it was definitely a diamond and probably worth about six thousand pounds. She'd joked with him, saying she wished she had thirty more, but sadly, she had just this one.

Except, she *did* have thirty more. Because that was how many were in the bag when she'd found them in the loft.

Carly Nichols had never even heard of cubic zirconia. Not until she bought enough of it to swap for the real diamonds she'd found in the bag that day.

She knew Jeff had been unfaithful. It was one of the things that had surprised her most during the investigation into Kate's murder.

The day she'd made the decision to throw him out was the day she'd plucked up the courage to go into the loft. She had it all planned.

She'd get his suitcases, fill them with his clothes and leave them by the door for when he got home. It was when she'd placed the suitcases by the loft hatch that she noticed the box of wedding photographs and had sat looking through them, the memories of happier days. She'd looked around and everything up there was another memory. The little electric fire they'd bought and huddled around when they shared their first flat, the old tape recorder her mother had given to them, the boxes of their children's clothes. Carly had touched them, smelt them, her heart aching as she did so. Then, she spotted the two unfamiliar bags over in the corner. When she'd opened them and saw the money, her mind had raced. Her husband, the police officer. Was he a criminal? Where had it all come from? What the hell had he been involved in?

Then she'd opened the second, smaller bag. More money, a black box filled with gold rings and the little black bag of diamonds. She'd sat there, staring at them in disbelief. Every scenario went through her mind. Maybe she should call the police, maybe she should confront Jeff. Or just maybe, she should take it all.

At that moment, she came up with the plan.

She couldn't swap the money or the rings for fakes, he'd spot it a mile away, plus she had no idea where or how to obtain such things. But, the diamonds, they could be switched. She'd counted them out and found a supplier of cubic zirconia, bought thirty-one pieces and swapped them two weeks after finding the bags in the loft. Two days after that, she threw Jeff out. He would never suspect that she'd been in the loft; he knew she never went up there.

Then, she waited. Carried on as normal. She knew there was a risk that he'd discover the switch and suspect her, confront her even, but she held the ace. Whatever he was involved in was clearly criminal and she'd just threaten to report him. What were the chances that he'd dare to admit he was bent?

Now, the case against Jeff Nichols was closed. It was over. The police weren't looking for anyone else.

And they certainly weren't looking for any diamonds.

EPILOGUE

Jeff Nichols was sentenced to life. The judge recommended that he was never to be released from prison. He continued to pay 'Bones' until the money ran out. He is now on Rule 43.

The lock-ups were searched and a total of 1.8 million pounds' worth of stolen property was recovered. Three members of the Doyle family were given custodial sentences for handling stolen goods.

Tom Hudson was buried next to his mother, dressed in full uniform. His warrant card was placed in his hand.

Anna Markinson is yet to sit her inspector's exam and remains a detective sergeant in Hale Street CID. Steve has so far kept his promise.

Joni Summers still works at The Gables. She's training to become an intermediary for people with speech and language problems. She loves it.

Mo Chase left The Gables and now works in a dry-cleaners. She hates it.

Ellie Sands passed away peacefully in her sleep. Her nephew Miles was at her bedside. And so was Joni.

Sheridan passed the pictures that Andrew Longford gave her to the cold-case team. They are currently trying to identify the man with the beard in the brown coat.

Jeff Nichols' father still visits him in prison. His mother refuses to go with him.

Sam and Maud moved in with Sheridan. Maud spends every other weekend at Joni's. She still likes eating Jaffa Cakes.

Carly Nichols still lives with her parents and children in Norfolk. She plans to buy herself a house someday. A rather nice house.

ACKNOWLEDGEMENTS

I bet that all of you who know you're going to be mentioned here have gone straight to this part of the book. You have, haven't you? Thought so.

Firstly, I want to thank you . . . the reader. Whoever you are, wherever you are, without you I'd just be a woman sitting at a laptop writing stories that no one ever reads. Thank you for buying my book. You are always in my mind as I write; I want you to hopefully fall in love with the characters, or hate the bad ones. I want you to feel satisfied from the first page to the last. Because this is the reason I do what I do. For you to maybe escape for a while. Of course, it pays the bills as well! Cheers everyone. Right, I'd better move on to others that I need to thank.

So, in no particular order (okay, there is a bit of an order because Susan Doherty has to be first):

Susie, I hope you know that I couldn't have done this without you. You've been there every step of the way, from the first chapter to the last. You were there when I was signed by Broo (more about Broo later) and when we got the phone call to say we'd landed a publisher (more about Vic later) and everything in between.

Just never forget that you are my strength, my muse, my soulmate and my IT genius when I hit the wrong button and my screen turns a funny colour.

Thank you for the endless nights we sat up talking about plots, characters and how amazing it would be if my books were one day out there, being read and *hopefully* enjoyed. And now we're here. Blimey, we did it. I think a cup of tea (not tea) is in order. Anyway, enough about you, I've got loads of other people to thank.

Next, my gatekeepers: Michael Doherty, Breda Byrne, Lorraine Burns, Detective Sergeant Jane Edwards (retired) and Katharine Robinson.

You are always the first to read my manuscripts, even before I send them to my agent. Please know that I will not be paying you for your services. I just wanted to make that clear. But know that you're all wonderful and you all take so much time to give me your honest feedback.

Michael, I'm honoured to have you on board, to spend precious time with you and your wonderful knowledge of . . . well everything, actually. You are the official Moogle. I adore your enthusiasm for my manuscripts and your infectious sense of humour. Looking forward to many more walks, talks and playing more golf with you, even if it is just to witness your beautifully strange swing . . . how do you even hit the ball?

Breda (LC now retired), as busy as you are, you always give time to others, but can you give more time to me please? I'm important, you know. Are you bored yet? And remember no matter what happens, I will always be there for BredasBootCamp. And you win the quote of the year award when, after reading my novel you rang and said those immortal words . . . '*Yes, it was really good. By the way, have you heard of M. W. Craven? He's brilliant.*' None taken.

Lorraine, your unerring ability to figure things out is both endearing and annoying. I'm going to buy you a pen that isn't red so that when you send my manuscript back, I don't feel like I'm back in the fifth year at school, getting my homework marked. Your mind is quite exquisite, and I fear you missed your vocation as a detective. Thank you for all the time you took to give me your brutally honest feedback. I *will* get you one day. You just wait.

Detective Sergeant Jane Edwards (retired), can you believe it's been twenty-three years since you first had the pleasure of working with me? So many fab memories from back in the day, and we're still here, the very best of friends. Thank you so much for your help on this book. For pointing out the things that probably wouldn't happen and stopping me from making a muppet of myself. We've had so many laughs over the years and there are so many more to come with me and Susie, you and Kev. Can I just ask though, please stop asking me to do the impression of the two pieces of toast sat in a toaster. Let it go. It was only funny once. PS: When are we going to Vegas?

Katharine Robinson, how have you put up with me all these years? Sorry that I spun your chair round so fast that time and you were ill for the rest of the day. Sorry that when we first worked together, I shared details of my morning *routine* with you. Sorry that I wrapped your whole office and everything in it in toilet roll. Actually, I'm not sorry about that one. It was hilarious. Thank you for spending so much time checking my manuscript and squealing with delight when you found an error. You're a bloody amazing woman, never forget that.

Supt Sonia Humphreys, I love that I can ring you and ask the most bizarre questions and you always unflinchingly give me the answer. Your knowledge is sublime, and I probably owe you a lot of those emergency sausage rolls we relied on to get us through those '*morning after*' mornings. Did we really stake the place out until it opened? We had no shame. I have laughed with you until things have shot out of my nose (probably a Tunnock's teacake). Thank you for being as proud of me as I am of you, ma'am. If Paula from Tesco's could see us now, eh?

Paul Sturman, my firearms '*go to*' expert and all-round bloody nice bloke. Thank you for always being there when I need you. You're still one of the many people who can take the piss out of me and get away with it. I loved working with you back in the day (was it really *that* long ago?). When I eventually get back to Norfolk, we're going out for a beer.

Rob Willis, for being one of the most genuine and hard-working police officers I have ever had the pleasure of working with. Oh and I stole your name for one of the characters, just changed the surname slightly. Don't worry, I didn't make you one of the bad guys.

Rosemary Wyatt, registered intermediary with the Ministry of Justice. Speech and language therapist MRCSLT (retired). When I first contacted you, needing expert advice on head injuries and speech therapy, you didn't hesitate. Thank you so much for all the time you spent helping me and all it cost me was a cup of coffee and a slice of carrot cake. You are a star and I think I probably owe you another piece of cake very soon.

Fraser Ritchie, crime scene investigator. Fraz, you are so patient and knowledgeable and never bat an eyelid when I ask you very strange questions. One day, I'll just send you an email to see how you are and how the weather is and not end it with '*so, if a body has been left to decompose for a few years . . .*' Thank you so much for all your help. You will forever be my CSI expert.

Julie Tomkins, I know you're not expecting to be mentioned here, so . . . *surprise*! What can I say? I could start by thanking you for being the best teacher I ever had. For being there for me (you know what I'm talking about) and for saving me when I got really drunk at school and the headmaster wanted to expel me. You're a legend.

Broo Doherty, the tall one. Blimey, what a journey . . . and it all started with you. Thank you for your unerring belief in me, your infectious enthusiasm and how you worry about me when I start bouncing around the room. You are a dream of an agent and I love working with you. One day, we will go out to lunch, and I'll actually eat something.

Helen Edwards, lovely Helen, I'm going to confess something now. I have absolutely no idea what it is you do exactly. I mean, I kind of know but it's all a bit technical for my tiny brain. I love it when I ask you a question and follow it with, 'Do I need to know how this works?' And you answer, 'No.' You are wonderful, I hope you know that.

Victoria Haslam, my totally wonderful editor. Thank you so much for everything, you really are a gem. I know you love Sheridan Holler as much as I do, but I think we both know that you love Maud the most. Thank you for believing in me. I know we're going to have a blast.

Russel D McLean, my wonderful dev editor. You *get* Sheridan and I love that. Thank you for all your hard work and wonderful sense of humour. And for always worrying about Maud. She'll be fine. *Never* kill off the cat.

Everyone at DHH Literary Agency, what a wonderful family you are and I am so proud to be a part of it. You also know how to throw the best parties. Keep doing what you do, because you're all rather good at it.

Yvonne Poles, thank you. For everything. You probably don't know how much you did for me. Thank you for your patience, your kindness and for keeping me sane. You know what I mean.

The Coven, you know who you are. I know who you are. The strongest, funniest and most supportive group of women I have never met. One day, and you know it will happen, we shall actually get together. There will be cats. There will be chips. There will be copious amounts of '*not tea*'. There will be a kitten battle ship and HHHHs. I love you all very much. Not in a creepy way.

Alison Black, thank you for giving me 'Sheila' and I hope you enjoy the book, but you can't just skip to the bits with her in it! Congratulations for winning the '*I Need A Character Name*' Twitter competition. If I'm ever up in your neck of the woods, I might pop in for a cuppa. I need to meet your gorgeous dog, Willow.

Now to my amazing Twitter 'followers' who I no longer call followers, but friends. I love the interaction with all of you. Thank you for putting up with and 'liking' all the ridiculous stuff I put out there. But now you know that I don't just make things out of wonky veg, or write poignant poetry to hopefully get you through the tough times. I hope you all stick around, because I will always endeavour to make you smile.

The Library Boys, you know who you are. Thank you for enlightening me with your wonderful Scouse language. I did notice that you were more than willing to educate me with a *lot* of swear words, most of which I haven't used . . . yet. Cheers boys, I owe you a beer. A lot of beer.

Cookie Dude, okay, judge me if you must, but I want to mention my cat, the legendary Cookie Dude. He's not here any more and I miss him. He was the most incredible character and I loved him very much. If you want to imagine him, he is basically Maud. But a boy. But he was kind of girlie too. And he would eat *anything*. And I mean . . . *anything*.

As I write these acknowledgments, I know there will be others involved in this process who I haven't met yet. So, I'm going to thank you in advance. For whatever you do and whoever you are . . . I know you're going to be bloody fabulous.

Lastly, I just want to say that I turned to a lot of people for their expert advice while writing this novel. However, on the odd occasion I may have made the decision to go very slightly off piste. If I have, then it's my responsibility and not theirs. Any mistakes are mine. (I had to say that so that people don't shout at me.) Right then, I think that's it. I have thoroughly enjoyed writing these acknowledgements; to be able to mention those who have been on this amazing journey with me has been very humbling. Anyway, must dash. Catch you all later. x

ABOUT THE AUTHOR

T. M. Payne was born in Lee-on-Solent, Hampshire and now lives on the Wirral with her wonderful partner. Having worked in the criminal justice system for eighteen years, the last fourteen of which were as a police case investigator within the Domestic Violence Unit, she has now taken a break to concentrate on her passion for writing crime novels. She is crazy about animals and if you walk past her with your dog, she will probably ask if she can pat it on the head. Or take it home with her. Or both. She loves laughing, Christmas, playing golf (badly), walking along New Brighton beach (not walking her dog because she hasn't got one), snow, sunshine, sunsets, family and friends. She dislikes beetroot.